THE DELIGHTS OF DETECTION

THE DELIGHTS
OF DETECTION

Edited with an Introduction
by JACQUES BARZUN

CRITERION BOOKS · NEW YORK

Acknowledgments

The Editor acknowledges with thanks the kindness of the following persons and firms for giving permission to reprint the stories listed below, which are held in copyright.

Doubleday and Company and Mrs. Hope Loresche for "The Greek Play" by H. C. Bailey, reprinted from *Meet Mr. Fortune*, 1942.

Alfred A. Knopf, Inc. for "The Unknown Peer" by E. C. Bentley, reprinted from *Trent Intervenes*, 1938.

Methuen and Company for "The Tragedy at Brookbend Cottage" by Ernest Bramah, reprinted from *Max Carrados*, 1914.

Miss D. E. Collins and Cassell and Company, Ltd. for "The Bottomless Well" by G. K. Chesterton, reprinted from *The Man Who Knew Too Much*, originally published by Harper and Brothers, 1922.

Edmund Crispin and Victor Gollancz and Company, Ltd. for "Otherwhere," reprinted from *Beware of the Trains*, 1953; first published in *Ellery Queen's Mystery Magazine*.

Dodd, Mead and Company for "A Case of Premeditation" by R. Austin Freeman, reprinted from *The Singing Bone*, 1912.

Michael Gilbert for "The Oyster Catcher," first published in *Ellery Queen's Mystery Magazine*.

Harry Kemelman for "The Nine-Mile Walk," first published in *Ellery Queen's Mystery Magazine*.

Doubleday and Company for "The Log Case" by Kenneth Livingston, reprinted from *The Dodd Cases*, 1934.

John D. MacDonald for "The Homesick Buick," first published in *Ellery Queen's Mystery Magazine*.

Daniel Pettiward and the *London Mystery Magazine* for "The Weir."

Dorothy Sayers for "The Professor's Manuscript," reprinted from *In the Teeth of the Evidence*, 1939; originally published by William Collins, Sons, Ltd.

Rex Stout and The Viking Press for "Murder Is No Joke," reprinted from *And Four To Go*, 1958.

Bayard Wendell and the Kingston Associates for "One Word at a Time."

In addition, the Editor wishes to express gratitude to the editors of *Ellery Queen's Mystery Magazine* for permitting him to reprint his translation of Beaumarchais and for generously relinquishing in his favor their first anthology rights to some of the stories listed above.

Table of Contents

HISTORIC TALES

Detection and the Literary Art

BY JACQUES BARZUN

It was a toss-up whether W. H. Auden or I should bring together for the reader of today a group of tales illustrating the art of detective fiction. Auden is as firm a devotee of the genre as I am, but it turned out in discussion that he prefers the long novels. This is a taste worthy of respect, but when several novels are reprinted together the volume bulks so large and heavy that no one can avoid calling it an omnibus, and although the exciting contents may indeed make it hard to put down, a doubt always remains whether anyone can pick it up.

The pleasant task fell to me, therefore, of collecting and introducing the short stories I like best in this popular but strangely misunderstood literary kind.

Because detective stories, short or long, are conventionally called cheap entertainment, and yet are read and written by talented people, absurd theories have been evolved about their significance and secret function. Some have said that the spectacle of crime and punishment purges the civilized man of fear and guilt; others, that it releases by a modern myth the animal instincts of the chase and the kill. Meanwhile, among those who perceive that all this is pretentious nonsense, many conclude that detective fiction can satisfy only a juvenile and unliterary taste. It rather adds to the confusion that the holders of these various views are thinking of different kinds of stories or of several kinds at once: they refer indiscriminately to "crime stories," "mystery stories," and "detective stories" as if they were all one.

What is morally worse—for it prevents the public from developing its own judgment—anthologists who understand the distinctions and who define the detective genre in their prefaces go on to fill their books with stories of crime and mystery absolutely devoid of detection. In the best of such books one is lucky to find four or five pieces out of fifteen or twenty that answer to the given description. No such insouciance would be tolerated elsewhere. An anthology of ghost stories is full of ghosts. A book labeled "westerns" does not include narratives of the mysterious East. A tale of love on Jones Beach would be deemed astray among sea stories. The present book accordingly seeks to set a precedent by sticking to its announced theme and offering varied examples of detection exclusively.

You naturally ask, "What are the distinguishing marks of the true genre and what peculiar delights does it afford the person of literary tastes?" It is not enough that one of the characters in the story should be called a detective—nor is it necessary. What is required is that the main interest of the story should consist in finding out, from circumstances largely physical, the true order and meaning of events that have been part disclosed and part concealed. Crime is attractive but incidental. An excellent detective story could be written about the identification of an amnesia victim. The reason why murder animates most detective story-telling is that the gravity of the deed gives assured momentum. Crime, moreover, makes plausible the concealment that arouses curiosity. But as the reader will see in Bayard Wendell's "One Word at a Time," the detective spirit adapts itself to many situations.

Certain readers, of course, are impatient with any detection that busies itself with physical clues. They mutter against "mechanical puzzles" and say that they cannot be bothered with material facts: the mysteries of the soul are so much more—mysterious. And they conclude that detective fiction, being of the order of riddles, can have no connection with literature.

They may be right in their judgment of particular works that are dull through being mechanical, but the condemnation of riddles is unjust. Tradition itself speaks for the riddle as a compelling literary device. From the Bible and the Greek dramatists to Dickens and Henry James, the discovery of who is who and what his actions mean has been the mainspring of great narratives. The stories of Joseph and Oedipus, the plots of *Bleak House* and "In the Cage," pose questions of identification and work out puzzles in the most exact sense of these terms.

In the ancient stories a single physical fact—a ring or other object, a footprint, a lock of hair—usually suffices to disclose identity and set off the dénouement. The object is symbolic and conventional rather than rationally convincing. What happens in modern detective fiction is that objects—and more than one in each tale—are taken literally and seriously. They are scanned for what they imply, studied as signs of past action and dark purpose. This search for history in things is anything but trivial. It reflects the way our civilization thinks about law and evidence, nature and knowledge. Our curiosity about objects has grown since the Greeks; we call the results science. By a parallel evolution of literature, the dominant kind of fiction is the prose narrative stuffed with material fact which we call the realistic novel. It blossomed a century and a half ago, with Scott and Balzac, and we are not surprised to find that the detective interest on the part of literary men dates from the same period of balanced rationalism and romanticism: detection is par excellence the romance of reason.

We see this new taste burgeoning in the eighteenth century in Voltaire's charming story of Zadig. We find it carried forward in the sketch by Beaumarchais which I reprint hereafter. And when Balzac follows this fictional tradition he attaches to it more than passing importance, for in an actual murder case we see him attempting to defend the accused by a memoir in which he pleads that: "Criminal investigation must retrace the deed morally *and physically*, for the proofs for and against are everywhere—*in people, places, and things.*" The emphatic italicizing is Balzac's own. A few years earlier, across the Channel, Sydney Smith had attacked the custom of denying legal advice to those charged with felony, by arguing that if "a footmark, a word, a sound, a tool dropped . . . are all essential to the detection of guilt," then the "same closeness of reasoning is necessary for the establishment of innocence."

From these and other examples it could be shown that the literary imagination of the first half of the nineteenth century was caught by what it understood of method in the new sciences (especially fossil reconstruction in geology) and by its sympathy with the new criminology, which called for the accurate use of physical evidence. At a time when Marsh's test for arsenic was hailed as a triumph which would eliminate the Borgias from our midst while saving those falsely accused, Europe and America thrilled to the descriptions of Leatherstocking's primitive way of tracking down friends and enemies with the aid of physical clues. Leggett's "The Rifle," not reprinted since 1830, will show how, in American fiction, crime was first brought home to a culprit by ballistics.

It remained for a genius to take this entrancing idea of detection and make it breed a distinctive literature by displaying it in an appropriate form. That genius was Edgar Allan Poe and the form was the short story, of which he was also the original theorist. "The Murders in the Rue Morgue," published in 1841, put an end to the episodic or casual use of detection. And when four years later Poe had written his three other detective tales, all the elements of the genre were in hand. What was to follow could only be elaboration, embellishment, and complication—most of it agreeable, some of it superior to the original in polish, but none of it transcending the first creation.

As the present collection shows, I continue to think the short story the true medium of detection. Pleasant as it is to begin a novel that promises a crowd of actors and incidents, of clues and disquisitions upon clues, the pleasure is soon marred by the apparently unavoidable drawback of a subplot and its false leads. The poet

C. Day Lewis, writing, as Nicholas Blake, the excellent *Minute for Murder*, apologizes for this fault by having his detective refer to "the monstrous red herring" that delayed the solution. Looking back over many a novel that is monster-ridden in this way, one cannot help thinking of the story as it was first conceived, without this artificial bustle and bulge which exists only to be deflated by a sentence or two near the end.

If this is true today, when a detective novel is also a slim volume, what are we to say of the earlier phase of expansion after Poe's sober contribution? When his idea was first stretched out to fill the dominant form, the novel meant a "tangled skein" of 150,000 words. The French *romans policiers* à la Gaboriau, the milder melodramas of Anna Katherine Green, and even the best novels of the 1920's from the hand of Agatha Christie or Dorothy Sayers were massive constructions in which a great many innocent people had to behave suspiciously if the main business was to be kept long enough out of the reader's sight. Conan Doyle himself went against sound instinct, though by another route, and concocted those intolerable middle sections which potbelly three out of four of his longer tales. The astute reader reads them once, at the age of twelve, and skips them forever after.

I grant that the short story also has its perils and defects, especially if for lack of invention it returns to the state of anecdote, that is, makes the dénouement hinge on one small point instead of on a chain of inferences drawn from several facts. Nothing is duller than the tale of the criminal who, having endured long questioning with aristocratic aplomb, turns green and claws the air because he is caught in a lie. The same holds true of the lost button, the spent match, the missing envelope—no matter how ingenious the situation or how skilfully built up the suspense, no solitary clue is good enough to satisfy the reader who knows what detection is and insists on getting it.

Ideally, the short detective story is a sequence of five parts, for which it is a pity that Greek names cannot at this late date be invented. First comes the preamble, philosophic in tone, and if possible paradoxical or otherwise arresting. It sets the mood by providing a sample of what Poe called ratiocination. However you pronounce it, ratiocination is a heart-warming prospect. The detective theorizes upon some aspect of life which the story will bear out, though he himself does not as yet know this. Next comes the predicament—mysterious, horrible, grotesque, or merely puzzling —the variation from the norm which invites inquiry. The commonplace mind, represented by the client or by some other embodiment of the *ewig-Watsonisches*, tries to assimilate the unusual and fails. But the superior mind, the detective intellect, seen through a cloud of smoke, discerns the true question and feels immortal inklings upon him—as may be gathered from the irritating silence which follows his voluble beginning.

Further events soon disconcert both the common and the superior minds, but, again, only the latter recovers. This is the signal for a little discourse on method, possibly given socratically, by questions and answers that dispose of the obvious hypothesis and leave everything in an engaging confusion. It is time for the detective to act on his still-hidden "deductions." He tests "places, people, and things." The sheep separate themselves from the goat, and the ensuing violence—confession, arrest, suicide—prepares the way for explanations.

These may of course be artfully distilled through the two or three closing sections of the tale, but if the end is not to be a wordy anticlimax, some provocation of sharp surprise must be kept to the last. We know that the culprit is the smooth solicitor with the pincenez, but we still cannot see how he could have been in London and Buenos Aires at the same time. The final lecturette which leads up to this disclosure, far from being a rehash, is an illumination which is also an emotional peak, because it releases the tension of intelligent curiosity we have labored under from the beginning.

To be sure, "form" in narrative is rather a metaphorical guide than a commandment, and the combining of incident and ratiocination in the detective short story can be widely varied, as R. Austin Freeman proved in *The Singing Bone*, from which I have chosen "A Case of Premeditation." In that volume he created the two-part invention, telling first the events in forward motion, as they occurred, then once again in reverse, as the detective reconstructs their sequence and meaning. To sustain interest in such a twice-told tale requires great generalship and a faultless choice of facts, for the repetition bares the machinery to the author's own practical criticism as well as the reader's. Unless the parts are solid and well-knit, what we accepted readily on a first recital will sound feeble or improbable when served up again to suit a new pattern and a diminished suspense.

All that I have been saying about the genre could be summed up in one word: the detective story is a *tale*. The pleasure it affords is that of any narrative in which the ancient riddle of who is who unravels itself to an accompaniment of worldly wisdom. In the detective tale proper there is a double satisfaction answering a double curiosity—what can the solution be? and how was the solution arrived at? But to recapture this innocent pleasure one must be sophisticated enough to abdicate other sophistications.

II

The case for the detective story cannot of course stop on this dogmatic note, for certain merits of the genre and certain objections to it are yet to be named. Among the objections is that of sameness— "read one and you have read them all." My description of the form could even be cited in support of the charge; it would be foolish to deny that detection in literature submits to very rigid canons. It is an art of symmetry, it seeks the appearance of logical necessity, like classical tragedy, and like tragedy it cherishes the unity of place—the locked room, the ship or train in motion. Its successes thus partake always of the tour de force. As Yeats rightly remarked, "The technique is *supairb*."

But these very limitations, when appreciated, draw our eyes to the points of difference between one tale and another. Indeed, superficial sameness is a common attribute of tales, in contrast with the surface variety we expect of novels and novelistic short stories. If you read Boccaccio and Margaret of Navarre and Bandello and the *Cent Nouvelles Nouvelles* and the *Contes Drôlatiques*, you will find these tales as alike among themselves as any comparable number of detective stories. In the one group, lovers plot against husbands and are either successful or ridiculous. In the other, the detective is confronted by the inexplicable and he reasons his way to the explanation, with or without apprehending a culprit. Fairy tales also betray a strong family likeness. There is a task set and an ogre to be conquered before the princess' hand is available; and generally everything comes in threes. Still, one can distinguish the masterpieces from the dull imitations, whatever the genre, by the art with which the formula has been vivified.

What one seems to miss in the tale is the novel's lifelike looseness, the illusion of uncontrived actuality. One is conscious of *listening to a tale*, which is why I suggest that the enjoyment of detective stories requires a superior sophistication. Again, I concede that the reader who goes to novels in order to learn something new about human character will be disappointed in detection. The tale may teach nothing but its own neatness, and its effect then is to bring a smile to the lips rather than a commotion to the soul. These are two orders of pleasure, not necessarily two degrees of it.

But if what I say is true, what becomes of the connection we observed, at least historically, between detective fiction and the realistic novel? To perceive the connection one must turn from form to substance. The raw material of detection consists of the physical objects that surround action. These become literary substance when the detective imagination has chosen and arranged them so that some are clues while others produce atmosphere, verisimilitude, suspense. In detection details are numerous and must be instantly convincing. We are ready to swallow long descriptions of houses and their furnishings, we are greedy for the contents of posthumous pockets, we long to master time tables, speeds of vehicles, and procedures for collecting evidence, provided always that these records of matter moving through time and space conform to the common standards of credibility. That is the reason why many years ago Father Ronald Knox laid down as one of the laws of detective fiction: "There must be no Chinamen."

For this cryptic rule, which its author said he could not explain, is in fact the principle of the realistic novel: the world of magic and mystery yields to a sense of reality based on the persuasiveness of things. To be sure, the great novels of the realistic school portray character even more painstakingly than things, whereas detection rightly keeps character subordinate. But detection makes up for this neglect by giving intelligence a place which it has in no other literary form. Only in the detective tale is the hero demonstrably as bright as the author says he is.

Some readers of course are by temperament impatient with small details. Trollope tells us that he did not like stories in which he had to remember what happened at a given hour on the Tuesday, or how many yards from the milestone the lady was abducted. But in so saying he is telling us about himself rather than criticizing the genre. His own work is full of little points to remember about people, church politics, and county snobbery. We follow him because, as we say, we gain an understanding of English life as well as of humankind. What do we gain from the details of detection? An understanding, first, of the silent life of things, and next, of the spectacle of mind at work. This is no doubt why detective feats have been, since Voltaire and Poe, the delight of intellectuals. The emotion called forth is that of seeing order grow out of confusion. This is no mean or despicable emotion: it can match in intensity the light of recognition which Aristotle declared the strongest effect of tragedy.

To experience this pleasure of discovery one must be willing to explore, as minutely and lovingly as the author desires, the nature and connections of the inanimate—including the corpse. One must be attentive to the interlinked traces of human action upon the material world. No doubt this is an acquired taste, like the taste for reading the history of the earth in rocks and rivers. But a generation reared on Proust's crumb of cake in the teacup should readily concede that bits of matter matter.

To those who acknowledge this, the attempt to "improve" the detective story and make it "a real novel" seems a proof of bad judgment. Replacing clues with "psychology" and intelligible plot with dubious suspense is childish tinkering. Far from "maturing" detection and giving us genuine novels with "real" characters, the so-called stories of suspense have only obscured a true genre and further muddled the criticism of it. The name itself is meaningless. Any good tale is a "story of suspense." What we are in fact given in the new mongrel form is "stories of anxiety," which cater for the contemporary wish to feel vaguely disturbed. I do not question the pleasure derived from this sort of self-abuse. I merely decline to call it superior to another pleasure which is totally different. And I hope I need not add that I enjoy and admire, each in its own kind, a great many of the tales now confused with detection, from Dashiell Hammett's *Red Harvest* to Stanley Ellin's *Broker's Special* and from Agatha Christie's *Witness for the Prosecution* to Anthony Boucher's *Elsewhen*.

The truth remains that it cannot improve a genre to drain out its essence, fill the void with second-hand soul-searching and arty verbal tricks, and pretend that the result is at once the classic article and something loftier. When I hunger for "real characters," I am satisfied by nothing less than Stendhal, Balzac, Meredith, James, Dickens, Hardy, or Joyce. When I want to read about "the psychology of a murderer," I go to Dostoevsky, Büchner, Victor Hugo, Stevenson, or Shakespeare: I do not want it from Miss Mary Limpet or Mr. Sterling Brass, who write in the *I Did It* and *I Done It* manners respectively.

Again, the detective tale is not the place to make us appreciate the moral burdens of the times by presenting a detective who (I am quoting the review) is "middle-aged, humane, and embittered," so that his detection gives "glimpses of man's callous indifference to man." Finally, detective fiction has more to offer the reader than an incomplete Baedeker to some unfamiliar region of the world. All these novelties are but inferior substitutes for detection, the genius of which, conceivably, is played out. All forms eventually die. Yet if we are to believe Mr. Anthony Boucher, the most alert observer of the tendencies affecting the genre, "there seems to be something of an upswing in the pure basic detective story, the logical and well-clued whodunit." (*New York Times*, June 12, 1960)

Meanwhile, from the modern deviations one can reason backward to certain critical conclusions. If you ask the ordinary reader which of the Sherlock Holmes short stories he likes best, the chances are that he will say: "The Speckled Band." The vision of the snake coming down the bell pull is the utmost thrill he expects from detection. To the connoisseur, however, the tale is one of Doyle's weaker efforts. It stands far below, say, "The Six Napoleons," which I would have reprinted if I had not taken it for granted that any reader of this book is at this very moment leaning his elbow on the complete Sherlock Holmes. Now the point of the contrast is not that "sensationalism" is out of place because detection is "intellectual." Turn to Ernest Bramah's "Brookbend Cottage" and you will see how compatible detection can be with thrills and fireworks. The point is rather that in any combination of the detective interest with anything else, the something else must remain the junior partner.

By this principle we can see why it is so rare that a detective tale of French or German authorship is true to its name. The old *roman policier* tradition hangs over it and makes one groan. Fanciful "reconstructions" of the crime, inane accusations, a vicious love of coincidence, a smug acceptance of chance solutions—all this, saturated with the unhealthy flavor of the state police, generally spoils the dish. Simenon's long-winded irrelevancies are the same thing modern style, that is, with morbid coloring added. What shall one say of the Oriental adaptation of our genre? To believe, among other things, that a criminal can for professional purposes conceal himself inside the upholstery of an armchair demands an effort of nonvisualization that few Western readers will be willing to make. The fact that the author of such inventions has taken the pseudonym of Edogawa Rampo only adds a touch of resentment to our dismay.

Yet strict naturalism is not enough, either, as we see in the so-called novels of police routine. These works are a little too conscientiously instructive and sociological. They should be taken in moderation, unless one is a salesman and able to find a narcissistic pleasure in seeing other patient men ring doorbells. I repeat: nothing less than the play of the detective intelligence upon the physical world will give us a detective tale. It might seem at first sight as if Mr. Kemelman's admirable "Nine-Mile Walk" destroyed the rule: what is his story but a few words overheard and analyzed? This is mere appearance. The detection is genuinely of the physical conditions surrounding the deed and implied by the one short sentence—an exemplary work as well as a tour de force.

III

But am I not still a good way from showing that detective fiction is a branch of literature in the honorific sense of belles-lettres? Is not detection perhaps a frivolous by-product of legal and scientific writing, a *jeu d'esprit* for tired professional men who lack the energy to tackle poetry? Behind these questions lurks a general suspicion about style. The literary conscience demands that anything called literature show mastery not only of structure but also of tone and diction. The manner of these is not prescribed, but the commonplace will degrade a narrative, however ingenious, to the rank of popular journalism.

Detective stories have been written, certainly, which show complete indifference to the felicities of feeling and expression. But this is true in equal measure of every type of story. Nick Carter has his counterparts in all genres, and we must judge detective fiction as we do other kinds, by the best examples. It is no concession to admit that there would be no genre to speak of and no art to criticize if detective stories gave us but stock situations interlarded with footprints and tobacco ash. It is the shuttling between the infinity of possible human actions and their equally varied physical setting that gives the detective story-teller the chance to be original, adroit, revelatory. And success here as elsewhere calls for the fundamental literary powers.

The supreme quality in our special genre is of course invention, which is to say imagination. Because the light shines on all the material circumstances these must seem fresh, at least in function, and yet sufficiently common to be plausible—streets and moors and stairs and potting sheds must be recognizable and in no way fanciful. Incidents, likewise, must show a studious regard for the norms and conventions of life and yet avoid that predictability which is the mark of journalism in the derogatory sense. Only art, the art of words, will support a writer who tries to walk this narrow path. It is style that in the fictions of Dorothy Sayers or Rex Stout, of E. C. Bentley or G. K. Chesterton, makes their works at once worthy of belief and pleasurable to read. Here again, as in classical tragedy, the illusion works, artificiality disappears, thanks to a scrupulous attention to language. And as in Racine, a few clichés must be accepted as part of the convention: when "tangled skeins" are out of date we must tolerate the detective's happy thought that his work resembles "the fitting together of a jigsaw puzzle."

Nor is literature in abeyance because we consent to character drawing being in detective fiction a secondary concern. For in these tales characters must none the less move and talk agreeably to their role—and to ourselves. We must know them at least as well as we know the many people, not our intimates, with whom we deal in daily life. By a right use of the Jamesian "point of view" the writer of detection allows us to see into his actors far enough to recognize their type and judge their ostensible motives. Were we to go farther we would see too much: the writer would have given away what it is his business to keep hidden until circumstances speak. In this half concealment lies an art which is none other than literary.

The one exception to this deliberate superficiality is the portrait of the detective, and here too the literature can show some triumphs. Sherlock Holmes is as fully a character as Mr. Pickwick. And by virtue of Doyle's almost unique success in giving a soul to the detective's partner—the common man—we have in the two a companion pair to Don Quixote and Sancho Panza, a contrast and concert capable of occupying our imaginations apart from the tales in which the two figure. Similarly in Nero Wolfe and Archie Goodwin this old pattern of the knight and his squire, which is as old as the *Iliad,* is repeated with conspicuous success in the American idiom.

It does not of course take such a partnership to prove that writers of detective tales can animate their heroes with a picturesque variety. From Father Brown to Peter Wimsey the range is wide. There is in fact but one limit that must not be transgressed; the detective cannot be a fool. I have no use for those ineffectual little men who are always mislaying their belongings and nursing a head cold, yet manage to track down desperate murderers. An all-embracing awareness of physical surroundings and great powers of ratiocination being the spectacle we look for, we are cheated when amiable bumblers hold the stage and succeed by accident at the last minute. They are as unconstitutional in their way as the "poison unknown to science" which kills before the cork is out of the bottle. And my objection to ineffectuality goes for the same paradox in any other form—the great Cointreau, let us say, who is always drinking and hiccuping, and who ends his cases snoring face down on the table while the prisoner is led away in a whiskey-scented haze. Poe decided once for all that the detective should be a man of independent mind, an eccentric possibly, something of an artist even in his "scientific" work, and in any case a creature of will and scope superior to the crowd. He is, in short, the last of the heroes. It follows that to produce him the author must be at least his equal in observation and vocabulary: wit, learning, and repartee consti-tute the hallmark of detective literature.

The final grace of the perfect tale is its ornamentation. I mean by this the small touches which, while they fit the working parts of the plot, give them a characteristic coloring. Thus in Mr. Mac-Donald's story the atmosphere of a small American town is ren-dered by a quantity of suitably superfluous details (such as the character and reputation of the twins), while by means of still others the adventure as a whole is bathed in irony. A similar effect in Michael Gilbert's "Oyster Catcher" strengthens there also the contrast between modern lab-work analysis and old-style ratiocina-tion. Indeed, an exact measure of levity in detection shows the master's hand, for as Arthur Machen pointed out long ago, the true tone of the genre springs from the alliance of murder and mirth. The laughter is a touch sardonic and must never degenerate into hilarity. The joke of death is on us. Conan Doyle and Dorothy Sayers, among the classics, understood this better than anyone else. What finer-humored critique of detection itself, and at the same time what more brilliant invention, than the casual reference in the Holmes story to the case which hinged on "how far the parsley had sunk into the butter upon a hot day"?

A muffled irony is perhaps as much as our later sensibility will stand, but some such injection of butter and parsley is needed if we are to preserve our proper distance from what is after all ugly business. Murder and detection in real life can give pleasure to very few. The one evokes anger and misery, the other boredom. Only when transmuted into literature by the artificial light of reason and the arbitrary rearrangement of parts do these social and anti-social realities begin to afford delight: after a time, the horrors perpetrated by Burke and Hare become the stuff of DeQuincey's *Murder Considered as One of the Fine Arts*—the first model of still another genre. But since Poe's great feat, we need no longer depend on Burke and Hare and DeQuincey, nor on the four or five disciples of the last-named who have reshaped for us the incidents of actual crime. We have for our solace and edification the literary genre I have tried to describe and am about to show at its best—abundant, variegated, illustrious, classical—the detective story.

CLASSIC TALES

The Tragedy at Brookbend Cottage

BY ERNEST BRAMAH

"Max," said Mr. Carlyle, when Parkinson had closed the door behind him, "this is Lieutenant Hollyer, whom you consented to see."

"To hear," corrected Carrados, smiling straight into the healthy and rather embarrassed face of the stranger before him. "Mr. Hollyer knows of my disability?"

"Mr. Carlyle told me," said the young man, "but, as a matter of fact, I had heard of you before, Mr. Carrados, from one of our men. It was in connection with the foundering of the *Ivan Saratov*."

Carrados wagged his head in good-humored resignation.

"And the owners were sworn to inviolable secrecy!" he exclaimed. "Well, it is inevitable, I suppose. Not another scuttling case, Mr. Hollyer?"

"No, mine is quite a private matter," replied the lieutenant. "My sister, Mrs. Creake—but Mr. Carlyle would tell you better than I can. He knows all about it."

"No, no; Carlyle is a professional. Let me have it in the rough, Mr. Hollyer. My ears are my eyes, you know."

"Very well, sir. I can tell you what there is to tell, right enough, but I feel that when all's said and done it must sound very little to another, although it seems important to me."

"We have occasionally found trifles of significance ourselves," said Carrados encouragingly. "Don't let that deter you."

This was the essence of Lieutenant Hollyer's narrative:

"I have a sister, Millicent, who is married to a man called Creake . . . She is about twenty-eight now and he is at least fifteen years older. Neither my mother (who has since died) nor I cared very much about Creake. We had nothing particular against him, except, perhaps, the moderate disparity of age, but none of us appeared to have anything in common. He was a dark, taciturn man, and his moody silence froze up conversation. As a result, of course, we didn't see much of each other."

"This, you must understand, was four or five years ago, Max," interposed Mr. Carlyle officiously.

Carrados maintained an uncompromising silence. Mr. Carlyle blew his nose and contrived to impart a hurt significance into the operation. Then Lieutenant Hollyer continued:

"Millicent married Creake after a very short engagement. It was a frightfully subdued wedding—more like a funeral to me. The man professed to have no relations and apparently he had scarcely any friends or business acquaintances. He was an agent for something or other and had an office off Holborn. I suppose he made a living out of it then, although we knew practically nothing of his private affairs, but I gather that it has been going down since, and I suspect that for the past few years they have been getting along almost entirely on Millicent's little income. You would like the particulars of that?"

"Please," assented Carrados.

"When our father died about seven years ago, he left three thousand pounds. It was invested in Canadian stock and brought in a little over a hundred a year. By his will my mother was to have the income of that for life and on her death it was to pass to Millicent, subject to the payment of a lump sum of five hundred pounds to me. But my father privately suggested to me that if I should have no particular use for the money at the time, he would propose my letting Millicent have the income of it until I did want it, as she would not be particularly well off. You see, Mr. Carrados, a great deal more had been spent on my education and advancement than on her; I had my pay, and, of course, I could look out for myself better than a girl could."

"Quite so," agreed Carrados.

"Therefore I did nothing about that," continued the lieutenant. "Three years ago I was over again but I did not see much of them. They were living in lodgings. That was the only time since the marriage that I have seen them until last week. In the meanwhile our mother had died and Millicent had been receiving her income. She wrote me several letters at the time. Otherwise we did not correspond much, but about a year ago she sent me their new address—Brookbend Cottage, Mulling Common—a house that they had taken. When I got two months' leave I invited myself there as a matter of course, fully expecting to stay most of my time with them, but I made an excuse to get away after a week. The place was dismal and unendurable, the whole life and atmosphere indescribably depressing." He looked round with an instinct of caution, leaned forward earnestly, and dropped his voice. "Mr. Carrados, it is my absolute conviction that Creake is only waiting for a favourable opportunity to murder Millicent."

"Go on," said Carrados quietly. "A week of the depressing surroundings of Brookbend Cottage would not alone convince you of that, Mr. Hollyer."

"I am not so sure," declared Hollyer doubtfully. "There was a feeling of suspicion and—before me—polite hatred that would have gone a good way towards it. All the same there *was* something more definite. Millicent told me this the day after I went there. There is no doubt that a few months ago Creake deliberately planned to poison her with some weed-killer. She told me the circumstances in a rather distressed moment, but afterwards she refused to speak of it again—even weakly denied it—and, as a matter of fact, it was with the greatest difficulty that I could get her at any time to talk about her husband or his affairs. The gist of it was that she had the strongest suspicion that Creake doctored a bottle of stout which he expected she would drink for her supper when she was alone. The weed-killer, properly labeled, but also in a beer bottle, was kept with other miscellaneous liquids in the same cupboard as the beer but on a high shelf. When he found that it had miscarried he poured away the mixture, washed out the bottle and put in the dregs from another. There is no doubt in my mind that if he had come back and found Millicent dead or dying he would have contrived it to appear that she had made a mistake in the dark and drunk some of the poison before she found out."

"Yes," assented Carrados. "The open way; the safe way."

"You must understand that they live in a very small style, Mr. Carrados, and Millicent is almost entirely in the man's power. The only servant they have is a woman who comes in for a few hours every day. The house is lonely and secluded. Creake is sometimes away for days and nights at a time, and Millicent, either through pride or indifference, seems to have dropped off all her old friends and to have made no others. He might poison her, bury the body in the garden, and be a thousand miles away before any one began even to inquire about her. What am I to do, Mr. Carrados?"

"He is less likely to try poison than some other means now," pondered Carrados. "That having failed, his wife will always be on her guard. He may know, or at least suspect, that others know. No.... The common-sense precaution would be for your sister to leave the man, Mr. Hollyer. She will not?"

"No," admitted Hollyer, "she will not. I at once urged that." The young man struggled with some hesitation for a moment and then blurted out: "The fact is, Mr. Carrados, I don't understand Millicent. She is not the girl she was. She hates Creake and treats him with a silent contempt that eats into their lives like acid, and yet she is so jealous of him that she will let nothing short of death part them. It is a horrible life they lead. I stood it for a week and I must say, much as I dislike my brother-in-law, that he has something to put up with. If only he got into a passion like a man and killed her it wouldn't be altogether incomprehensible."

"That does not concern us," said Carrados. "In a game of this kind one has to take sides and we have taken ours. It remains for us to see that our side wins. You mentioned jealousy, Mr. Hollyer. Have you any idea whether Mrs. Creake has real ground for it?"

"I should have told you that," replied Lieutenant Hollyer. "I happened to strike up with a newspaper man whose office is in the same block as Creake's. When I mentioned the name he grinned. 'Creake,' he said, 'oh, he's the man with the romantic typist, isn't he?' 'Well, he's my brother-in-law,' I replied. 'What about the typist?' Then the chap shut up like a knife. 'No, no,' he said, 'I didn't know he was married. I don't want to get mixed up in anything of that sort. I only said that he had a typist. Well, what of that? So have we; so has every one.' There was nothing more to be got out of him, but the remark and the grin meant—well, about as usual, Mr. Carrados."

Carrados turned to his friend.

"I suppose you know all about the typist by now, Louis?"

"We have had her under efficient observation, Max," replied Mr. Carlyle, with severe dignity.

"Is she unmarried?"

"Yes; so far as ordinary repute goes, she is."

"That is all that is essential for the moment. Mr. Hollyer opens up three excellent reasons why this man might wish to dispose of his wife. If we accept the suggestion of poisoning—though we have only a jealous woman's suspicion for it—we add to the wish the determination. Well, we will go forward on that. Have you got a photograph of Mr. Creake?"

The lieutenant took out his pocket-book.

"Mr. Carlyle asked me for one. Here is the best I could get."

Carrados rang the bell.

"This, Parkinson," he said, when the man appeared, "is a photograph of a Mr. —. What first name, by the way?"

"Austin," put in Hollyer, who was following everything with a boyish mixture of excitement and subdued importance.

"—of a Mr. Austin Creake. I may require you to recognize him."

Parkinson glanced at the print and returned it to his master's hand.

"May I inquire if it is a recent photograph of the gentleman, sir?" he asked.

"About six years ago," said the lieutenant, taking in this new actor in the drama with frank curiosity. "But he is very little changed."

"Thank you, sir. I will endeavor to remember Mr. Creake, sir."

Lieutenant Hollyer stood up as Parkinson left the room. The interview seemed to be at an end.

"Oh, there's one other matter," he remarked. "I am afraid that I did rather an unfortunate thing while I was at Brookbend. It seemed to me that as all Millicent's money would probably pass into Creake's hands sooner or later I might as well have my five hundred pounds, if only to help her with afterwards. So I broached the subject and said that I should like to have it now as I had an opportunity for investing."

"And you think?"

"It may possibly influence Creake to act sooner than he otherwise might have done. He may have got possession of the principal even and find it very awkward to replace it."

"So much the better. If your sister is going to be murdered it may as well be done next week as next year so far as I am concerned. Excuse my brutality, Mr. Hollyer, but this is simply a case to me and I regard it strategically. Now Mr. Carlyle's organization can look after Mrs. Creake for a few weeks, but it cannot look after her forever. By increasing the immediate risk we diminish the permanent risk."

"I see," agreed Hollyer. "I'm awfully uneasy but I'm entirely in your hands."

"Then we will give Mr. Creake every inducement and every opportunity to get to work. Where are you staying now?"

"Just now with some friends at St. Albans."

"That is too far." The inscrutable eyes retained their tranquil depth but a new quality of quickening interest in the voice made Mr. Carlyle forget the weight and burden of his ruffled dignity. "Give me a few minutes, please. The cigarettes are behind you, Mr. Hollyer." The blind man walked to the window and seemed to look out over the cypress-shaded lawn. The lieutenant lit a cigarette and Mr. Carlyle picked up *Punch*. Then Carrados turned round again.

"You are prepared to put your own arrangements aside?" he demanded of his visitor.

"Certainly."

"Very well. I want you to go down now—straight from here—to Brookbend Cottage. Tell your sister that your leave is unexpectedly cut short and that you sail to-morrow."

"The *Martian*?"

"No, no; the *Martian* doesn't sail. Look up the movements on your way there and pick out a boat that does. Say you are transferred. Add that you expect to be away only two or three months and that you really want the five hundred pounds by the time of your return. Don't stay in the house long, please."

"I understand, sir."

"St. Albans is too far. Make your excuse and get away from there to-day. Put up somewhere in town, where you will be in reach of the telephone. Let Mr. Carlyle and myself know where you are. Keep out of Creake's way. I don't want actually to tie you down to the house, but we may require your services. We will let you know at the first sign of anything doing and if there is nothing to be done we must release you."

"I don't mind that. Is there nothing more that I can do now?"

"Nothing. In going to Mr. Carlyle you have done the best thing possible; you have put your sister into the care of the shrewdest man in London." Whereat the object of this quite unexpected eulogy found himself becoming covered with modest confusion.

"Well, Max?" remarked Mr. Carlyle tentatively when they were alone.

"Well, Louis?"

"Of course, it wasn't worth while rubbing it in before young Hollyer, but, as a matter of fact, every single man carries the life of any other man—only one, mind you—in his hands, do what you will."

"Provided he doesn't bungle," acquiesced Carrados.

"Quite so."

"And also that he is absolutely reckless of the consequences."

"Of course."

"Two rather large provisos. Creake is obviously susceptible to both. Have you seen him?"

"No. As I told you, I put a man on to report his habits in town. Then, two days ago, as the case seemed to promise some interest— for he certainly is deeply involved with the typist, Max, and the thing might take a sensational turn at any time—I went down to Mulling Common myself. Although the house is lonely it is on the electric tram route. You know the sort of market-garden rurality that about a dozen miles out of London offers—alternate bricks and cabbages. It was easy enough to get to know about Creake locally. He mixes with no one there, goes into town at irregular times but generally every day, and is reputed to be devilish hard to get money out of. Finally, I made the acquaintance of an old fellow who used to do a day's gardening at Brookbend occasionally. He has a cottage and a garden of his own with a greenhouse, and the business cost me the price of a pound of tomatoes."

"Was it—a profitable investment?"

"As tomatoes, yes; as information, no. The old fellow had the fatal disadvantage from our point of view of labouring under a grievance. A few weeks ago Creake told him that he would not require him again as he was going to do his own gardening in future."

"That is something, Louis."

"If only Creake was going to poison his wife with hyoscyamine and bury her, instead of blowing her up with a dynamite cartridge and claiming that it came in among the coal."

"True, true. Still—"

"However, the chatty old soul had a simple explanation for everything that Creake did. Creake was mad. He had even seen him flying a kite in his garden where it was bound to get wrecked among the trees. A lad of ten would have known better, he declared. And certainly the kite did get wrecked, for I saw it hanging over the road myself. But that a sane man should spend his time 'playing with a toy' was beyond him."

"A good many men have been flying kites of various kinds lately," said Carrados. "Is he interested in aviation?"

"I dare say. He appears to have some knowledge of scientific subjects. Now what do you want me to do, Max?"

"Will you do it?"

"Implicitly—subject to the usual reservations."

"Keep your man on Creake in town and let me have his reports after you have seen them. Lunch with me here now. Phone up to your office that you are detained on unpleasant business and then give the deserving Parkinson an afternoon off by looking after me while we take a motor run round Mulling Common. If we have time we might go on to Brighton, feed at the 'Ship,' and come back in the cool."

"Amiable and thrice lucky mortal," sighed Mr. Carlyle, his glance wandering round the room.

But, as it happened, Brighton did not figure in that day's itinerary. It had been Carrados' intention merely to pass Brookbend Cottage on this occasion, relying on his highly developed faculties, aided by Mr. Carlyle's description, to inform him of the surroundings. A hundred yards before they reached the house he had given an order to his chauffeur to drop into the lowest speed and they were leisurely drawing past when a discovery by Mr. Carlyle modified their plans.

"By Jupiter!" that gentleman suddenly exclaimed, "there's a board up, Max. The place is to be let."

Carrados picked up the tube again. A couple of sentences passed and the car stopped by the roadside, a score of paces past the limit of the garden. Mr. Carlyle took out his notebook and wrote down the address of a firm of house agents.

"You might raise the bonnet and have a look at the engines, Harris," said Carrados. "We want to be occupied here for a few minutes."

"This is sudden; Hollyer knew nothing of their leaving," remarked Mr. Carlyle.

"Probably not for three months yet. All the same, Louis, we will go on to the agents and get a card to view, whether we use it to-day or not."

A thick hedge, in its summer dress effectively screening the house beyond from public view, lay between the garden and the road. Above the hedge showed an occasional shrub; at the corner nearest to the car a chestnut flourished. The wooden gate, once white, which they had passed, was grimed and rickety. The road itself was still the unpretentious country lane that the advent of the electric car had found it. When Carrados had taken in these details there seemed little else to notice. He was on the point of giving Harris the order to go on when his ear caught a trivial sound.

"Some one is coming out of the house, Louis," he warned his friend. "It may be Hollyer, but he ought to have gone by this time."

"I don't hear any one," replied the other, but as he spoke a door banged noisily and Mr. Carlyle slipped into another seat and ensconced himself behind a copy of *The Globe*.

"Creake himself," he whispered across the car, as a man appeared at the gate. "Hollyer was right; he is hardly changed. Waiting for a car, I suppose."

But a car very soon swung past them from the direction in which Mr. Creake was looking and it did not interest him. For a minute or two longer he continued to look expectantly along the road. Then he walked slowly up the drive back to the house.

"We will give him five or ten minutes," decided Carrados. "Harris is behaving very naturally."

Before even the shorter period had run out they were repaid. A telegraph-boy cycled leisurely along the road, and, leaving his machine at the gate, went up to the cottage. Evidently there was no reply, for in less than a minute he was trundling past them back again. Round the bend an approaching tram clanged its bell noisily, and, quickened by the warning sound, Mr. Creake again appeared, this time with a small portmanteau in his hand. With a backward glance he hurried on towards the next stopping-place, and, boarding the car as it slackened down, he was carried out of their knowledge.

"Very convenient of Mr. Creake," remarked Carrados, with quiet satisfaction. "We will now get the order and go over the house in his absence. It might be useful to have a look at the wire as well."

"It might, Max," acquiesced Mr. Carlyle a little dryly. "But if it is, as it probably is, in Creake's pocket, how do you propose to get it?"

"By going to the post office, Louis."

"Quite so. Have you ever tried to see a copy of a telegram addressed to some one else?"

"I don't think I have ever had occasion yet," admitted Carrados. "Have you?"

"In one or two cases I have perhaps been an accessory to the act. It is generally a matter either of extreme delicacy or considerable expenditure."

"Then for Hollyer's sake we will hope for the former here." And Mr. Carlyle smiled darkly and hinted that he was content to wait for a friendly revenge.

A little later, having left the car at the beginning of the straggling High Street, the two men called at the village post office. They had already visited the house agent and obtained an order to view Brookbend Cottage, declining with some difficulty the clerk's persistent offer to accompany them. The reason was soon forthcoming. "As a matter of fact," explained the young man, "the present tenant is under *our* notice to leave."

"Unsatisfactory, eh?" said Carrados, encouragingly.

"He's a corker," admitted the clerk, responding to the friendly tone. "Fifteen months and not a doit of rent have we had. That's why I should have liked—"

"We will make every allowance," replied Carrados.

The post office occupied one side of the stationer's shop. It was not without some inward trepidation that Mr. Carlyle found himself committed to the adventure. Carrados, on the other hand, was the personification of bland unconcern.

"You have just sent a telegram to Brookbend Cottage," he said to the young lady behind the brass-work lattice. "We think it may have come inaccurately and should like a repeat." He took out his purse. "What is the fee?"

The request was evidently not a common one. "Oh," said the girl uncertainly, "wait a minute, please." She turned to a pile of tele-gram duplicates behind the desk and ran a doubtful finger along the upper sheets. "I think this is all right. You want it repeated?"

"Please." Just a tinge of questioning surprise gave point to the courteous tone.

"It will be fourpence. If there is an error the amount will be re-funded."

Carrados put down his coin and received his change.

"Will it take long?" he inquired carelessly, as he pulled on his glove.

"You will most likely get it within a quarter of an hour," she replied.

"Now you've done it," commented Mr. Carlyle, as they walked back to their car. "How do you propose to get that telegram, Max?"

"Ask for it," was the laconic explanation.

And, stripping the artifice of any elaboration, he simply asked for it and got it. The car, posted at a convenient bend in the road, gave him a warning note as the telegraph-boy approached. Then Car-rados took up a convincing attitude with his hand on the gate while Mr. Carlyle lent himself to the semblance of a departing friend. That was the inevitable impression when the boy rode up.

"Creake, Brookbend Cottage?" inquired Carrados, holding out his hand, and without a second thought the boy gave him the en-velope and rode away on the assurance that there would be no reply.

"Some day, my friend," remarked Mr. Carlyle, looking nerv-ously towards the unseen house, "your ingenuity will get you into a tight corner."

"Then my ingenuity must get me out again," was the retort. "Let us have our 'view' now. The telegram can wait."

An untidy workwoman took their order and left them standing at the door. Presently a lady whom they both knew to be Mrs. Creake appeared.

"You wish to see over the house?" she said, in a voice that was utterly devoid of any interest. Then, without waiting for a reply, she turned to the nearest door and threw it open.

"This is the drawing-room," she said, standing aside.

They walked into a sparsely furnished, damp-smelling room and made a pretense of looking round, while Mrs. Creake remained silent and aloof.

"The dining-room," she continued, crossing the narrow hall and opening another door.

Mr. Carlyle ventured a genial commonplace in the hope of inducing conversation. The result was not encouraging. Doubtless they would have gone through the house under the same frigid guidance had not Carrados been at fault in a way that Mr. Carlyle had never known him fail before. In crossing the hall he stumbled over a mat and almost fell.

"Pardon my clumsiness," he said to the lady. "I am, unfortunately, quite blind. But," he added, with a smile, to turn off the mishap, "even a blind man must have a house."

The man who had eyes was surprised to see a flood of color rush into Mrs. Creake's face.

"Blind!" she exclaimed, "oh, I beg your pardon. Why did you not tell me? You might have fallen."

"I generally manage fairly well," he replied. "But, of course in a strange house—"

She put her hand on his arm very lightly.

"You must let me guide you, just a little," she said.

The house, without being large, was full of passages and inconvenient turnings. Carrados asked an occasional question and found Mrs. Creake quite amiable without effusion. Mr. Carlyle followed them from room to room in the hope, though scarcely the expectation, of learning something that might be useful.

"This is the last one. It is the largest bedroom," said their guide. Only two of the upper rooms were fully furnished and Mr. Carlyle at once saw, as Carrados knew without seeing, that this was the one which the Creakes occupied.

"A very pleasant outlook," declared Mr. Carlyle.

"Oh, I suppose so," admitted the lady vaguely. The room, in fact, looked over the leafy garden and the road beyond. It had a French window opening on to a small balcony, and to this, under the strange influence that always attracted him to light, Carrados walked.

"I expect that there is a certain amount of repair needed?" he said, after standing there a moment.

"I am afraid there would be," she confessed.

"I ask because there is a sheet of metal on the floor here," he continued. "Now that, in an old house, spells dry-rot to the wary observer."

"My husband said that the rain, which comes in a little under the window, was rotting the boards there," she replied. "He put that down recently. I had not noticed anything myself."

It was the first time she had mentioned her husband; Mr. Carlyle pricked up his ears.

"Ah, that is a less serious matter," said Carrados. "May I step out on to the balcony?"

"Oh, yes, if you like to." Then, as he appeared to be fumbling at the catch, "Let me open it for you."

But the window was already open, and Carrados, facing the various points of the compass, took in the bearings.

"A sunny, sheltered corner," he remarked. "An ideal spot for a deck-chair and a book."

She shrugged her shoulders half-contemptuously.

"I dare say," she replied, "but I never use it."

"Sometimes, surely," he persisted mildly. "It would be my favourite retreat. But then—"

"I was going to say that I had never even been out on it, but that would not be quite true. It has two uses for me, both equally romantic; I occasionally shake a duster from it, and when my husband returns late without his latchkey he wakes me up and I come out here and drop him mine."

Further revelation of Mr. Creake's nocturnal habits was cut off, greatly to Mr. Carlyle's annoyance, by a cough of unmistakable significance from the foot of the stairs. They had heard a trade cart drive up to the gate, a knock at the door, and the heavy-footed woman tramp along the hall.

"Excuse me a minute, please," said Mrs. Creake.

"Louis," said Carrados, in a sharp whisper, the moment they were alone, "stand against the door."

With extreme plausibility Mr. Carlyle began to admire a picture so situated that while he was there it was impossible to open the door more than a few inches. From that position he observed his confederate go through the curious procedure of kneeling down on the bedroom floor and for a full minute pressing his ear to the sheet of metal that had already engaged his attention. Then he rose to his feet, nodded, dusted his trousers, and Mr. Carlyle moved to a less equivocal position.

"What a beautiful rose-tree grows up your balcony," remarked Carrados, stepping into the room as Mrs. Creake returned. "I suppose you are very fond of gardening?"

"I detest it," she replied.

"But this *Gloire*, so carefully trained—?"

"Is it?" she replied. "I think my husband was nailing it up recently." By some strange fatality Carrados' most aimless remarks seemed to involve the absent Mr. Creake. "Do you care to see the garden?"

The garden proved to be extensive and neglected. Behind the house was chiefly orchard. In front, some semblance of order had been kept up; here it was lawn and shrubbery, and the drive they had walked along. Two things interested Carrados: the soil at the foot of the balcony, which he declared on examination to be particularly suitable for roses, and the fine chestnut-tree in the corner by the road.

As they walked back to the car Mr. Carlyle lamented that they had learned so little of Creake's movements.

"Perhaps the telegram will tell us something," suggested Carrados. "Read it, Louis."

Mr. Carlyle cut open the envelope, glanced at the enclosure, and in spite of his disappointment could not restrain a chuckle.

"My poor Max," he explained, "you have put yourself to an amount of ingenious trouble for nothing. Creake is evidently taking a few days' holiday and prudently availed himself of the Meteorological Office forecast before going. Listen: '*Immediate prospect*

for London warm and settled. Further outlook cooler but fine.'
Well, well; I did get a pound of tomatoes for *my* fourpence."

"You certainly scored there, Louis," admitted Carrados, with humorous appreciation. "I wonder," he added speculatively, "whether it is Creake's peculiar taste usually to spend his week-end holiday in London."

"Eh?" exclaimed Mr. Carlyle, looking at the words again, "by gad, that's rum, Max. They go to Weston-super-Mare. Why on earth should he want to know about London?"

"I can make a guess, but before we are satisfied I must come here again. Take another look at that kite, Louis. Are there a few yards of string hanging loose from it?"

"Yes, there are."

"Rather thick string—unusually thick for the purpose?"

"Yes; but how do you know?"

As they drove home again Carrados explained, and Mr. Carlyle sat aghast, saying incredulously: "Good God, Max, is it possible?"

An hour later he was satisfied that it was possible. In reply to his inquiry some one in his office telephoned him the information that "they" had left Paddington by the four-thirty for Weston.

It was more than a week after his introduction to Carrados that Lieutenant Hollyer had a summons to present himself at The Turrets again. He found Mr. Carlyle already there and the two friends awaiting his arrival.

"I stayed in all day after hearing from you this morning, Mr. Carrados," he said, shaking hands. "When I got your second message I was all ready to walk straight out of the house. That's how I did it in the time. I hope everything is all right?"

"Excellent," replied Carrados. "You'd better have something before we start. We probably have a long and perhaps an exciting night before us."

"And certainly a wet one," assented the lieutenant. "It was thundering over Mulling way as I came along."

"That is why you are here," said his host. "We are waiting for a certain message before we start, and in the meantime you may as well understand what we expect to happen. As you saw, there is a thunderstorm coming on. The Meteorological Office morning forecast predicted it for the whole of London if the conditions remained. That was why I kept you in readiness. Within an hour it is now inevitable that we shall experience a deluge. Here and there damage will be done to trees and buildings; here and there a person will probably be struck and killed."

"Yes."

"It is Mr. Creake's intention that his wife should be among the victims."

"I don't exactly follow," said Hollyer, looking from one man to the other. "I quite admit that Creake would be immensely relieved if such a thing did happen, but the chance is surely an absurdly remote one."

"Yet unless we intervene it is precisely what a coroner's jury will decide has happened. Do you know whether your brother-in-law has any practical knowledge of electricity, Mr. Hollyer?"

"I cannot say. He was so reserved, and we really knew so little of him—"

"Yet in 1896 an Austin Creake contributed an article on 'Alternating Currents' to the American *Scientific World*. That would argue a fairly intimate acquaintanceship."

"But do you mean that he is going to direct a flash of lightning?"

"Only into the minds of the doctor who conducts the post-mortem, and the coroner. This storm, the opportunity for which he has been waiting for weeks, is merely the cloak to his act. The weapon which he has planned to use—scarcely less powerful than lightning but much more tractable—is the high voltage current of electricity that flows along the tram wire at his gate."

"Oh!" exclaimed Lieutenant Hollyer, as the sudden revelation struck him.

"Some time between eleven o'clock to-night—about the hour when your sister goes to bed—and one-thirty in the morning—the time up to which he can rely on the current—Creake will throw a stone up at the balcony window. Most of his preparation has long been made; it only remains for him to connect up a short length to the window handle and a longer one at the other end to tap the live wire. That done, he will wake his wife in the way I have said. The moment she moves the catch of the window—and he has carefully filed its parts to ensure perfect contact—she will be electrocuted as effectually as if she sat in the executioner's chair in Sing Sing Prison."

"But what are we doing here!" exclaimed Hollyer; starting to his feet, pale and horrified. "It is past ten now and anything may happen."

"Quite natural, Mr. Hollyer," said Carrados, reassuringly, "but you need have no anxiety. Creake is being watched, the house is being watched, and your sister is as safe as if she slept to-night in Windsor Castle. Be assured that whatever happens he will not be allowed to complete his scheme; but it is desirable to let him implicate himself to the fullest limit. Your brother-in-law, Mr. Hollyer, is a man with a peculiar capacity for taking pains."

"He is a damned cold-blooded scoundrel!" exclaimed the young officer fiercely. "When I think of Millicent five years ago—"

"Well, for that matter, an enlightened nation has decided that electrocution is the most humane way of removing its superfluous citizens," suggested Carrados, mildly. "He is certainly an ingenious-minded gentleman. It is his misfortune that in Mr. Carlyle he was fated to be opposed by an even subtler brain—"

"No, no! Really, Max!" protested the embarrassed gentleman.

"Mr. Hollyer will be able to judge for himself when I tell him that it was Mr. Carlyle who first drew attention to the significance of the abandoned kite," insisted Carrados, firmly. "Then, of course, its object became plain to me—as indeed to any one. For ten minutes, perhaps, a wire must be carried from the overhead line to the chestnut-tree. Creake has everything in his favour, but it is just within possibility that the driver of an inopportune tram might notice the appendage. What of that? Why, for more than a week he has seen a derelict kite with its yards of trailing string hanging in the tree. A very calculating mind, Mr. Hollyer. It would be interesting to know what line of action Mr. Creake has mapped out for himself afterwards. I expect he has half a dozen artistic little touches up his sleeve. Possibly he would merely singe his wife's hair, burn her feet with a red-hot poker, shiver the glass of the French window, and be content with that to let well enough alone. You see, lightning is so varied in its effects that whatever he did or did not do would be right. He is in the impregnable position of the body showing all the symptoms of death by lightning shock and nothing else but lightning to account for it—a dilated eye, heart contracted in systole, bloodless lungs shrunk to a third the normal weight, and all the rest of it. When he has removed a few outward traces of his work Creake might quite safely 'discover' his dead wife and rush off for the nearest doctor. Or he may have decided to arrange a convincing alibi, and creep away, leaving the discovery to another. We shall never know; he will make no confession."

"I wish it was well over," admitted Hollyer. "I'm not particularly jumpy, but this gives me a touch of the creeps."

"Three more hours at the worst, Lieutenant," said Carrados, cheerfully. "Ah-ha, something is coming through now."

He went to the telephone and received a message from one quarter; then made another connection and talked a few minutes with some one else.

"Everything working smoothly," he remarked between times over his shoulder. "Your sister has gone to bed, Mr. Hollyer."

Then he turned to the house telephone and distributed his orders.

"So we," he concluded, "must get up."

By the time they were ready a large closed motor car was waiting. The lieutenant thought he recognized Parkinson in the well-swathed form beside the driver, but there was no temptation to linger for a second on the steps. Already the stinging rain had lashed the drive into the semblance of a frothy estuary; all round the lightning jagged its course through the incessant tremulous glow of more distant lightning, while the thunder only ceased its muttering to turn at close quarters and crackle viciously.

"One of the few things I regret missing," remarked Carrados, tranquilly; "but I hear a good deal of color in it."

The car slushed its way down to the gate, lurched a little heavily across the dip into the road, and, steadying as it came upon the straight, began to hum contentedly along the deserted highway.

"We are not going direct?" suddenly inquired Hollyer, after they had travelled perhaps half a dozen miles. The night was bewildering enough but he had the sailor's gift for location.

"No; through Hunscott Green and then by a field path to the orchard at the back," replied Carrados. "Keep a sharp look-out for the man with the lantern about here, Harris," he called through the tube.

"Something flashing just ahead, sir," came the reply, and the car slowed down and stopped.

Carrados dropped the near window as a man in glistening water-proof stepped from the shelter of a lich-gate and approached.

"Inspector Beedel, sir," said the stranger, looking into the car.

"Quite right, Inspector," said Carrados. "Get in."

"I have a man with me, sir."

"We can find room for him as well."

"We are very wet."

"So shall we all be soon."

The lieutenant changed his seat and the two burly forms took places side by side. In less than five minutes the car stopped again, this time in a grassy country lane.

"Now we have to face it," announced Carrados. "The inspector will show us the way."

The car slid round and disappeared into the night, while Beedel led the party to a stile in the hedge. A couple of fields brought them to the Brookbend boundary. There a figure stood out of the black foliage, exchanged a few words with their guide and piloted them along the shadows of the orchard to the back door of the house.

"You will find a broken pane near the catch of the scullery window," said the blind man.

"Right, sir," replied the inspector. "I have it. Now who goes through?"

"Mr. Hollyer will open the door for us. I'm afraid you must take off your boots and all wet things, Lieutenant. We cannot risk a single spot inside."

They waited until the back door opened, then each one divested himself in a similar manner and passed into the kitchen, where the remains of a fire still burned. The man from the orchard gathered together the discarded garments and disappeared again.

Carrados turned to the lieutenant.

"A rather delicate job for you now, Mr. Hollyer. I want you to go up to your sister, wake her, and get her into another room with as little fuss as possible. Tell her as much as you think fit and let her understand that her very life depends on absolute stillness when she is alone. Don't be unduly hurried, but not a glimmer of a light, please."

Ten minutes passed by the measure of the battered old alarm on the dresser shelf before the young man returned.

"I've had rather a time of it," he reported, with a nervous laugh, "but I think it will be all right now. She is in the spare room."

"Then we will take our places. You and Parkinson come with me to the bedroom. Inspector, you have your own arrangements. Mr. Carlyle will be with you."

They dispersed silently about the house. Hollyer glanced apprehensively at the door of the spare room as they passed it, but within was as quiet as the grave. Their room lay at the other end of the passage.

"You may as well take your place in the bed now, Hollyer," directed Carrados when they were inside and the door closed. "Keep well down among the clothes. Creake has to get up on the balcony, you know, and he will probably peep through the window, but he dare come no farther. Then when he begins to throw up stones slip on this dressing-gown of your sister's. I'll tell you what to do after."

The next sixty minutes drew out into the longest hour that the lieutenant had ever known. Occasionally he heard a whisper pass between the two men who stood behind the window curtains, but he could see nothing. Then Carrados threw a guarded remark in his direction.

"He is in the garden now."

Something scraped slightly against the outer wall. But the night was full of wilder sounds, and in the house the furniture and the boards creaked and sprung between the yawling of the wind among the chimneys, the rattle of the thunder and the pelting of the rain. It was a time to quicken the steadiest pulse, and when the crucial moment came, when a pebble suddenly rang against the pane with a sound that the tense waiting magnified into a shivering crash, Hollyer leapt from the bed on the instant.

"Easy, easy," warned Carrados, feelingly. "We will wait for another knock." He passed something across. "Here is a rubber glove. I have cut the wire but you had better put it on. Stand just for a moment at the window, move the catch so that it can blow open a little, and drop immediately. Now."

Another stone had rattled against the glass. For Hollyer to go through his part was the work merely of seconds, and with a few touches Carrados spread the dressing-gown to more effective disguise about the extended form. But an unforeseen and in the circumstances rather horrible interval followed, for Creake, in accordance with some detail of his never-revealed plan, continued to shower missile after missile against the panes until even the unimpressionable Parkinson shivered.

"The last act," whispered Carrados, a moment after the throwing had ceased. "He has gone round to the back. Keep as you are. We take cover now." He pressed behind the arras of an extemporized wardrobe, and the spirit of emptiness and desolation seemed once more to reign over the lonely house.

From half a dozen places of concealment ears were straining to catch the first guiding sound. He moved very stealthily, burdened, perhaps, by some strange scruple in the presence of the tragedy that he had not feared to contrive, paused for a moment at the bedroom door, then opened it very quietly, and in the fickle light read the consummation of his hopes.

"At last!" they heard the sharp whisper drawn from his relief. "At last!"

He took another step and two shadows seemed to fall upon him from behind, one on either side. With primitive instinct a cry of terror and surprise escaped him as he made a desperate movement to wrench himself free, and for a short second he almost succeeded in dragging one hand into a pocket. Then his wrists slowly came together and the handcuffs closed.

"I am Inspector Beedel," said the man on his right side. "You are charged with the attempted murder of your wife, Millicent Creake."

"You are mad," retorted the miserable creature, falling into a desperate calmness. "She has been struck by lightning."

"No, you blackguard, she hasn't," wrathfully exclaimed his brother-in-law, jumping up. "Would you like to see her?"

"I also have to warn you," continued the inspector impassively, "that anything you say may be used as evidence against you."

A startled cry from the farther end of the passage arrested their attention.

"Mr. Carrados," called Hollyer, "oh, come at once."

At the open door of the other bedroom stood the lieutenant, his eyes still turned towards something in the room beyond, a little empty bottle in his hand.

"Dead!" he exclaimed tragically, with a sob, "with this beside her. Dead just when she would have been free of the brute."

The blind man passed into the room, sniffed the air, and laid a gentle hand on the pulseless heart.

"Yes," he replied. "That, Hollyer, does not always appeal to the woman, strange to say."

The Bottomless Well

BY GILBERT K. CHESTERTON

In an oasis, or green island, in the red and yellow seas of sand that stretch beyond Europe towards the sunrise, there can be found a rather fantastic contrast, which is none the less typical of such a place, since international treaties have made it an outpost of the British occupation. The site is famous among archaeologists for something that is hardly a monument, but merely a hole in the ground. But it is a round shaft, like that of a well, and probably a part of some great irrigation works of remote and disputed date, perhaps more ancient than anything in that ancient land. There is a green fringe of palm and prickly pear round the black mouth of the well; but nothing of the upper masonry remains except two bulky and battered stones standing like pillars of a gateway of nowhere, in which some of the more transcendental archaeologists, in certain moods at moonrise or sunset, think they can trace the faint lines of figures or features of more than Babylonian monstrosity; while the more rationalistic archaeologists, in the more rational hours of daylight, see nothing but two shapeless rocks. It may have been noticed, however, that all Englishmen are not archaeologists. Many of those assembled in such a place for official and military purposes have hobbies other than archaeology. And it is a solemn fact that the English in this Eastern exile have contrived to make a small golf links out of the green scrub and sand; with a comfortable clubhouse at one end of it and this primeval monument at the other. They did not actually use this archaic abyss as a bunker, because it was by tradition unfathomable, and even for practical purposes unfathomed. Any sporting projectile sent into it might be counted most literally as a lost ball. But they often sauntered round it in their interludes of talking and smoking cigarettes, and one of them had just come down from the clubhouse to find another gazing somewhat moodily into the well.

Both the Englishmen wore light clothes and white pith helmets and puggrees, but there, for the most part, their resemblance ended. And they both almost simultaneously said the same word, but they said it on two totally different notes of the voice.

"Have you heard the news?" asked the man from the club. "Splendid."

"Splendid," replied the man by the well. But the first man pronounced the word as a young man might say it about a woman, and the second as an old man might say it about the weather, not without sincerity, but certainly without fervor.

And in this the tone of the two men was sufficiently typical of them. The first, who was a certain Captain Boyle, was of a bold and boyish type, dark, and with a sort of native heat in his face that did not belong to the atmosphere of the East, but rather to the ardors and ambitions of the West. The other was an older man and certainly an older resident, a civilian official—Horne Fisher; and his drooping eyelids and drooping light mustache expressed all the paradox of the Englishman in the East. He was much too hot to be anything but cool.

Neither of them thought it necessary to mention what it was that was splendid. That would indeed have been superfluous conversation about something that everybody knew. The striking victory over a menacing combination of Turks and Arabs in the north, won by troops under the command of Lord Hastings, the veteran of so many striking victories, was already spread by the newspapers all over the Empire, let alone to this small garrison so near to the battlefield.

"Now, no other nation in the world could have done a thing like that," cried Captain Boyle, emphatically.

Horne Fisher was still looking silently into the well; a moment later he answered: "We certainly have the art of unmaking mistakes. That's where the poor old Prussians went wrong. They could only make mistakes and stick to them. There is really a certain talent in unmaking a mistake."

"What do you mean," asked Boyle, "what mistakes?"

"Well, everybody knows it looked like biting off more than he could chew," replied Horne Fisher. It was a peculiarity of Mr. Fisher that he always said that everybody knew things which about one person in two million was ever allowed to hear of. "And it was certainly jolly lucky that Travers turned up so well in the nick of time. Odd how often the right thing's been done for us by the second in command, even when a great man was first in command. Like Colborne at Waterloo."

"It ought to add a whole province to the Empire," observed the other.

"Well, I suppose the Zimmernes would have insisted on it as far as the canal," observed Fisher, thoughtfully, "though everybody knows adding provinces doesn't always pay much nowadays."

Captain Boyle frowned in a slightly puzzled fashion. Being cloudily conscious of never having heard of the Zimmernes in his life, he could only remark, stolidly:

"Well, one can't be a Little Englander."

Horne Fisher smiled, and he had a pleasant smile.

"Every man out here is a Little Englander," he said. "He wishes he were back in Little England."

"I don't know what you're talking about, I'm afraid," said the younger man, rather suspiciously. "One would think you didn't really admire Hastings or—or—anything."

"I admire him no end," replied Fisher. "He's by far the best man for this post; he understands the Moslems and can do anything with them. That's why I'm all against pushing Travers against him, merely because of this last affair."

"I really don't understand what you're driving at," said the other, frankly.

"Perhaps it isn't worth understanding," answered Fisher, lightly, "and, anyhow, we needn't talk politics. Do you know the Arab legend about that well?"

"I'm afraid I don't know much about Arab legends," said Boyle, rather stiffly.

"That's rather a mistake," replied Fisher, "especially from your point of view. Lord Hastings himself is an Arab legend. That is perhaps the very greatest thing he really is. If his reputation went it would weaken us all over Asia and Africa. Well, the story about that hole in the ground, that goes down nobody knows where, has always fascinated me, rather. It's Mohammedan in form now, but I shouldn't wonder if the tale is a long way older than Mohammed. It's all about somebody they call the Sultan Aladdin, not our friend of the lamp, of course, but rather like him in having to do with genii or giants or something of that sort. They say he commanded the giants to build him a sort of pagoda, rising higher and higher above all the stars. The Utmost for the Highest, as the people said when they built the Tower of Babel. But the builders of the Tower of Babel were quite modest and domestic people, like mice, compared with Old Aladdin. They only wanted a tower that would reach heaven—a mere trifle. He wanted a tower that would pass heaven and rise above it, and go on rising for ever and ever. And Allah cast him down to earth with a thunderbolt, which sank into the earth, boring a hole deeper and deeper, till it made a well that was without a bottom as the tower was to have been without a top. And down that inverted tower of darkness the soul of the proud Sultan is falling forever and ever."

"What a queer chap you are," said Boyle. "You talk as if a fellow could believe those fables."

"Perhaps I believe the moral and not the fable," answered Fisher. "But here comes Lady Hastings. You know her, I think."

The clubhouse on the golf links was used, of course, for many other purposes besides that of golf. It was the only social center of the garrison beside the strictly military headquarters; it had a billiard room and a bar, and even an excellent reference library for those officers who were so perverse as to take their profession seriously. Among these was the great general himself, whose head of silver and face of bronze, like that of a brazen eagle, were often to be found bent over the charts and folios of the library. The great Lord Hastings believed in science and study, as in other severe ideals of life, and had given much paternal advice on the point to young Boyle, whose appearances in that place of research were rather more intermittent. It was from one of these snatches of study that the young man had just come out through the glass doors of the library on to the golf links. But, above all, the club was so appointed as to serve the social conveniences of ladies at least as much as gentlemen, and Lady Hastings was able to play the queen in such a society almost as much as in her own ballroom. She was eminently calculated and, as some said, eminently inclined to play such a part. She was much younger than her husband, an attractive and some-times dangerously attractive lady; and Mr. Horne Fisher looked after her a little sardonically as she swept away with the young soldier. Then his rather dreary eye strayed to the green and prickly growths round the well, growths of that curious cactus formation in which one thick leaf grows directly out of the other without stalk or twig. It gave his fanciful mind a sinister feeling of a blind growth without shape or purpose. A flower or shrub in the West grows to the blossom which is its crown, and is content. But this was as if hands could grow out of hands or legs grow out of legs in a nightmare. "Always adding a province to the Empire," he said, with a smile, and then added, more sadly, "but I doubt if I was right, after all!"

A strong but genial voice broke in on his meditations and he looked up and smiled, seeing the face of an old friend. The voice was, indeed, rather more genial than the face, which was at the first glance decidedly grim. It was a typically legal face, with angular jaws and heavy, grizzled eyebrows; and it belonged to an eminently legal character, though he was now attached in a semimilitary capacity to the police of that wild district. Cuthbert Grayne was perhaps more of a criminologist than either a lawyer or a policeman, but in his more barbarous surroundings he had proved successful in turning himself into a practical combination of all three. The discovery of a whole series of strange Oriental crimes stood to his credit. But as few people were acquainted with, or attracted to, such a hobby or branch of knowledge, his intellectual life was somewhat solitary. Among the few exceptions was Horne Fisher, who had a curious capacity for talking to almost anybody about almost anything.

"Studying botany, or is it archaeology?" inquired Grayne. "I shall never come to the end of your interests, Fisher, I should say that what you don't know isn't worth knowing."

"You are wrong," replied Fisher, with a very unusual abruptness and even bitterness. "It's what I do know that isn't worth knowing. All the seamy side of things, all the secret reasons and rotten motives and bribery and blackmail they call politics. I needn't be so proud of having been down all these sewers that I should brag about it to the little boys in the street."

"What do you mean? What's the matter with you?" asked his friend. "I never knew you taken like this before."

"I'm ashamed of myself," replied Fisher. "I've just been throwing cold water on the enthusiasms of a boy."

"Even that explanation is hardly exhaustive," observed the criminal expert.

"Damned newspaper nonsense the enthusiasms were, of course," continued Fisher, "but I ought to know that at that age illusions can be ideals. And they're better than the reality, anyhow. But there is one very ugly responsibility about jolting a young man out of the rut of the most rotten ideal."

"And what may that be?" inquired his friend.

"It's very apt to set him off with the same energy in a much worse direction," answered Fisher; "a pretty endless sort of direction, a bottomless pit as deep as the bottomless well."

Fisher did not see his friend until a fortnight later, when he found himself in the garden at the back of the clubhouse on the opposite side from the links, a garden heavily colored and scented with sweet semitropical plants in the glow of a desert sunset. Two other men were with him, the third being the now celebrated second in command, familiar to everybody as Tom Travers, a lean, dark man, who looked older than his years, with a furrow in his brow and something morose about the very shape of his black mustache. They had just been served with black coffee by the Arab now officiating as the temporary servant of the club, though he was a figure already familiar, and even famous, as the old servant of the general. He went by the name of Said, and was notable among other Semites for that unnatural length of his yellow face and height of his narrow forehead which is sometimes seen among them, and gave an irrational impression of something sinister, in spite of his agreeable smile.

"I never feel as if I could quite trust that fellow," said Grayne, when the man had gone away. "It's very unjust, I take it, for he was certainly devoted to Hastings, and saved his life, they say. But Arabs are often like that, loyal to one man. I can't help feeling he might cut anybody else's throat, and even do it treacherously."

"Well," said Travers, with a rather sour smile, "so long as he leaves Hastings alone the world won't mind much."

There was a rather embarrassing silence, full of memories of the great battle, and then Horne Fisher said, quietly:

"The newspapers aren't the world, Tom. Don't you worry about them. Everybody in your world knows the truth well enough."

"I think we'd better not talk about the general just now," remarked Grayne, "for he's just coming out of the club."

"He's not coming here," said Fisher. "He's only seeing his wife to the car."

As he spoke, indeed, the lady came out on the steps of the club, followed by her husband, who then went swiftly in front of her to open the garden gate. As he did so she turned back and spoke for a moment to a solitary man still sitting in a cane chair in the shadow of the doorway, the only man left in the deserted club save for the three that lingered in the garden. Fisher peered for a moment into the shadow, and saw that it was Captain Boyle.

The next moment, rather to their surprise, the general reappeared and, remounting the steps, spoke a word or two to Boyle in his turn. Then he signaled to Said, who hurried up with two cups of coffee, and the two men re-entered the club, each carrying his cup in his hand. The next moment a gleam of white light in the growing darkness showed that the electric lamps had been turned on in the library beyond.

"Coffee and scientific researches," said Travers, grimly. "All the luxuries of learning and theoretical research. Well, I must be going, for I have my work to do as well." And he got up rather stiffly, saluted his companions, and strode away into the dusk.

"I only hope Boyle *is* sticking to scientific researches," said Horne Fisher. "I'm not very comfortable about him myself. But let's talk about something else."

They talked about something else longer than they probably imagined, until the tropical night had come and a splendid moon painted the whole scene with silver; but before it was bright enough to see by Fisher had already noted that the lights in the library had been abruptly extinguished. He waited for the two men to come out by the garden entrance, but nobody came.

"They must have gone for a stroll on the links," he said.

"Very possibly," replied Grayne. "It's going to be a beautiful night."

A moment or two after he had spoken they heard a voice hailing them out of the shadow of the clubhouse, and were astonished to perceive Travers hurrying towards them, calling out as he came:

"I shall want your help, you fellows," he cried. "There's something pretty bad out on the links."

They found themselves plunging through the club smoking room and the library beyond, in complete darkness, mental as well as material. But Horne Fisher, in spite of his affectation of indifference, was a person of a curious and almost transcendental sensibility to atmospheres, and he already felt the presence of something more than an accident. He collided with a piece of furniture in the library, and almost shuddered with the shock, for the thing moved as he could never have fancied a piece of furniture moving. It seemed to move like a living thing, yielding and yet striking back. The next moment Grayne had turned on the lights, and he saw he had only stumbled against one of the revolving bookstands that had swung round and struck him; but his involuntary recoil had revealed to him his own subconscious sense of something mysterious and monstrous. There were several of these revolving bookcases standing here and there about the library; on one of them stood the two cups of coffee, and on another a large open book. It was Budge's book on Egyptian hieroglyphics, with colored plates of strange birds and gods, and even as he rushed past, he was conscious of something odd about the fact that this, and not any work of military science, should be open in that place at that moment. He was even conscious of the gap in the well-lined bookshelf from which it had been taken, and it seemed almost to gape at him in an ugly fashion, like a gap in the teeth of some sinister face.

A run brought them in a few minutes to the other side of the ground in front of the bottomless well, and a few yards from it, in a moonlight almost as broad as daylight, they saw what they had come to see.

The great Lord Hastings lay prone on his face, in a posture in which there was a touch of something strange and stiff, with one elbow erect above his body, the arm being doubled, and his big, bony hand clutching the rank and ragged grass. A few feet away was Boyle, almost as motionless, but supported on his hands and knees, and staring at the body. It might have been no more than shock and accident; but there was something ungainly and unnatural about the quadrupedal posture and the gaping face. It was as if his reason had fled from him. Behind, there was nothing but the clear blue southern sky, and the beginning of the desert, except for the two great broken stones in front of the well. And it was in such a light and atmosphere that men could fancy they traced in them enormous and evil faces, looking down.

Horne Fisher stooped and touched the strong hand that was still clutching the grass, and it was as cold as a stone. He knelt by the body and was busy for a moment applying other tests; then he rose again, and said, with a sort of confident despair:

"Lord Hastings is dead."

There was a stony silence, and then Travers remarked, gruffly: "This is your department, Grayne; I will leave you to question Captain Boyle. I can make no sense of what he says."

Boyle had pulled himself together and risen to his feet, but his face still wore an awful expression, making it like a new mask or the face of another man.

"I was looking at the well," he said, "and when I turned he had fallen down."

Grayne's face was very dark. "As you say, this is my affair," he said. "I must first ask you to help me carry him to the library and let me examine things thoroughly."

When they had deposited the body in the library, Grayne turned to Fisher and said, in a voice that had recovered its fullness and confidence, "I am going to lock myself in and make a thorough examination first. I look to you to keep in touch with the others and make a preliminary examination of Boyle. I will talk to him later. And just telephone to headquarters for a policeman, and let him come here at once and stand by till I want him."

Without more words the great criminal investigator went into the lighted library, shutting the door behind him, and Fisher, without replying, turned and began to talk quietly to Travers. "It is curious," he said, "that the thing should happen just in front of that place."

"It would certainly be very curious," replied Travers, "if the place played any part in it."

"I think," replied Fisher, "that the part it didn't play is more curious still."

And with these apparently meaningless words he turned to the shaken Boyle and, taking his arm, began to walk him up and down in the moonlight, talking in low tones.

Dawn had begun to break abrupt and white when Cuthbert Grayne turned out the lights in the library and came out on to the links. Fisher was lounging about alone, in his listless fashion; but the police messenger for whom he had sent was standing at attention in the background.

"I sent Boyle off with Travers," observed Fisher, carelessly; "he'll look after him, and he'd better have some sleep, anyhow."

"Did you get anything out of him?" asked Grayne. "Did he tell you what he and Hastings were doing?"

"Yes," answered Fisher, "he gave me a pretty clear account, after all. He said that after Lady Hastings went off in the car the general asked him to take coffee with him in the library and look up a point about local antiquities. He himself was beginning to look for Budge's book in one of the revolving bookstands when the general found it in one of the bookshelves on the wall. After looking at some of the plates they went out, it would seem, rather abruptly, on to the links, and walked towards the old well; and while Boyle was looking into it he heard a thud behind him, and turned round to find the general lying as we found him. He himself dropped on his knees to examine the body, and then was paralyzed with a sort of terror and could not come nearer to it or touch it. But I think very little of that; people caught in a real shock of surprise are sometimes found in the queerest postures."

Grayne wore a grim smile of attention, and said, after a short silence:

"Well, he hasn't told you many lies. It's really a creditably clear and consistent account of what happened, with everything of importance left out."

"Have you discovered anything in there?" asked Fisher.

"I have discovered everything," answered Grayne.

Fisher maintained a somewhat gloomy silence, as the other resumed his explanation in quiet and assured tones.

"You were quite right, Fisher, when you said that young fellow was in danger of going down dark ways towards the pit. Whether or no, as you fancied, the jolt you gave to his view of the general had anything to do with it, he has not been treating the general well for some time. It's an unpleasant business, and I don't want to dwell on it; but it's pretty plain that his wife was not treating him well, either. I don't know how far it went, but it went as far as concealment, anyhow; for when Lady Hastings spoke to Boyle it was to tell him she had hidden a note in the Budge book in the library. The general overheard, or came somehow to know, and he went straight to the book and found it. He confronted Boyle with it, and they had a scene, of course. And Boyle was confronted with something else; he was confronted with an awful alternative in which the life of one old man meant ruin and his death meant triumph and even happiness."

"Well," observed Fisher, at last, "I don't blame him for not telling you the woman's part of the story. But how do you know about the letter?"

"I found it on the general's body," answered Grayne, "but I found worse things than that. The body had stiffened in the way rather peculiar to poisons of a certain Asiatic sort. Then I examined the coffee cups, and I knew enough chemistry to find poison in the dregs of one of them. Now, the general went straight to the bookcase, leaving his cup of coffee on the bookstand in the middle of the room. While his back was turned, and Boyle was pretending to examine the bookstand, he was left alone with the coffee cup. The poison takes about ten minutes to act, and ten minutes' walk would bring them to the bottomless well."

"Yes," remarked Fisher, "and what about the bottomless well?"

"What has the bottomless well got to do with it?" asked his friend.

"It has nothing to do with it," replied Fisher. "That is what I find utterly confounding and incredible."

"And why should that particular hole in the ground have anything to do with it?"

"It is a particular hole in your case," said Fisher. "But I won't insist on that just now. By the way, there is another thing I ought to tell you. I said I sent Boyle away in charge of Travers. It would be just as true to say I sent Travers in charge of Boyle."

"You don't mean to say you suspect Tom Travers?" cried the other.

"He was a deal bitterer against the general than Boyle ever was," observed Horne Fisher, with a curious indifference.

"Man, you're not saying what you mean," cried Grayne. "I tell you I found the poison in one of the coffee cups."

"There was always Said, of course," added Fisher, "either for hatred or hire. We agreed he was capable of almost anything."

"And we agreed he was incapable of hurting his master," retorted Grayne.

"Well, well," said Fisher, amiably, "I dare say you are right; but I should just like to have a look at the library and the coffee cups."

He passed inside, while Grayne turned to the policeman in attendance and handed him a scribbled note, to be telegraphed from headquarters. The man saluted and hurried off; and Grayne, following his friend into the library, found him beside the bookstand in the middle of the room, on which were the empty cups.

"This is where Boyle looked for Budge, or pretended to look for him, according to your account," he said.

As Fisher spoke he bent down in a half-crouching attitude, to look at the volumes in the low, revolving shelf, for the whole bookstand was not much higher than an ordinary table. The next moment he sprang up as if he had been stung.

"Oh, my God!" he cried.

Very few people, if any, had ever seen Mr. Horne Fisher behave as he behaved just then. He flashed a glance at the door, saw that the open window was nearer, went out of it with a flying leap, as if over a hurdle, and went racing across the turf, in the track of the disappearing policeman. Grayne, who stood staring after him, soon saw his tall, loose figure, returning, restored to all its normal limpness and air of leisure. He was fanning himself slowly with a piece of paper, the telegram he had so violently intercepted.

"Lucky I stopped that," he observed. "We must keep this affair as quiet as death. Hastings must die of apoplexy or heart disease."

"What on earth is the trouble?" demanded the other investigator.

"The trouble is," said Fisher, "that in a few days we should have had a very agreeable alternative—of hanging an innocent man or knocking the British Empire to hell."

"Do you mean to say," asked Grayne, "that this infernal crime is not to be punished?"

Fisher looked at him steadily.

"It is already punished," he said.

After a moment's pause he went on. "You reconstructed the crime with admirable skill, old chap, and nearly all you said was true. Two men with two coffee cups did go into the library and did put their cups on the bookstand and did go together to the well, and one of them was a murderer and had put poison in the other's cup. But it was not done while Boyle was looking at the revolving bookcase. He did look at it, though, searching for the Budge book with the note in it, but I fancy that Hastings had already moved it to the shelves on the wall. It was part of that grim game that he should find it first.

"Now, how does a man search a revolving bookcase? He does not generally hop all round it in a squatting attitude, like a frog. He simply gives it a touch and makes it revolve."

He was frowning at the floor as he spoke, and there was a light under his heavy lids that was not often seen there. The mysticism that was buried deep under all the cynicism of his experience was awake and moving in the depths. His voice took unexpected turns and inflections, almost as if two men were speaking.

"That was what Boyle did; he barely touched the thing, and it went round as easily as the world goes round. Yes, very much as the world goes round, for the hand that turned it was not his. God, who turns the wheel of all the stars, touched that wheel and brought it full circle, that His dreadful justice might return."

"I am beginning," said Grayne, slowly, "to have some hazy and horrible idea of what you mean."

"It is very simple," said Fisher, "when Boyle straightened himself from his stooping posture, something had happened which he had not noticed, which his enemy had not noticed, which nobody had noticed. The two coffee cups had exactly changed places."

The rocky face of Grayne seemed to have sustained a shock in silence; not a line of it altered, but his voice when it came was unexpectedly weakened.

"I see what you mean," he said, "and, as you say, the less said about it the better. It was not the lover who tried to get rid of the husband, but—the other thing. And a tale like that about a man like that would ruin us here. Had you any guess of this at the start?"

"The bottomless well, as I told you," answered Fisher, quietly; "that was what stumped me from the start. Not because it had anything to do with it, because it had nothing to do with it."

He paused a moment, as if choosing an approach, and then went on: "When a man knows his enemy will be dead in ten minutes, and takes him to the edge of an unfathomable pit, he means to throw his body into it. What else should he do? A born fool would have the sense to do it, and Boyle is not a born fool. Well, why did not Boyle do it? The more I thought of it the more I suspected there was some mistake in the murder, so to speak. Somebody had taken somebody there to throw him in, and yet he was not thrown in. I had already an ugly, unformed idea of some substitution or reversal of parts; then I stooped to turn the bookstand myself, by accident, and I instantly knew everything, for I saw the two cups revolve once more, like moons in the sky."

After a pause, Cuthbert Grayne said, "And what are we to say to the newspapers?"

"My friend, Harold March, is coming along from Cairo today," said Fisher. "He is a very brilliant and successful journalist. But for all that he's a thoroughly honorable man, so you must not tell him the truth."

Half an hour later Fisher was again walking to and fro in front of the clubhouse, with Captain Boyle, the latter by this time with a very buffeted and bewildered air; perhaps a sadder and a wiser man.

"What about me, then?" he was saying. "Am I cleared? Am I not going to be cleared?"

"I believe and hope," answered Fisher, "that you are not going to be suspected. But you are certainly not going to be cleared. There must be no suspicion against him, and therefore no suspicion against you. Any suspicion against him, let alone such a story against him, would knock us endways from Malta to Mandalay. He was a hero as well as a holy terror among the Moslems. Indeed, you might almost call him a Moslem hero in the English service. Of course he got on with them partly because of his own little dose of Eastern blood; he got it from his mother, the dancer from Damascus; everybody knows that."

"Oh," repeated Boyle, mechanically, staring at him with round eyes, "everybody knows that."

"I dare say there was a touch of it in his jealousy and ferocious vengeance," went on Fisher. "But, for all that, the crime would ruin us among the Arabs, all the more because it was something like a crime against hospitality. It's been hateful for you and it's pretty horrid for me. But there are some things that damned well can't be done, and while I'm alive that's one of them."

"What do you mean?" asked Boyle, glancing at him curiously. "Why should you, of all people, be so passionate about it?"

Horne Fisher looked at the young man with a baffling expression.

"I suppose," he said, "it's because I'm a Little Englander."

"I can never make out what you mean by that sort of thing," answered Boyle, doubtfully.

"Do you think England is so little as all that?" said Fisher, with a warmth in his cold voice, "that it can't hold a man across a few thousand miles? You lectured me with a lot of ideal patriotism, my young friend; but it's practical patriotism now for you and me, and with no lies to help it. You talked as if everything always went right with us all over the world, in a triumphant crescendo culminating in Hastings. I tell you everything has gone wrong with us here, except Hastings. He was the one name we had left to conjure with, and that mustn't go as well, no, by God! It's bad enough that a gang of infernal Jews should plant us here, where there's no earthly English interest to serve, and all hell beating up against us, simply because Nosey Zimmern has lent money to half the Cabinet. It's bad enough that an old pawnbroker from Bagdad should make us fight his battles; we can't fight with our right hand cut off. Our one score was Hastings and his victory, which was really somebody else's victory. Tom Travers has to suffer, and so have you."

Then, after a moment's silence, he pointed towards the bottomless well and said, in a quieter tone:

"I told you that I didn't believe in the philosophy of the Tower of Aladdin. I don't believe in the Empire growing until it reaches the sky; I don't believe in the Union Jack going up and up eternally like the Tower. But if you think I am going to let the Union Jack go down and down eternally, like the bottomless well, down into the blackness of the bottomless pit, down in defeat and derision, amid the jeers of the very Jews who have sucked us dry—no I won't, and that's flat; not if the Chancellor were blackmailed by twenty millionaires with their gutter rags, not if the Prime Minister married twenty Yankee Jewesses, not if Woodville and Carstairs had shares in twenty swindling mines. If the thing is really tottering, God help it, it mustn't be we who tip it over."

Boyle was regarding him with a bewilderment that was almost fear, and had even a touch of distaste.

"Somehow," he said, "there seems to be something rather horrid about the things you know."

"There is," replied Horne Fisher. "I am not at all pleased with my small stock of knowledge and reflection. But as it is partly responsible for your not being hanged, I don't know that you need complain of it."

And, as if a little ashamed of his first boast, he turned and strolled away towards the bottomless well.

The Log Case

BY KENNETH LIVINGSTON

"However," I broke off, "I mustn't start talking shop on a holiday."

"Rot," said Cedric Dodd, tapping the hard ground rhythmically with his walking stick as he strode along. "Rot. Why not? The idea that your professional man dislikes talking shop when off duty is pure bunkum. If a couple of stockbrokers were killed together in a railway smash or a motor accident, I'll wager that before they had been half an hour on the other side they would be eagerly discussing the probable value of their holdings to their respective estates. However, to return to what you were saying, I maintain that nine out of ten so-called detective problems are in reality so simple that they contain no problem at all. Such difficulties as they present arise solely from the investigator's blindness or deafness or failure to take proper thought at the right moment. He usually misses the really significant point simply because it is too obvious to be seen."

Few would have recognized in the speaker the man whom one of our leading periodicals had recently described as "England's most celebrated criminal investigator," for he was clad in a Norfolk jacket and shorts and carried a knapsack on his back; but then,

67

few would have been likely to be there in any case to attempt such a recognition, for the time was half-past six in the morning, and we were trudging along a deserted lane in glorious June sunshine, having been already on the road for well over an hour. The air had that delicious freshness, the clouds that clear brilliance, which are peculiar to the early morning hours, and as my sadly material mind turned to the coffee and bacon and eggs to which every step brought us nearer I had to acknowledge that there was more in my friend's methods of holiday-making than I had thought when he dragged me out of bed at five o'clock that morning.

"Probably you are right," I replied, "All the same . . ." But Dodd was not listening.

A turn in the lane had brought us into a long, straight stretch, towards the end of which we could see a log blocking the road. But it was not the log that had caused Dodd's lapse—it was something that lay just ahead of it; and indeed, as we quickened our pace it became increasingly obvious that an accident had occurred.

"There's a motorbike there," said Dodd, breaking into a run.

"And that looks like the rider lying on the left," I added.

And so it proved. Ignoring for the moment the overturned cycle, we made for the crumpled figure beyond it; but the briefest examination was sufficient to assure us that the man, an elderly, grey-haired clergyman, was dead.

"And he's been here some hours, too," said Dodd. "Probably all night. Let's see if we can find out who he is."

A cautious investigation of the dead man's pockets soon produced a leather letter case containing, among various other papers, an addressed and opened envelope. "Here we are," said Dodd, reading the superscription. " 'The Rev. Septimus Shorter, D.D., Badley Grammar School, Near Badley, Sussex.' No doubt the headmaster. And the school is along on the main road, not a quarter of a mile from here. I happened to notice it on the map."

"He was probably returning there late last night," I suggested. "Though I should have thought they would have found him before this if it's as close as you say."

"They may not have missed him yet," Dodd answered. "It's by no means unlikely, especially if he's a bachelor, that he intended to let himself in."

He spoke somewhat abstractedly, for he was on his knees in the roadway, methodically completing his examination of the dead man's wounds.

"See there," he said, indicating the shattered skull, "that's what killed him." But I much preferred not to see. Dodd busied himself for some time longer, exploring the damage with professional curiosity and zeal, even feeling the limbs all over and examining the palms of the hands. "Just like a doctor," I thought. "They're quite as interested in you when you're dead as when you're alive—probably more so."

Meanwhile I turned my attention to the cause of the accident. "But what a darned careless thing," I exclaimed, "to leave a thing like that lying across the road!"

Dodd, rising at last from his labours, eyed the log curiously. Part of the branch of an oak tree, fairly thick, and of about four feet in length, it lay straight across the pathway, leaving only a narrow passage through which a motorcyclist might, in broad daylight, have just managed to squeeze. "Sawn off," he said. "And not recently, either." He tried to lift it, but soon let the end fall back again.

"Too heavy to move?" I asked.

"No. It could be done. But unless one were pretty hefty one would have to roll or lug it along. The question is—where did it come from? And again, how did it get here?"

Crossing to the side of the lane, he began to range about like a retriever searching for a lost scent. "Ah," he exclaimed suddenly, pointing with his stick, "here we are!"

He had moved a few paces farther up the lane, on the left; and when I joined him there I saw that he was looking at a long, discoloured patch in the grass verge of the lane. A glance was sufficient to show that in size and shape it corresponded with the log in the roadway.

"By Jove!" I murmured. "Someone's moved the thing from here."

"Looks like it," Dodd agreed. "And if that is so, it raises a rather curious and interesting point." His eye travelled from the patch where the log had lain to the position it now occupied. "If you or I wanted to drag a heavy log from there into the roadway, we should naturally move it as little as possible. Here, opposite where it originally lay, is the place where one would expect to find it, yet whoever was responsible for its presence in the road actually took the trouble to drag it some paces back."

I looked at Dodd in amazement, ignoring the finer aspects of the question in the horror aroused by the main implication of his remarks.

"But surely you are not suggesting that someone did this deliberately?" I exclaimed.

Dodd shrugged. "After all," I went on, somewhat nettled by his professional readiness to see a crime in every occurrence, "you must remember that this is not a motoring road. No cars would come down here; in fact, I doubt even if many cyclists would. Moreover, don't forget that there's a school close by, and it's just the sort of thing a group of mischievous boys would do, to play around with a log like this, and then thoughtlessly leave it stuck in the middle of the road."

Dodd glanced from the log to the body and back again. "Hm!" he said noncommittally.

"And again," I went on, warming to my work as I noticed that he seemed to be considering my theory, "that would account for your difficulty about the log having been moved farther than necessary. They would lug it about all over the place, and finally just leave it anywhere. And that disposes of the question of the weight, too; a number of boys could move it easily enough."

"Hm!" said Dodd again. "All the same, I should like to have a look round. Supposing you go off now to the school and give the alarm, and leave me here to amuse myself until you come back? It's not far; you go straight on until you come to the main road; then turn to the right, and you'll be almost on top of it."

II

I set off as directed, leaving Dodd sniffing round the damaged cycle with his usual inquisitiveness, and soon found myself turning up the drive of a large red-brick, ivy-covered building, one end of which was obviously the headmaster's private residence. As I approached, a tall, thin figure emerged from the main entrance of the school and came towards me. No doubt my hurried gait and grave demeanour warned him that my errand was an important one, for he greeted me abruptly and authoritatively with the single word "Yes?"

"A man who worries overmuch," I thought at once, watching the weary, ungenial expression of his grey, lined face.

"I'm afraid there has been an accident," I explained rapidly. "We have found someone in the lane down the road who, I think, belongs to the school."

"A clergyman?" he asked, somewhat pompously. "Grey-haired and of heavy build?"

I nodded.

"Ah!" he said, with a note of excitement in his voice. "We have just discovered that he's not in the building. You say he's had an accident?"

I nodded again and gave him a brief account of our discovery of the body, adding that my friend was a doctor and that there was no doubt that the unfortunate man in the lane was dead. My collocutor thereupon introduced himself as the late headmaster's second in command, Talbot by name, and taking me through the school buildings to the private quarters, rang up the local hospital.

"We've no ambulance here in Badley, so they may be some little time," he said as he replaced the receiver. "Meanwhile I'll come back with you and make sure that it is poor Shorter."

A big bell set up a raucous clamour as we re-entered the main buildings, and almost at once a procession of jostling boys began to race down the long corridor.

"Chapel," my guide explained briefly; and reminiscences of my own youth, and of the penalties of unpunctuality, recurred to me vividly as I noticed one small urchin feverishly struggling into his coat as he ran.

After a momentary delay, during which Mr. Talbot conferred in low but magisterial tones with a begowned pedagogue who just then came whirling along the corridor, presumably on his way to officiate at the early morning prayers, we set off on our short walk to the scene of the tragedy; and I took advantage of the opportunity to give my companion a more detailed account of what had happened. He listened in silence until I referred to the possibility of the log having been left in its dangerous position by some of the boys, when he gave a low whistle, and his face grew graver still.

"By Jove," he murmured. "You don't say so! That looks ugly."

"But of course it's only a theory," I hastened to add, "and the disastrous consequences would in any case be a pure accident."

"That may be," he said dubiously. "But, nevertheless, the thing will take on a rather nasty colour. You see, as it happens—I suppose there can be no harm in my telling you this—we've had a little trouble recently—one of our periodical outbreaks of smoking—and the Head was supposed to have been temporarily in bad odour. Nothing serious, of course, you understand," he added quickly, obviously beginning to regret having said so much. "A little disciplinary action which appears to have been unusually resented."

"But surely," I objected, "not to the extent of their doing a thing like that deliberately? And in any case, even supposing that it was a deliberate piece of mischief, they could not possibly know who would be the victim of it."

"As to that," Talbot answered gloomily, "it was common knowledge. The Head had friends in Badley whom he was constantly visiting, and he always returned by that route. Not that I'm suggesting for a moment that there's anything in it," he added hastily, "but it's the talk and tittle-tattle that gets about which I'm afraid of. You see," he went on in his somewhat didactic manner that reminded me of the lecture room, "this may mean the headmastership for me—though heaven knows I would not have wished it to come in this way—so that I have every reason to be jealous of the honour of the school and anxious that nothing should retard its welfare."

I understood now the involuntary note of excitement which I had detected in his voice when I first broke the news to him—the natural and, to my mind, understandable excitement of a man who suddenly finds his greatest ambition about to be realized.

"Here we are," I said, as we turned into the lane and saw in the near distance the solitary figure of Cedric Dodd standing, as if lost in thought, in the centre of the pathway. "And perhaps by now," I went on hopefully, "he will be able to throw more light on the affair, for if there is anything to be discovered here, you can be sure that Cedric Dodd will find it."

"Cedric Dodd!" Talbot exclaimed, almost standing still in his surprise. "Surely you don't mean *the* Cedric Dodd?"

I nodded, quickening my pace again as Dodd advanced towards us.

"But you said your friend was a doctor," Talbot objected.

"So he was, originally." We were now within earshot of the subject of our conversation, so that for the moment my new acquaintance was unable to continue.

"This is a bad business, Mr. Dodd," the schoolmaster said, when I had formally introduced the two and he had indentified the body as that of his late colleague. "Your friend here tells me that there's a possibility of some of our boys having been concerned in it." He threw a vicious glance at the fatal log. "It certainly looks as if the confounded thing had been stuck there deliberately," he added.

"Not a doubt of it," Dodd agreed quietly. I could see that he was watching our new acquaintance closely.

"Mr. Talbot has been telling me that the Head has been a little unpopular lately," I put in. "So that there is, as it turns out, some slight support for my theory in the facts."

Dodd cocked an eyebrow at Talbot. "But surely—?" he said. "British schoolboys?"

Talbot flushed. "No, no," he agreed hastily. "Of course not. The thing's unthinkable."

"Even British schoolboys occasionally number a black sheep in the flock," I pointed out.

At this Dodd grinned openly.

"My friend is not the monster he seems," he told Talbot. "Nor has he so poor an opinion of our youth as you might think. It is merely that, like many a detective before him, he is over-zealous in defense of his pet theory. And after all," he went on, with a sudden change to seriousness, "why should he not be? As he says, there are boys and boys; and we are all very much in the dark at present. Have a look round, Gregory, while I talk to Mr. Talbot, and see what you make of things."

"Certainly," I agreed, with an alacrity which was wholly assumed. And, remembering our interrupted conversation, I added jauntily: "I'll look for that really significant point of which you were speaking."

III

I set about my task in the methodical manner I had learned from Dodd. First I examined the body, and more particularly the wound—though not without some inward qualms, for the head was lying in a pool of blood; but it told me very little. I could find no trace of broken bones, and this, in conjunction with the comparatively clean nature of the wound, made it at least clear that the rider had been shot forward over his handlebars, curvetting through the air and striking the ground with his head at a point just above the forehead.

The force of the impact had shattered the skull, either killing him outright, or rendering him unconscious so that he had bled to death where he lay. His round, black clerical hat, almost new, which was lying near the body, confirmed my theory of the fall, being merely a little dusty and otherwise quite undamaged; it had obviously fallen from its owner's head as he circled through the air. As for the cycle, the front wheel was buckled, as might have been expected, and the handlebars scratched; otherwise I could discern no sign of serious damage. The log I had already examined with Dodd, and I could find now nothing to alter our original theory that it had been placed in its fatal position by human agency, either deliberately or through gross carelessness. The fact that it had been carried some way farther than it need have been seemed to point to the second of these alternatives.

"Well," asked Dodd, as I rejoined him and Talbot, "what do you make of it?"

"Very little," I answered, assuming the casual tone of one who could say more if he wished.

Dodd nodded. "And that little," he said, playing up to me nobly, "you prefer for the time being to keep to yourself, eh?"

At that moment a diversion was created by the arrival of a car at the head of the lane, which proved to be a Morris Oxford belonging to the local hospital, and sent, with some good sense, in place of the ambulance. The car backed gingerly down the lane, and, with some difficulty, for the late Dr. Shorter had been a heavy man, we succeeded in disposing of the body on the back seat. It proved even more grisly a job than my recent examination of the body, so that I was not sorry when the car drove off, and Talbot, who had arranged to attend at the hospital later in the day, suggested our returning with him to the school for breakfast.

Personally I found that our recent activities had taken away all vestige of the appetite upon which I had no long time since been congratulating myself, and as for Talbot, his face resembled that of a man who has lately crossed the Channel in rough weather; but Dodd accepted the offer with alacrity.

During our brief walk back to the school, and throughout the late breakfast which we ate at the master's table in the big, empty dining hall, Dodd carried on a spasmodic conversation with Talbot, asking a number of questions about the routine of the school and the other members of its staff. Talbot answered freely enough, though I could see that his pedantic manner amused Dodd as much as it did me.

"You yourself, I presume, are not in Holy Orders?" Dodd asked at last.

"Alas, no," Talbot replied. "All the rest of us are mere laymen."

He helped himself to toast and marmalade, and in a tone of elaborate unconcern enquired whether Dodd could hold out any hope that the boys had had no hand in moving "that infernal log." His solicitude for the honour of his charges struck me as a distinctly pleasing trait in an otherwise somewhat irritating personality. Dodd shook his head. "Who can say?" he replied vaguely, and thereupon relapsed into a silence which lasted for some minutes. I could see that he was deep in thought, and I found myself wondering with no little curiosity how he would approach his somewhat novel task, and whether, for that matter, he intended to approach it at all. Indeed, the spectacle of Cedric Dodd tracking down mischievous schoolboys struck me as having something incongruous, if not actually comical, about it.

"Perhaps," Talbot suggested as we rose from the table, "you would care to have a look round and see us at our work?" He spoke with some awkwardness and was obviously relieved when the invitation was accepted. I had by now decided that he was loath to part with us, but that for some reason, probably not unconnected with the question of fees, he hesitated to engage my friend's services outright.

Hardly, however, had we emerged from the dining hall into the long, dark corridor when Dodd, with a muttered exclamation, clapped his hand to his pocket, and after a feverish search announced that he had left his cigarette case at our lodgings and must return at once to retrieve it. Talbot, of course, could make no demur, but he looked surprised and even a little suspicious; and it occurred to me that Dodd might haven taken the trouble to concoct a less obvious pretext for his withdrawal.

"I'll be back in under an hour," he said, "and with Mr. Talbot's permission I'll rejoin you here. In the meanwhile," he added solemnly to Talbot, with a mischievous wink at me, "I'm sure Mr. Pierce will be only too pleased to spend the time in looking a little further into your problem. I think, Gregory," he finished breezily, "that the line of enquiry we spoke of at breakfast should prove the most promising."

I stared at him in complete astonishment, for we had been alone at breakfast for five minutes at the most, during which time he had met my tentative enquiry as to the progress, if any, of the investigation with an obstinate silence; but before I could devise a way of ridding myself of the unwelcome responsibility thus thrust upon me, my exasperating friend had bidden us a rapid au revoir and set off at a brisk pace, no doubt chuckling to himself at the quandary in which he had left me.

IV

One thing at least was obvious: Dodd's supposed departure was no more than a ruse designed to cover his absence during some enquiry connected with the case and which he wished to conduct alone. But far less obvious, unfortunately, was the answer to the question that next presented itself. What part had he intended me to play in the meanwhile? Was it possible that he desired Talbot to be detained at all costs? Again, had his parting instructions, so far from being a joke at my expense, contained some obscure hint which I was too dense to grasp? It was a pretty problem, and I solved it in what I conceived to be the only sensible way. I would obey his instructions to the letter—by continuing the investigation on the spot and, to the best of my ability, in the manner in which Dodd himself, had he been present, would have conducted it. Indeed, it occurred to me as even possible that Dodd's mysterious quest might not take him very far afield, and that he might reappear at any moment to confound us with some brilliant solution.

Meanwhile, however, something had to be done, if only to maintain my spurious reputation in the eyes of my host, and so, chiefly in order to gain time in which to devise some course of action, I jumped at his suggestion that we should adhere to our original plan and begin with a tour of the classrooms.

"Are any members of the staff away today?" I inquired.

"No. We are at full strength at present."

This, at least, was satisfactory. I felt that I might profitably take a look at each one of the late Dr. Shorter's colleagues, to see if there were any strong men among them, any man strong enough to lift a heavy log....

"And now, as regards last night: The boys, I take it, couldn't be out late without the fact being known; but what of the staff? Is there any particular time at which they are supposed to be in?"

Talbot glanced at me keenly. He realized, no doubt, the drift of my question. If the log had been placed in the road by anyone other than schoolboys, with the deliberate intention of causing "grievous bodily harm" to the doctor, it would probably have been placed there at the latest possible time, in order to avoid the risk of its being seen and removed by some passing wayfarer, or the even greater risk of its not being seen and consequently causing injury to the wrong person. In any event, the information for which I was asking would prove useful if, as was more than likely, outside testimony became available to establish the latest hour at which the log was *not* in position.

"As to the boys," Talbot answered decidedly, "I am positive that none would be out after regulation hours. Second prep begins at seven o'clock, and they must all be in by then. But the members of the staff are, of course, in a different position. I can't answer for their movements during the evening. Apart from those taking prep or on special duty, they would be free from about five o'clock onwards; though as far as I remember we were all present at dinner, which is at half-past seven."

"But they couldn't get in at all hours of the night?"

"Oh, no. The back gates are locked when second prep begins. The front entrance remains open until ten o'clock, and after that the janitor is on duty to admit anyone who happens to be late."

"I see. We will have a word with him presently, if we may, and also, possibly, with some of the boys—the ringleaders of the recent rumpus, for choice. And meanwhile," I continued, "it would certainly be a help if you could find out whether any of the staff admit to being late last night."

We made a tour of the classrooms, the occupants of which gazed at me curiously. The death of its headmaster had thrown the school into a flutter, and it was obvious that little work would be done that morning. Talbot introduced me to each of the masters in turn, without making any attempt to account for my presence; and I think most of them, thanks to my clothes, mistook me for an important representative of the Boy Scout movement, and began to anticipate with no little concern an outbreak of shorts and jackknives as a result of my visit. As we were leaving each room Talbot, apparently as an afterthought, returned to collect the information I had asked for, explaining that he had been called upon to furnish to the authorities, as a matter of form, particulars of the whereabouts of every member of the staff on the previous evening from eight o'clock onwards.

For some time we drew blank—and incidentally obtained an insight into the dullness of a master's life at a country school, for not only was each of our witnesses indoors before the janitor came on duty at ten o'clock, but every one was also able to give a satisfactory account of his movements, and to substantiate it by naming another or others in whose company he had passed the evening. At last, however, we lighted upon a possible suspect in the shape of a wasp-ish, bewhiskered little man named Jacks, who, in answer to Talbot's question, averred snappishly that on the previous evening he had been for a long country walk from which he had not returned until close upon eleven. I made a mental note to interrogate him further if necessary, though his small build and obvious lack of physical strength were in themselves almost sufficient to exonerate him.

We next inquired for the steward and janitor, only to learn, however, that that official had been absent on leave for the last two days, having been called away on urgent family business. "In that case," said Talbot, "Sergeant Wren is our man. He acts as janitor when the steward is off duty. He is our gymnasium instructor, and quite one of the characters of the school. A rough diamond—but a splendid man at his job."

As he spoke he led the way through a large quadrangle to an old wooden door studded with nails, rather resembling the entrance to a jail, and pushing this open we found ourselves within a large gymnasium, smelling of canvas and equipped with every modern device for the development of the muscles of small boys. The first class of the day was just assembling, and for some little time we con-tented ourselves with remaining discreetly in the background, watching the class at work. Sergeant Wren, nicknamed "The Bird," as Talbot informed me in an undertone, was a huge, upright-standing man, with a long nose, bushy eyebrows, a wide forehead, and rugged features that revealed the downright, dominating character of an army instructor of the old school. After calling the roll—each boy answering to his name with a prompt "sum, Instructor"—the burly sergeant, who was clad in a white sweater and trousers, conducted the class through a series of exercises, reeling off the while a monotonous patter of directions and instructions, mingled with less formal remarks of a facetious nature.

It was a class of the older boys, and as I watched them awaiting in line their turn to join the swift-moving stream that doubled steadily to the leather vaulting horse, each boy, when he reached it, taking off from a springboard and soaring neatly over, returning again to take his place in the rear of the line, I reflected that it was surely impossible for these nice-looking lads to have been guilty of an act as unsporting and un-English as that into which we were enquiring.

Suddenly a big heavy lout of a boy missed his spring, and instead of vaulting over the horse, landed asprawl across it. Amid a shout of laughter the sergeant smartly planted a resounding smack upon the tight target thus offered, after which, stepping upon the springboard, he lifted down the victim of the mishap and deposited him upon the ground with as much ease as if the boy had been five instead of fifteen.

"Take off with the right foot, placin' the 'ands lightly on the 'orse, knees bent, landin' easily on the toes," he chanted monotonously, "and no talking in the ranks, if you please."

At that moment, catching the sergeant's eye, Talbot lifted a finger. The tune changed. "The class will carry on at the vaultin'-'orse in a quiet *and* horderly manner, and without 'orseplay." The joke, clearly an old favourite, was nevertheless as well received as if it had but that moment been conceived.

As Sergeant Wren came over to us my eyes took in the easy stride, the rippling muscles, the resolute, hawk-like features. Here was a man with whom it would be dangerous to trifle, a man quick to strike in anger, a man, too, easily capable of lifting about a big boy, a big log. . . . I pulled myself up short, hearing suddenly a mischievous elfin chuckle, as it were from the ghost of Cedric Dodd.

"Now, Sergeant," I said easily, when Talbot had formally introduced me, "I want to ask you one or two questions about the events of last night."

Was it my imagination, or had Sergeant Wren changed colour? Why did he shift his eyes? Why did he find the cool gymnasium suddenly so warm? The inhuman zest of the hunter entered my blood, and I spoke in a tone quite other than I had intended to use—a tone deliberately over-suave, ominously polite, suggestive of a lawyer luring a witness into a trap.

"You remained in the building all the evening?"

"I did, sir. I was on dooty."

"I think the steward was away?"

"Yes, sir, 'e was, and 'e still is."

"And last night you took his duty as doorkeeper in his absence?"

"I did, sir."

Why, again, was he answering my questions with such a show of punctilious accuracy?

"Tell me, Sergeant, exactly what does that mean? You don't, I presume, stand in front of the door all the evening?"

To my annoyance, Talbot took it upon himself to answer this.

"No," he explained. "There is a small room off the hall known as the steward's room, which has a sliding grille opening into the hall, through which the boys get their letters and parcels; and when the janitor comes on duty for the evening he would sit there and answer the door when he hears the bell."

"I see." I turned again, somewhat pointedly, to the sergeant. "So that, had the doctor returned last night, you would have admitted him?"

"Oh, no." It was still Talbot who officiously answered; but I noticed that the sergeant looked relieved, as if at last he saw where my questions were leading. "The Head wouldn't come in at the school entrance. He would let himself in at his private house, on the left wing of the building."

"Thank you, Mr. Talbot." Once more I turned to the sergeant.

"And at what time do you think the Head would have returned?"

"That, of course, is difficult, not to say impossible, to answer, at least as regards last night," said Talbot. "But it was known that he always kept late hours and was seldom in before twelve."

I thanked Talbot again, wondering whether he noticed the tone in which I did so. It was obvious that I should receive no further answers from Sergeant Wren until I asked a question which he and he alone could answer. With a patience which, I thought, would have earned the approbation of Cedric Dodd himself, I tried again.

"Now, Sergeant," and this time I literally turned my back on Talbot, with an action so marked that even he could not fail to notice it, "apart from the headmaster's private house, as to which, of course, you know nothing, could anyone have entered the main school after ten o'clock without being seen by you?"

"No, sir. That I *can* say."

"You are positive?"

"Quite."

"And you saw no one?"

The sentence, half statement, half question, slipped out with such casual ease that I began to think I had mistaken my vocation. The sergeant, wholly unaware of the trap it contained, answered readily: "No, sir; no one at all."

"And you admitted no one?"

"Quite correct, sir." Again I noticed the relief in his voice. My heart was now beating wildly with the excitement of the chase, for incredible as it seemed, it was now evident that I was on the right trail; but before I could push my advantage home the irrepressible Talbot broke in once again.

"Except, of course, Mr. Jacks, Sergeant; you have forgotten Mr. Jacks."

The sergeant hesitated; fortunately he was not sufficiently quick-witted to have seized the point already, and in that moment of hesitation I saw my chance.

"One moment, Talbot," I said, in a quick, authoritative rasp very different to the smooth tones in which I had previously spoken.

"Leave this to me, please. Now, Sergeant Wren, did you, or did you not, admit Mr. Jacks last night?"

The sergeant glanced here and there, moistened his lips, hesitated, stammered, in a manner pitiful to see.

"Mr. Jacks," he said. "Mr. Jacks. . . . Let me see now . . . Let me think . . . Mr. Jacks . . ."

I turned away.

"Well," I said, with a shrug that clearly indicated my opinion of his evidence, "we can settle the point easily enough by consulting Mr. Jacks himself. Meanwhile," I went on, turning to Talbot, "I think we had better continue our enquiries in some more private place. I have one or two very pertinent questions to put to our friend the sergeant here."

v

Seated magisterially at the table in the late headmaster's private study, whither Talbot had conducted us, with the sergeant standing limply before me and an impressed and astounded Talbot impatiently awaiting the arrival of the hastily summoned Mr. Jacks, I began to feel that I had hitherto been inclined to overrate the difficulty of detective work. Close and careful observation, the exercise of a little acumen, a quick and ready intellect, and perhaps a certain flair for perceiving in what direction the truth was most likely to lie— these, I now saw, were all that were necessary for ultimate success.

My pleasant reverie was interrupted by the appearance of Mr. Jacks—fussy, snappy, and obviously not at all pleased at being summoned from his duties in such a peremptory manner.

"I am sorry to have to trouble you again, Mr. Jacks," I said, blending sternness with urbanity in a manner worthy of a long-seasoned London magistrate. "But there is just one question I want to put to you. At what time exactly did you return from your walk last night?"

Mr. Jacks, without answering, gazed at me for a moment or two without obvious disfavour, after which, with a jerk of the head in my direction and addressing Mr. Talbot, he asked brusquely: "What's it all about?"

Talbot started in some embarrassment. "Mr. Pierce is investigating the doctor's death," he explained stiffly.

Mr. Jacks surveyed me again—at some length.

"Oh," he said. "And on whose authority?"

"On mine," Talbot answered with dignity.

"Oh," said Jacks again, somewhat taken aback. "Then I suppose that's all right. Well, Mr.—I forget your name—if you want to know, I went for a walk at about nine o'clock, I returned at about eleven, I did not meet Dr. Shorter either going or coming, and I had nothing whatever to do with his death. Further, it may interest you to know that I can't prove a word of what I say—and I've no intention of trying."

"I see. Thank you, Mr. Jacks. And one thing more—who let you in on your return?"

At this—as it seemed to him—further proof of the net that was being spread for him, Mr. Jacks turned to Talbot, bristling with indignation to his very whiskers.

"I decline to answer any further questions until I have consulted my solicitor," he snapped.

At any other time I should have rather enjoyed baiting the waspish little man further, but just now the information we required of him was of such vital importance that I hastened to smooth away the misunderstanding.

"Come, Mr. Jacks," I said soothingly; "let me assure you that no suspicions of any sort attach to you. We merely wish to verify, by reference to you, the various statements we have already taken from others."

"Oh," said Mr. Jacks. "Oh. You do? Very well, then. As a matter of fact, I let myself in."

"With a key?"

"No. Without a key. I haven't got a key. There was no one about, and the door was unfastened, so naturally I walked in."

"Thank you, Mr. Jacks. We are very much obliged to you."

Now that we had obviously finished with him, Mr. Jacks seemed in no great haste to depart. I had done my best to give him the impression that the sergeant's presence was due to nothing more significant than our desire to take a statement from him, but the man's dejected appearance was in itself a sufficient contradiction of this; and by the time Talbot had succeeded in getting his peppery little colleague out of the room I felt sure that any further attempts at secrecy would be useless.

"Sergeant Wren," I said sternly, when the three of us were alone together again, "I think it is now time you told us where you were at eleven o'clock last night, when Mr. Jacks returned and found the door unattended."

Sergeant Wren, as if slightly dazed, turned his huge frame heavily in his chair and regarded me with a gaze that was almost vacant.

"Aye," he said listlessly. "You've got me there. And I suppose I may as well make a clean breast of it sooner as later. Once you gentlemen begin ferreting things out, there ain't much chance of getting away with it."

Up to then Talbot, I think, had been to a certain extent in the dark, and I myself had not expected an actual confession of guilt such as we were apparently about to hear; so that I felt somewhat like an amateur angler who, casting his line casually into waters from which no great catch is to be expected, suddenly finds himself struggling with a fish of embarrassing size.

It was a simple enough story that he had to tell us, and throughout his short recital I found it difficult to withhold a certain measure of sympathy for the man. Indeed—so strange are the twists in our mental make-up and so elastic our moral senses—only by reminding myself that in effect he had committed the crime of murder was I able to refrain from wishing that my chance enquiries that morning had met with less success.

It all began, apparently, by one of the sergeant's friends getting himself into what the sergeant called "a little bit o' trouble with the police," though in effect it was bad enough to necessitate his leaving the country. The sergeant made this possible for him by "wangling" the cash at the tuckshop, which was under his sole charge; and he admitted with characteristic simplicity—I was almost going to say honesty—that, having found this an easy matter, he went a step further and "took a bit for himself as well." The spectacle of the sergeant "cooking" the books would, under less tragic circumstances, have been comic; and of course Dr. Shorter ultimately found him out.

Then arose a situation which has often arisen before, and will continue to arise so long as human nature remains what it is. Dr. Shorter was a Christian—that is to say, he was enough of a Christian to forgive the offense and magnanimously allow the culprit another chance, but not enough of a Christian to refrain from mentioning the matter again. With unctuous enthusiasm he proceeded to take charge of the sergeant's soul, and to make it clear that his honour, his livelihood, and even his personal freedom depended solely upon the doctor's magnanimity. It was a kind of innocent blackmail, levied no doubt with the best of intentions; but to a rough-and-ready man like the sergeant, accustomed to being respected and obeyed, one can well understand that it was intolerable. At every turn he was faced with the threat of exposure; he had to listen to constant homilies, to suffer the indignity of continual veiled allusions and mysterious admonishments in public, and even to attend church twice every Sunday, where, he declared, the doctor on several occasions preached directly *at* him. Finally, as was inevitable, the thing got on his mind, and gradually he conceived for the doctor such a hatred as only those who have suffered long and constantly at the hands of another can know. The last straw had been added to the weight of his hatred when, on the preceding day, he had received through the good offices of a retired major in his old regiment the offer of a post as gymnastic instructor to a famous school at a salary far greater than that he was receiving, only to find himself in danger of having to refuse it because the doctor declared that he should consider it his duty to reveal his, the sergeant's, lapse to his new employers.

As for the actual crime, it had been committed as a result of prolonged temptation. The log was an old friend; he had often sat upon it to smoke a quiet pipe on returning from a solitary ramble; and it was not unnatural that, seeing the doctor make off that evening on his motorbicycle, he had wished, in the fury of his heart, that some convenient accident might remove his enemy from his path—some such accident, for example, as might befall if the cyclist were to collide in the dark with an unexpected obstacle in his path. From this it was but a step to the fiendish suggestion to which in the end he had succumbed; and shortly before eleven he had slipped away from his post and, in a mood of reckless malevolence, had engineered the "accident" that would mean so much to him.

The round bald patch in the middle of his head glistened with perspiration by the time he had done; and as for Talbot, his drawn, lined face, never very cheerful at the best of times, was grey with worry and concern. It was clear that, in spite of what he had heard, he still retained a sneaking liking for the sergeant, and hardly less clear that he had no great regard for the sergeant's victim.

"Good God, Sergeant," he said, with a curious, childish petulance, "you must have been mad."

"Maybe I was, Mr. Talbot," the sergeant answered miserably. "But there it is."

Talbot looked at me. "I suppose there can be no question, from the legal standpoint, that he . . . that he has . . ." The question tailed off.

"None whatever, I'm afraid." After all, the man deserved little sympathy; he was, in effect, a thief and a murderer self-confessed. "In the eyes of the law," I continued aloud, with what was perhaps unnecessary harshness, "he who does an act in the hope, and with the intention, of causing the death of another must be answerable for the results; and if he succeeds is clearly guilty of murder."

"Exactly!" said Cedric Dodd. "But *did* he succeed?"

VI

The door had opened as I was speaking, and my friend stood regarding us curiously.

"From what I have just heard," he went on, before any of us could recover from the surprise of his sudden appearance, "I presume that you have succeeded in clearing up the matter of the log?"

"Yes," I said, though already I spoke with ebbing confidence. "We have."

"And the person responsible?"

"He is here," I said. "Sergeant Wren."

"Very well," said Dodd, and with hardly more than a glance at the despondent figure by the window he crossed the room, picked up the telephone, and asked for the local police station.

During the moment or two of waiting that ensued my thoughts raced furiously. Already, by his queer initial question, Dodd seemed to have taken some of the wind out of my sails. A moment ago I had been confidently conducting the final stage of what had seemed a wholly successful investigation; now I began to ask myself how much, in effect, I had really achieved, and even to doubt the correctness of my conclusions. And yet—had not the sergeant confessed? Surely even Cedric Dodd would be unable to deny the force of that!

"Police station? Inspector Berry, please." There was a lazy softness in his voice—the purr of a man well pleased with his work. "That you, Inspector? . . . Dodd speaking. They've got your other man for you. . . . No, you must thank my colleague, Gregory Pierce, for that. . . . Right, I will." He rang off. "Sergeant," he announced curtly, "I am instructed to detain you here until Inspector Berry arrives. You will be charged, I suppose, with attempting to commit grievous bodily harm."

The sergeant raised his head, and in his eyes I saw an unforgettable look—the look of a man who, after abandoning hope and seeing himself in his imagination already dead, is suddenly confronted with a prospect of renewed life.

"Attempting to commit grievous bodily harm." The phrase seemed to ring through the room; Sergeant Wren, speechless, gazed and gazed at Dodd, as a starving man gazes at the sight of food, as a man lost in an underground cavern gazes at a sudden distant glimpse of daylight.

Dodd took a chair. "You were quite correct in what you were

saying," he said. "If this man here had attempted to cause the death of another, however indirectly, and had succeeded in that attempt, he would be guilty of murder in the eyes of the law; but, fortunately for him, he chose a method so indirect that it was hardly likely to succeed—nor did it succeed."

"Then—do you mean that the doctor has recovered after all?" Talbot asked, and his eagerness was obviously sincere.

Dodd shook his head. "No," he said, "I am afraid you mustn't expect any such happy issue as that. But this man here did not kill him. However," he went on more briskly, turning to me, "I should like first of all to hear what has been happening in my absence."

Alas, how difficult were my brief, halting explanations from the royal recital I had foreseen; and how clearly, as I proceeded, did the fact emerge that in truth I had done no more than anyone else could have done—no more, indeed, than stumble upon a solution that the least expert of enquiries must at once have elicited! I saw now that my quarry had been no careful, cunning villain, hiding his guilt beneath an air of disarming innocence, but a trembling, conscience-stricken wretch, ready to break down and confess at the first suspicious glance from the eye of justice.

"A queer case," said Dodd when I had finished. "It is not often that a man genuinely confesses to a crime he hasn't committed. And it was fortunate for him that there happened to be someone on hand to investigate the matter thoroughly, though there were, as it turned out, various fairly obvious indications that the affair was not as simple as it appeared to be, and one in particular that would at once have gone far to exculpate the sergeant from immediate responsibility. You will remember, Gregory," he went on, "that I invited you this morning to look for it yourself."

"You did," I admitted. "But even now I don't know what it was or how I came to miss it."

For a moment Dodd's mischievous smile flickered on his face. "You missed it, I'm afraid, by not being thorough enough," he said. "The point I speak of concerned the hat—the clerical hat that lay by the doctor's side."

"But I didn't miss that," I protested. "I examined it most carefully."

"I dare say," Dodd answered. "But you didn't do with it the one thing that was really necessary. For, after all, what are hats for?"

"To wear, I suppose."

"Exactly. And you didn't try that hat on the dead man's head, to see if he *could* wear it. Had you done so, you would have seen that it didn't fit. It was several sizes too small."

Not for the first time in our acquaintanceship, I gazed at Dodd in envious admiration.

"I never thought of it," I ejaculated.

"No," Dodd answered, with another swift smile. "And really, I suppose, in a way, it wasn't so very obvious. And yet, after all, hats *are* made primarily to wear, you know. However," he went on, "you will be more interested now to hear what I did do than what you didn't." He paused for a moment, as if to take a swift survey of what he had to say, and as he did so the still, somnolent silence of the hot summer morning was broken by the remote call of the cuckoo.

"The first thing that was obvious in this case," said Cedric Dodd, "was that the log, however it had got where it was found, was not responsible for the death. The condition of the body alone proved that; and that of the cycle, and even of the log itself, confirmed it. When a cycle strikes an obstacle on the ground, the rider is shot forward over the handlebars, his head strikes the ground, his face is torn and grazed, *and so are his hands,* for he will instinctively throw them out to save himself. But in this case the wound was clean, there was no grazing of the face, and the hands were untouched. Then again, assuming that the cycle had struck the log, the condition of both was curious. If the force of the impact had been such as to throw the rider with sufficient violence to kill him, the front tyre would probably have burst and the machine generally be far more damaged than was actually the case; moreover, the log itself would have been grazed by the low-built engine passing over it, and there were no signs of this on the log.

"I had already asked myself why the cyclist's headlight had failed to reveal the log in time; and the answer to this was now clear. It had not failed to reveal it; on the contrary, the rider had seen it and dismounted, to meet his death subsequently by a blow on the head from some blunt instrument, delivered by a human hand.

"It was at this point that the full significance of the curious position of the log flashed upon me. You will remember that, heavy as it was, it had not been heaved straight onto the road opposite the spot where it had originally lain, as one would expect; it had actually been dragged some little way back along the lane. And now the reason for this, too, was plain. If the man had been struck down by someone *before he reached the log,* the murderer, in order to give the necessary appearance of accident to the scene, would have had either to shift the body forward beyond the log, or the log back behind the body. As the body lay in a pool of blood, he was obliged to adopt the latter course.

"All this, however, left me very little the wiser as to the actual perpetrator of the crime. After you, Gregory, had gone off to the school I stood in the roadway, surveying the scene, and I had to confess that for the moment I found myself completely floored. And yet it was unlikely that a crime of this kind could have been committed without the murderer leaving some trace behind, and I accordingly fell back upon my usual plan of looking for something so obvious that no one had considered it worth looking at. I had, of course, already seen the hat, and noticed that it was undamaged, but as this fact appeared, on the face of it, to be against my general theory rather than for it, I had explained it, somewhat carelessly perhaps, by assuming that the hat had either been removed before the blow or had fallen off in a scuffle immediately preceding it. But now I picked it up and examined it again, and while I was doing so the elementary idea occurred to me of making sure first of all that it was in fact the deceased's hat.

"The rest, of course, was easy. That hat simply gave the whole thing away. The moment I found that it didn't fit I saw that the hat's undamaged condition, far from being against my theory, abundantly supported it. It was undamaged because it was not the dead man's hat, and if it was not the dead man's hat, it was in all probability the murderer's. Why? Because the doctor's hat had, after all, been damaged by the blow, as, when one comes to think of it, it would inevitably have been; and consequently the murderer, if he wished to give his crime the appearance of an accident, could not leave the hat behind, for when a man falls off a bicycle his hat, especially if it be a clerical hat, does not remain glued to his head until he strikes the ground. The murderer could not afford to leave his victim's crushed and bloody hat behind, but neither could he afford to leave no hat behind, and so he was obliged to leave his own.

"There was also another point on which the hat threw considerable light. Up to then I had been assuming that the crime was premeditated; now I felt pretty sure that it was not. I had taken it for granted that the hand that rolled the log into position was the hand that struck the fatal blow; but the discovery that that hand was a clergyman's suggested other possibilities. A clergyman might strike—and kill—in a sudden access of anger or in self-protection, but it was unlikely that he would have deliberately planned a dastardly murder involving the preparation of the ground beforehand. I therefore inclined to the opinion that the log had been placed in position by someone else; probably, as was suggested, by the boys, possibly by some person with malevolent intentions; and for this reason I thought it better, when you two turned up, to say as little as possible about the discoveries I had made, particularly as I had already determined to follow up the main clue myself and to leave you to deal with the secondary matter of the log.

"My own task was easy enough, for it was obvious that I should not have far to look. My quarry was a clergyman, and, if my assumption that the crime was unpremeditated was correct, he was probably a local resident. If not, I had the hat to help me, for it was new, and bore the name of the maker, through whom it could be traced; or it was even possible that enquiries in the district would reveal from whom and by whom it had been bought. However, there proved to be no necessity for any of these steps, for on calling at the vicarage I found the vicar prostrate, and soon had no difficulty in forcing the whole story from him."

It was not until after lunch, when Dodd and I sat with Talbot over our coffee, preparatory to setting forth once more on our interrupted walking tour, that I heard the rest of the story. The tragedy itself, as Dodd had surmised, had been entirely unpremeditated—and the origin of it nothing more unusual than a girl. Indeed, had the vicar—a tall, wiry young fellow to look at—been possessed of physical courage in proportion to his size, it need never have happened at all. But he had been nurtured, I suppose, in a softer school than the big, browbeating doctor, so that the sudden translation of their dispute from the realm of argument to that of brute force had produced in him the most ignoble and the most dangerous of human emotions—blind, ungovernable fear.

He and the girl in question had grown up together, and, as often happens, had partly drifted and partly been pushed by relations into a somewhat tepid bethrothal. Tepid, at least, on her side, but not on his; for when the girl found herself carried off her feet by the impetuous wooing of the older man, with whom she must have fallen seriously in love, the unfortunate vicar became frantic with grief. He excused his subsequent actions—his refusal to accept his former fiancée's decision, his constant pestering of the girl and her new lover, and his insincere threats of legal action, on the grounds that the two were unsuited to each other by reason of the disparity in their ages, and that the girl was the victim of a temporary infatuation of which no true gentleman would take advantage.

It must not be imagined that all this was common knowledge. For one thing, the original engagement had never actually been announced, though it had been taken for granted by all concerned; and for another, the doctor seems to have kept his relations with the girl remarkably quiet, even to the point of making them look more like an illicit intrigue than a genuine wooing. At all events, the extraordinary fact remains that Talbot himself was wholly unaware of his chief's matrimonial intentions—which gives a certain colour to the accusation recklessly launched by the vicar on the fatal night and productive of the final tragedy.

For some days previously the doctor had resolutely refused to see the vicar, and when, on the evening in question, he received a frantic and peremptory note demanding a private interview at the vicarage, he still took no notice. For some reason the vicar apparently thought he would keep the appointment, perhaps because the girl happened to be away; at all events, he waited in for his rival all the evening, and, when the latter failed to turn up, set out, late as it was, to walk to the school and once more force his presence upon the doctor. As a matter of fact, unknown to him, the girl had already returned; indeed, she and the doctor had actually passed the evening together.

On his way to the school the vicar almost fell over the log, and at the same time saw and heard the approach of the motorcycle. Fearing an accident, he stood in the middle of the roadway, waving his arms and shouting; the cyclist saw him in time, pulled up, and dismounted; and the vicar then discovered that he had been fortunate—or unfortunate—enough to intercept the very man he was so anxious to see.

There, in that dark lane, late at night, the two faced each other; and there, after a bitter quarrel in which both seem to have completely lost their tempers, the vicar hurled at his enemy the accusation to which I have referred. The doctor, a man of fierce temper at the best of times, saw red; and snatching from the vicar's hand the heavy country stick he was carrying, fell back upon the argument he was accustomed to find so effective when dealing with his boys, and began to thrash his adversary unmercifully.

There are some men upon whom brute force has an utterly unnerving effect, and the vicar, unfortunately, was one of them. He must have been almost beside himself with fear and indignation when, chancing to regain possession of his stick, he launched at the doctor's head the brutal blow that killed him; and it was fear, and nothing else, that afterwards lent cunning to his brain, showing him how to take full advantage of the way of escape that Providence had opened in his path, a way which, but for Dodd's intervention, might have left him to live out his life with a dreadful secret, the memory of which would have caused his sensitive soul suffering that is too awful to contemplate.

The Professor's Manuscript

BY DOROTHY L. SAYERS

"See here, Monty," said Mr. Hopgood (travelling representative for Messrs. Brotherhood, Ltd.) to Mr. Egg (travelling representative for Messrs. Plummett & Rose); "while you're here, why don't you have a go at old Professor Pindar? I should say he was just about in your line."

Mr. Egg brought his mind back—a little unwillingly—from the headlines in his morning paper ("SCREEN STAR'S MARRIAGE ROMANCE PLANE DASH"—"CONTINENT COMB-OUT FOR MISSING FINANCIER"—"BUDGET INCOME-TAX REMISSION POSSIBILITY"), and inquired who Professor Pindar might be when he was at home.

"He's a funny old bird that's come and settled down at Wellingtonia House," replied Mr. Hopgood. "You know, where the Fennells used to live. Bought the place last January and moved in about a month ago. Writes books, or something. I went along yesterday to see if there was anything doing in our way. Heard he was a retired sort of old party. Thought he might be good for a case of Sparkling Pompayne or something else in the soft drinks line. Quite rude to me, he was. Called it 'gut-rot,' and spilled a piece of poetry about 'windy waters.' Shouldn't have expected such strong expressions from a brainy-looking old gent like him. Apologised for taking up his time, of course, and said to myself, 'Here's where young Monty gets in with his matured spirits and fine old fruity.' Thought I'd give you the tip, that's all—but suit yourself, of course."

Mr. Egg thanked Mr. Hopgood, and agreed that Professor Pindar sounded like a useful prospect.

"One gets to see him all right, then?" he asked.

"Yes—only you have to state your business," said Mr. Hopgood. "Housekeeper's a bit of a dragon. No good trying on the old tale of being sent round by his dear friend Mr. So-and-so, because, for one thing, he's got no friends round here and, for another, they know that one."

"In that case—" began Mr. Egg; but Mr. Hopgood did not appear to notice that he had said anything odd, and he felt it was hardly worth while to start an argument, especially as the morning was getting on, and he had not yet read about the film-star's marriage dash or the country-house arson suspicions. He turned his attention to these, discovered that the romance was the lady's fifth marriage and that the fire was thought to be yet another ramification of the insurance ramp, went on to ascertain that the person detained the day before in Constantinople was not, after all, the absconding head of Mammoth Industries, Ltd., and that the hope of sixpence off the income-tax was little more than the *Daily Trumpet* correspondent's dream of wish-fulfillment, and then embarked upon a juicy leader-page article headed "CAN COMMERCIAL TRAVELLERS BE CHRISTIANS?—by One of Them," which interested him, not so much because he had any doubts about commercial morality as because he fancied he knew who the author was.

Before very long, however, his own commercial conscience (which was sensitive) reminded him that he was wasting his employer's time, and he went out to inquire into a complaint received from the landlord of the Ring of Bells that the last case of Plummett & Rose's Superior Old Tawny (full body, fine masculine flavour) was not up to sample, owing to alleged faulty corking.

Having disposed of this little unpleasantness, and traced the trouble to the fact that the landlord had thoughtlessly run the main pipe of a new heating installation behind the racks housing the Superior Old Tawny, Mr. Egg asked to be directed to Wellingtonia House.

"It's about five miles out of the town," said the landlord. "Take the road to Great Windings, turn off to the left by the tower they call Grabb's Folly and then it's down the lane on the right past the old water-mill. Biggish place with a high brick wall, right down in the hollow. Damp, in my opinion. Shouldn't care to live there myself. All right if you like peace and quietness, but I prefer to see a bit of life myself. So does the missis. But this old chap ain't married, so I suppose it's all right for him. Lives there alone with a housekeeper and a handy-man and about fifty million tons of books. I was sorry to hear he'd taken the house. What we want there is a family with a bit of money, to bring some trade into the town."

"Not a rich man, then?" asked Mr. Egg, mentally substituting a cheaper line for the Cockburn 1896 (a grand ancient wine thirty-five years in bottle) with which he had hoped to tempt the Professor.

"He may have," replied the landlord; "must have, I suppose, since he's bought the place freehold. But what's the odds if he don't spend it? Never goes anywhere. No entertaining. Bit of a crank, by what they tell me."

"Butcher's meat?" inquired Mr. Egg.

"Oh, yes," said the landlord, "and only the best cuts. But what's one old gentleman's steak and chop when you come to think of it? That don't make a lot of difference in the week's turn-over."

However, the thought of the steak and chops comforted Mr. Egg as he drove by Grabb's Folly and the old watermill and turned down the little, winding lane between high hedgerows starred with dog-violets and the lesser celandine. Grilled meat and wine went together almost as certainly as nut-cutlets and home-made lemonade.

The door of Wellingtonia House was opened by a middle-aged woman in an apron, at sight of whom Mr. Egg instantly dismissed the manner he used for domestic servants and substituted the one reserved for persons "out of the top drawer," as he phrased it. A pre-War gentlewoman in a post-War job, he decided. He produced his card and stated his business frankly.

"Well," said the housekeeper. She looked Mr. Egg searchingly up and down. "Professor Pindar is a very busy man, but he may like to see you. He is very particular about his wines—especially vintage port."

"Vintage port, madam," replied Mr. Egg, "is a speciality with us."

"*Real* vintage port?" asked the housekeeper, smiling.

Mr. Egg was hurt, though he tried not to show it. He mentioned a few of Messrs. Plummett & Rose's choicer shipments, and produced a list.

"Come in," said the housekeeper. "I'll take the list to Professor Pindar. He may like to see you himself, though I can't promise. He is very hard at work upon his book, and he can't possibly spare very much time."

"Certainly not, madam," said Mr. Egg, stepping in and wiping his boots carefully. They were perfectly clean, but the ritual was part of his regular routine, as laid down by *The Salesman's Handbook.* ("Be clean and courteous; raise your hat, And wipe your boots upon the mat: Such proofs of gentlemanly feeling Are to the ladies most appealing.") "In my opinion," he added, as he followed his conductress through a handsome hall and down a long and thickly carpeted passage, "more sales are lost through being too persistent than through not being persistent enough. There's a little verse, madam, that I try to bear in mind: 'Don't stay too long; the customer has other things to do than sitting in the parlour and listening to you; And if, through your loquacity, she lets the dinner burn, She will not soon forget it, and it does you a bad turn.' I will just show the professor my list, and if he is not interested, I will promise to go away at once."

The housekeeper laughed. "You are more reasonable than most of them," she said, and showed him into a large and lofty room, lined from floor to ceiling with bookshelves. "Wait here a minute, and I will see what Professor Pindar says."

She was gone for some time, and Mr. Egg, being left to contem-

plate, with awe and some astonishment, the array of learning all
about him, became restless, and even a little reckless. He walked
about the library, trying to ascertain from the titles of the books
what Professor Pindar was professor of. His interests, however,
appeared to be catholic, for the books dealt with many subjects. One
of them, a stout, calf-bound octavo in a long row of calf-bound
octavos, attracted Mr. Egg's attention. It was an eighteenth-century
treatise on brewing and distilling, and he extended a cautious finger
to hook it from the shelf. It was, however, too tightly wedged
between a bound collection of pamphlets and a play by Ben Jonson
to come out easily, and he abandoned the attempt. Curiosity made
him next tiptoe over to the formidable great desk strewn with
manuscripts. This gave more information. In the centre, near the
typewriter, lay a pile of neatly typed sheets, embellished with
footnotes and a good many passages of what looked to Mr. Egg
like Greek, though it might, of course, have been Russian or
Arabic, or any other language with a queer alphabet. The half-
finished page upon the blotter broke off abruptly with the words:
"This was the opinion of St. Augustine, though Clement of
Alexandria expressly declares—" Here the sentence ended, as
though the writer had paused to consult his authority. The open
folio on the table was, however, neither St. Augustine nor Clement
of Alexandria, but Origen. Close beside it stood a metal strong-box
with a combination-lock, which Mr. Egg judged to contain some
rare manuscript or other.

The sound of a hand upon the door-handle caused him to start
guiltily away from the table, and when the door opened he had
whisked round with his back to the desk and was staring abstractedly at a shelf crammed with immense tomes, ranging from
Aristotle's works to a Jacobean *Life of Queen Elizabeth*.

Professor Pindar was a very bent and tottery old gentleman, and
the hairiest person Mr. Egg had ever set eyes upon. His beard began
at his cheekbones and draped his chest as far as the penultimate
waistcoat-button. Over a pair of very sharp grey eyes, heavy grey
eyebrows hung like a pent-house. He wore a black skull-cap, from
beneath which more grey hair flowed so as to conceal his collar.

He wore a rather shabby black velvet jacket, grey trousers, which had forgotten the last time they had ever seen a trousers-press, and a pair of carpet slippers, over which grey woollen socks wreathed themselves in folds. His face (what could be seen of it) was thin, and he spoke with a curious whistle and click due to an extremely ill-fitting set of dentures.

"Hso you are the young man from the wine-merchant's, hish, click," said the Professor. "Hsit down. Click." He waved his hand to a chair some little distance away, and himself shuffled to the desk and seated himself. "You brought me a list—where have I— ah! yesh! click! here it is, hish. Let me hsee." He fumbled about himself and produced a pair of steel spectacles. "Hish! yesh! Very interesting. What made you think of calling on me, click, hey? Hish."

Mr. Egg said that he had been advised to call by Messrs. Brother-hood's representative.

"I thought, sir," he said, ingenuously, "that if you disapproved so much of soft drinks, you might appreciate something more, shall we say, full-bodied."

"You did, did you?" said the Professor. "Very shrewd of you. Click! Hsmart of you, hish. Got some good hish stuff here." He waved the list. "Don't believe in highclassh wine-merchants touting for customers shthough. Infra dig. Hey?"

Mr. Egg explained that the pressure of competition had driven Messrs. Plummett & Rose to this undoubtedly rather modern ex-pedient. "But of course, sir," he added, "we exercise our discretion. I should not dream of showing a gentleman like yourself the list we issue to licensed houses."

"Humph!" said Professor Pindar. "Well—" He entered upon a discussion of the wine-list, showing himself remarkably knowl-edgeable for an aged scholar whose interests were centred upon the Fathers of the Church. He was, he said, thinking of laying down a small cellar, though he should have to get some new racks installed, since the former owners had allowed that part of the establishment to fall into decay.

Mr. Egg ventured on a mild witticism about "rack and ruin,"

and booked a useful little order for some Warre, Dow & Cockburn
ports, together with a few dozen selected burgundies, to be delivered in a month's time, when the cellar accommodation should
be ready for them.

"You are thinking of settling permanently in this part of the
country, sir?" he ventured, as he rose (mindful of instructions) to
take his leave.

"Yes. Why not, hey?" snapped the Professor.

"Very glad to hear it, sir," said Monty. "Always very glad to
hear of a good customer, you know."

"Yes, of coursh," replied Professor Pindar. "Naturally. I exsh-
pect to be here till I have finished my book, at any rate. May take
years, click! *Hishtory of the Early Chrishtian Chursh*, hish, click."
Here his teeth seemed to take so alarming a leap from his jaws that
Mr. Egg made an instinctive dive forward to catch them, and
wondered why the Professor should have hit on a subject and title so
impossible of pronunciation.

"But that means nothing to *you*, I take it, hey?" concluded the
Professor, opening the door.

"Nothing, I'm sorry to say, sir," said Mr. Egg, who knew where
to draw the line between the pretence of interest and the confession
of ignorance. "Like the Swan of Avon, if I may put it that way, I
have small Latin and less Greek, and that's the only resemblance
between me and him, I'm afraid."

The Professor laughed, perilously, and followed up this exercise
with a terrific click.

"Mrs. Tabbitt!" he called, "show this gentleman out."

The housekeeper reappeared and took charge of Mr. Egg, who
departed, full of polite thanks for esteemed favours.

"Well," thought Montague Egg, "that's a puzzler, that is. All the
same, it's no business of mine, and I don't want to make a mistake.
I wonder who I could ask. Wait a minute. Mr. Griffiths—he's the
man. He'd know in a moment."

It so happened that he was due to return to town that day. He
attended to his business and then, as soon as he was free, went round

to call upon a very good customer and friend of his, who was the senior partner in the extremely respectable publishing firm of Griffiths & Seabright. Mr. Griffiths listened to his story with considerable interest.

"Pindar?" said he. "Never heard of him. Early Fathers of the Church, eh? Well, Dr. Abcock is the man for that. We'll ring him up. Hullo! is that Dr. Abcock? Sorry to bother you, but have you ever heard of a Professor Pindar who writes your kind of stuff? You haven't? . . . I don't know. Wait a moment."

He took down various stout volumes and consulted them.

"He doesn't seem to hold any English or Scotch professorship," he observed, presently. "Of course, it might be foreign or American—did he speak with any sort of accent, Egg?—No?—Well, that proves nothing, of course. Anybody can get a professorship from those odd American universities. Well, never mind, Doctor, don't bother. Yes, a book. I rather wanted to get the thing vetted. I'll let you know again later."

He turned to Monty.

"Nothing very definite there," he said, "but I'll tell you what I'll do. I'll call on this man—or perhaps it will be better to write. I'll say I've heard about the work and would like to make an offer for it. That might produce something. You're a bit of a terror, aren't you, Egg? Have a spot of one of your own wares before you go."

It was some time before Mr. Egg heard again from Mr. Griffiths. Then a letter was forwarded to him in York, whither his travels had taken him.

"Dear Egg,

"I wrote to your Professor, and with a good bit of trouble extracted an answer and a typescript. Now, there's no doubt at all about the MS. It's first-class, of its kind. Rather unorthodox, in some ways, but stuffed as full of scholarship as an egg (sorry) is of meat. But his letter was what I should call evasive. He doesn't say where he got his professorship. Possibly he bestowed the title on himself, *honoris causa*. But the book is so darned

good that I'm going to make a stiff push to get it for G. &
S. I'm writing to ask the mysterious Professor for an
appointment and will send you a line if I get it."

The next communication reached Mr. Egg in Lincoln.

"Dear Egg,
    "Curiouser and curiouser. Professor Pindar absolutely
refuses to see me or to discuss his book with me, though
he is ready to consider an offer. Abcock is getting excited
about it, and has written to ask for further information
on several controversial points in the MS. We cannot
understand how a man of such remarkable learning and
ability should have remained all this time unknown to
the experts in his particular subject. I think our best
chance is to get hold of old Dr. Wilverton. He knows
all about everything and everybody, only he is so very
eccentric that it is rather difficult to get anything out of
him. But you can be sure of one thing—the man who
wrote that book is a bona fide scholar, so your doubts
must have been ill-founded. But I'm immensely grateful
to you for putting me on to Professor Pindar, whoever
he is. The work will make a big noise in the little world
of learning."

Mr. Egg had returned to London before he heard from Mr. Griffiths again. Then he was rung up and requested, in rather excited
tones, to come round and meet the great and eccentric Dr. Lovell
Wilverton at Mr. Griffiths' house. When he got there, he found the
publisher and Dr. Abcock seated by the fire, while a strange little
man in a check suit and steel spectacles ramped irritably up and
down the room.

"It's no use," spluttered Dr. Wilverton, "it's no use to tell
me. I know. I say I *know*. The views expressed—the style—the—
everything points the same way. Besides, I tell you, I've seen that
passage on Clement of Alexandria before. Poor Donne! He was a
most brilliant scholar—*the* most brilliant scholar who ever passed
through my hands. I went to see him once, at that horrible little
hut on the Essex Marshes that he retired to after the—collapse, you

know—and he showed me the stuff then. Mistaken? Of course
I'm not mistaken. I'm never mistaken. Couldn't be. I've often
wondered since where that manuscript went to. If only I'd been
in England at the time I should have secured it. Sold with the rest
of his things, for junk, I suppose, to pay the rent."

"Just a moment, Wilverton," said Dr. Abcock, soothingly.
"You're going too fast for us. You say this *History of the Early
Christian Church* was written by a young man called Roger Donne,
a pupil of yours, who unfortunately took to drink and went to live
in very great poverty in a hut on the Essex Marshes. Now it turns
up, in typescript, which you say Donne wouldn't have used,
masquerading as the work of an old person calling himself Professor
Pindar, of Wellingtonia House, in Somerset. Are you suggesting
that Pindar stole the manuscript or bought it from Donne? Or
that he is Donne in disguise?"

"Of course he isn't Donne," said Dr. Wilverton, angrily. "I told
you, didn't I? Donne's dead. He died last year when I was in Syria.
I suppose this old imposter bought the manuscript at the sale."

Mr. Egg smote his thigh with his palm.

"Why, of course, sir," he said. "The deed-box I saw on the
table. That would have the original manuscript in it, and this old
professor-man just copied it out on his own typewriter."

"But what for?" asked Mr. Griffiths. "It's a remarkable book,
but it's not a thing one would get a lot of money out of."

"No," agreed Monty, "but it would be an awfully good proof
that the professor really was what he pretended to be. Suppose the
police made investigations—there was the professor, and there was
the book, and any expert they showed it to (unless they had the
luck to hit on Dr. Lovell Wilverton, of course) would recognize it
for the work of a really learned gentleman."

"Police?" said Dr. Abcock, sharply. "Why the police? Who do
you suppose this Pindar really is?"

Mr. Egg extracted a newspaper cutting from his pocket.

"Him, sir," he said. "Greenholt, the missing financier, who
absconded with all the remaining assets of Mammoth Industries,
Ltd., just a week before Professor Pindar came and settled at

Wellingtonia House. Here's his description: sixty years old, grey eyes, false teeth. Why, a bunch of hair and a bad set of dentures, a velvet coat and skullcap, and there you are. There's your Professor Pindar. I did think the hair was just a bit overdone. And that Mrs. Tabbitt was a lady, all right, and here's a photo of Mrs. Greenholt. Take away the make-up and scrag her hair back in a bun, and they're as like as two peas."

"Great heavens!" exclaimed Mr. Griffiths. "And they've been combing Europe for the fellow. Egg, I shouldn't wonder if you're right. Give me the 'phone. We'll get on to Scotland Yard. Hullo! Give me Whitehall 1212."

"You seem to be something of a detective, Mr. Egg," said Dr. Lovell Wilverton, later in the evening, when word had come through of the arrest of Robert Greenholt at Wellingtonia House. "Do you mind telling me what first put this idea into your head?"

"Well, sir," replied Mr. Egg, modestly, "I'm not a brainy man, but in my line one learns to size a party up pretty quickly. The first thing that seemed odd was that this Professor wouldn't see my friend, Hopgood, of Brotherhood, Ltd., till he knew where he came from, and then, when he did see him, told him he couldn't stick soft drinks. Now, you know, sir, as a rule, a busy gentleman won't see a commercial at all if he's not interested in the goods. It's one of our big difficulties. It looked as though the Professor wanted to be seen, in his character as a professor, by anybody and everybody, provided that it wasn't anybody who knew too much about books and so on. Then there was the butcher. He supplied steaks and chops to the household, which looked like a gentleman with good teeth; but when I got there, I found a hairy old boy whose dental plate was so wonky he could hardly have chewed scrambled eggs with it. But the thing that really bothered me was the books in that library. I'm no reader, unless it's a crook yarn or something of that kind, but I visit a good many learned gentlemen, and I've now and again cast my eye on their shelves, always liking to improve myself. Now, there were three things in that library that weren't like the library of any gentleman that uses his books. First, the books were all mixed up, with different subjects alongside one another, instead of all the same subject together. Then, the books were too neat, all big books in one place and all small ones in another. And then they were too snug in the shelves. No gentleman that likes books or needs to consult them quickly keeps them as tight as that—they won't come out when you want them and besides, it breaks the bindings. That's true, I know, because I asked a friend of mine in the second-hand book business. So you see," said Mr. Egg, persuasively, "Greek or no Greek, I couldn't believe that gentleman ever read any of his books. I expect he just bought up somebody's library—or you can have 'em delivered by the yard; it's often done by rich gentlemen who get their libraries done by furnishing firms."

"Bless my soul," said Dr. Lovell Wilverton, "is Saul also among the prophets? You seem to be an observant man, Mr. Egg."

"I try to be," replied Mr. Egg. "Never miss a chance of learning for that words spells ' £ ' plus 'earning.'—You'll find that in *The Salesman's Handbook*. Very neat, sir, don't you think?"

The Unknown Peer

BY E. C. BENTLEY

When Philip Trent went down to Lackington, with the mission of throwing some light upon the affair of Lord Southrop's disappearance, it was without much hope of adding anything to the simple facts already known to the police and made public in the newspapers. Those facts were plain enough, pointing to but one sad conclusion.

In the early morning of Friday, the 23rd of September, a small touring-car was found abandoned by the shore at Merwin Cove, some three miles along the coast from the flourishing Devonian resort of Brademouth. It had been driven off the road over turf to the edge of the pebble beach.

Examined by the police, it was found to contain a heavy overcoat, a folding stool, and a case of sketching materials with a sketching-block on the back seat; a copy of Anatole France's *Mannequin d'Osier*, two pipes, some chocolate, a flask of brandy, and a pair of binoculars in the shelves before the driving-seat; and in the pockets a number of maps and the motoring papers of Lord Southrop, of Hingham Blewitt, near Wymondham, in Norfolk.

Inquiries in the neighbourhood led to the discovery that a similar car and its driver were missing from the Crown Inn at Lackington, a small place a few miles inland; and later the car was definitely recognized.

In the hotel register, however, the owner had signed his name as L. G. Coxe; and it was in that name that a room had been booked by telephone early in the day. A letter, too, addressed to Coxe, had been delivered at the Crown, and had been opened by him on his arrival about 6:30. A large suitcase had been taken up to his room, where it still lay, and the mysterious Coxe had deposited an envelope containing £35 in banknotes in the hotel safe. He had dined in the coffee-room, smoked in the lounge for a time, then gone out again in his car, saying nothing of his destination. No more had been seen or heard of him.

Some needed light had been cast on the affair when Lord Southrop was looked up in *Who's Who*—for no one in the local force had ever heard of such a peer. It appeared that his family name was Coxe, and that he had been christened Lancelot Graham; that he was the ninth baron, was thirty-three years old, and had succeeded to the title at the age of twenty-six; that he had been educated at Harrow and Trinity, Cambridge; that he was unmarried, and that his heir was a first cousin, Lambert Reeves Coxe. No public record of any kind, nor even any "recreation" was noted in this unusually brief biography, which, indeed, bore the marks of having been compiled in the office, without any assistance from its subject.

Trent, however, had heard something more than this about Lord Southrop. Sir James Molloy, the owner of the *Record*, who had sent Trent to Lackington, had met everybody, including even the missing peer, who was quite unknown in society. Society, according to Molloy, was heartily detested and despised by Lord Southrop. His interests were exclusively literary and artistic, apart from his taste in the matter of wine, which he understood better than most men. He greatly preferred Continental to English ways of life, and spent much of his time abroad. He had a very large income, for most of which he seemed to have no use. He had good health and a kindly disposition; but he had a passion for keeping himself to himself, and had indulged it with remarkable success. One of his favourite amusements was wandering about the country alone in his car, halting here and there to make a sketch, and staying always at out-of-the-way inns under the name he had used at Lackington.

Lord Southrop had been, however, sufficiently like other men to fall in love, and Molloy had heard that his engagement to Adela Tindal was on the point of being announced at the time of his disappearance. His choice had come as a surprise to his friends; for though Miss Tindal took art and letters as seriously as himself, she was, as an authoress, not at all averse to publicity. She enjoyed being talked about, Molloy declared; and talked about she had certainly been—especially in connection with Lucius Kelly, the playwright. Their relationship had not been disguised; but a time came when Kelly's quarrelsome temper was no longer to be endured, and she refused to see any more of him.

All this was quite well known to Lord Southrop, for he and Kelly had been friends from boyhood; and the knowledge was a signal proof of the force of his infatuation. On all accounts, in Molloy's judgment, the match would have been a complete disaster; and Trent, as he thought the matter over in the coffee-room of the Crown, was disposed to agree with him.

Shortly before his arrival that day, a new fact for his first dispatch to the *Record* had turned up. A tweed cap had been found washed up by the waves on the beach between Brademouth and Merwin Cove; and the people at the Crown were sure that it was Lord Southrop's. He had worn a suit of unusually rough, very light-grey homespun tweed, the sort of tweed that, as the headwaiter at the Crown vividly put it, you could smell half a mile away; and his cap had been noted because it was made of the same stuff as the suit. After a day and a half in salt water, it had still an aroma of Highland sheep. Apart from this and its colour, or absence of colour, there was nothing by which it could be identified; not even a maker's name; but there was no reasonable doubt about its being Lord Southrop's, and it seemed to settle the question, if question there were, of what had happened to him. It was, Trent reflected, just like an eccentric intellectual—with money—to have his caps made for him, and from the same material as his clothes.

It was these garments, together with the very large horn-rimmed spectacles which Lord Southrop affected, which had made most impression on the headwaiter. Otherwise, he told Trent, there was nothing unusual about the poor gentleman, except that he seemed a bit absentminded-like. He had brought a letter to the table with him—the waiter supposed it would be the one that came to the hotel for him—and it had seemed to worry him. He had read and reread it all through his dinner, what there was of it; he didn't have only some soup and a bit of fish. Yes, sir; consommé and a nice fillet of sole, like there is this evening. There was roast fowl, but he wouldn't have that, nor nothing else. Would Trent be ordering his own dinner now?

"Yes, I want to—but the fish is just what I won't have," Trent decided, looking at the menu. "I will take the rest of the hotel dinner." An idea occurred to him. "Do you remember what Lord Southrop had to drink? I might profit by his example."

The waiter produced a fly-blown wine-list. "I can tell you that, sir. He had a bottle of this claret here, Chateau Margaux 1922."

"You're quite sure? And did he like it?"

"Well, he didn't leave much," the waiter answered. Possibly, Trent thought, he took a personal interest in unfinished wine. "Were you thinking of trying some of it yourself, sir? It's our best claret."

"I don't think I will have your best claret," Trent said, thoughtfully scanning the list. "There's a Beychevelle 1924 here, costing eighteenpence less, which is good enough for me. I'll have that." The waiter hurried away, leaving Trent to his reflections in the deserted coffee-room.

Trent had learned from the police that the numbers of the notes left in the charge of the hotel had been communicated by telephone to Lord Southrop's bank in Norwich, the reply being that these notes had been issued to him in person ten days before. Trent had also been allowed to inspect the objects, including the maps, found in the abandoned car. Lackington he found marked in pencil with a cross; and working backwards across the country he found similar crosses at the small towns of Hawbridge, Wringham, and Candley. The police, acting on these indications, had already established that "L. G. Coxe" had passed the Thursday, Wednesday and Tuesday nights respectively at inns in these places; and they had learned already of his having started from Hingham Blewitt on the Monday.

Trent, finding no more to be done at Lackington, decided to follow this designated trail in his own car. On the morning after his talk with the waiter at the Crown he set out for Hawbridge. The distances in Lord Southrop's progress, as marked, were not great by the most direct roads; but it could be guessed that he had been straying about to this and that point of interest—not, Trent imagined, to sketch, for there had been no sketches found among his belongings. Hawbridge was reached in time for lunch; and at the Three Bells Inn Trent again found matter for thought in a conversation—much like the chat which he had already enjoyed at the Crown Inn—with the headwaiter. So it was again at the Green Man in Wringham that evening. The next day, however, when Trent dined at the Running Stag in Candley, the remembered record of Lord Southrop's potations took a different turn. What Trent was told convinced him that he was on the right track.

The butler and housekeeper at Hingham Blewitt, when Trent spoke with them the following day, were dismally confident that Lord Southrop would never be seen again. The butler had already given to the police investigator from Devon what little information he could. He admitted that none of it lent the smallest support to the idea that Lord Southrop had been contemplating suicide; that he had, in fact, been unusually cheerful, if anything, on the day of his departure. But what, the butler asked, could a person think? Especially, the housekeeper observed, after the cap was found. Lord Southrop was, of course, eccentric in his views; and you never knew—here the housekeeper, with a despondent head-shake, paused, leaving unspoken the suggestion that a man who did not think or behave like other people might go mad at any moment.

Lord Southrop, they told Trent, never left any address when he went on one of these motoring tours. What he used to say was, he never knew where he was going till he got there. But this time he did have one object in mind, though what it was or where it was the butler did not know; and the police-officer, when he was informed, did not seem to make any more of it. What had happened was that, a few days before Lord Southrop started out, he had been rung up by some one on the phone in his study; and as the door of the room was open, the butler, in passing through the hall, had happened to catch a few words of what he said.

He had told this person he was going next Tuesday to visit the old moor; and that if the weather was right he was going to make a sketch. He had said, "You remember the church and chapel!"—the butler heard that distinctly; and he had said that it must be over twenty years. "What must be over twenty years?" Trent wanted to know. Impossible to tell: Lord Southrop had said just that.

The butler had heard nothing further. He thought the old moor might perhaps be Dartmoor or Exmoor, seeing where it was that Lord Southrop had disappeared. Trent thought otherwise, but he did not discuss the point. "There's one thing you can perhaps tell me," he said. "Lord Southrop was at Harrow and Cambridge, I believe. Do you know if he went to a preparatory school before Harrow?"

"I can tell you that, sir," the housekeeper said. "I have been with the family since I was a girl. It was Marsham House he went to, near Sharnsley in Derbyshire. The school was founded by his lordship's grandfather's tutor, and all the Coxe boys have gone there for two generations. It stands very high as a school, sir; the best families send their sons there."

"Yes, I've heard of it," Trent said. "Should you say, Mrs. Pillow, that Lord Southrop was happy as a schoolboy—popular, I mean, and fond of games, and so forth?"

Mrs. Pillow shook her head decisively. "He always hated school, sir; and as for games, he had to play them, of course, but he couldn't abide them. And he didn't get on with the other boys—he used to say he wouldn't be a sheep, just like all the other something sheep— he learned bad language at school, if he didn't learn anything else.

But at Cambridge—that was very different. He came alive there for the first time—so he used to say."

In Norwich, that same afternoon, Trent furnished himself with a one-inch Ordnance Survey map of a certain section of Derbyshire. He spent the evening at his hotel with this and a small-scale map of England, on which he marked the line of small towns which he had already visited; and he drew up, not for publication, a brief and clear report of his investigation so far.

The next morning's run was long. He had lunch at Sharnsley, where he made a last and very gratifying addition to his string of coffee-room interviews. Marsham House, he learnt, stood well outside Sharnsley on the verge of the Town Moor; which, as the map had already told him, stretched its many miles away to the south and west. He learnt, too, what and where were "the church and chapel," and was thankful that his inquiring mind had not taken those simple terms at their face value.

An hour later he halted his car at a spot on the deserted road that crossed the moor; a spot whence, looking up the purple slope, he could see its bareness broken by a huge rock, and another less huge, whose summits pierced the skyline. They looked, Trent told himself, not more unlike what they were called than rocks with names usually do. Away to the right of them was a small clump of trees, the only ones in sight, to which a rough cart-track led from the road; and from that point, he thought an artist might well consider that the church and chapel and their background made the best effect. He left his car and took the path through the heather.

Arrived at the clump, which stood well above the road, he looked over a desolate scene. If anyone had met Lord Southrop there, they would have had the world to themselves. Not a house or hut was in sight, and no live thing but the birds. He looked about for traces of any human visitor; and he had just decided that nothing of the sort could reasonably be expected, after the lapse of a week, when something white, lodged in the root of a fir tree, caught his eye.

It was a small piece of torn paper, penciled on one side with lines and shading the look of which he knew well. A rapid search discovered another piece near by among the heather. It was all that the wind had left undispersed of an artist's work; but for Trent, as he scanned the remnants closely, it was enough.

His eyes turned now over a wider range; for this, though to him it spelt certainty, was not what he had been looking for. Slowly following the track over the moor, he came at length to the reason for its existence—a small quarry, to all appearance long abandoned. A roughly circular pond of muddy water, some fifty yards across, filled the lower part of it; and about the margin was a confusion of stony fragments, broken and rusted implements, bits of rotting wood and smashed earthenware—a typical scene of industrial litter. With his arm bare to the shoulder Trent could feel no bottom to the pond. If it held any secret, that opaque yellow water kept it well.

There was no soil to take a footprint near the pond. For some time he raked among the débris in which the track ended, finding nothing. Then, as he turned over a broken fire-bucket, something flashed in the sunlight. It was a small, flat fragment of glass, about as large as a threepenny piece, with one smooth and two fractured edges. Trent examined it thoughtfully. It had no place in his theory; it might mean nothing. On the other hand . . . he stowed it carefully in his note-case along with the remnants of paper.

Two hours later, at the police headquarters in Derby, he was laying his report and maps, with the objects found on the moor, before Superintendent Allison, a sharp-faced, energetic officer, to whom Trent's name was well known.

It was well known also to Mr. Gurney Bradshaw, head of the firm of Bradshaw & Co., legal advisers to Lord Southrop and to his father before him. He had, at Trent's telephoned request, given him an appointment at three o'clock; and he appeared at that hour on the day after his researches in Derbyshire. Mr. Bradshaw, a courteous but authoritative old gentleman, wore a dubious expression as they shook hands.

"I cannot guess," he said, "what it is that you wish to put before me. It seems to me a case in which we should get the Court to presume death with the minimum of difficulty; and I wish I thought otherwise, for I had known Lord Southrop all his life, and I was much attached to him. Now I must tell you that I have asked a third party to join us here—Mr. Lambert Coxe, who perhaps you know is the heir to the title and to a very large estate. He wrote me yesterday that he had just returned from France, and wanted to know what the position was; and I thought he had better hear what you have to say, so I asked him for the same time as yourself."

"I know of him as a racing man," Trent said, "I had no idea he was what you say until I saw it in the papers."

The buzzer on the desk-telephone sounded, and Bradshaw put it to his ear. "Show him in," he said.

Lambert Coxe was a tall, spare, hard-looking man with a tanned, clean-shaven face, and a cordless monocle screwed into his left eye. As they were introduced he looked at the other with a keen and curious scrutiny.

"And now," Bradshaw said, "let us hear your statement, Mr. Trent."

Trent put his folded hands on the table. "I will began by making a suggestion which may strike you gentlemen as an absurd one. It's this. The man who drove that car to Lackington, and afterwards down to the seashore, was not Lord Southrop."

Both men stared at him blankly; then Bradshaw, composing his features, said impassively, "I shall be interested to hear your reasons for thinking so. You have not a name for making absurd suggestions, Mr. Trent, but I may call this an astonishing one."

"I should damned well think so," observed Coxe.

"I got the idea originally," Trent said, "from the wine which this man chose to drink with his dinner at the Crown Inn before the disappearance. Do you think that absurd?"

"There is nothing absurd about wine," Mr. Bradshaw replied with gravity. "I take it very seriously myself. Twice a day, as a rule," he added.

"Lord Southrop, I am told, also took it seriously. He had the reputation of a first-rate connoisseur. Now this man I'm speaking of had little appetite that evening, it seems. The dinner they offered him consisted mainly of soup, fillet of sole, and roast fowl."

"I am sure it did," Bradshaw said grimly. "It's what you get nine times out of ten in English hotels. Well?"

"This man took only the soup and the fish. And with it he had a bottle of claret."

The solicitor's composure deserted him abruptly.

"Claret!" he exclaimed.

"Yes, claret, and a curious claret too. You see, mine host of the Crown kept a perfectly good Beychevelle 1924—I had some myself. But he had also a Margaux 1922; and I suppose because it was an older wine he thought it ought to be dearer, so he marked it in his list eighteenpence more than the other. That was the wine which was chosen by our traveller that evening. What do you think of it? With a fish dinner he had claret, and he chose a wine of a bad year, when he could have had a wine of 1924 for less money."

While Coxe looked his bewilderment, Mr. Bradshaw got up and began to pace the room slowly. "I will admit so much," he said. "I cannot conceive of Lord Southrop doing such a thing if he was in his right mind."

"If you still think it was he, and that he was out of his senses," Trent rejoined, "there was a method in his madness. Because the night before, at Hawbridge, he chose one of those wines bearing the name of a chateau which doesn't exist, and is merely a label that sounds well; and the night before that, at Wringham, he had two whiskies and soda just before dinner, and another inferior claret at an excessive price on top of them. I have been to both the inns and got these facts. But when I worked back to Candley, the first place where Lord Southrop stayed after leaving home, it was another story. I found he had picked out about the best thing on the list, a Rhine wine, which hardly anybody ever asked for. The man who ordered that, I think, was really Lord Southrop."

Bradshaw pursed up his mouth. "You are suggesting that some-one in Lord Southrop's car was impersonating him at the other three places, and that, knowing his standing as a connoisseur, this man did his ignorant best to act up to it. Very well; but Lord South-rop signed the register in his usual way at those places. He received and read a letter addressed to him at Lackington. The motor tour as a whole was just such a haphazard tour as he had often made before. The description given of him at Lackington was exact—the clothes, the glasses, the abstracted manner. The cap that was washed up was certainly his. No, no, Mr. Trent. We are bound to assume that it was Lord Southrop; and the presumption is that he drove down to the sea and drowned himself. The alternative is that he was staging a sham suicide, so as to be able to disappear; and there is no sense in that."

"Just so," observed Lambert Coxe. "What you say about the wine may be all right as far as it goes, Mr. Trent, but I agree with Mr. Bradshaw. Southrop committed suicide; and if he was insane enough to do that, he was insane enough to go wrong about his drinks."

Trent shook his head. "There are other things to be accounted for. I'm coming to them. And the clothes and the cap and the rest are all part of my argument. This man was wearing Lord Southrop's tweed suit just because it was so easily identifiable. He knew all about Lord Southrop and his ways. He had letters from Lord Southrop in his possession, and had learnt to imitate his writing. It was he who wrote and posted that letter addressed to L. G. Coxe; and he made a pretence of being worried by it. He knew that Lord Southrop's notes could be traced; so he left them at the bureau to clinch the thing. And, of course, he did not drown himself. He only threw the cap into the sea. What he may have done is to change out of those conspicuous clothes, put them in a bag which he had in the car, and which contained another suit in which he proceeded to dress himself. He may then have walked, with his bag, the few miles into Brademouth, and travelled to London by the 12:15— quite a popular train, in which you can get a comfortable sleeping-berth."

"So he may," Bradshaw agreed with some acidity, while Lambert Coxe laughed shortly. "But what I am interested in is facts, Mr. Trent."

"Well, here are some. A few days before Lord Southrop set out from his place in Norfolk, someone rang him up in his library. The door was ajar, and the butler heard a little of what he said to the caller. He said he was going on the following Tuesday to visit a place he called the old moor, as if it was a place as well known to the other as to himself. He said, "You remember the church and the chapel," and that it must be over twenty years; and that he was going to make a sketch."

Coxe's face darkened. "If Southrop was alive," he sneered, "I am sure he would appreciate your attention to his private affairs. What are we supposed to gather from all this keyhole business?"

"I think we can gather," Trent said gently, "that some person, ringing Lord Southrop up about another matter, was told incidentally where Lord Southrop expected to be on that Tuesday—the day, you remember, when he suddenly developed a taste for bad wine in the evening. Possibly the information gave this person an idea, and he had a few days to think it over. Also we can gather that Lord Southrop was talking to someone who shared his recollection of a moor which they had known over twenty years ago—that's to say, when he was at the prep school age, as he was thirty-three this year. And then I found that he had been at a school called Marsham House, on the edge of Sharnsley Town Moor in Derbyshire. So I went off there to explore; and I discovered that the church and chapel were a couple of great rocks on the top of the moor, about two miles from the school. If you were there with your cousin, Mr. Coxe, you may remember them."

Coxe was drumming on the table with his fingers. "Of course I do," he said aggressively. "So do hundreds of others who were at Marsham House. What about it?"

Bradshaw, who was now fixing him with an attentive eye, held up a hand. "Come, come, Mr. Coxe," he said. "Don't let us lose our tempers. Mr. Trent is helping to clear up what begins to look like an even worse business than I thought. Let us hear him out peaceably, if you please."

"I am in the sketching business myself," Trent continued, "so I looked about for what might seem the best view-point for Lord Southrop's purpose. When I went to the spot, I found two pieces of torn-up paper, the remains of a pencil sketch; and that paper is of precisely the same quality as the paper of Lord Southrop's sketching-block, which I was able to examine at Lackington. The sketch was torn from the block and destroyed, I think, because it was evidence of his having been to Sharnsley. That part of the moor is a wild, desolate place. If someone went to meet Lord Southrop there, as I believe, he could hardly have had more favourable circumstances for what he meant to do. I think it was he who appeared in the car at Wringham that evening; and I think it was on Sharnsley Moor, not at Lackington, that Lord Southrop—disappeared."

Bradshaw half rose from his chair. "Are you not well, Mr. Coxe?" he asked.

"Perfectly well, thanks," Coxe answered. He drew a deep breath, then turned to Trent. "And so that's all you have to tell us. I can't say that—"

"Oh, no, not nearly all," Trent interrupted him. "But let me tell you now what I believe it was that really happened. If the man who left the moor in Lord Southrop's car was not Lord Southrop, I wanted an explanation of the masquerade that ended at Lackington. What would explain it was the idea that the man who drove the car down to Devonshire had murdered him, and then staged a sham suicide for him three hundred miles away. That would have been an ingenious plan. It would have depended on everyone making the natural assumption that the man in the car was Lord Southrop, and how was anyone to imagine that he wasn't?

"Lord Southrop was the very reverse of a public character. He lived quite out of the world; he had never been in the news; very few people knew what he looked like. He depended on all this for maintaining his privacy in the way he did when touring in his car—staying always at small places where there was no chance of his being recognized, and pretending not to be a peer. The murderer knew all about that, and it was the essence of his plan. The people at the inns would note what was conspicuous about the traveller; all that they could say about his face would be more vague, and would fit Lord Southrop well enough, so long as there was no striking difference in looks between the two men. Those big horn-rims are a disguise in themselves."

Bradshaw rubbed his hands slowly together. "I suppose it could happen so," he said. "What do you think, Mr. Coxe?"

"It's just a lot of ridiculous guesswork," Coxe said impatiently. "I've heard enough of it, for one." He rose from his chair.

"No, no, don't go, Mr. Coxe," Trent advised him. "I have some more of what you prefer—facts, you know. They are important, and you ought to hear them. Thinking as I did, I looked about for any places where a body could be concealed. In that bare and featureless expanse I could find only one: an old, abandoned quarry in the hillside, with a great pond of muddy water at the bottom of it. And by the edge of it I picked up a small piece of broken glass.

"Yesterday evening this piece of glass was shown by a police-officer and myself to an optician in Derby. He stated that it was a fragment of a monocle, what they call a spherical lens, so that he could tell us all about it from one small bit. Its formula was not a common one—minus 5; so that it had been worn by a man very short-sighted in one eye. The police think that as very few people wear monocles, and hardly any of them would wear one of that power, an official inquiry should establish the names of those who had been supplied with such a glass in recent years. You see," Trent went on, "this man had dropped and broken his glass on the stones while busy about something at the edge of the pond. Being a tidy man, he picked up all the pieces that he could see; but he missed this one."

Lambert Coxe put a hand to his throat. "It's infernally stuffy in here," he muttered. "I'll open a window, if you don't mind." Again he got to his feet; but the lawyer's movement was quicker. "I'll see to that," he said; and stayed by the window when he had opened it.

Trent drew a folded paper from his pocket. "This is a telegram I received just before lunch from Superintendent Allison, of the Derbyshire police. I have told him all I am telling you." He unfolded the paper with deliberation. "He says that the pond was dragged this morning, and they recovered the body of a man who had been shot in the head from behind. It was stripped to the underclothing and secured by a chain to a pedal bicycle.

"That, you see, clears up the question how the murderer got to the remote spot where Lord Southrop was. He couldn't go there in a car, because he would have had to leave it there. He used a cycle, because there was to be a very practical use for the machine afterwards. The police believe they can trace the seller of the cycle, because it is in perfectly new condition, and he may give them a line on the buyer."

Bradshaw, his hands thrust into his pockets, stared at Coxe's ghastly face as he inquired, "Has the body been identified?"

"The superintendent says the inquest will be the day after tomorrow. He knows whose body I believe it is, so he will already be sending down to Hingham Blewitt about evidence of identity. He says my own evidence will probably not be required until a later stage of the inquest, after a charge has been—"

A sobbing sound came from Lambert Coxe. He sprang to his feet, pressing his hands to his temples; then crashed unconscious to the floor.

While Trent loosened his collar, the lawyer splashed water from the bottle on his table upon the upturned face. The eyelids began to flicker. "He'll do," Bradshaw said coolly. "My congratulations, Mr. Trent. This man is not a client of mine, so I may say that I don't think he will enjoy the title for long—or the money, which was what really mattered, I have reason to believe. He's dropped his monocle again, you see. I happen to know, by the way, that he has been half-blind in that eye since it was injured by a cricket ball at Marsham."

The Greek Play

BY H. C. BAILEY

Mr. Fortune was concentrated on an investigation. In this state of mind, he is not aware of time or persons. He was in his garden. Some of the long experiments in producing his ideal sweet pea flowered about him in colours of the freshness of his own innocent complexion. He sniffed delicately, he sniffed profoundly. The sweet pea of his dreams was to give him the rich waved grace of the moderns with the deeper fragrance of the old. And his round face became wistful.

On this sorrow came the voice of a person of great personality. His black Persian, Darius, sat down on the lawn, gazed with large golden eyes, and announced that instant attention was required. Reggie awoke and came hastily. Darius lay on his back and stretched, exhibiting a stomach for homage. It was rubbed respectfully. Darius sang a small song, curled up on the hand and kissed it, rose, walked away with his tail in the air. "Darlin'," Reggie murmured to his swaggering hinder end.

"My dear child!" he was rebuked. Mrs. Fortune came towards him.

"Oh, Peter!" Reggie blinked at her. She was dressed not for gardening, but for a garden party, in something filmy that revealed her adorably and shimmered apple-green and gold. He looked down at his crumpled grey flannel, and again at her and with alarm.

"You are, you really are," he murmured.

"Why aren't you dressed?" said Mrs. Fortune severely.

"I am. For this world. I didn't know we were going to heaven."

"You're not. You're going to Logate. Run away and make yourself respectable."

Reggie groaned. "Black coat?"

"Yes, dear. Full fig. Run. You've only half an hour for lunch and all."

But under pressure he can be very quick and neat. He sat down in the clothes of ceremony before she had finished her fish. He gave his whole mind to that, salmon trout in mayonnaise. He stopped and turned to the parlourmaid. "Tell Elise that chives in a fish salad are an error." He tasted the wine. "And you've got the Carbonnieux too cold."

"Don't be peevish, child," Mrs. Fortune smiled.

"I'm not. Only alert. The faculties have been aroused. And earnest." He proceeded swiftly by way of lamb in aspic to a soufflé. "Ah! Tell Elise that all is forgiven. And a few strawberries, please." He dealt with them; he was drinking his coffee while the soufflé still occupied Mrs. Fortune. "Why are we going to Logate, Joan?" he murmured.

"To see a Greek play, dear."

"My only aunt!" Reggie gazed at her. "What is Logate, Joan?"

"My dear child! Logate School. The girls' school. You know all about it."

"Do I?" Reggie said plaintively. "Fancy knowin' all about a girls' school! Well, well. Why did you marry that kind of man?"

Mrs. Fortune stood up. "You're not amusing." She looked down at him. "This is merely futile. It's no use being innocent to me, my child. You won't be let off. I told you ages ago we were going to the play at Logate."

"P'r'aps I wasn't listening, dear," Reggie sighed.

"Probably not. But you always hear," said she. "Come along, Reginald."

And he went. He did in fact know something about Logate. Everybody does. It is one of the more magnificent of those schools which were founded last century when the wild hope that girls might be educated first dazzled England. From the private adventure of a determined woman it grew into an established institution, with governors and endowments, and drew to its walls the daughters of people of importance. He knew also that his wife had acquaintance among those fortunate maidens, and he remembered with painful clearness that she had talked of an invitation to some festivity there. Her desire to take him into social crowds is the only tragic element in their married life.

He lay back in the car and contemplated her; an occupation always comforting. "Well, well," he murmured. "What is this play, Joan?"

"The Antigone."

"Oh, ah! When I was at Oxford a dear old don told me that nobody was educated who hadn't read the Antigone. So I did. In translation. And these young things are doing it in Greek! Well, well. The advance of women."

"They haven't done one in Greek before. That's the new classical mistress. Nan says she's a tiger."

Reggie's eyelids drooped. "Is that so?" he murmured. "Nan. Who is Nan?"

"You know. My young godchild, Nan Bundy. We're really going to see her."

"And very nice too," Reggie murmured. "Nice legs. Is she Antigone?"

Mrs. Fortune laughed. "Heavens, no! How could she?"

"Nohow. Contrariwise. Would that matter?"

"It is a glorious part," Mrs. Fortune sighed. She was herself the Rosalind of men's dreams before she decided to be a wife.

"Yes. Yes. Resolute young woman. And we're going to see a schoolgirl play it."

"Nan says she's wonderfully good," said Mrs. Fortune. "It's a girl called Nora Brown." Reggie's eyes were nearly closed, but he continued to look at her. "Of course, she's not likely to get near it. But still Antigone ought to be a girl—it's like Juliet; you want a girl and a great actress too—and nobody is both at once. But sometimes a girl is wonderful." She began to talk about acting. This is most unusual. And Reggie ceased to look at her. His mind played with a doubt whether it was the Greek play that he was being taken to see. But he did not say so. He has been married some time.

Logate School is established in a vast house in a park. Both were originally constructed for an eighteenth-century profiteer. The park keeps unspoilt its artificial lake, its delusive vistas, its sham ruins, its copied statues and temples.

The house has a huge portico to disguise the obvious fact that its front door is at the back. They went into what had been a good hall before its proportions were destroyed. Logate is much organized. The guests who enter there abandon freedom and walk in a straight and narrow path under continual orders from the staff.

"Oh, my hat!" Reggie muttered. "Joan! I want to go home." And they were passed into the presence of the head mistress and it was announced that they were Mr. and Mrs. Fortune.

He raised frightened eyes and saw a small, intense woman. Her set smile of welcome flickered. "Mr. Fortune?" she repeated. "How do you do?" It seemed that he caused her some surprise, some curiosity, if such a woman could be curious about a man.

"Do you know our chairman?" She passed him on to the Bishop of Lanchester. That plump and crimson prelate gurgled slightly and took pains to be affable. He made a mild joke about Mrs. Fortune being too young, oh, far too young, to have a daughter at Logate. He obviously desired to know who had sent Reggie an invitation. "Not a daughter, but a goddaughter," said Mrs. Fortune. "So we feel quite parental about Logate." The Bishop said it was very natural, the Bishop said he was delighted, and they were taken with ceremony to the terraced lawns which made a theatre for the play, they were set in the seats of the mighty. Reggie looked sideways at his wife. "Why do they love us so?" he murmured. "This is very alarmin', Joan."

"The penalty of fame, dear. Be a brave little man." She began to talk to the mistress presiding over that block of seats.

Reggie gazed about him. The lawns were cut like broad steps out of the slope on the top of which behind them the great house stood. Each lawn had its rows of chairs. At the foot of the slope on an open space between banks of rhododendrons a stage was built, with the front of a Greek palace for scenery. On either side and beyond the park displayed its green vistas set with sham antiquities—here a ruined Gothic tower, there a classic temple.

Mrs. Fortune compelled him into her conversation with the mistress, who was delivering a lecture on the play: "Terribly sad, you see. Quite dreadful. Of course, it's very grand. Some people feel it's not nice for girls. The theme, you see—a girl defying the law and killing herself. You're meant to think she's a martyr to her own sense of right. An immortal protest, of course. But perhaps it is unsettling for girls."

"You think so?" Reggie murmured.

Mrs. Fortune was indignant. "It's a noble play! I can't imagine it could do anybody harm."

"Especially in Greek," Reggie murmured. "Do girls get Greek plays on their nerves? I was only a boy."

"Girls are so serious," said the mistress. "So earnest. One has to be very careful." She gave them copies of the play and fussed on to somebody else.

"Curious symptoms," Reggie mumbled.

"Why?" Mrs. Fortune turned to him. "What are you thinking of?"

"Vague suggestions of collective hysteria; or getting the general wind up. As you say—why?"

"I suppose it's first-night nervousness."

"Yes. I wonder. Yes. Well, well, what exactly did Antigone do?" He opened the book of the words. "Oh, ah! She was told not to bury her brother because he died fighting against her city, and she went and did it. So the king shut her up in a tomb and she said it

was hard she couldn't have the life of other girls, but she'd done her
duty and she hanged herself."

"Don't, Reggie. It's grand."

"I know. I'm not feelin' facetious, Joan." He looked about him
and his round face was grave and plaintive, like an earnest child's.
Important parents and the governing body filled the seats about
them. The head mistress and the Bishop, side by side, glanced at
them and leaned over to say amiable nothings. And the play began.

Antigone was on the stage, a girl not more than common tall,
slim as a boy in her Greek dress, not pretty beside the buxom fair-
ness of her sister, Ismene. But she held the eye, she had dignity, she
was desperately earnest, and the other only a girl in fancy dress. Her
dark face was individual, a face to remember, proud, wistful, with
a brow and a chin.

It is a quiet scene, to show Antigone as a girl who believes that she
has a duty—to break the law. This Antigone was very quiet. But
when she had gone, when the chorus were doing physical exercises
in front of the stage and chanting a hymn to dawn, Reggie murmured: "Yes, she looks like somebody."

Mrs. Fortune was gravely interested. "She's feeling it, poor child.
Did you notice the sister? Little pig!"

"Yes, missing a bit, wasn't she?"

"Missing! She was deliberately spoiling it. Playing as jealous as
could be."

The bullying King Creon, a robust damsel who wore her beard
with a swagger and spoke in a shout, came on to hear that Antigone
had buried her dead and defied him, and she was brought prisoner
before him to declare she obeyed "unwritten laws, eternal in the
heavens." Her voice rang clear, she had a good gesture.

"She is rather out of the way, what?" Reggie murmured. "Know
her again, wouldn't you?"

"Very sincere and natural," Mrs. Fortune frowned a little.
"Passionate, yes." Ismene returned to be companion of her sister's
fate. She was very nice and pretty about it. She made a mess of
Antigone's lovely dignity.

The chorus chanted the great ode to love as if it were a cheery hymn, and Antigone came to say her farewell to light and life. She looked desperate enough. Her voice throbbed. She was feeling the agony. "Unwept and unfriended"—she stopped, she held out her arms and let them fall, she looked up to the sky. And the raucous voice of the prompter rattled out the next line.

"Ah!" Mrs. Fortune flushed. "How ghastly!" But the prompter gave the words and the chorus giggled. Antigone was shattered. She went on with her speech in a hurry. She had no more reality. She was a girl saying a lesson and caring for nothing but to get to the end. "Behold me, what things at the hands of what men I suffer." She was gone.

"Oh, that was a shame," Mrs. Fortune whispered, her hand on Reggie's. "She was being rather fine."

"Yes. Yes. As you say." Reggie looked at her with closing eyes.

The chorus, very brisk and lively, chanted that she came of a noble family, but Fate's everlasting hands availed to reach her, and a messenger came and described how in her tomb prison he "saw the maiden hanged, about her neck some shred of linen served her for a noose," and the chorus remarked that to be happy one must be wise, and marched off.

The audience began to chatter and move. Reggie was in no hurry. The head mistress and the Bishop stopped in passing. "A great play," said the Bishop.

"Oh, yes. Yes. And a very interestin' performance," Reggie murmured.

"I thought Antigone did wonderfully," said Mrs. Fortune.

"I am afraid she found it rather difficult." The head mistress lingered. "But she has ability."

"Yes. Strikin' child. Yes," Reggie murmured.

"Very hard for her." The head mistress looked at him keenly. "Do you know Miss Hopkins perhaps?"

"Is that the prompter?" said Mrs. Fortune with some ferocity.

"Oh, dear, no." The head mistress frowned. "That was Miss Evans, who has always produced our plays. Miss Hopkins has just taken charge of the classical side. She persuaded us to attempt a

Greek tragedy. She has worked night and day for this performance."

"She found an Antigone," said Mrs. Fortune.

The head mistress slowly followed her bishop. But Reggie sat
still, watching with dreamy eyes the rest of the governing body
depart. "Well, well," he sighed, and turned to his wife with a smile.
"And now, Joan—what was I brought here for?"

Her eyes met his large and solemn. "Nan Bundy asked us."

"Yes. You told me so. I also believe it. What exactly did she say?"

"Do you think there's something wrong here?"

"My dear girl! Oh, my dear girl. I've been thinkin' somebody
thought so ever since we left home."

"And now?" she said eagerly.

"And now I think hysteria's catchin'. Don't you catch it, Joan.
What did the sinful child say?"

"She said, 'Do bring the Cherub.' "

"Nobody respects me," Reggie sighed. "Is that all?"

"No. She said it again in a postscript, 'Do bring the Cherub.
Things are being perfectly foul and I want to tell him.' "

"Oh, my aunt!" Reggie moaned. "More nerves."

"The letter did sound like nerves. But that isn't like Nan."

"No. No. She's more like an ice. Say strawberry Melba. Well,
well, let's find the minx."

"She was in the chorus," said Mrs. Fortune.

They went down to the level turf about the stage where proud
parents were waiting for their daughters to emerge from the dress-
ing tent behind the rhododendrons. The pretty Ismene came out
of it with a large woman who had been handsome in a florid way.
The woman was in a hurry, but Ismene chattered past. "Oh, Miss
Evans, isn't she impossible? ... But, Miss Evans..."

"Well, well. So that's the assertive prompter." Reggie watched
her with dreamy curiosity.

"I should like to box her ears," said Mrs. Fortune.

Miss Evans had to be introduced to Ismene's mamma. She spared
time to be gushing. Then she hurried away towards the house.
Reggie continued to watch her. She passed into the crowd on the

terrace. She was talking to some of the governors. She vanished. "Oh, you lambs!" A buxom young person of vivid colour rushed upon them. "Bless you! Wasn't it the putrid limit? Poor old Nobs."

"Referrin' to Antigone, Miss Bundy?" Reggie inquired.

"Yes, Mr. Fortune," she said demurely. "Oh, Cherub, you are a darling to come. Angel face!"

"Thankin' you for these kind words—why am I brought to your maiden revels?"

"Well, I ask you! Wasn't it absolutely foul? Half of them rotting her and the Evanly one braying at her. Hoppy's furious. Poor old Nobs, she's wishing she was dead."

"Poor girl," Mrs. Fortune sighed. "I think she did wonderfully, Nan. Could I speak to her? I'd like to tell her so."

"You're a dear; she doesn't want to speak to anybody just now. She's in the tent still. Wants to get alone. She's like that when she's down."

"Yes. Yes. This show bein' a kind of climax. Now we'll begin at the beginning, Nan. Who is Antigone that Miss Evans and friends crab her?"

Nan stared at him. "Golly!" she said. "You're awfully clever. Yes, that is the beginning. I say, let's come out of the mob." She took them away to a stone seat in a hollow of the green slope, remote, and commanding wide spaces of loveliness from the lake to the temple above. "Shan't have anybody sneaking here."

"Oh! That's the state of society," Reggie murmured.

"We're a happy family, I don't think," said Miss Bundy. "Look here, you know the sort of shop this is. Absolutely it. Nobody wanted unless Father's somebody. That went all right. Things were very jolly when I came five years ago. Nothing mattered but the games, and they were top-hole. Then the old head went and we got this woman. She's a highbrow. Her strong suit is ideals. She's always blethering about the old noble purpose of Logate's to raise the standard of woman's capacity. Well, of course that sort of thing got people's backs up frightfully."

"Miss Bundy has no use for an intellectual head?"

"I don't mind, bless you. The woman's not bad, if she wouldn't preach. We wanted a change. The place was jolly slack. But naturally people hated it. Talked all sorts of rot. There was a yarn the mistresses were frightfully sick she got the job—thought one of themselves ought to have had it—the Evanly one was favourite. Somebody put it about the governors wouldn't back her up. But she carried on and went on stiffening things. And then she brought in scholarship girls. You know—entrance scholarships open to anybody. We'd never had that before. Six a year. She caught some rum fish. Clever kids from nowhere, looking like nothing on earth, didn't want to do anything but sap. That didn't make a happy home. Of course, they got treated like absolute outsiders, and some of the mistresses backed 'em and some gave 'em jip, specially the Evanly one. Then the Head brought in a new mistress or two of her own sort and Hoppy. Hoppy's a tiger. She's classics. That put the Evanly one's nose right out of joint. The Evanly one had always run the idea that a little classics was classy, being her subject, so she got the smart set."

"Miss Evans likes the aristocracy?" Reggie murmured.

"She's a priceless snob," said Miss Bundy. "If a girl has a title somewhere or there's money about, the Evanly one's all over her. Well, in comes Hoppy and takes the top classics away from her. More trouble. The slackers have a rotten time and so there's the smart set against Hoppy and fawning round good Evans. Like that fatty Edith—you saw her—Ismene."

"Yes. Yes. Flaccid type," Reggie yawned. "Thyroid trouble perhaps. When were you coming to Antigone?"

"Poor old Nobs! She's a scholarship girl. Wouldn't think it, would you? I'm sorry—I'm a snob myself. But I mean she don't look the usual book grub."

"No. No. Not a grub. She might have a brain."

"She looks someone quite unusual," said Mrs. Fortune. "It's a fine face, Nan."

"Not one of the undistinguished proletariat. No," Reggie murmured. "By the way—to reach at last the beginning—who is she? What's her name, for instance?"

Nan said "Hush!" And her eyes directed his to Antigone. The

girl had changed out of her Greek dress to the school uniform—
grey serge tunic, white blouse and tie in the Logate white and grey
colours—an austere garb which on the day of festival nobody else
was wearing. Nan called out, "I say, Nobs, old thing!" The girl
looked, frowned, and hurried on into the loneliness of the park.
"Sorry," said Nan. "She's like that when she's upset. Can't bear
anybody. And I'm by way of being a pal."

Reggie watched her. She seemed to have a determined purpose.
"Often upset, is she?"

"She's had a rotten time. She's poor."

"Oh, yes. Hence the uniform—when the rest of you are in purple
and fine linen."

"Of course, she's got other clothes—but nothing nice—just like
her to wear the school rags on a show day. Sort of defiance. She's
like that. You see, the other scholarship girls—well, they've got
people of sorts, but Nobs came from a village school."

"Is that so?" Reggie murmured: he was still watching the determined march of Antigone. "From the village school straight to
the exclusive and expensive Logate. Well, well!"

"Oh, she did. She's a wonder. There was a mistress who got keen
on her and coached her and she took the first school. She's not a bit
like what you'd think either. She's jolly good at games, and awfully
decent. But she's had a beastly time. Just because she's specially
poor and nobody. We are a lot of snobs. The Evanly one's had a
particular down on her lately. Only Hoppy's kind of taken her up.
Hoppy don't make favourites, but if you can do anything she shoves
you along. Well, you saw what happened to-day—that was pretty
ghastly, wasn't it? That's the way things are. Now you know why
I wanted you to come, Cherub." She took Reggie's hand for a swift
moment.

Antigone had vanished in the hollows of the park where the
portico of the temple shimmered grey. Reggie turned and gazed at
Miss Bundy. "My dear girl! Oh, my dear girl!" he sighed.

"I wrote about it to Father and he said it was like a school story—"

"Yes. Yes. So it is, you know. The persecuted heroine has only
got to save somebody's life and you'll all live happily ever after."

"You don't believe that," said Nan; and her frank eyes challenged him.

"You think not? Why wouldn't I?"

"You can see there's something wrong with the jolly old place."

"Oh, yes. Yes. That is indicated."

"Well, you can make people take notice. You can do things."

"My dear girl! Oh, my dear girl!" Reggie moaned again. "Not me, no. They never let me do anything till everything's happened. By the way—reachin' finally the beginning—what is her name?"

"Nora—Nora Brown. She hasn't got any people. An aunt or something brought her up. In a cottage."

A short sturdy young woman came out of the tent in the rhododendrons and stood looking all ways.

"That's Hoppy," said Nan. "Like to speak to her?"

Reggie said "Help!" Behind her horn spectacles Miss Hopkins looked very brisk and strenuous.

She saw Nan and made for her and called her sharply, asking if Nora had been seen.

"She came out some time ago. I say, Miss Hopkins—I want to introduce you. This is Mr. Fortune—and Mrs. Fortune. My godmother, you know. They were awfully interested in the play."

"How do you do? I'm sorry it wasn't more successful," said Miss Hopkins. "Where did Nora go, Nan?"

"I think I can show you," said Reggie. "Allow me. This way." He walked on, and Miss Hopkins, having no choice, went with him. He stepped out.

Nan made a comical face at Mrs. Fortune. "Snubs to us." They followed some way behind.

Miss Hopkins was saying, "I've no doubt I can find her."

"I hope so," Reggie murmured, and went on with her.

Miss Hopkins looked at him keenly. "Are you *the* Mr. Fortune?"

"Yes. The one you mean. Yes. Any objection?"

"Not the least. Were you asked to come here?"

"By Nan Bundy. Not professionally. Any reason why I should be?"

"I don't know," said Miss Hopkins. "You seem rather interested in finding Nora Brown."

"And you," Reggie murmured.

"If you saw the play you can guess why. She was upset. I don't like her going off alone."

"No. No. That was my view. What do you know about her?"

"If you've been talking to Nan you know all that I know."

"But you thought I might have been called in professionally. What for?"

"I don't understand detective work, Mr. Fortune."

"Nobody does," Reggie murmured. "Nobody can. You never know what you're looking for, so you have to look for everything." He stopped. He looked about him. "I lost her somewhere here. Takin' one thing with another, I should say she went into that place." He pointed to the temple. "Let's see."

It was a small bad copy of a Doric temple in wood painted to look like stone. They stood under the portico. Lacking windows, the interior was dark. "Oh, Heaven!" Miss Hopkins gasped. Reggie ran in.

Nora's body hung swaying from a beam. Her school tie was knotted about her neck, knotted again to one of the hooks in the beam from which lamps had hung. Under her feet a bench was overturned.

He set that up again, he held her body in one arm and cut the tie and laid her on the ground. . . .

"Is she dead?" Miss Hopkins whispered.

"Not yet. Not quite." He took off his coat, he began to work at the processes of artificial respiration. "There's a bad chance. Have you got a school hospital or anything? With doctor complete? Good. Run away and find her. Say Mr. Fortune's lookin' after a girl who's had an accident and wants her here quick. Don't tell anyone else. Then warn the hospital to have hot-water bottles and a mustard plaster ready. Hurry!" He laboured on with rhythmic movements and called, "Joan!"

She was already watching him, she and Nan.

"Go and bring the car."

"Oh, let me—I'll run," Nan cried.

"You stay here," said Reggie.

"Can't I do something? Can't I do anything? It's so dreadful."

"You can rub her legs," Reggie grunted, and worked on. . . .

Miss Hopkins came back panting. "Dr. Headley, Mr. Fortune."
Reggie turned his sweating face and saw a gaunt businesslike
woman. "Heard all about it?"

"Miss Hopkins told me how you found her." Dr. Headley knelt
beside the girl. "She's far gone."

"Yes. Yes. I came late. My error. I didn't think of this."

Dr. Headley stared at him. "How could you? You didn't know
her, did you?"

"Know nothing about her," Reggie grunted.

"She's a very clever girl. Very highly strung. I'm afraid she's not
been happy here."

"You're not surprised, what?" Reggie glanced at her.

"Poor child," said Dr. Headley.

"Yes. Yes. That's better," Reggie murmured. "You carry on
now." He wiped his face and watched. . . . "Steady." He bent again
over the girl. . . . "Yes. Keep going. I think so. Yes. I think so. She's
coming." . . .

"Oh, Cherub!" Nan gasped. "Is it really—will she be all right?"

"It'll be a fight for her," Reggie said gently. "I'll fight, Nan."

Mrs. Fortune laid her hand on his shoulder. They looked at each
other. "You—" she said with a sigh of content.

Reggie touched the hand. "Well, Doctor—my car's here. We'll
get her to hospital. I think I'd better do a venesection." They
wrapped the girl in a rug and laid her in the big car. "Oh, Miss
Hopkins—you'll have to tell your head mistress—say Mr. Fortune
has taken charge and considers it a grave case. Nan! Hop up by
Joan and show her the best way to your hospital. Just a moment."
He went again into the temple, looked round it with searching eyes,
stood on the bench and cut down the remains of the tie. "All right."
The car glided away with him. . . .

Some time afterwards he came out of the hospital and Miss Hopkins and Nan met him eagerly. "She's doing as well as she could," he said.

Mrs. Fortune came and put her arm round Nan. "You'll see the head mistress, Mr. Fortune?" Miss Hopkins asked.

"Oh, yes. Yes. I'm going to. You might tell her, would you?" He turned away, he contemplated with dreamy eyes the expanse of the park, and Miss Hopkins stared at him and departed. "I say, Nan," he murmured. "Take Joan and give her some tea." He wandered away, but not to the house. He had the air of a man strolling aimlessly; in time he reached the temple, and then, drifting still more casually, he went over the turf about it, in and out among trees and shrubs and so towards the house by a corkscrew route, and once he stopped for some time and was much interested in a clump of hawthorns.

The last of the visitors were departing. From their talk he learnt that they had been told Antigone had met with an accident. He went into the hall. A few of the staff were there, getting rid of the lingerers. Miss Hopkins met him. "Come to the head mistress's room, please."

"Oh, my hat!" Reggie smiled. "Sounds as if I were going to be swished."

Miss Hopkins did not approve of this frivolity. She marched ahead of him. The ample form of Miss Evans swept upon them. "Is that Mr. Fortune? Pray forgive me, how is poor Nora?"

Reggie spread out his hands. "Not a nice case," he murmured.

"Such a dreadful thing," said Miss Evans.

The head mistress had the Bishop in her room, and other pompous men. "Oh. Oh, I should like to speak to you alone," Reggie said plaintively.

"These gentlemen are members of the governing body," the head mistress explained.

"Well, well!" Reggie murmured, and contemplated them with benign curiosity.

The Bishop cleared his throat. "I am sure Mr. Fortune will understand that we are gravely concerned as a body—a terrible affair for the school."

"Yes. And for the girl," Reggie murmured.

"Quite. Quite. I feel that most deeply. We all feel it." He proceeded to introduce them—General Cutts, Lord Stourmouth, Sir
Ingram Stow.

The head mistress interrupted. "How is Nora, Mr. Fortune?"

"I can promise you nothing," Reggie said slowly.

The head mistress put her hand to her brow and sighed. "Poor
child, poor child."

"Dear me," said the Bishop. "Her condition is serious?"

"Oh, yes. Yes. Quite serious."

Sir Ingram Stow leaned forward. "You understand, Mr. Fortune, we're asking you for your opinion, an expert medical opinion:
is the child likely to recover?"

Reggie looked at him with closing eyes. "I've given you my
opinion. It's not a case in which I can promise anything."

"You're not very definite, sir," said the General.

"No. I'm not feeling definite," Reggie murmured.

"I suppose you can tell us if the girl will return to consciousness."
The General glared.

"Oh, she has. And gone to sleep. Why did you want to know?"

"Naturally, we want to know," the General cried. "Are you
being frank with us, sir? We want to know if the girl has given any
reason for her attempt to commit suicide. We have a right to know."

"She hasn't. I didn't ask her. You won't be able to ask her. What
happened and why it happened will be a matter for the police. Is that
quite frank?"

"What, sir? You propose to inform the police? Then let me tell
you, sir, I protest—in the strongest way I protest. It would be a
most irresponsible and reckless abuse of your professional position.
A scandalous interference which I should resent by every means in
my power. We should all resent it."

"Would you really?" Reggie murmured. He surveyed them with
curiosity. "You'd better not."

Lord Stourmouth, a little dry man, opened his mouth for the first
time, and he said, "You're talking nonsense, Cutts."

The Bishop cleared his throat. "I am bound to say, I feel you are
wrong, General."

"Pray allow me," Sir Ingram Stow stood up, a tall and handsome person making the most of himself. "Our first thought must be for the interests of the school. That is what influences the General."

"It's our duty, sir, our duty," the General gobbled.

"I feel that deeply. Now we must all see that to call in the police would be disastrous to the school. The publicity would be hideous. The school could never recover from such a scandal. We are also bound to consider the interests of this unhappy girl. Nothing could be more cruel than to make her or her memory the subject of a police investigation. I'm afraid, Stourmouth, you don't realize the suggestions, the insinuations about her which would be inevitable. It would be a cruel wrong to inflict—and without any reason. What happened is not in doubt. She was found by her own mistress hanging there in the temple."

"Did you really think you could hush it up?" Reggie murmured.

"I have made no such suggestion, Mr. Fortune. It is obvious that an inquest must follow her death. That cannot be avoided and none of us would wish to avoid it. There is nothing to conceal. But I protest in the strongest manner against calling in the police to turn it into a sensational case."

"So do I, begad! Making a scandal of it," the General cried. "Make the place a byword. Getting the school in all the papers. That's what comes of taking these scholarship girls. But I won't have it, sir. I'll see the Chief Constable myself."

"Don't worry. He knows all about it," said Reggie. "I telephoned from the hospital. Also to Scotland Yard."

The General glared at him. "Confounded impertinence!"

"You think so?" Reggie murmured. "Well, well." He turned to the head mistress. "I'll see Nora before I go," he said gently. "And Dr. Headley has my telephone number." He held out his hand. "I'm seeing this through."

"Thank you very much." Her eyes met his.

"Good-night, gentlemen." He looked them over. "Nora is not to be seen. There'll be a policeman at the hospital." He went out.

Stourmouth followed him. "Just a word, Mr. Fortune." He took

Reggie into a little lobby where the hats of the governors hung. "You know you're right, of course. So do I. Cutts is an ass and Stow is a snob."

"Yes. Not quite a home of peace, Logate," Reggie murmured. He contemplated the hats with grave interest. And Stow and Cutts came in a hurry to seize theirs. Reggie stood aside and watched them depart. He gazed dreamily at Stourmouth. "Yes. That's one of the factors. Good-night." . . .

When he came out of the hospital Nan was waiting with Mrs. Fortune in the car. She jumped down to meet him. "What, Nan?" he smiled. "You don't have to worry any more."

"Oh, Cherub—"

"Yes. My show now. You've done rather well. But you've done your bit. Go and sleep. You can."

The car carried him away. He lit a cigar and slid low in his corner. "Reggie, was that true?" said Mrs. Fortune.

"Oh, yes. Yes. The girl's comin' through. But I don't want it advertised just yet. She didn't hang herself."

"Ah, thank God!"

"Cause for satisfaction. Yes. They might have maddened her into suicide. Possibly that was in somebody's nice mind. Then it would have been a very difficult case."

Mrs. Fortune shuddered. "But what a devilish thing! Has she told you who did it?"

"She doesn't know. I don't know. That's one of the problems."

"One!" Mrs. Fortune cried.

Reggie looked at her with the large bewildered eyes of a child. "Only one, yes," he said plaintively. "By the way—two men comin' to dinner—the Chief Constable and Bell—I rang up Elise."

Mrs. Fortune laughed. "Martha!" she said and made a face at him. It is a term of abuse employed for his careful interest in domestic affairs. "Do I dine with you?"

"My only aunt! Please. I don't want to talk shop. I want my nice dinner. You're a necessary element, Joan."

"Pig," said she. "Essentially pig."

To the surprise of the Chief Constable of the county, an earnest, zealous official, they talked at dinner of roses and wine, of shoes and ships and sealing wax, of cabbages and kings. When Mrs. Fortune was gone and the cigars were lit, Reggie turned to the bewildered man. "Very nice of you to come over. Rather a complex case. Going to work out nasty. I thought you'd like to have it all before you at the start. This is what we've got." And he gave a sketch of his adventures at Logate.

The Chief Constable shook a sage head. "Shocking affair, however you take it. Quite right, Mr. Fortune, we can't overlook it. But you know in my experience adolescent girls do very queer things. And these clever ones are the most uncertain. I should have said myself it looked like a plain case of attempted suicide. She thought everybody was persecuting her and the play put it into her head to hang herself. Just the way these tragedies do happen with young women."

"Yes. That's what you're meant to think. I daresay that's the way it was meant to happen. Quite an ingenious mind workin' at Logate."

"Looks a bit too natural to me," said Bell. "They put on a play in which a girl hangs herself, and the girl who takes the part goes and does it quick. I'd work the case over before I passed it for suicide."

"Certainly we shall have to investigate," said the Chief Constable. "But I've no doubt myself any jury would say it was attempted suicide."

"Oh, no. No. If it gets to a jury, I shall be givin' evidence. And I shall say it was attempted murder. The girl has two bruises on her head, one at the back, that's the larger—one on her brow. She couldn't have made them hanging herself. The inference is she was struck from behind and she fell. When she came to herself in hospital, the only sensible thing she said was, 'Who hit me?' That is one of the problems."

"Murder? At Logate? It's one of the best girls' schools in the country." The Chief Constable was horrified. "You might say it's a girls' Eton."

"Yes. You might. That's an interesting factor. These things do happen in the best society. But not often."

"You say who did it is one of the problems, Mr. Fortune," Bell grinned. "It's the whole problem, isn't it?"

"For police purposes, yes. For the girl, no. And speakin' scientifically, it's a minor matter. The main problem bein'—why was it done?"

"Motive, eh?" said the Chief Constable. "Take it as suicide, you've got that plain enough. But taking it as murder, the motive's a puzzle. You make out there's been a lot of feeling at Logate against the scholarship girls concentrated on this one. Do you mean to say some of the other girls tried to murder her?"

"Oh, no. No. But thus two further problems are suggested. Who did start the trouble at Logate? And who is Nora Brown? Providin' us with lines of inquiry."

"About the school—" said the Chief Constable anxiously. "It isn't quite fair to talk about starting the trouble. There has been friction at Logate and it dates from the coming of this head mistress. Not her fault, I daresay. You know what big schools are. A new head comes. There are people who think somebody else ought to have had the job. The new head makes changes. More people get discontented and annoyed. And so on. It's very common."

Reggie blew smoke rings. "Yes. Quite. Yes. So some people wanted another woman head mistress. Who would they be?"

"Well, you know there was a strong feeling that one of the mistresses who'd been at Logate some time ought to have had the appointment."

"I see. Yes. Which one?"

"I couldn't give you a name." The Chief Constable was embarrassed. "You're not suggesting one of the mistresses would murder the girl? If you'll excuse my saying so, Mr. Fortune, I don't think you ought to have that kind of idea about Logate. All the mistresses are ladies."

Bell grunted. "Have you found that makes much difference, sir? I haven't."

The Chief Constable was shocked. "Well, I don't agree. But leaving out that—why on earth should one of the mistresses want to murder one of the girls? It's a mad idea."

"I daresay a mistress often wants to," Reggie smiled. "But it is unusual for her to try. Motive inadequate, as you say."

"I don't see anything like a motive myself," said Bell. "You can't always get to a reasonable motive. This is the kind of case I wouldn't expect one. The evidence is, there's a lot of bad blood in this girls' school—grievances and quarrelling and persecution. Given all that, you'll often find a woman run mad."

"Kind of hysteria, you mean?" the Chief Constable said. "Well, I suppose that's possible. You'll pardon me, Mr. Fortune, I can't help thinking it's not so certain we need look beyond the poor girl herself. An hysterical young woman meaning suicide often tries to make it look like murder."

"Sometimes. Yes. Ever tried to hit yourself hard behind the ear? Not easy, even in hysterics. I'm afraid you can't turn it into suicide. Do you know anyone on the governing body?"

The Chief Constable stared. "I know General Cutts."

"Yes. So he indicated. And Sir Ingram Stow?"

"I've met Stow. Why?"

"Well, they want to hush it up, you know."

"Mr. Fortune, you don't suggest that I—"

"Oh, no. No. You couldn't, anyway. But it wouldn't look well to play into their hands. What do you know about 'em?"

"General Cutts was my commanding officer, sir."

"You have my sympathy. And Stow?"

"I've merely met him. He's of a good old family, a rich man, a very pleasant fellow. Why do you ask all this?"

"Well, you know, it seemed to me that Cutts and Stow don't love the other governors. I suppose they were against this new head mistress, they were against the respectable and exclusive Logate takin' scholarship girls, and specially they're against this girl Nora Brown. That is, they've been backin' the trouble in the school."

"I can't let that pass, Mr. Fortune. Of course, it's well known General Cutts is opposed to the new policy at Logate and Sir Ingram Stow has supported him."

"Oh! You knew that," said Reggie sharply. "You didn't tell us. Rather a pity, isn't it?"

"I don't understand you, Mr. Fortune. There is no secret about their opinions. They're gentlemen of the highest reputation."

"Everybody always is in this kind of case," Bell grunted. "These are gentlemen and the mistresses are ladies. All the same, a girl nearly got murdered among 'em."

"But this is preposterous," the Chief Constable cried.

"Oh, no. No. Summary of facts by Superintendent Bell. Let's expand it. These two gentlemen have been behind the trouble in the school which produced the persecution of Nora Brown. Somebody attempts to murder her and they try to prevent inquiry into the case. And the attempt wasn't wholly feminine. What do you know about that?" He held out a specimen box containing a small piece of black fluff.

The Chief Constable gaped. "Came off a silk hat, what?" said Bell.

"Yes. It came off a silk hat. Onto a hawthorn bough by the temple where I found it. With a man's footprints adjacent. Also the blow which knocked Nora out was beyond a woman's strength. Assistance of a man in the crime is strongly indicated."

"And a gentleman," Bell grinned.

"But it's bewildering," the Chief Constable gasped. "Surely, Mr. Fortune, you can't believe these gentlemen would murder a girl because of their opinions on school policy. The idea is crazy!"

"Oh, yes. Yes. Quite. To keep poor girls out of Logate by murderin' one who got in—that isn't a business proposition. But a man did try to murder her and these men are tryin' to hush it up. And when you kindly assisted in our first line of inquiry, who started the trouble at Logate leadin' to the persecution of Nora, you put us onto these same men. That was very helpful of you." He smiled at the scared Chief Constable. "Convergin' evidence, isn't it?"

"It's very strange," the Chief Constable stammered. "But the connection—what connection is there between the change of policy at Logate and this girl? She didn't come till lately."

"Till after the trouble began. Yes. The inference is, they started the trouble for other reasons, but when Nora Brown got into the school they found they had special reasons for turning it against her. Hence the persecution. Possibly with hopes of her suicide. In other words, Nora Brown is somebody who had to be murdered for her own sake."

The Chief Constable rubbed his brow. "I can't believe the General—I'd answer for him absolutely—"

"Yes. I should say he's merely an ass," Reggie murmured.

"You suspect Stow, then? But what possible reason?"

"I haven't the slightest idea," said Reggie.

The Chief Constable stared at him pathetically. "Of course, there must be an investigation, a thorough investigation. What would you like me to do?"

"Nothing. And do it carefully. Leave your man on guard over Nora. The woman doctor's all right. But a policeman is a good scarecrow for criminals. You might have some plain-clothes men watchin' to see if Stow comes to the school or has anybody go from the school to him. I'll attend to Miss Brown senior."

"Senior?" The Chief Constable gaped.

"Yes. The hypothetical aunt. Followin' the second line of inquiry, who is Nora Brown? Well, this being thus, that's all. You'll want to be goin'. Many thanks." He got rid of an unhappy man.

Bell filled a pipe and cocked an eyebrow. "Told him a lot, didn't you, sir? You talk about converging evidence. I'd say you haven't got any evidence to take to a jury."

"Not much. No." Reggie pulled out of his pocket the tie by which the girl was hanged. "What do you think of that?"

Bell turned it over. "Good knots, sailor's knots."

"Yes. Stow was in the navy. I looked him up."

Bell grunted. "Well, that's another pointer. But it's not much, is it? Looks like one of those cases where you feel sure but you can't put the man in the dock. Clever fellow."

"I wonder," Reggie murmured. "Very ingenious mind somewhere."

"If you hadn't been at this school to-day, the girl would have been cut down dead; nobody would have thought of anything but suicide. Stow would have had a nice quiet little inquest and been on velvet."

"Yes. That is so," Reggie smiled. "But I don't think he's feeling on velvet to-night."

"I don't know. I don't see where you're going to get your evidence, even now."

Reggie stood up. "The hypothetical aunt, my Bell."

"That's all very well. You may find some connection with Stow. You may find a motive for him killing the girl. But that don't make evidence he tried."

"My little ray of sunshine." Reggie contemplated him with affection. "Are we downhearted? No. We've saved the girl. Come to bed. We'll seek Aunt bright and early."

So early in the morning they drove away to the cottage of Miss Brown. It stood sixty miles from Logate and far from anywhere, in a flat and lonely country, a small cottage, at the end of a small village, looking from the outside homely and well kept. To their knocking at the door no answer came. Bell strode off to the nearest neighbours. He was told that they didn't know nothing but they thought Miss Brown was gone away. A motorcar did come to her place the night afore and she went off in it and they never see her come back.

Superintendent Bell becomes annoyed when he meets attempts to frustrate his investigations. "Somebody's been very quick." He frowned at Reggie. "What's the game?"

"Somebody's got the wind up," Reggie smiled.

"Do you think Stow's made away with her?"

"It could be," Reggie murmured. "She knows something we mustn't know."

"That don't make sense to my mind. This woman's been living here with the girl; brought her up; let her go to Logate. And it's only when she gets there Stow meddles with her. Why did he wait?"

"Yes. Why did he? Interestin' question. You'd better ask Miss Brown."

"I'm going to have a job to find her."

"Oh, my dear chap! What about the advertised resources of our highly organized police force?"

"I'll set 'em to work," Bell frowned.

"Yes. Yes. You make 'em find out where she's gone," Reggie smiled. "I want to know where she came from." He left Bell working the telephone in the village post office. He went to call on the village school.

He found the mistress who had coached Nora for her scholarship, a worn and weary woman, but of a quick intelligence. She would tell him nothing till he told her what had happened to the girl. Then all she knew and all she thought was laid before him. She had always considered Nora a girl of uncommon ability and character; she had never heard of any relations, friends, enemies, anybody who took an interest in her. Miss Brown was an ordinary woman, rather dull, rather reserved, kind enough in a stolid way. She came to the village when Nora was a baby, a year old or less. Nobody knew where from. Miss Brown kept much to herself; having money enough to live on, considered herself above the village people. She had not wanted Nora to go to Logate, but gave way.

"I see. Yes." Reggie smiled. "You forced her hand."

"I'd have done anything to give the child her chance," the mistress said fiercely. "I told her so."

"Yes. Did she know anything about Logate?"

"She'd never heard of it. She only objected because she thought it was what she called a school for the gentry."

"I see. And what was Miss Brown? Not gentry?"

"Oh, dear, no. She'd been a hospital nurse, I believe. I heard her say once she'd been trained at Exeter."

"Is that so?" Over Reggie's face came a slow benign smile. "And her age?"

"I couldn't say. Forty—fifty. I have a photograph of her with Nora. You can form your own opinion. That was taken five years ago."

Reggie studied a photograph of a neat woman with a fat and stolid face. "Splendid," he murmured. "Yes. Say forty plus now. At the Exeter hospital twenty plus years back. What's her colouring?"

"Oh, fair, florid, blue eyes and brown hair."

"Thanks very much. I may take the photograph?"

"You'll let me have it back? It's the only one I have of Nora at that age."

"Yes. Charmin' child. She is still. Yes. You shall have it safe. Thanks very much. Nora's had a good friend." He held out his hand.

"You're working for her, aren't you?" There were tears in the tired eyes.

"I'm for her," said Reggie gently. "Good-bye. I shall remember you." . . .

Some days afterwards the Chief of the Criminal Investigation Department saw in the personal column of the morning papers this advertisement:

> DEWES: Any person having knowledge of Mrs. Veronica Dewes, who died at Beton, Devon, January 1915, is desired to inform the Criminal Investigation Department, Scotland Yard.

He was not pleased. He was making trouble about it in the Department when his telephone rang.

"Is that Lomas? Fortune speaking. From Beton, Devon. Good-morning. Seen the papers?"

"Good Gad!" Lomas groaned. "I might have known it was you."

"You might. Yes. Didn't you? Dear, dear. Never at your brightest in the morning. Any news of the vanished Miss Brown?"

"Bell thinks she's sailed for Canada. He's wirelessing the ship. If it is the woman, we'll have her held on the other side."

"Good. And Stow?"

"Stow hasn't run. He's at his place in the country. We can't find any evidence he went to her cottage. He was out driving his own car that night. What's this new hare you've started?"

"Not new. No. Same old hare. Miss Brown. After training in the Exeter hospital Miss Brown became district nurse at this charmin' place. Mrs. Dewes was living here. Young wife of a man said to have been killed in the war. In 1914 she had a baby, christened Veronica. Miss Brown nursed her. In 1915, she died, Miss Brown still nursing her. Baby also died. Cause of death in the register pneumonia for both. Doctor who gave the certificate is dead. Shortly after these deaths, Miss Brown vanished from Beton."

"Queer story. So you want to find the relations of Mrs. Dewes? We'll look the man up in the casualty lists."

"Yes. I want to know who they were. I also want an exhumation order."

"What? Good Gad! For bodies buried fourteen years? You can't make out anything now, can you?"

"It depends what I find."

"You suspect foul play?"

"Oh, yes. Yes. Something wrong. Put it through."

"It's very unusual."

"My only aunt!" the telephone moaned. "Here I am livin' in a fishermen's pub, and you talk about what's usual. Get on with it."

But official objections might have delayed that order long if General Blaker had not called at Scotland Yard. It was some time before he interested Lomas. He had to explain why Jimmy Dewes was the best subaltern a man ever had and how he was killed at Le Cateau. But then he became relevant. Jimmy was the son of old Colonel Dewes and married without his father's consent and the old man wouldn't allow him a penny—didn't believe in early marriages for soldiers—poor old man, never thought there was a world war coming to kill all the lads off. Mrs. Dewes was a charming girl, dear creature, but the old man wouldn't look at her. So, naturally, when Jimmy was killed she was too proud to go to the old fellow—carried on as she could, till she died, poor thing, she and her baby, first winter of the war. Probably pined away when her man was gone—too many of 'em did. There was old Dewes left without a soul of his name. He didn't last long.

"What became of his money?" said Lomas.

"Oh, he made no will—it went to the next of kin, a young cousin, a baronet. Stow the name is—Ingram Stow." . . .

Under a red Devon cliff Reggie lay watching the sea. The girl child who delivered the telegrams of Beton came to him. He read this message:

YOU WIN. INSTRUCTING COUNTY POLICE. ARRANGE WITH
THEM. LOMAS.

He scrambled to his feet and made for the village telephone.

When the sun came over the cliff in the morning men began to dig into one of the nameless mounds in the little churchyard. They found the mother's coffin and the baby's lying side by side, and the tarnished plates. "All right. Carry on." He walked slowly away.

Some hours later he came out of the mortuary in Exeter and strolled to the railway station. The Cornish express roared through, the slip carriage from it slid to the platform and Lomas jumped out. "My dear old thing," Reggie beamed at him. "All ready for you. Come along."

"Has it gone all right?"

"Oh, yes. Yes. Very nice and neat."

Reggie put him into a taxi and said to the driver, "The mortuary."

"Good Gad!" Lomas gasped. "You don't want to show me—"

"Oh, yes. You'd better have a look."

"My dear fellow! I can't help you with this sort of thing."

"Not help, no. I've finished. There's nothing to be done with the mother. We can hope she died a natural death. But the baby—well, it's very interesting."

Lomas shuddered. "The baby didn't?"

"No. No. That is indicated."

They came to the mortuary and Reggie led him in. The woman's coffin was covered. In the baby's lay something wrapped in a shroud. Reggie beckoned to an attendant. "Unroll that again." It was lifted out and from the shroud came a pillow case. "There's the baby. A feather pillow with a few stones for makeweight. See? The baby didn't die. Miss Brown wasn't wholly inhuman. So we can hope the mother died by nature."

"Good Gad!" said Lomas. "I suppose that's what you had in your head all the time."

"Yes. Yes." Over Reggie's face came a slow benign smile. "That was the workin' hypothesis. Well, well. Now we can get on."

They went back to their cab. "Lunch is indicated. A grave but placid lunch. You'll want to wind up the case with the police down here. Then we'll go back and deal with Stow."

"It's not so easy to deal with Stow," Lomas frowned. "This doesn't make evidence that he tried to murder the girl at Logate. What have we got? It was to his interest as the next heir to old Dewes to have this woman and her baby dead. The probability is he tried to arrange something with Miss Brown."

"Oh, yes. Yes. I should say she told him the baby was dead, hadn't the heart to kill it, but took the price for its death. She retired on that and brought the girl up. Thus making the best of both worlds. Then the child turned out clever and the village school mistress took her up and got her into Logate. Miss Brown not knowin' enough to object. Thus Stow found a girl looking like the Dewes family in Logate and called Brown. That must have hit him hard. If anybody came along who knew the Dewes, there'd be questions. She's a strikin' child. I suppose he looked up Miss Brown and decided he had to get rid of the girl. And he made a very good try."

"That's all very well. No doubt that's how it all happened. There's a very good chance of proving the girl heiress to the Dewes estate and showing Stow up. What do you think of the evidence for a criminal charge against him? If we can catch this Miss Brown and frighten her into telling the truth, we might make something of the fraud of the baby's death. But for the attempt to murder the girl at Logate, we're where we were. No case."

"Yes. As you say," Reggie murmured. "No case. But we might ask him about it. Very interestin'."

"Oh, I'll ask him," said Lomas. "But he's in touch with Logate. He must know we've got nothing more there. If you think he'll give himself away, you're hopeful."

"Yes. Perhaps you're right," Reggie sighed. "A sad world."

So they went to lunch and when Lomas had settled his business with the police took a train for Logate's county town. Reggie nearly missed it. He explained that he had been writing letters.

That evening they conferred with the Chief Constable, and having laid the case before that amazed man, arranged with him to drive over in the morning and interrogate Stow in his own house. When they were leaving, "By the way," said Reggie, "have you kept your men watching Stow?"

"Watched his house night and day, Mr. Fortune. And Logate. Made nothing of it. He's seen none of the school people. He's kept very quiet. Of course, he must know the girl's doing well and that would scare him. I have rather wondered he didn't try to bolt when he got that Miss Brown out of the country."

Reggie looked at him with dreamy eyes. "Yes. That's interestin', isn't it? Good-night."

The Chief Constable's car came to their hotel while they were still at an early breakfast. "Come on, Lomas." Reggie pushed back his chair. "All is best though oft we doubt—you're much better without that coffee. I wonder where they got it." And Lomas groaned and followed.

The Chief Constable was brisk. " 'Morning. 'Morning. I thought we'd better lose no time. Seen the papers, Mr. Lomas?"

"I'm not awake yet," Lomas mumbled.

"They've got onto it. Look." And Lomas read:

EXHUMATION IN DEVON

In the little fishing village of Beton on the Devonshire coast an exhumation was made yesterday by order of the Home Office. Two coffins were removed to Exeter. It is understood that a sensational discovery was made. Further developments in a case in another part of the country are expected.

"That's as good as a straight tip to Sir Ingram Stow, isn't it?" said the Chief Constable. "If he's read that he'll be off."

"You think so?" Reggie murmured. "You've still got a man watching his house."

"I have, Mr. Fortune. And I sent off another on a motorbike as soon as I read this."

"Then that is that," Reggie sighed.

Lomas looked at him without affection, but his round face had a dreamy calm.

By Stow's gate a motorcyclist tinkering with his machine waved them on. They came to the house, a big new place built onto an old one. "Been using the Dewes money," Lomas frowned.

They were told by an aggrieved butler that Sir Ingram was still at breakfast. "He will see me at once," said Lomas. They were put into the library and he came.

He was visibly a weaker man than he had been at Logate. He had shrunken, he was pale. He greeted the Chief Constable with a show of joviality; he was shy of Reggie, anxiously civil to Lomas. "I must suppose you've come on business, sir. I'm quite at your orders. What can I do?"

"You'd better sit down," said Lomas. "I want to hear your account of your actions on the day Nora Brown was hanged at Logate."

"My actions?" Stow laughed. "I had no actions, so to speak. I went to Logate to see the play, saw it, went back to the school-house and was talking there till we heard the poor child had hanged herself."

"Oh, no. No." Reggie said. "That's not our information. The evidence is you went to the temple. You found the girl there. You struck her behind the ear and knocked her out. You took off her tie and hanged her. Then you went back to the schoolhouse and talked."

"The evidence?" Stow gasped. "She's told you that?"

"She?" said Reggie, and he laughed. "Didn't you think she would?"

"It's a lie!" Stow cried.

"Oh! She is lying? Which she do you mean?" He leaned forward, watching the man's fear with smiling curiosity.

"The girl, of course." Stow licked his lips. "I don't understand."

"There's more evidence than the girl's," said Reggie. "You know that. Do you choose to tell your story?"

Stow looked at him white and shaking. "What do you mean, my story? I don't know what you've heard. I—"

But Reggie was not listening. There was the sound of a car outside. He made for the window. He watched a moment and turned quickly. "Here she is," he said with a chuckle and hurried out.

He came back grasping the arm of a large woman. She was red. She was protesting incoherently. She was Miss Evans.

"Oh, yes. Yes." Reggie's placid voice cut across hers. "Much obliged to you. We wanted you. He says it wasn't his idea at all."

Stow huddled in his chair. "I swear it wasn't," he muttered. "She thought of it like that. She said—"

"Ah, you hound!" the woman cried. She plucked at her bag, she pulled out a pistol and fired into his face. As she turned the pistol on herself, they flung themselves upon her. . . .

"And that is that," Reggie sighed, watching the car drive her away to gaol. "One of my neater cases, Lomas, old thing." He lit a cigar. "We couldn't have hanged Stow. Now we've got 'em both. I daresay the late Stow told the truth in the end. I expect she put him up to the hanging. Feminine insight about it."

"No doubt she did," Lomas agreed. "That's why she shot when the fellow rounded on her."

"It could be. Yes. I should say she was mad at losing what she played for. Always being frustrated."

"What do you mean?"

"That she wasn't going to be Lady Stow. When he wanted to get at the girl he had this disgruntled woman ready to be used. But she wouldn't do murder for nothing. Sort of woman who'd stood out for the top price. Marriage. I should say it was because she thought that was right off, she put a pistol in her bag when she came to call."

"But what brought her this morning?"

"My dear chap! Oh, my dear chap!" Reggie smiled. "She reads the papers."

"Good Gad! That cursed paragraph." Lomas stared at him. "That was you, of course."

"Yes. Yes. I thought it might draw her," Reggie murmured. "It did, didn't it? Quite a neat case."

A Case of Premeditation

BY R. AUSTIN FREEMAN

1. THE ELIMINATION OF MR. PRATT

The wine merchant who should supply a consignment of *petit vin* to a customer who had ordered, and paid for, a vintage wine, would render himself subject to unambiguous comment. Nay! more; he would be liable to certain legal penalties. And yet his conduct would be morally indistinguishable from that of the railway company which, having accepted a first-class fare, inflicts upon the passenger that kind of company which he has paid to avoid. But the corporate conscience, as Herbert Spencer was wont to explain, is an altogether inferior product to that of the individual.

Such were the reflections of Mr. Rufus Pembury when, as the train was about to move out of Maidstone (West) station, a coarse and burly man (clearly a denizen of the third-class) was ushered into his compartment by the guard. He had paid the higher fare, not for cushioned seats, but for seclusion or, at least, select companionship. The man's entry had deprived him of both, and he resented it.

But if the presence of this stranger involved a breach of contract, his conduct was a positive affront—an indignity; for, no sooner had the train started than he fixed upon Mr. Pembury a gaze of impertinent intensity, and continued thereafter to regard him with a stare as steady and unwinking as that of a Polynesian idol. It was offensive to a degree, and highly disconcerting withal. Mr. Pembury fidgeted in his seat with increasing discomfort and rising temper. He looked into his pocket-book, read one or two letters and sorted a collection of visiting-cards. He even thought of opening his umbrella. Finally, his patience exhausted and his wrath mounting to boiling-point, he turned to the stranger with frosty remonstrance.

"I imagine, sir, that you will have no difficulty in recognizing me, should we ever meet again—which God forbid."

"I should recognize you among ten thousand," was the reply, so unexpected as to leave Mr. Pembury speechless.

"You see," the stranger continued impressively, "I've got the gift of faces. I never forget."

"That must be a great consolation," said Pembury.

"It's very useful to me," said the stranger, "at least, it used to be, when I was a warder at Portland—you remember me, I dare say: my name is Pratt. I was assistant-warder in your time. God-for-saken hole, Portland, and mighty glad I was when they used to send me up to town on reckernizing duty. Holloway was the house of detention then, you remember; that was before they moved to Brixton."

Pratt paused in his reminiscences, and Pembury, pale and gasping with astonishment, pulled himself together.

"I think," said he, "you must be mistaking me for some one else."

"I don't," replied Pratt. "You're Francis Dobbs, that's who you are. Slipped away from Portland one evening about twelve years ago. Clothes washed up on the Bill next day. No trace of fugitive. As neat a mizzle as ever I heard of. But there are a couple of photo-graphs and a set of fingerprints at the Habitual Criminals Register. P'r'aps you'd like to come and see 'em?"

"Why should I go to the Habitual Criminals Register?" Pembury demanded faintly.

"Ah! Exactly. Why should you? When you are a man of means, and a little judiciously invested capital would render it unnecessary?"

Pembury looked out of the window, and for a minute or more preserved a stony silence. At length he turned suddenly to Pratt. "How much?" he asked.

"I shouldn't think a couple of hundred a year would hurt you," was the calm reply.

Pembury reflected awhile. "What makes you think I am a man of means?" he asked presently.

Pratt smiled grimly. "Bless you, Mr. Pembury," said he, "I know all about you. Why, for the last six months I have been living within half-a-mile of your house."

"The devil you have!"

"Yes. When I retired from the service, General O'Gorman engaged me as a sort of steward or caretaker of his little place at Baysford—he's very seldom there himself—and the very day after I came down, I met you and spotted you, but, naturally, I kept out of sight myself. Thought I'd find out whether you were good for anything before I spoke, so I've been keeping my ears open and I find you are good for a couple of hundred."

There was an interval of silence, and then the ex-warder resumed—

"That's what comes of having a memory for faces. Now there's Jack Ellis, on the other hand; he must have had you under his nose for a couple of years, and yet he's never twigged—he never will either," added Pratt, already regretting the confidence into which his vanity had led him.

"Who is Jack Ellis?" Pembury demanded sharply.

"Why, he's a sort of supernumerary at the Baysford Police Station; does odd jobs; rural detective, helps in the office and that sort of thing. He was in the Civil Guard at Portland, in your time, but he got his left forefinger chopped off, so they pensioned him, and, as he was a Baysford man, he got this billet. But he'll never reckernize you, don't you fear."

"Unless you direct his attention to me," suggested Pembury.

"There's no fear of that," laughed Pratt. "You can trust me to sit quiet on my own nest-egg. Besides, we're not very friendly. He came nosing round our place after the parlourmaid—him a married man, mark you! But I soon boosted him out, I can tell you; and Jack Ellis don't like me now."

"I see," said Pembury reflectively; then, after a pause, he asked: "Who is this General O'Gorman? I seem to know the name."

"I expect you do," said Pratt. "He was governor of Dartmoor when I was there—that was my last billet—and, let me tell you, if he'd been at Portland in your time, you'd never have got away."

"How is that?"

"Why, you see, the general is a great man on bloodhounds. He kept a pack at Dartmoor and, you bet, those lags knew it. There were no attempted escapes in those days. They wouldn't have had a chance."

"He has the pack still, hasn't he?" asked Pembury.

"Rather. Spends any amount of time on training 'em, too. He's always hoping there'll be a burglary or a murder in the neighbourhood so as he can try 'em, but he's never got a chance yet. P'r'aps the crooks have heard about 'em. But, to come back to our little arrangement: what do you say to a couple of hundred, paid quarterly, if you like?"

"I can't settle the matter off-hand," said Pembury. "You must give me time to think it over."

"Very well," said Pratt. "I shall be back at Baysford tomorrow evening. That will give you a clear day to think it over. Shall I look in at your place to-morrow night?"

"No," replied Pembury; "you'd better not be seen at my house, nor I at yours. If I meet you at some quiet spot, where we shan't be seen, we can settle our business without any one knowing that we have met. It won't take long, and we can't be too careful."

"That's true," agreed Pratt. "Well, I'll tell you what. There's an avenue leading up to our house; you know it, I expect. There's no lodge, and the gates are always ajar, excepting at night. Now I shall be down by the six-thirty at Baysford. Our place is a quarter of an hour from the station. Say you meet me in the avenue at a quarter to seven."

"That will suit me," said Pembury; "that is, if you are sure the bloodhounds won't be straying about the grounds."

"Lord bless you, no!" laughed Pratt. "D'you suppose the general lets his precious hounds stray about for any casual crook to feed with poisoned sausage? No, they're locked up safe in the kennels at the back of the house. Hallo! This'll be Swanley, I expect. I'll change into a smoker here and leave you time to turn the matter over in your mind. So long. To-morrow evening in the avenue at a quarter to seven. And, I say, Mr. Pembury, you might as well bring the first instalment with you—fifty, in small notes or gold."

"Very well," said Mr. Pembury. He spoke coldly enough, but there was a flush on his cheeks and an angry light in his eyes, which, perhaps, the ex-warder noticed; for when he had stepped out and shut the door, he thrust his head in at the window and said threateningly—

"One more word, Mr. Pembury-Dobbs: no hanky-panky, you know. I'm an old hand and pretty fly, I am. So don't you try any chickery-pokery on me. That's all." He withdrew his head and disappeared, leaving Pembury to his reflections.

The nature of those reflections, if some telepathist—transferring his attention for the moment from hidden courtyards or missing thimbles to more practical matters—could have conveyed them into the mind of Mr. Pratt, would have caused that quondam official some surprise and, perhaps, a little disquiet. For long experience of the criminal, as he appears when in durance, had produced some rather misleading ideas as to his behaviour when at large. In fact, the ex-warder had considerably under-estimated the ex-convict.

Rufus Pembury, to give his real name—for Dobbs was literally a *nom de guerre*—was a man of strong character and intelligence. So much so that, having tried the criminal career and found it not worth pursuing, he had definitely abandoned it. When the cattle-boat that picked him up off Portland Bill had landed him at an American port, he brought his entire ability and energy to bear on legitimate commercial pursuits, and with such success that, at the end of ten years, he was able to return to England with a moderate competence. Then he had taken a modest house near the little town of Baysford, where he had lived quietly on his savings for the last two years, holding aloof without much difficulty from the rather exclusive local society; and here he might have lived out the rest of his life in peace but for the unlucky chance that brought the man Pratt into the neighbourhood. With the arrival of Pratt his security was utterly destroyed.

There is something eminently unsatisfactory about a black-mailer. No arrangement with him has any permanent validity. No undertaking that he gives is binding. The thing which he has sold remains in his possession to sell over again. He pockets the price of emancipation, but retains the key of the fetters. In short, the blackmailer is a totally impossible person.

Such were the considerations that had passed through the mind of Rufus Pembury, even while Pratt was making his proposals; and those proposals he had never for an instant entertained. The ex-warder's advice to him to "turn the matter over in his mind" was unnecessary. For his mind was already made up. His decision was arrived at in the very moment when Pratt had disclosed his identity. The conclusion was self-evident. Before Pratt appeared he was living in peace and security. While Pratt remained, his liberty was precarious from moment to moment. If Pratt should disappear, his peace and security would return. Therefore Pratt must be eliminated.

It was a logical consequence.

The profound meditations, therefore, in which Pembury re-mained immersed for the remainder of the journey, had nothing whatever to do with the quarterly allowance; they were concerned exclusively with the elimination of ex-warder Pratt.

Now Rufus Pembury was not a ferocious man. He was not even cruel. But he was gifted with a certain magnanimous cynicism which ignored the trivialities of sentiment and regarded only the main issues. If a wasp hummed over his teacup, he would crush that wasp; but not with his bare hand. The wasp carried the means of aggression. That was the wasp's look-out. *His* concern was to avoid being stung.

So it was with Pratt. The man had elected, for his own profit, to threaten Pembury's liberty. Very well. He had done it at his own risk. That risk was no concern of Pembury's. *His* concern was his own safety.

When Pembury alighted at Charing Cross, he directed his steps (after having watched Pratt's departure from the station) to Buckingham Street, Strand, where he entered a quiet private hotel. He was apparently expected, for the manageress greeted him by his name as she handed him his key.

"Are you staying in town, Mr. Pembury?" she asked.

"No," was the reply. "I go back to-morrow morning, but I may be coming up again shortly. By the way, you used to have an encyclopaedia in one of the rooms. Could I see it for a moment?"

"It is in the drawing-room," said the manageress. "Shall I show you?—but you know the way, don't you?"

Certainly Mr. Pembury knew the way. It was on the first floor; a pleasant old-world room looking on the quiet old street; and on a shelf, amidst a collection of novels, stood the sedate volumes of *Chambers' Encyclopaedia*.

That a gentleman from the country should desire to look up the subject of "hounds" would not, to a casual observer, have seemed unnatural. But when from hounds the student proceeded to the article on blood, and thence to one devoted to perfumes, the observer might reasonably have felt some surprise; and this surprise might have been augmented if he had followed Mr. Pembury's subsequent proceedings, and specially if he had considered them as the actions of a man whose immediate aim was the removal of a superfluous unit of the population.

Having deposited his bag and umbrella in his room, Pembury set forth from the hotel as one with a definite purpose; and his footsteps led, in the first place, to an umbrella shop on the Strand, where he selected a thick rattan cane. There was nothing remarkable in this, perhaps; but the cane was of an uncomely thickness and the salesman protested. "I like a thick cane," said Pembury.

"Yes, sir; but for a gentleman of your height" (Pembury was a small, slightly-built man) "I would venture to suggest—"

"I like a thick cane," repeated Pembury. "Cut it down to the proper length and don't rivet the ferrule on. I'll cement it on when I get home."

His next investment would have seemed more to the purpose, though suggestive of unexpected crudity of method. It was a large Norwegian knife. But not content with this he went on forthwith to a second cutler's and purchased a second knife, the exact duplicate of the first. Now, for what purpose could he want two identically similar knives? And why not have bought them both at the same shop? It was highly mysterious.

Shopping appeared to be a positive mania with Rufus Pembury. In the course of the next half-hour he acquired a cheap hand-bag, an artist's black-japanned brush-case, a three-cornered file, a stick of elastic glue and a pair of iron crucible-tongs. Still insatiable, he repaired to an old-fashioned chemist's shop in a by-street, where he further enriched himself with a packet of absorbent cotton-wool and an ounce of permanganate of potash; and, as the chemist wrapped up these articles, with the occult and necromantic air peculiar to chemists, Pembury watched him impassively.

"I suppose you don't keep musk?" he asked carelessly.

The chemist paused in the act of heating a stick of sealing-wax, and appeared as if about to mutter an incantation. But he merely replied: "No, sir. Not the solid musk; it's so very costly. But I have the essence."

"That isn't as strong as the pure stuff, I suppose?"

"No," replied the chemist, with a cryptic smile, "not *so* strong, but strong enough. These animal perfumes are so very penetrating, you know; and so lasting. Why, I venture to say that if you were to sprinkle a table-spoonful of the essence in the middle of St. Paul's, the place would smell of it six months hence."

"You don't say so!" said Pembury. "Well, that ought to be enough for anybody. I'll take a small quantity, please, and, for goodness' sake, see that there isn't any on the outside of the bottle. The stuff isn't for myself, and I don't want to go about smelling like a civet cat."

"Naturally you don't, sir," agreed the chemist. He then produced an ounce bottle, a small glass funnel and a stoppered bottle labelled "Ess. Moschi," with which he proceeded to perform a few trifling feats of legerdemain.

"There, sir," said he, when he had finished the performance, "there is not a drop on the outside of the bottle, and, if I fit it with a rubber cork, you will be quite secure."

Pembury's dislike of musk appeared to be excessive, for, when the chemist had retired into a secret cubicle as if to hold converse with some familiar spirit (but actually to change half-a-crown), he took the brush-case from his bag, pulled off its lid, and then, with the crucible-tongs, daintily lifted the bottle off the counter, slid it softly into the brush-case, and, replacing the lid, returned the case and tongs to the bag. The other two packets he took from the counter and dropped into his pocket, and, when the presiding wizard, having miraculously transformed a single half-crown into four pennies, handed him the product, he left the shop and walked thoughtfully back towards the Strand. Suddenly a new idea seemed to strike him. He halted, considered for a few moments and then strode away northward to make the oddest of all his purchases.

The transaction took place in a shop in the Seven Dials, whose strange stock-in-trade ranged the whole zoological gamut, from water-snails to Angora cats. Pembury looked at a cage of guinea-pigs in the window and entered the shop.

"Do you happen to have a dead guinea-pig?" he asked.

"No; mine are all alive," replied the man, adding, with a sinister grin: "But they're not immortal, you know."

Pembury looked at the man distastefully. There is an appreciable difference between a guinea-pig and a blackmailer. "Any small mammal would do," he said.

"There's a dead rat in that cage, if he's any good," said the man. "Died this morning, so he's quite fresh."

"I'll take the rat," said Pembury; "he'll do quite well."

The little corpse was accordingly made into a parcel and deposited in the bag, and Pembury, having tendered a complimentary fee, made his way back to the hotel.

After a modest lunch he went forth and spent the remainder of the day transacting the business which had originally brought him to town. He dined at a restaurant and did not return to his hotel until ten o'clock, when he took his key, and tucking under his arm a parcel that he had brought in with him, retired for the night. But before undressing—and after locking his door—he did a very strange and unaccountable thing. Having pulled off the loose ferrule from his newly-purchased cane, he bored a hole in the bottom of it with the spike end of the file. Then, using the latter as a broach, he enlarged the hole until only a narrow rim of the bottom was left. He next rolled up a small ball of cotton-wool and pushed it into the ferrule; and having smeared the end of the cane with elastic glue, he replaced the ferrule, warming it over the gas to make the glue stick.

When he had finished with the cane, he turned his attention to one of the Norwegian knives. First, he carefully removed with the file most of the bright, yellow varnish from the wooden case or handle.

Then he opened the knife, and, cutting the string of the parcel that he had brought in, took from it the dead rat which he had bought at the zoologist's. Laying the animal on a sheet of paper, he cut off its head, and, holding it up by the tail, allowed the blood that oozed from the neck to drop on the knife, spreading it over both sides of the blade and handle with his finger.

Then he laid the knife on the paper and softly opened the window. From the darkness below came the voice of a cat, apparently perfecting itself in the execution of chromatic scales; and in that direction Pembury flung the body and head of the rat, and closed the window. Finally, having washed his hands and stuffed the paper from the parcel into the fire-place, he went to bed.

But his proceedings in the morning were equally mysterious. Having breakfasted betimes, he returned to his bedroom and locked himself in. Then he tied his new cane, handle downwards, to the leg of the dressing-table. Next, with the crucible-tongs, he drew the little bottle of musk from the brush-case, and, having assured himself, by sniffing at it, that the exterior was really free from odour, he withdrew the rubber cork. Then, slowly and with infinite care, he poured a few drops—perhaps half-a-teaspoonful—of the essence on the cotton-wool that bulged through the hole in the ferrule, watching the absorbent material narrowly as it soaked up the liquid. When it was saturated he proceeded to treat the knife in the same fashion, letting fall a drop of the essence on the wooden handle—which soaked it up readily. This done, he slid up the window and looked out. Immediately below was a tiny yard in which grew, or rather survived, a couple of faded laurel bushes. The body of the rat was nowhere to be seen; it had apparently been spirited away in the night. Holding out the bottle, which he still held, he dropped it into the bushes, flinging the rubber cork after it.

His next proceeding was to take a tube of vaseline from his dressing-bag and squeeze a small quantity onto his fingers. With this he thoroughly smeared the shoulder of the brush-case and the inside of the lid, so as to ensure an air-tight joint. Having wiped his fingers, he picked the knife up with the crucible-tongs, and, dropping it into the brush-case, immediately pushed on the lid. Then he heated the tips of the tongs in the gas flame to destroy the scent, packed the tongs and brush-case in the bag, untied the cane—carefully avoiding contact with the ferrule—and, taking up the two bags, went out, holding the cane by its middle.

There was no difficulty in finding an empty compartment, for first-class passengers were few at that time in the morning. Pembury waited on the platform until the guard's whistle sounded, when he stepped into the compartment, shut the door and laid the cane on the seat with its ferrule projecting out of the off-side window, in which position it remained until the train drew up in Baysford station.

Pembury left his dressing-bag at the cloak-room, and, still grasping the cane by its middle, he sallied forth. The town of Baysford lay some half-a-mile to the east of the station; his own house was a mile along the road to the west; and half-way between his house and the station was the residence of General O'Gorman. He knew the place well. Originally a farmhouse, it stood on the edge of a great expanse of flat meadows and communicated with the road by an avenue, nearly three hundred yards long, of ancient trees. The avenue was shut off from the road by a pair of iron gates, but these were merely ornamental, for the place was unenclosed and accessible from the surrounding meadows—indeed, an indistinct footpath crossed the meadows and intersected the avenue about half-way up.

On this occasion Pembury, whose objective was the avenue, elected to approach it by the latter route; and at each stile or fence that he surmounted, he paused to survey the country. Presently the avenue arose before him, lying athwart the narrow track, and, as he entered it between two of the trees, he halted and looked about him.

He stood listening for a while. Beyond the faint rustle of leaves no sound was to be heard. Evidently there was no one about, and, as Pratt was at large, it was probable that the general was absent.

And now Pembury began to examine the adjacent trees with more than a casual interest. The two between which he had entered were respectively an elm and a great pollard oak, the latter being an immense tree whose huge, warty bole divided about seven feet from the ground into three limbs, each as large as a fair-sized tree, of which the largest swept outwards in a great curve half-way across the avenue. On this patriarch Pembury bestowed especial attention, walking completely round it and finally laying down his bag and cane (the latter resting on the bag with the ferrule off the ground) that he might climb up, by the aid of the warty out-growths, to examine the crown; and he had just stepped up into the space between the three limbs, when the creaking of the iron gates was followed by a quick step in the avenue. Hastily he let himself down from the tree, and, gathering up his possessions, stood close behind the great bole.

"Just as well not to be seen," was his reflection, as he hugged the tree closely and waited, peering cautiously round the trunk. Soon a streak of moving shadow heralded the stranger's approach, and he moved round to keep the trunk between himself and the intruder. On the footsteps came, until the stranger was abreast of the tree; and when he had passed Pembury peeped round at the retreating figure. It was only the postman, but then the man knew him, and he was glad he had kept out of sight.

Apparently the oak did not meet his requirements, for he stepped out and looked up and down the avenue. Then, beyond the elm, he caught sight of an ancient pollard hornbeam—a strange, fantastic tree whose trunk widened out trumpet-like above into a broad crown, from the edge of which multitudinous branches uprose like the limbs of some weird hamadryad.

That tree he approved at a glance, but he lingered behind the oak until the postman, returning with brisk step and cheerful whistle, passed down the avenue and left him once more in solitude. Then he moved on with a resolute air to the hornbeam.

The crown of the trunk was barely six feet from the ground. He could reach it easily, as he found on trying. Standing the cane against the tree—ferrule downwards, this time—he took the brush-case from the bag, pulled off the lid, and, with the crucible-tongs, lifted out the knife and laid it on the crown of the tree, just out of sight, leaving the tongs—also invisible—still grasping the knife. He was about to replace the brush-case in the bag, when he appeared to alter his mind. Sniffing at it, and finding it reeking with the sickly perfume, he pushed the lid on again and threw the case up into the tree, where he heard it roll down into the central hollow of the crown. Then he closed the bag, and, taking the cane by its handle, moved slowly away in the direction whence he had come, passing out of the avenue between the elm and the oak.

His mode of progress was certainly peculiar. He walked with excessive slowness, trailing the cane along the ground, and every few paces he would stop and press the ferrule firmly against the earth, so that, to any one who should have observed him, he would have appeared to be wrapped in an absorbing reverie.

Thus he moved on across the fields, not, however, returning to the high road, but crossing another stretch of fields until he emerged into a narrow lane that led out into the High Street. Immediately opposite to the lane was the police station, distinguished from the adjacent cottages only by its lamp, its open door and the notices pasted up outside. Straight across the road Pembury walked, still trailing the cane, and halted at the station door to read the notices, resting his cane on the doorstep as he did so. Through the open doorway he could see a man writing at a desk. The man's back was towards him, but, presently, a movement brought his left hand into view, and Pembury noted that the forefinger was missing. This, then, was Jack Ellis, late of the Civil Guard at Portland.

Even while he was looking the man turned his head, and Pembury recognized him at once. He had frequently met him on the road between Baysford and the adjoining village of Thorpe, and always at the same time. Apparently Ellis paid a daily visit to Thorpe—perhaps to receive a report from the rural constable—and he started between three and four and returned between seven and a quarter past.

Pembury looked at his watch. It was a quarter past three. He moved away thoughtfully (holding his cane, now, by the middle), and began to walk slowly in the direction of Thorpe—westward.

For a while he was deeply meditative, and his face wore a puzzled frown. Then, suddenly, his face cleared and he strode forward at a brisker pace. Presently he passed through a gap in the hedge, and, walking in a field parallel with the road, took out his purse—a small pigskin pouch. Having frugally emptied it of its contents, excepting a few shillings, he thrust the ferrule of his cane into the small compartment ordinarily reserved for gold or notes.

And thus he continued to walk on slowly, carrying the cane by the middle and the purse jammed on the end.

At length he reached a sharp double curve in the road whence he could see back for a considerable distance; and here, opposite a small opening, he sat down to wait. The hedge screened him effectually from the gaze of passers-by—though these were few enough— without interfering with his view.

A quarter of an hour passed. He began to be uneasy. Had he been mistaken? Were Ellis's visits only occasional instead of daily, as he had thought? That would be tiresome though not actually disastrous. But at this point in his reflections a figure came into view, advancing along the road with a steady swing. He recognized the figure. It was Ellis.

But there was another figure advancing from the opposite direction: a labourer, apparently. He prepared to shift his ground, but another glance showed him that the labourer would pass first. He waited. The labourer came on and, at length, passed the opening, and, as he did so, Ellis disappeared for a moment in a bend of the road. Instantly Pembury passed his cane through the opening in the hedge, shook off the purse and pushed it into the middle of the footway. Then he crept forward, behind the hedge, towards the approaching official, and again sat down to wait. On came the steady tramp of the unconscious Ellis, and, as it passed, Pembury drew aside an obstructing branch and peered out at the retreating figure. The question now was, would Ellis see the purse? It was not a very conspicuous object.

The footsteps stopped abruptly. Looking out, Pembury saw the police official stoop, pick up the purse, examine its contents and finally stow it in his trousers pocket. Pembury heaved a sigh of relief; and, as the dwindling figure passed out of sight round a curve in the road, he rose, stretched himself and strode away briskly.

Near the gap was a group of ricks, and, as he passed them, a fresh idea suggested itself. Looking round quickly he passed to the farther side of one and, thrusting his cane deeply into it, pushed it home with a piece of stick that he picked up near the rick, until the handle was lost among the straw. The bag was now all that was left, and it was empty—for his other purchases were in the dressing-bag, which, by the way, he must fetch from the station. He opened it and smelt the interior, but, though he could detect no odour, he resolved to be rid of it if possible.

As he emerged from the gap a wagon jogged slowly past. It was piled high with sacks, and the tail-board was down. Stepping into the road, he quickly overtook the wagon, and, having glanced round, laid the bag lightly on the tail-board. Then he set off for the station.

On arriving home he went straight up to his bedroom, and, ringing for his housekeeper, ordered a substantial meal. Then he took off his clothes and deposited them, even to his shirt, socks and necktie, in a trunk, wherein his summer clothing was stored with a plentiful sprinkling of naphthol to preserve it from the moth. Taking the packet of permanganate of potash from his dressing-bag, he passed into the adjoining bathroom, and, tipping the crystals into the bath, turned on the water. Soon the bath was filled with a pink solution of the salt, and into this he plunged, immersing his entire body and thoroughly soaking his hair. Then he emptied the bath and rinsed himself in clear water, and, having dried himself, returned to the bedroom and dressed himself in fresh clothing. Finally he took a hearty meal, and then lay down on the sofa to rest until it should be time to start for the rendezvous.

Half-past six found him lurking in the shadow by the station-approach, within sight of the solitary lamp. He heard the train come in, saw the stream of passengers emerge, and noted one figure detach itself from the throng and turn on to the Thorpe Road. It was Pratt, as the lamp-light showed him; Pratt, striding forward to the meet-ing-place with an air of jaunty satisfaction and an uncommonly creaky pair of boots.

Pembury followed him at a safe distance, and rather by sound than sight, until he was well past the stile at the entrance to the foot-path. Evidently he was going on to the gates. Then Pembury vaulted over the stile and strode away swiftly across the dark meadows.

When he plunged into the deep gloom of the avenue, his first act was to grope his way to the hornbeam and slip his hand up onto the crown and satisfy himself that the tongs were as he had left them. Reassured by the touch of his fingers on the iron loops, he turned and walked slowly down the avenue. The duplicate knife—ready opened—was in his left inside breast-pocket, and he fingered its handle as he walked.

Presently the iron gate squeaked mournfully, and then the rhyth-mical creak of a pair of boots was audible, coming up the avenue. Pembury walked forward slowly until a darker smear emerged from the surrounding gloom, when he called out—

"Is that you, Pratt?"

"That's me," was the cheerful, if ungrammatical response, and, as he drew nearer, the ex-warder asked: "Have you brought the rhino, old man?"

The insolent familiarity of the man's tone was agreeable to Pembury: it strengthened his nerve and hardened his heart. "Of course," he replied; "but we must have a definite understanding, you know."

"Look here," said Pratt, "I've got no time for jaw. The General will be here presently; he's riding over from Bingfield with a friend. You hand over the dibs and we'll talk some other time."

"That is all very well," said Pembury, "but you must understand—" He paused abruptly and stood still. They were now close to the hornbeam, and, as he stood, he stared up into the dark mass of foliage.

"What's the matter?" demanded Pratt. "What are you staring at?" He, too, had halted and stood gazing intently into the darkness.

Then, in an instant, Pembury whipped out the knife and drove it, with all his strength, into the broad back of the ex-warder, below the left shoulder-blade.

With a hideous yell Pratt turned and grappled with his assailant. A powerful man and a competent wrestler, too, he was far more than a match for Pembury unarmed, and, in a moment, he had him by the throat. But Pembury clung to him tightly, and, as they trampled to and fro and round and round, he stabbed again and again with the viciousness of a scorpion, while Pratt's cries grew more gurgling and husky. Then they fell heavily to the ground, Pembury underneath. But the struggle was over. With a last bubbling groan, Pratt relaxed his hold and in a moment grew limp and inert. Pembury pushed him off and rose, trembling and breathing heavily.

But he wasted no time. There had been more noise than he had bargained for. Quickly stepping up to the hornbeam, he reached up for the tongs. His fingers slid into the looped handles; the tongs grasped the knife, and he lifted it out from its hiding-place and carried it to where the corpse lay, depositing it on the ground a few feet from the body. Then he went back to the tree and carefully pushed the tongs over into the hollow of the crown.

At this moment a woman's voice sounded shrilly from the top of the avenue.

"Is that you, Mr. Pratt?" it called.

Pembury started and then stepped back quickly, on tiptoe, to the body. For there was the duplicate knife. He must take that away at all costs.

The corpse was lying on its back. The knife was underneath it, driven in to the very haft. He had to use both hands to lift the body, and even then he had some difficulty in disengaging the weapon. And, meanwhile, the voice, repeating its question, drew nearer.

At length he succeeded in drawing out the knife and thrust it into his breast-pocket. The corpse fell back, and he stood up gasping.

"Mr. Pratt! Are you there?" The nearness of the voice startled Pembury, and turning sharply, he saw a light twinkling between the trees. And then the gates creaked loudly and he heard the crunch of a horse's hoofs on the gravel.

He stood for an instant bewildered—utterly taken by surprise. He had not reckoned on a horse. His intended flight across the meadows towards Thorpe was now impracticable. If he were over-taken he was lost, for he knew there was blood on his clothes and his hands were wet and slippery—to say nothing of the knife in his pocket.

But his confusion lasted only for an instant. He remembered the oak tree; and, turning out of the avenue, he ran to it, and, touching it as little as he could with his bloody hands, climbed quickly up into the crown. The great horizontal limb was nearly three feet in diameter, and, as he lay out on it, gathering his coat closely round him, he was quite invisible from below.

He had hardly settled himself when the light which he had seen came into full view, revealing a woman advancing with a stable lantern in her hand. And, almost at the same moment, a streak of brighter light burst from the opposite direction. The horseman was accompanied by a man on a bicycle.

The two men came on apace, and the horseman, sighting the woman, called out: "Anything the matter, Mrs. Parton?" But, at that moment, the light of the bicycle lamp fell full on the prostrate corpse. The two men uttered a simultaneous cry of horror; the woman shrieked aloud; and then the horseman sprang from the saddle and ran forward to the body.

"Why," he exclaimed, stooping over it, "it's Pratt;" and, as the cyclist came up and the glare of his lamp shone on a great pool of blood, he added: "There's been foul play here, Hanford."

Hanford flashed his lamp around the body, lighting up the ground for several yards.

"What is that behind you, O'Gorman?" he said suddenly; "isn't it a knife?" He was moving quickly towards it when O'Gorman held up his hand.

"Don't touch it!" he exclaimed. "We'll put the hounds onto it. They'll soon track the scoundrel, whoever he is. By God! Hanford, this fellow has fairly delivered himself into our hands." He stood for a few moments looking down at the knife with something uncommonly like exultation, and then, turning quickly to his friend, said: "Look here, Hanford; you ride off to the police station as hard as you can pelt. It is only three-quarters of a mile; you'll do it in five minutes. Send or bring an officer and I'll scour the meadows meanwhile. If I haven't got the scoundrel when you come back, we'll put the hounds onto this knife and run the beggar down."

"Right," replied Hanford, and without another word he wheeled his machine about, mounted and rode away into the darkness.

"Mrs. Parton," said O'Gorman, "watch that knife. See that nobody touches it while I go and examine the meadows."

"Is Mr. Pratt dead, sir?" whimpered Mrs. Parton.

"Gad! I hadn't thought of that," said the general. "You'd better have a look at him; but mind! nobody is to touch that knife or they will confuse the scent."

He scrambled into the saddle and galloped away across the meadows in the direction of Thorpe; and, as Pembury listened to the diminuendo of the horse's hoofs, he was glad that he had not attempted to escape; for that was the direction in which he had meant to go, and he would surely have been overtaken.

As soon as the general was gone, Mrs. Parton, with many a terror-stricken glance over her shoulder, approached the corpse and held the lantern close to the dead face. Suddenly she stood up, trembling violently, for footsteps were audible coming down the avenue. A familiar voice reassured her.

"Is anything wrong, Mrs. Parton?" The question proceeded from one of the maids who had come in search of the elder woman, escorted by a young man, and the pair now came out into the circle of light.

"Good God!" ejaculated the man. "Who's that?"

"It's Mr. Pratt," replied Mrs. Parton. "He's been murdered."

The girl screamed, and then the two domestics approached on tiptoe, staring at the corpse with the fascination of horror.

"Don't touch that knife," said Mrs. Parton, for the man was about to pick it up. "The general's going to put the bloodhounds onto it."

"Is the general here, then?" asked the man; and, as he spoke, the drumming of hoofs, growing momentarily louder, answered him from the meadow.

O'Gorman reined in his horse as he perceived the group of servants gathered about the corpse. "Is he dead, Mrs. Parton?" he asked.

"I am afraid so, sir," was the reply.

"Ha! Somebody ought to go for the doctor; but not you, Bailey. I want you to get the hounds ready and wait with them at the top of the avenue until I call you."

He was off again into the Baysford meadows, and Bailey hurried away, leaving the two women staring at the body and talking in whispers.

Pembury's position was cramped and uncomfortable. He dared not move, hardly dared to breathe, for the women below him were not a dozen yards away; and it was with mingled feelings of relief and apprehension that he presently saw from his elevated station a group of lights approaching rapidly along the road from Baysford. Presently they were hidden by the trees, and then, after a brief interval, the whirr of wheels sounded on the drive and streaks of light on the tree-trunks announced the new arrivals. There were three bicycles, ridden respectively by Mr. Hanford, a police inspector and a sergeant; and, as they drew up, the general came thundering back into the avenue.

"Is Ellis with you?" he asked, as he pulled up.

"No, sir," was the reply. "He hadn't come in from Thorpe when we left. He's rather late to-night."

"Have you sent for a doctor?"

"Yes, sir, I've sent for Dr. Hills," said the inspector, resting his bicycle against the oak. Pembury could smell the reek of the lamp as he crouched. "Is Pratt dead?"

"Seems to be," replied O'Gorman, "but we'd better leave that to the doctor. There's the murderer's knife. Nobody has touched it. I'm going to fetch the bloodhounds now."

"Ah! that's the thing," said the inspector. "The man can't be far away." He rubbed his hands with a satisfied air as O'Gorman cantered away up the avenue.

In less than a minute there came out from the darkness the deep baying of a hound followed by quick footsteps on the gravel. Then into the circle of light emerged three sinister shapes, loose-limbed and gaunt, and two men advancing at a shambling trot.

"Here, inspector," shouted the general, "you take one; I can't hold 'em both."

The inspector ran forward and seized one of the leashes, and the general led his hound up to the knife, as it lay on the ground. Pembury, peering cautiously round the bough, watched the great brute with almost impersonal curiosity; noted its high poll, its wrinkled forehead and melancholy face as it stooped to snuff suspiciously at the prostrate knife.

For some moments the hound stood motionless, sniffing at the knife; then it turned away and walked to and fro with its muzzle to the ground. Suddenly it lifted its head, bayed loudly, lowered its muzzle and started forward between the oak and the elm, dragging the general after it at a run.

The inspector next brought his hound to the knife, and was soon bounding away to the tug of the leash in the general's wake.

"They don't make no mistakes, they don't," said Bailey, addressing the gratified sergeant, as he brought forward the third hound; "you'll see—" But his remark was cut short by a violent jerk of the leash, and the next moment he was flying after the others, followed by Mr. Hanford.

The sergeant daintily picked the knife up by its ring, wrapped it in his handkerchief and bestowed it in his pocket. Then he ran off after the hounds.

Pembury smiled grimly. His scheme was working out admirably in spite of the unforeseen difficulties. If those confounded women would only go away, he could come down and take himself off while the coast was clear. He listened to the baying of the hounds, gradually growing fainter in the increasing distance, and cursed the dilatoriness of the doctor. Confound the fellow! Didn't he realize that this was a case of life or death?

Suddenly his ear caught the tinkle of a bicycle bell; a fresh light appeared coming up the avenue and then a bicycle swept up swiftly to the scene of the tragedy, and a small elderly man jumped down by the side of the body. Giving his machine to Mrs. Parton, he stooped over the dead man, felt the wrist, pushed back an eyelid, held a match to the eye and then rose. "This is a shocking affair, Mrs. Parton," said he. "The poor fellow is quite dead. You had better help me to carry him to the house. If you two take the feet I will take the shoulders."

Pembury watched them raise the body and stagger away with it up the avenue. He heard their shuffling steps die away and the door of the house shut. And still he listened. From far away in the meadows came, at intervals, the baying of the hounds. Other sounds there was none. Presently the doctor would come back for his bicycle, but, for the moment, the coast was clear. Pembury rose stiffly. His hands had stuck to the tree where they had pressed against it, and they were still sticky and damp. Quickly he let himself down to the ground, listened again for a moment, and then, making a small circuit to avoid the lamplight, softly crossed the avenue and stole away across the Thorpe meadows.

The night was intensely dark, and not a soul was stirring in the meadows. He strode forward quickly, peering into the darkness and stopping now and again to listen; but no sound came to his ears, save the now faint baying of the distant hounds. Not far from his house, he remembered, was a deep ditch spanned by a wooden bridge, and towards this he now made his way; for he knew that his appearance was such as to convict him at a glance. Arrived at the ditch, he stooped to wash his hands and wrists; and, as he bent forward, the knife fell from his breast-pocket into the shallow water at the margin. He groped for it, and, having found it, drove it deep into the mud as far out as he could reach. Then he wiped his hands on some water-weed, crossed the bridge and started homewards.

He approached his house from the rear, satisfied himself that his housekeeper was in the kitchen, and, letting himself in very quietly with his key, went quickly up to his bedroom. Here he washed thoroughly—in the bath, so that he could get rid of the discoloured water—changed his clothes and packed those that he took off in a portmanteau.

By the time he had done this the gong sounded for supper. As he took his seat at the table, spruce and fresh in appearance, quietly cheerful in manner, he addressed his housekeeper. "I wasn't able to finish my business in London," he said. "I shall have to go up again tomorrow."

"Shall you come home the same day?" asked the housekeeper.

"Perhaps," was the reply, "and perhaps not. It will depend on circumstances."

He did not say what the circumstances might be, nor did the housekeeper ask. Mr. Pembury was not addicted to confidences. He was an eminently discreet man: and discreet men say little.

2. RIVAL SLEUTH-HOUNDS

Related by Christopher Jervis, M.D.

The half-hour that follows breakfast, when the fire has, so to speak, got into its stride, and the morning pipe throws up its clouds of incense, is, perhaps, the most agreeable in the whole day. Especially so when a sombre sky, brooding over the town, hints at streets pervaded by the chilly morning air, and hoots from protesting tugs upon the river tell of lingering mists, the legacy of the lately-vanished night.

The autumn morning was raw: the fire burned jovially. I thrust my slippered feet towards the blaze and meditated, on nothing in particular, with cat-like enjoyment. Presently a disapproving grunt from Thorndyke attracted my attention, and I looked round lazily. He was extracting, with a pair of office shears, the readable portions of the morning paper, and had paused with a small cutting between his finger and thumb. "Bloodhounds again," said he. "We shall be hearing presently of the revival of the ordeal by fire."

"And a deuced comfortable ordeal, too, on a morning like this," I said, stroking my legs ecstatically. "What is the case?"

He was about to reply when a sharp rat-tat from the little brass knocker announced a disturber of our peace. Thorndyke stepped over to the door and admitted a police inspector in uniform, and I stood up, and, presenting my dorsal aspect to the fire, prepared to combine bodily comfort with attention to business.

"I believe I am speaking to Dr. Thorndyke," said the officer, and, as Thorndyke nodded, he went on: "My name, sir, is Fox, Inspector Fox of the Baysford Police. Perhaps you've seen the morning paper?"

Thorndyke held up the cutting, and, placing a chair by the fire, asked the inspector if he had breakfasted.

"Thank you, sir, I have," replied Inspector Fox. "I came up to town by the late train last night so as to be here early, and stayed at an hotel. You see, from the paper, that we have had to arrest one of our own men. That's rather awkward, you know, sir."

"Very," agreed Thorndyke.

"Yes; it's bad for the force and bad for the public too. But we had to do it. There was no way out that we could see. Still, we should like the accused to have every chance, both for our sake and his own, so the chief constable thought he'd like to have your opinion on the case, and he thought that, perhaps, you might be willing to act for the defence."

"Let us have the particulars," said Thorndyke, taking a writing-pad from a drawer and dropping into his armchair. "Begin at the beginning," he added, "and tell us all you know."

"Well," said the inspector, after a preliminary cough, "to begin

with the murdered man: his name is Pratt. He was a retired prison
warder, and was employed as steward by General O'Gorman, who
is a retired prison governor—you may have heard of him in connection with his pack of bloodhounds. Well, Pratt came down
from London yesterday evening by a train arriving at Baysford at
six-thirty. He was seen by the guard, the ticket collector and the
outside porter. The porter saw him leave the station at six-thirty-
seven. General O'Gorman's house is about half-a-mile from the
station. At five minutes to seven the general and a gentleman named
Hanford and the general's housekeeper, a Mrs. Parton, found Pratt
lying dead in the avenue that leads up to the house. He had apparently been stabbed, for there was a lot of blood about, and a knife—
a Norwegian knife—was lying on the ground near the body. Mrs.
Parton had thought she heard some one in the avenue calling out
for help, and, as Pratt was just due, she came out with a lantern. She
met the general and Mr. Hanford, and all three seem to have caught
sight of the body at the same moment. Mr. Hanford cycled down to
us, at once, with the news; we sent for a doctor, and I went back
with Mr. Hanford and took a sergeant with me. We arrived at
twelve minutes past seven, and then the general, who had galloped
his horse over the meadows each side of the avenue without having
seen anybody, fetched out his bloodhounds and led them up to the
knife. All three hounds took up the scent at once—I held the leash
of one of them—and they took us across the meadows without a
pause or a falter, over stiles and fences, along a lane, out into the
town, and then, one after the other, they crossed the road in a bee-
line to the police station, bolted in at the door, which stood open,
and made straight for the desk, where a supernumerary officer,
named Ellis, was writing. They made a rare to-do, struggling to
get at him, and it was as much as we could manage to hold them
back. As for Ellis, he turned as pale as a ghost."

"Was any one else in the room?" asked Thorndyke.

"Oh, yes. There were two constables and a messenger. We led
the hounds up to them, but the brutes wouldn't take any notice of
them. They wanted Ellis."

"And what did you do?"

"Why, we arrested Ellis, of course. Couldn't do anything else—especially with the general there."

"What had the general to do with it?" asked Thorndyke.

"He's a J.P. and a late governor of Dartmoor, and it was his hounds that had run the man down. But we must have arrested Ellis in any case."

"Is there anything against the accused man?"

"Yes, there is. He and Pratt were on distinctly unfriendly terms. They were old comrades, for Ellis was in the Civil Guard at Portland when Pratt was warder there—he was pensioned off from the service because he got his left forefinger chopped off—but lately they had had some unpleasantness about a woman, a parlourmaid of the general's. It seems that Ellis, who is a married man, paid the girl too much attention—or Pratt thought he did—and Pratt warned Ellis off the premises. Since then they had not been on speaking terms."

"And what sort of a man is Ellis?"

"A remarkably decent fellow he always seemed; quiet, steady, good-natured; I should have said he wouldn't have hurt a fly. We all liked him—better than we liked Pratt, in fact; poor Pratt was what you'd call an old soldier—sly, you know, sir—and a bit of a sneak."

"You searched and examined Ellis, of course?"

"Yes. There was nothing suspicious about him except that he had two purses. But he says he picked up one of them—a small, pigskin pouch—on the footpath of the Thorpe road yesterday afternoon; and there's no reason to disbelieve him. At any rate, the purse was not Pratt's."

Thorndyke made a note on his pad, and then asked: "There were no blood-stains or marks on his clothing?"

"No. His clothing was not marked or disarranged in any way."

"Any cuts, scratches, or bruises on his person?"

"None whatever," replied the inspector.

"At what time did you arrest Ellis?"

"Half-past seven exactly."

"Have you ascertained what his movements were? Had he been near the scene of the murder?"

"Yes; he had been to Thorpe and would pass the gates of the avenue on his way back. And he was later than usual in returning, though not later than he has often been before."

"And now, as to the murdered man; has the body been examined?"

"Yes; I had Dr. Hills's report before I left. There were no less than seven deep knife-wounds, all on the left side of the back. There was a great deal of blood on the ground, and Dr. Hills thinks Pratt must have bled to death in a minute or two."

"Do the wounds correspond with the knife that was found?"

"I asked the doctor that, and he said 'Yes,' though he wasn't going to swear to any particular knife. However, that point isn't of much importance. The knife was covered with blood, and it was found close to the body."

"What has been done with it, by the way?" asked Thorndyke.

"The sergeant who was with me picked it up and rolled it in his handkerchief to carry in his pocket. I took it from him, just as it was, and locked it in a dispatch-box."

"Has the knife been recognized as Ellis's property?"

"No, sir, it has not."

"Were there any recognizable footprints or marks of a struggle?" Thorndyke asked.

The inspector grinned sheepishly. "I haven't examined the spot, of course, sir," said he, "but, after the general's horse and the bloodhounds and the general on foot and me and the gardener and the sergeant and Mr. Hanford had been over it twice, going and returning, why, you see, sir—"

"Exactly, exactly," said Thorndyke. "Well, inspector, I shall be pleased to act for the defence; it seems to me that the case against Ellis is in some respects rather inconclusive."

The inspector was frankly amazed. "It certainly hadn't struck me in that light, sir," he said.

"No? Well, that is my view; and I think the best plan will be for me to come down with you and investigate matters on the spot."

The inspector assented cheerfully, and, when we had provided him with a newspaper, we withdrew to the laboratory to consult time-tables and prepare for the expedition.

"You are coming, I suppose, Jervis?" said Thorndyke.

"If I shall be of any use," I replied.

"Of course you will," said he. "Two heads are better than one, and, by the look of things, I should say that ours will be the only ones with any sense in them. We will take the research case, of course, and we may as well have a camera with us. I see there is a train from Charing Cross in twenty minutes."

For the first half-hour of the journey Thorndyke sat in his corner, alternately conning over his notes and gazing with thoughtful eyes out of the window. I could see that the case pleased him, and was careful not to break in upon his train of thought. Presently, however, he put away his notes and began to fill his pipe with a more companionable air, and then the inspector, who had been wriggling with impatience, opened fire.

"So you think, sir, that you see a way out for Ellis?"

"I think there is a case for the defence," replied Thorndyke. "In fact, I call the evidence against him rather flimsy."

The inspector gasped. "But the knife, sir? What about the knife?"

"Well," said Thorndyke, "what about the knife? Whose knife was it? You don't know. It was covered with blood. Whose blood? You don't know. Let us assume, for the sake of argument, that it was the murderer's knife. Then the blood on it was Pratt's blood. But if it was Pratt's blood, when the hounds had smelt it they should have led you to Pratt's body, for blood gives a very strong scent. But they did not. They ignored the body. The inference seems to be that the blood on the knife was not Pratt's blood."

The inspector took off his cap and gently scratched the back of his head. "You're perfectly right, sir," he said. "I'd never thought of that. None of us had."

"Then," pursued Thorndyke, "let us assume that the knife was Pratt's. If so, it would seem to have been used in self-defence. But this was a Norwegian knife, a clumsy tool—not a weapon at all— which takes an appreciable time to open and requires the use of two free hands. Now, had Pratt both hands free? Certainly not after the attack had commenced. There were seven wounds, all on the left side of the back; which indicates that he held the murderer locked in his arms and that the murderer's arms were around him. Also, incidentally, that the murderer is right-handed. But, still, let us assume that the knife was Pratt's. Then the blood on it was that of the murderer. Then the murderer must have been wounded. But Ellis was not wounded. Then Ellis is not the murderer. The knife doesn't help us at all."

The inspector puffed out his cheeks and blew softly. "This is getting out of my depth," he said. "Still, sir, you can't get over the bloodhounds. They tell us distinctly that the knife is Ellis's knife and I don't see any answer to that."

"There is no answer because there has been no statement. The bloodhounds have told you nothing. You have drawn certain inferences from their actions, but those inferences may be totally wrong and they are certainly not evidence."

"You don't seem to have much opinion of bloodhounds," the inspector remarked.

"As agents for the detection of crime," replied Thorndyke, "I regard them as useless. You cannot put a bloodhound in the witness-box. You can get no intelligible statement from it. If it possesses any knowledge, it has no means of communicating it. The fact is," he continued, "that the entire system of using bloodhounds for criminal detection is based on a fallacy. In the American plantations these animals were used with great success for tracking runaway slaves. But the slave was a known individual. All that was required was to ascertain his whereabouts. That is not the problem that is presented in the detection of a crime. The detective is not concerned in establishing the whereabouts of a known individual, but in discovering the identity of an unknown individual. And for this purpose bloodhounds are useless. They may discover such identity, but they cannot communicate their knowledge. If the criminal is unknown they cannot identify him: if he is known, the police have no need of the bloodhounds.

"To return to our present case," Thorndyke resumed, after a

pause; "we have employed certain agents—the hounds—with whom we are not *en rapport*, as the spiritualists would say; and we have no 'medium.' The hound possesses a special sense—the olfactory— which in man is quite rudimentary. He thinks, so to speak, in terms of smell, and his thoughts are untranslatable to beings in whom the sense of smell is undeveloped. We have presented to the hound a knife, and he discovers in it certain odorous properties; he discovers similar or related odorous properties in a tract of land and a human individual—Ellis. We cannot verify his discoveries or ascertain their nature. What remains? All that we can say is that there appears to exist some odorous relation between the knife and the man Ellis. But until we can ascertain the nature of that relation, we cannot estimate its evidential value or bearing. All the other 'evidence' is the product of your imagination and that of the general. There is, at present, no case against Ellis."

"He must have been pretty close to the place when the murder happened," said the inspector.

"So, probably, were many other people," answered Thorndyke; "but had he time to wash and change? Because he would have needed it."

"I suppose he would," the inspector agreed dubiously.

"Undoubtedly. There were seven wounds which would have taken some time to inflict. Now we can't suppose that Pratt stood passively while the other man stabbed him—indeed, as I have said, the position of the wounds shows that he did not. There was a struggle. The two men were locked together. One of the murderer's hands was against Pratt's back; probably both hands were, one clasping and the other stabbing. There must have been blood on one hand and probably on both. But you say there was no blood on Ellis, and there doesn't seem to have been time or opportunity for him to wash."

"Well, it's a mysterious affair," said the inspector; "but I don't see how you are going to get over the bloodhounds."

Thorndyke shrugged his shoulders impatiently. "The blood-hounds are an obsession," he said. "The whole problem really centres around the knife. The questions are, Whose knife was it?

and what was the connection between it and Ellis? There is a problem, Jervis," he continued, turning to me, "that I submit for your consideration. Some of the possible solutions are exceedingly curious."

As we set out from Baysford station, Thorndyke looked at his watch and noted the time. "You will take us the way that Pratt went," he said.

"As to that," said the inspector, "he may have gone by the road or by the footpath; but there's very little difference in the distance."

Turning away from Baysford, we walked along the road westward, towards the village of Thorpe, and presently passed on our right a stile at the entrance to a footpath.

"That path," said the inspector, "crosses the avenue about half-way up. But we'd better keep on the road." A quarter of a mile further on we came to a pair of rusty iron gates one of which stood open, and, entering, we found ourselves in a broad drive bordered by two rows of trees, between the trunks of which a long stretch of pasture meadows could be seen on either hand. It was a fine avenue, and, late in the year as it was, the yellowing foliage clustered thickly overhead.

When we had walked about a hundred and fifty yards from the gates, the inspector halted.

"This is the place," he said; and Thorndyke again noted the time.

"Nine minutes exactly," said he. "Then Pratt arrived here about fourteen minutes to seven, and his body was found at five minutes to seven—nine minutes after his arrival. The murderer couldn't have been far away then."

"No, it was a pretty fresh scent," replied the inspector. "You'd like to see the body first, I think you said, sir?"

"Yes; and the knife, if you please."

"I shall have to send down to the station for that. It's locked up in the office."

He entered the house, and, having dispatched a messenger to the police station, came out and conducted us to the outbuilding where the corpse had been deposited. Thorndyke made a rapid examination of the wounds and the holes in the clothing, neither of which presented anything particularly suggestive. The weapon used had evidently been a thick-backed, single-edged knife similar to the one described, and the discolouration around the wounds indicated that the weapon had a definite shoulder like that of a Norwegian knife, and that it had been driven in with savage violence.

"Do you find anything that throws any light on the case?" the inspector asked, when the examination was concluded.

"That is impossible to say until we have seen the knife," replied Thorndyke; "but while we are waiting for it, we may as well go and look at the scene of the tragedy. These are Pratt's boots, I think?" He lifted a pair of stout laced boots from the table and turned them up to inspect the soles.

"Yes, those are his boots," replied Fox, "and pretty easy they'd have been to track, if the case had been the other way about. Those Blakey's protectors are as good as a trademark."

"We'll take them, at any rate," said Thorndyke; and, the inspector having taken the boots from him, we went out and retraced our steps down the avenue.

The place where the murder had occurred was easily identified by a large dark stain on the gravel at one side of the drive, half-way between two trees—an ancient pollard hornbeam and an elm. Next to the elm was a pollard oak with a squat, warty bole about seven feet high, and three enormous limbs, of which one slanted half-way across the avenue; and between these two trees the ground was covered with the tracks of men and hounds superimposed upon the hoof-prints of a horse.

"Where was the knife found?" Thorndyke asked.

The inspector indicated a spot near the middle of the drive, almost opposite the hornbeam, and Thorndyke, picking up a large stone, laid it on the spot. Then he surveyed the scene thoughtfully, looking up and down the drive and at the trees that bordered it, and, finally, walked slowly to the space between the elm and the oak, scanning the ground as he went. "There is no dearth of footprints," he remarked grimly, as he looked down at the trampled earth.

"No, but the question is, whose are they?" said the inspector.

"Yes, that is the question," agreed Thorndyke; "and we will begin the solution by identifying those of Pratt."

"I don't see how that will help us," said the inspector. "We know he was here."

Thorndyke looked at him in surprise, and I must confess that the foolish remark astonished me too, accustomed as I was to the quick-witted officers from Scotland Yard.

"The hue and cry procession," remarked Thorndyke, "seems to have passed out between the elm and the oak; elsewhere the ground seems pretty clear." He walked round the elm, still looking earnestly at the ground, and presently continued: "Now here, in the soft earth bordering the turf, are the prints of a pair of smallish feet wearing pointed boots; a rather short man, evidently, by the size of foot and length of stride, and he doesn't seem to have belonged to the procession. But I don't see any of Pratt's; he doesn't seem to have come off the hard gravel." He continued to walk slowly towards the hornbeam with his eyes fixed on the ground. Suddenly he halted and stooped with an eager look at the earth; and, as Fox and I approached, he stood up and pointed. "Pratt's footprints—faint and fragmentary, but unmistakable. And now, inspector, you see their importance. They furnish the time factor in respect of the other footprints. Look at this one and then look at that." He pointed from one to another of the faint impressions of the dead man's foot.

"You mean that there are signs of a struggle?" said Fox.

"I mean more than that," replied Thorndyke. "Here is one of Pratt's footprints treading into the print of a small, pointed foot; and there at the edge of the gravel is another of Pratt's nearly obliterated by the tread of a pointed foot. Obviously the first pointed footprint was made before Pratt's, and the second one after his; and the necessary inference is that the owner of the pointed foot was here at the same time as Pratt."

"Then he must have been the murderer!" exclaimed Fox.

"Presumably," answered Thorndyke; "but let us see whither he went. You notice, in the first place, that the man stood close to this tree"—he indicated the hornbeam—"and that he went towards the elm. Let us follow him. He passes the elm, you see, and you will observe that these tracks form a regular series leading from the hornbeam and not mixed up with the marks of the struggle. They were, therefore, probably made after the murder had been perpetrated. You will also notice that they pass along the backs of the trees—outside the avenue, that is; what does that suggest to you?"

"It suggests to me," I said, when the inspector had shaken his head hopelessly, "that there was possibly some one in the avenue when the man was stealing off."

"Precisely," said Thorndyke. "The body was found not more than nine minutes after Pratt arrived here. But the murder must have taken some time. Then the housekeeper thought she heard some one calling and came out with a lantern, and, at the same time, the general and Mr. Hanford came up the drive. The suggestion is that the man sneaked along outside the trees to avoid being seen. However, let us follow the tracks. They pass the elm and they pass on behind the next tree; but wait! There is something odd here." He passed behind the great pollard oak and looked down at the soft earth by its roots. "Here is a pair of impressions much deeper than the rest, and they are not a part of the track since their toes point towards the tree. What do you make of that?" Without waiting for an answer he began closely to scan the bole of the tree and especially a large, warty protuberance about three feet from the ground. On the bark above this was a vertical mark, as if something had scraped down the tree, and from the wart itself a dead twig had been newly broken off and lay upon the ground. Pointing to these marks Thorndyke set his foot on the protuberance, and, springing up, brought his eye above the level of the crown, whence the great boughs branched off.

"Ah!" he exclaimed. "Here is something much more definite." With the aid of another projection, he scrambled up into the crown of the tree, and, having glanced quickly round, beckoned to us. I stepped up on the projecting lump and, as my eyes rose above the crown, I perceived the brown, shiny impression of a hand on the edge. Climbing into the crown, I was quickly followed by the inspector, and we both stood up by Thorndyke between the three boughs. From where we stood we looked on the upper side of the great limb that swept out across the avenue; and there on its lichen-covered surface, we saw the imprints in reddish-brown of a pair of open hands.

"You notice," said Thorndyke, leaning out upon the bough, "that he is a short man; I cannot conveniently place my hands so low. You also note that he has both forefingers intact, and so is certainly not Ellis."

"If you mean to say, sir, that these marks were made by the murderer," said Fox, "I say it's impossible. Why, that would mean that he was here looking down at us when we were searching for him with the hounds. The presence of the hounds proves that this man could not have been the murderer."

"On the contrary," said Thorndyke, "the presence of this man with bloody hands confirms the other evidence, which all indicates that the hounds were never on the murderer's trail at all. Come now, inspector, I put it to you: Here is a murdered man; the murderer has almost certainly blood upon his hands; and here is a man with bloody hands, lurking in a tree within a few feet of the corpse and within a few minutes of its discovery (as is shown by the foot-prints); what are the reasonable probabilities?"

"But you are forgetting the bloodhounds, sir, and the murderer's knife," urged the inspector.

"Tut, tut, man!" exclaimed Thorndyke; "those bloodhounds are a positive obsession. But I see a sergeant coming up the drive, with the knife, I hope. Perhaps that will solve the riddle for us."

The sergeant, who carried a small dispatch-box, halted opposite the tree in some surprise while we descended, when he came forward with a military salute and handed the box to the inspector, who forthwith unlocked it, and, opening the lid, displayed an object wrapped in a pocket-handkerchief.

"There is the knife, sir," said he, "just as I received it. The handkerchief is the sergeant's."

Thorndyke unrolled the handkerchief and took from it a large-sized Norwegian knife, which he looked at critically and then handed to me. While I was inspecting the blade, he shook out the handkerchief and, having looked it over on both sides, turned to the sergeant.

"At what time did you pick up this knife?" he asked.

"About seven-fifteen, sir; directly after the hounds had started. I was careful to pick it up by the ring, and I wrapped it in the handkerchief at once."

"Seven-fifteen," said Thorndyke. "Less than half-an-hour after the murder. That is very singular. Do you observe the state of this handkerchief? There is not a mark on it. Not a trace of any bloodstain; which proves that when the knife was picked up, the blood on it was already dry. But things dry slowly, if they dry at all, in the saturated air of an autumn evening. The appearances seem to suggest that the blood on the knife was dry when it was thrown down. By the way, sergeant, what do you scent your handkerchief with?"

"Scent, sir!" exclaimed the astonished officer in indignant accents; "me scent my handkerchief! No, sir, certainly not. Never used scent in my life, sir."

Thorndyke held out the handkerchief, and the sergeant sniffed at it incredulously. "It certainly does seem to smell of scent," he admitted, "but it must be the knife." The same idea having occurred to me, I applied the handle of the knife to my nose and instantly detected the sickly-sweet odour of musk.

"The question is," said the inspector, when the two articles had been tested by us all, "was it the knife that scented the handkerchief or the handkerchief that scented the knife?"

"You heard what the sergeant said," replied Thorndyke. "There was no scent on the handkerchief when the knife was wrapped in it. Do you know, inspector, this scent seems to me to offer a very curious suggestion. Consider the facts of the case: the distinct trail leading straight to Ellis, who is, nevertheless, found to be without a scratch or a spot of blood; the inconsistencies in the case that I pointed out in the train, and now this knife, apparently dropped with dried blood on it and scented with musk. To me it suggests a carefully-planned, coolly-premeditated crime. The murderer knew about the general's bloodhounds and made use of them as a blind. He planted this knife, smeared with blood and tainted with musk, to furnish a scent. No doubt some object, also scented with musk, would be drawn over the ground to give the trail. It is only a suggestion, of course, but it is worth considering."

"But, sir," the inspector objected eagerly, "if the murderer had handled the knife, it would have scented him too."

"Exactly; so, as we are assuming that the man is not a fool, we may assume that he did not handle it. He will have left it here in readiness, hidden in some place whence he could knock it down, say, with a stick, without touching it."

"Perhaps in this very tree, sir," suggested the sergeant, pointing to the oak.

"No," said Thorndyke, "he would hardly have hidden in the tree where the knife had been. The hounds might have scented the place instead of following the trail at once. The most likely hiding-place for the knife is the one nearest the spot," and looking round, continued: "You see, that hornbeam is much the nearest, and its flat crown would be very convenient for the purpose—easily reached even by a short man, as he appears to be. Let us see if there are any traces of it. Perhaps you will give me a 'back up,' sergeant, as we haven't a ladder."

The sergeant assented with a faint grin, and stooping beside the tree in an attitude suggesting the game of leapfrog, placed his hands firmly on his knees. Grasping a stout branch, Thorndyke swung himself up on the sergeant's broad back, whence he looked down into the crown of the tree. Then, parting the branches, he stepped onto the ledge and disappeared into the central hollow.

When he re-appeared he held in his hands two very singular objects: a pair of iron crucible-tongs and an artist's brush-case of black-japanned tin. The former article he handed down to me, but the brush-case he held carefully by its wire handle as he dropped to the ground.

"The significance of these things is, I think, obvious," he said. "The tongs were used to handle the knife with and the case to carry it in, so that it should not scent his clothes or bag. It was very carefully planned."

"If that is so," said the inspector, "the inside of the case ought to smell of musk."

"No doubt,' said Thorndyke; "but before we open it, there is a rather important matter to be attended to. Will you give me the Vitogen powder, Jervis?"

I opened the canvas-covered "research case" and took from it an object like a diminutive pepper-caster—an iodoform dredger in fact—and handed it to him. Grasping the brush-case by its wire handle, he sprinkled the pale yellow powder from the dredger freely all round the pulloff lid, tapping the top with his knuckles to make the fine particles spread. Then he blew off the superfluous powder, and the two police officers gave a simultaneous gasp of joy; for now, on the black background, there stood out plainly a number of finger-prints, so clear and distinct that the ridge-pattern could be made out with perfect ease.

"These will probably be his right hand," said Thorndyke. "Now for the left." He treated the body of the case in the same way, and, when he had blown off the powder, the entire surface was spotted with yellow, oval impressions. "Now, Jervis," said he, "if you will put on a glove and pull off the lid, we can test the inside."

There was no difficulty in getting the lid off, for the shoulder of the case had been smeared with vaseline—apparently to produce an airtight joint—and, as it separated with a hollow sound, a faint, musky odour exhaled from its interior.

"The remainder of the inquiry," said Thorndyke, when I pushed the lid on again, "will be best conducted at the police station, where, also, we can photograph these finger-prints."

"The shortest way will be across the meadows," said Fox; "the way the hounds went."

By this route we accordingly travelled, Thorndyke carrying the brush-case tenderly by its handle.

"I don't quite see where Ellis comes in in this job," said the inspector, as we walked along, "if the fellow had a grudge against Pratt. They weren't chums."

"I think I do," said Thorndyke. "You say that both men were prison officers at Portland at the same time. Now doesn't it seem

likely that this is the work of some old convict who had been identified—and perhaps blackmailed—by Pratt, and possibly by Ellis too?
That is where the value of the finger-prints comes in. If he is an old
'lag' his prints will be at Scotland Yard. Otherwise they are not of
much value as a clue."

"That's true, sir," said the inspector. "I suppose you want to see
Ellis."

"I want to see that purse that you spoke of, first," replied Thorndyke. "That is probably the other end of the clue."

As soon as we arrived at the station, the inspector unlocked a safe
and brought out a parcel. "These are Ellis's things," said he, as he
unfastened it, "and that is the purse."

He handed Thorndyke a small pigskin pouch, which my colleague opened, and having smelt the inside, passed to me. The odour
of musk was plainly perceptible, especially in the small compartment at the back.

"It has probably tainted the other contents of the parcel," said
Thorndyke, sniffing at each article in turn, "but my sense of smell
is not keen enough to detect any scent. They all seem odourless to
me, whereas the purse smells quite distinctly. Shall we have Ellis in
now?"

The sergeant took a key from a locked drawer and departed for
the cells, whence he presently re-appeared accompanied by the
prisoner—a stout, burly man, in the last stage of dejection.

"Come, cheer up, Ellis," said the inspector. "Here's Dr. Thorndyke come down to help us and he wants to ask you one or two
questions."

Ellis looked piteously at Thorndyke, and exclaimed: "I know
nothing whatever about this affair, sir, I swear to God I don't."

"I never supposed you did," said Thorndyke. "But there are one
or two things that I want you to tell me. To begin with, that purse:
where did you find it?"

"On the Thorpe road, sir. It was lying in the middle of the footway."

"Had any one else passed the spot lately? Did you meet or pass
any one?"

"Yes, sir, I met a labourer about a minute before I saw the purse. I can't imagine why he didn't see it."

"Probably because it wasn't there," said Thorndyke. "Is there a hedge there?"

"Yes, sir; a hedge on a low bank."

"Ha! Well, now, tell me: is there any one about here whom you knew when you and Pratt were together at Portland? Any old lag—to put it bluntly—whom you and Pratt have been putting the screw on."

"No, sir, I swear there isn't. But I wouldn't answer for Pratt. He had a rare memory for faces."

Thorndyke reflected. "Were there any escapes from Portland in your time?" he asked.

"Only one—a man named Dobbs. He made off to the sea in a sudden fog and he was supposed to be drowned. His clothes washed up on the Bill, but not his body. At any rate, he was never heard of again."

"Thank you, Ellis. Do you mind my taking your finger-prints?"

"Certainly not, sir," was the almost eager reply; and the office inking-pad being requisitioned, a rough set of finger-prints was produced; and when Thorndyke had compared them with those on the brush-case and found no resemblance, Ellis returned to his cell in quite buoyant spirits.

Having made several photographs of the strange finger-prints, we returned to town that evening, taking the negatives with us; and while we waited for our train, Thorndyke gave a few parting injunctions to the inspector. "Remember," he said, "that the man must have washed his hands before he could appear in public. Search the banks of every pond, ditch and stream in the neighbourhood for footprints like those in the avenue; and, if you find any, search the bottom of the water thoroughly, for he is quite likely to have dropped the knife into the mud."

The photographs, which we handed in at Scotland Yard that same night, enabled the experts to identify the finger-prints as those of Francis Dobbs, an escaped convict. The two photographs—profile and full-face—which were attached to his record, were sent down to Baysford with a description of the man, and were, in due course, identified with a somewhat mysterious individual, who passed by the name of Rufus Pembury and who had lived in the neighbourhood as a private gentleman for some two years. But Rufus Pembury was not to be found either at his genteel house or elsewhere. All that was known was that, on the day after the murder, he had converted his entire "personalty" into "bearer securities," and then vanished from mortal ken. Nor has he ever been heard of to this day.

"And, between ourselves," said Thorndyke, when we were discussing the case some time after, "he deserved to escape. It was clearly a case of blackmail, and to kill a blackmailer—when you have no other defence against him—is hardly murder. As to Ellis, he could never have been convicted, and Dobbs, or Pembury, must have known it. But he would have been committed to the Assizes, and that would have given time for all traces to disappear. No, Dobbs was a man of courage, ingenuity and resource; and, above all, he knocked the bottom out of the great bloodhound superstition."

MODERN TALES

The Nine-Mile Walk

BY HARRY KEMELMAN

I had made an ass of myself in a speech I had given at the Good Government Association dinner, and Nicky Welt had cornered me at breakfast at the *Blue Moon*, where we both ate occasionally, for the pleasure of rubbing it in. I had made the mistake of departing from my prepared speech to criticize a statement my predecessor in the office of District Attorney had made to the press. I had drawn a number of inferences from his statement and had thus left myself open to a rebuttal which he had promptly made and which had the effect of making me appear intellectually dishonest. I was new to this political game, having but a few months before left the Law School faculty to become the Reform Party candidate for District Attorney. I said as much in extenuation, but Nicholas Welt, who could never drop his pedagogical manner (he was Snowdon Professor of English Language and Literature), replied in much the same tone that he would dismiss a request from a sophomore for an extension on a term paper, "That's no excuse."

Although he is only two or three years older than I, in his late forties, he always treats me like a schoolmaster hectoring a stupid pupil. And I, perhaps because he looks so much older with his white hair and lined, gnomelike face, suffer it.

"They were perfectly logical inferences," I pleaded.

"My dear boy," he purred, "although human intercourse is well-nigh impossible without inference, most inferences are usually wrong. The percentage of error is particularly high in the legal profession where the intention is not to discover what the speaker wishes to convey, but rather what he wishes to conceal."

I picked up my check and eased out from behind the table.

"I suppose you are referring to cross-examination of witnesses in court. Well, there's always an opposing counsel who will object if the inference is illogical."

"Who said anything about logic?" he retorted. "An inference can be logical and still not be true."

He followed me down the aisle to the cashier's booth. I paid my check and waited impatiently while he searched in an old-fashioned change purse, fishing out coins one by one and placing them on the counter beside his check, only to discover that the total was insufficient. He slid them back into his purse and with a tiny sigh extracted a bill from another compartment of the purse and handed it to the cashier.

"Give me any sentence of ten or twelve words," he said, "and I'll build you a logical chain of inferences that you never dreamed of when you framed the sentence."

Other customers were coming in, and since the space in front of the cashier's booth was small, I decided to wait outside until Nicky completed his transaction with the cashier. I remember being mildly amused at the idea that he probably thought I was still at his elbow and was going right ahead with his discourse.

When he joined me on the sidewalk I said, "A nine-mile walk is no joke, especially in the rain."

"No, I shouldn't think it would be," he agreed absently. Then he stopped in his stride and looked at me sharply. "What the devil are you talking about?"

"It's a sentence and it has eleven words," I insisted. And I repeated the sentence, ticking off the words on my fingers.

"What about it?"

"You said that given a sentence of ten or twelve words—"

"Oh, yes." He looked at me suspiciously. "Where did you get it?"

"It just popped into my head. Come on now, build your inferences."

"You're serious about this?" he asked, his little blue eyes glittering with amusement. "You really want me to?"

It was just like him to issue a challenge and then to appear amused when I accepted it. And it made me angry.

"Put up or shut up," I said.

"All right," he said mildly. "No need to be huffy. I'll play. Hm-m, let me see, how did the sentence go? 'A nine-mile walk is no joke, especially in the rain.' Not much to go on there."

"It's more than ten words," I rejoined.

"Very well." His voice became crisp as he mentally squared off to the problem. "First inference: the speaker is aggrieved."

"I'll grant that," I said, "although it hardly seems to be an inference. It's really implicit in the statement."

He nodded impatiently. "Next inference: the rain was unforeseen, otherwise he would have said, 'A nine-mile walk in the rain is no joke,' instead of using the 'especially' phrase as an afterthought."

"I'll allow that," I said, "although it's pretty obvious."

"First inferences should be obvious," said Nicky tartly.

I let it go at that. He seemed to be floundering and I didn't want to rub it in.

"Next inference: the speaker is not an athlete or an outdoors man."

"You'll have to explain that one," I said.

"It's the 'especially' phrase again," he said. "The speaker does not say that a nine-mile walk in the rain is no joke, but merely the walk —just the distance, mind you—is no joke. Now, nine miles is not such a terribly long distance. You walk more than half that in eighteen holes of golf—and golf is an old man's game," he added slyly. I play golf.

"Well, that would be all right under ordinary circumstances," I said, "but there are other possibilities. The speaker might be a soldier in the jungle, in which case nine miles would be a pretty good hike, rain or no rain."

"Yes," and Nicky was sarcastic, "and the speaker might be one-legged. For that matter, the speaker might be a graduate student writing a Ph.D. on humor and starting by listing all the things that are not funny. See here, I'll have to make a couple of assumptions before I continue."

"How do you mean?" I asked, suspiciously.

"Remember, I'm taking this sentence *in vacuo*, as it were. I don't know who said it or what the occasion was. Normally a sentence belongs in the framework of a situation."

"I see. What assumptions do you want to make?"

"For one thing, I want to assume that the intention was not frivolous, that the speaker is referring to a walk that was actually taken, and that the purpose of the walk was not to win a bet or something of that sort."

"That seems reasonable enough," I said.

"And I also want to assume that the locale of the walk is here."

"You mean here in Fairfield?"

"Not necessarily. I mean in this general section of the country."

"Fair enough."

"Then, if you grant those assumptions, you'll have to accept my last inference that the speaker is no athlete or outdoors man."

"Well, all right, go on."

"Then my next inference is that the walk was taken very late at night or very early in the morning—say, between midnight and five or six in the morning."

"How do you figure that one?" I asked.

"Consider the distance, nine miles. We're in a fairly well-populated section. Take any road and you'll find a community of some sort in less than nine miles. Hadley is five miles away, Hadley Falls is seven and a half, Goreton is eleven, but East Goreton is only eight and you strike East Goreton before you come to Goreton. There is local train service along the Goreton road and bus service along the others. All the highways are pretty well traveled. Would anyone have to walk nine miles in a rain unless it were late at night when no busses or trains were running and when the few automobiles that were out would hesitate to pick up a stranger on the highway?"

"He might not have wanted to be seen," I suggested.

Nicky smiled pityingly. "You think he would be less noticeable trudging along the highway than he would be riding in a public conveyance where everyone is usually absorbed in his newspaper?"

"Well, I won't press the point," I said brusquely.

"Then try this one: he was walking toward a town rather than away from one."

I nodded. "It is more likely, I suppose. If he were in a town, he could probably arrange for some sort of transportation. Is that the basis for your inference?"

"Partly that," said Nicky, "but there is also an inference to be drawn from the distance. Remember, it's a *nine-mile* walk and nine is one of the exact numbers."

"I'm afraid I don't understand."

That exasperated schoolteacher-look appeared on Nicky's face again. "Suppose you say, 'I took a ten-mile walk' or 'a hundred-mile drive'; I would assume that you actually walked anywhere from eight to a dozen miles, or that you rode between ninety and a hundred and ten miles. In other words, *ten* and *hundred* are round numbers. You might have walked *exactly* ten miles or just as likely you might have walked *approximately* ten miles. But when you speak of walking *nine* miles, I have a right to assume that you have named an exact figure. Now, we are far more likely to know the distance of the city from a given point than we are to know the distance of a given point from the city. That is, ask anyone in the city how far out Farmer Brown lives, and if he knows him, he will say, 'Three or four miles.' But ask Farmer Brown how far he lives from the city and he will tell you, 'Three and six-tenths miles—measured it on my speedometer many a time.' "

"It's weak, Nicky," I said.

"But in conjunction with your own suggestion that he could have arranged transportation if he had been in a city—"

"Yes, that would do it," I said. "I'll pass it. Any more?"

"I've just begun to hit my stride," he boasted. "My next inference is that he was going to a definite destination and that he had to be there at a particular time. It was not a case of going off to get help because his car broke down or his wife was going to have a baby or somebody was trying to break into his house."

"Oh, come now," I said, "the car breaking down is really the most likely situation. He could have known the exact distance from having checked the mileage just as he was leaving the town."

Nicky shook his head. "Rather than walk nine miles in the rain, he would have curled up on the back seat and gone to sleep, or at least stayed by his car and tried to flag another motorist. Remember, it's nine miles. What would be the least it would take him to hike it?"

"Four hours," I offered.

He nodded. "Certainly no less, considering the rain. We've agreed that it happened very late at night or very early in the morning. Suppose he had his breakdown at one o'clock in the morning. It would be five o'clock before he would arrive. That's daybreak. You begin to see a lot of cars on the road. The busses start just a little later. In fact, the first busses hit Fairfield around 5:30. Besides, if he were going for help, he would not have to go all the way to town—only as far as the nearest telephone. No, he had a definite appointment, and it was in a town, and it was for some time before 5:30."

"Then why couldn't he have got there earlier and waited?" I asked. "He could have taken the last bus, arrived around one o'clock, and waited until his appointment. He walks nine miles in the rain instead, and you said he was no athlete."

We had arrived at the Municipal Building where my office is. Normally, any arguments begun at the *Blue Moon* ended at the entrance to the Municipal Building. But I was interested in Nicky's demonstration and I suggested that he come up for a few minutes.

When we were seated I said, "How about it, Nicky, why couldn't he have arrived early and waited?"

"He could have," Nicky retorted. "But since he did not, we must assume that he was either detained until after the last bus left, or that he had to wait where he was for a signal of some sort, perhaps a telephone call."

"Then according to you, he had an appointment some time between midnight and 5:30—"

"We can draw it much finer than that. Remember, it takes him four hours to walk the distance. The last bus stops at 12:30 A.M. If he doesn't take that, but starts at the same time, he won't arrive at his destination until 4:30. On the other hand, if he takes the first bus in the morning, he will arrive around 5:30. That would mean that his appointment was for some time between 4:30 and 5:30."

"You mean that if his appointment were earlier than 4:30, he would have taken the last night bus, and if it were later than 5:30, he would have taken the first morning bus?"

"Precisely. And another thing: if he were waiting for a signal or a phone call, it must have come not much later than one o'clock."

"Yes, I see that," I said. "If his appointment is around five o'clock and it takes him four hours to walk the distance, he'd have to start around one."

He nodded, silent and thoughtful. For some queer reason I could not explain, I did not feel like interrupting his thoughts. On the wall was a large map of the county and I walked over to it and began to study it.

"You're right, Nicky," I remarked over my shoulder, "there's no place as far as nine miles away from Fairfield that doesn't hit another town first. Fairfield is right in the middle of a bunch of smaller towns."

He joined me at the map. "It doesn't have to be Fairfield, you know," he said quietly. "It was probably one of the outlying towns he had to reach. Try Hadley."

"Why Hadley? What would anyone want in Hadley at five o'clock in the morning?"

"The Washington Flyer stops there to take on water about that time," he said quietly.

"That's right, too," I said. "I've heard that train many a night when I couldn't sleep. I'd hear it pulling in and then a minute or two later I'd hear the clock on the Methodist Church banging out five." I went back to my desk for a timetable. "The Flyer leaves Washington at 12:47 A.M. and gets into Boston at 8:00 A.M."

Nicky was still at the map measuring distances with a pencil.

"Exactly nine miles from Hadley is the Old Sumter Inn," he announced.

"Old Sumter Inn," I echoed. "But that upsets the whole theory. You can arrange for transportation there as easily as you can in a town."

He shook his head. "The cars are kept in an enclosure and you have to get an attendant to check you through the gate. The attendant would remember anyone taking out his car at a strange hour. It's a pretty conservative place. He could have waited in his room until he got a call from Washington about someone on the Flyer—maybe the number of the car and the berth. Then he could just slip out of the hotel and walk to Hadley."

I stared at him, hypnotized.

"It wouldn't be difficult to slip aboard while the train was taking on water, and then if he knew the car number and the berth—"

"Nicky," I said portentously, "as the reform District Attorney who campaigned on an economy program, I am going to waste the taxpayers' money and call Boston long distance. It's ridiculous, it's insane—but I'm going to do it!"

His little blue eyes glittered and he moistened his lips with the tip of his tongue.

"Go ahead," he said hoarsely.

I replaced the telephone in its cradle.

"Nicky," I said, "this is probably the most remarkable coincidence in the history of criminal investigation: *A man was found murdered in his berth on last night's 12:47 from Washington!* He'd been dead about three hours, which would make it exactly right for Hadley."

"I thought it was something like that," said Nicky. "But you're wrong about its being a coincidence. It can't be. Where did you get that sentence?"

"It was just a sentence. It simply popped into my head."

"It couldn't have! It's not the sort of sentence that pops into one's head. If you had taught composition as long as I have, you'd know that when you ask someone for a sentence of ten words or so, you get an ordinary statement such as 'I like milk'— with the other words made up by a modifying clause like, 'because it is good for my health.' The sentence you offered related to a *particular situation*."

"But I tell you I talked to no one this morning. And I was alone with you at the *Blue Moon*."

"You weren't with me all the time I paid my check," he said sharply. "Did you meet anyone while you were waiting on the sidewalk for me to come out of the *Blue Moon*?"

I shook my head. "I was outside for less than a minute before you joined me. You see, a couple of men came in while you were digging out your change and one of them bumped me, as I thought I'd wait—"

"Did you ever see them before?"

"Who?"

"The two men who came in," he said, the note of exasperation creeping into his voice again.

"Why, no—they weren't anyone I knew."

"Were they talking?"

"I guess so. Yes, they were. Quite absorbed in their conversation, as a matter of fact—otherwise, they would have noticed me and I would not have been bumped."

"Not many strangers come into the *Blue Moon*," he remarked.

"Do you think it was they?" I asked eagerly. "I think I'd know them again if I saw them."

Nicky's eyes narrowed. "It's possible. There had to be two— one to trail the victim in Washington and ascertain his berth number, the other to wait here and do the job. The Washington man would be likely to come down here afterward. If there were theft as well as murder, it would be to divide the spoils. If it were just murder, he would probably have to come down to pay off his confederate."

I reached for the telephone.

"We've been gone less than half an hour," Nicky went on. "They were just coming in and service is slow at the *Blue Moon*. The one who walked all the way to Hadley must certainly be hungry and the other probably drove all night from Washington."

"Call me immediately if you make an arrest," I said into the phone and hung up.

Neither of us spoke a word while we waited. We paced the floor, avoiding each other almost as though we had done something we were ashamed of.

The telephone rang at last. I picked it up and listened. Then I said, "O. K." and turned to Nicky.

"One of them tried to escape through the kitchen but Winn had someone stationed at the back and they got him."

"That would seem to prove it," said Nicky with a frosty little smile.

I nodded agreement.

He glanced at his watch. "Gracious," he exclaimed, "I wanted to make an early start on my work this morning, and here I've already wasted all this time talking with you."

I let him get to the door. "Oh, Nicky," I called, "what was it you set out to prove?"

"That a chain of inferences could be logical and still not be true," he said.

"Oh."

"What are you laughing at?" he asked snappishly. And then he laughed too.

The Weir

Mr. and Mrs. Bobbin were driving home from the sea one evening in their very old Austin, Candida. They had just passed some large wrought-iron gates when Mrs. Bobbin grabbed Mr. Bobbin's arm, a thing she knew she must never do, and exclaimed, "Look, there's a woman waving."

"I know," said Mr. Bobbin, "I've been watching her for at least five minutes."

"She's hopping about as if she'd been stung by something."

"Too pretty to want a lift, I'm afraid," said Mr. Bobbin, pulling up.

The woman, wearing dark glasses and a sketchy pink-and-white sunbathing outfit, put her fashionably arranged head through Mr. Bobbin's open window.

"Can you please come at once," she said, panting. "I'm afraid it may be too late; my husband's fallen into the river."

"Better stay here, dear," said Mr. Bobbin firmly to Mrs. Bobbin, who took no notice. They followed the woman through a gap in the hedge; at least it was hardly a gap and the hawthorn branches

209

clawed at them fiercely, though the woman was in too much of a state to notice. Her brown arms and her hands on which were three costly looking rings were all white scratches. Only her back was smooth except for some scars between the shoulder-blades—two little sixpenny-sized circles, then a red mark and another circle. Mr. Bobbin pictured her being branded long ago and far away by bandits.

On the other side of the hedge was a field of standing hay. "It's the weir," called the woman, stumbling ahead. "He can't swim properly; neither can I. I don't know if anyone can get to him. The current's terribly strong."

They could hear the roar of the water ahead. In front was a footpath leading from the weir to the gate on the road some distance in front of the Bobbins' car. Mr. Bobbin followed the path through some bushes to the flimsy wooden bridge which spanned the river at the point where the water crashed down to the lower level. There was a balustrade on the downstream side which had given way in the middle. The broken ends were trailing in the water.

For a few seconds Mr. Bobbin, keeping well away from the edge, stood on the bridge and scanned the heaving water. It had been raining for a night and a day, and the river was at full spate—nearly forty feet wide—hurling itself down and then whipping back on itself. For about twenty feet it seethed and plunged. No swimmer on earth could have stood a chance against it.

Suddenly Mr. Bobbin saw a bare arm shoot out of the water and a few seconds later a head and shoulders were flung momentarily above the surface and then dragged violently back again. As the other two came up he looked round frantically for something that might be of help, although it was plain even from that brief glimpse that there was no life left in the body.

On the far side of the bridge, running along the bank in both directions, there was a grass path backed by high weeds and rushes growing out of marshy ground. On the down-stream side of the weir, a yard or so along the path, a plaid rug was spread. On it was a cherry-coloured jumper, a big basket, an open white handbag, two *Tatlers*, some cigarettes and two bottles of pale ale, one unstoppered and spilling over the rug. Some little way farther down, where the river was quieter and shallower and began to curl to the left, there was a rod resting on the bank, its line tugging in the water. Behind it on the grass were a canvas bag, a tweed hat and a box of flies.

Mr. Bobbin had to shout above the noise of the falling water. "Look, if I got that rod and hung on to one end while you two clung to the other, perhaps I might be able to wade into the river and catch hold of him when he next bobbed up. I'm afraid there's no chance at all of his being alive, though."

"No, we don't want another tragedy," the two women said almost together, the one in the sunbathing outfit adding, "It's terribly deep right up to the bank. I can't think what on earth made him go on to the bridge; he knew perfectly well it wasn't safe to lean on the rail."

"I wonder," said Mr. Bobbin, "how long he'll go on coming up for."

"He might for an awful long time," said the woman; "we used to throw logs and quite heavy things in and watch them coming up again for ages before they went downstream."

"Can we get a boat?"

"At the mill," said the woman, "there's an old punt. Blick, the waterman, would help you get it out. I was coming back from there when I saw him struggling in the water. Blick's scything just opposite the little island. He's nearly half a mile along the bank, otherwise I'd have gone to him instead of coming to the road." Although she was still breathless she had begun to speak with a sort of unnatural calm.

"You go for the punt, Beverley," said Mrs. Bobbin, and to the woman, "Come back to the car with me, my dear, and I'll give you some tea from the thermos. I'm afraid we've nothing stronger."

"I'd like a cigarette more than anything. I'll get mine." She walked over and picked up her cigarettes and her bag, shaking some of the spilt beer off the rug as she did so.

Mr. Bobbin trotted off down the tow-path between banks of willow-herb and purple loosestrife, just the sort of place he would have liked to linger in if it hadn't been for this body. Where the bushes came to an end and the roar of the weir, now hidden, subsided, there was a fence and a stile into a meadow. On the stile was a notice-board with "Private" on it. Mr. Bobbin could see the roof of the mill above a group of sycamores.

Between the mill and the stile was the island, and between the island and Mr. Bobbin a dark man in dark trousers and waistcoat was scything the nettles that were beginning to pour over the path.

"Been an accident," puffed Mr. Bobbin. "Fellow's drowned himself in the weir. Came for the punt. You the waterman Blick?"

"Drowned hisself!" said the man, flinging down his scythe. "Yes, I'm Blick; punt's yonder."

"Have to try to fish him out," said Mr. Bobbin as they approached the mill, half running, half walking.

It was a pretty little mill, now only used for housing the waterman and his family. There were beehives and fruit trees, and a clothes-line with huge pairs of combinations at one end and diminutive pairs of knickers at the other.

Three children were catching tiddlers in one of the three streams which converged at the mill, while an oldish man with a blue felt hat covering his face was apparently asleep in a green plush chair under a pear tree. A woman, obviously Mrs. Blick, hobbled out of the house and hurled a bucketful of something into the nettles. As Mr. Bobbin and Blick came up, the others, sensing drama, crowded round them.

"Gentleman here says chap's been drowned," said Blick.

"Who is it, sir, do you know?" asked the old man, Mrs. Blick's father, who had come to life and trundled over from his chair.

"Don't know," said Mr. Bobbin, "ginger-headed, I think. His wife found him in the water and came to the road to raise the alarm."

"Oh dear," said Mrs. Blick, sitting down heavily on the green chair and fanning herself with her apron, "that'll be poor Mr. Gringell."

Blick was scratching the back of his leathery neck.

"It'll take a devil of a time to get the old punt up there agin the stream," he said. "She leaks like a bleeding sieve, too. Quicker to carry her. Look here, you kids, nip up to the gardens and see if Mr. Heathcote's still there. Tell him we wants him quick."

"I'll give you a hand with the punt," said Mrs. Blick's father, Mr. Hopping; "would one of the landing-nets be any use do you reckon, sir?"

"Might be," said Mr. Bobbin.

It was an arduous business getting the big square punt out of the mud and tipping out the water that she'd shipped.

"They don't only use her for cutting weeds like," said Hopping, coming back with the landing-net and a groundsheet in time to miss the most punishing part of the operation.

They had carried the punt a bare sixty yards, puffing and sweating as they went, when Heathcote the agent, a muscular young man in whipcord trousers and a short-sleeved shirt, caught up with them. While he and Mr. Bobbin introduced themselves, the children who were tagging on behind were ordered back peremptorily by their father.

"What's all this about?" Heathcote asked, grabbing hold of a corner of the punt. "The boy said something about someone being drowned."

"Gentleman," said Blick, dashing sweat from his forehead with a lean hand, "says chap's tumbled in weir like. Looks like it must be Mr. Gringell."

"Blast that bloody bridge," Heathcote cried; "the Gringells have been told dozens of times that that handrail isn't safe. That's why we had to make that bit of the path private to stop strangers going on the bridge until we'd got it repaired. Is Pam—is Mrs. Gringell all right? Was she with him when it happened?"

"No, apparently not," said Mr. Bobbin; "she's in a bit of a state naturally. I didn't press her for any details."

"I met her starting off for the river well over an hour ago," Heathcote said. "She had a heavy basket full of beer bottles and stuff that she was taking down to where her husband was fishing so I went with her to help her carry it. I wish to God I'd stayed down there and kept an eye on Gringell."

"Look," said Mr. Bobbin, "let's change ends. My arm's dropping off. You mean you might have prevented him leaning on the rail?"

Heathcote was silent for a moment; then he said, "I suppose I ought to be more careful what I'm saying, but Gringell was a very queer customer. Desperately moody. He got very badly knocked about in the war. He had a leg that gave him almost continual pain, I believe."

"Are you suggesting that he might have done himself in deliberately?"

"Well, he was in a perfectly filthy temper when we arrived and didn't seem to want us anywhere near him, which is why, after a few minutes of his company, Pam and I just walked off and left him to simmer down. At least I had to go up to the gardens, anyway, to go over the accounts, and she parked her belongings and came with me. She was frightfully het up by that time. I think they'd been having a full-dress row about something during most of the day."

"What made her come back to the weir so soon?"

"Well, we were practically at the kitchen gardens—they're about ten minutes' walk past the mill—when she suddenly said she must go back to him. She didn't say so, but I think, you know, she must have had some sort of premonition. Once before, about six months ago, she told me she came into their room and found him half-way out of the window three storeys up. I suppose this time she was just too late."

They had reached the stile and were negotiating it with the punt. Heathcote didn't seem to be in the least exhausted. Mr. Bobbin was very tired.

"Do the Gringells own the place?" Mr. Bobbin managed to get out.

"Oh Lord, no! They're just here for the week-end. They come here a great deal. It's Sir Henry Harcourt's place. Sir Henry had to go into Podbury for a committee meeting and various odd jobs, otherwise he'd probably have been with them. I suppose it will be me who has to break the jolly news to him. Where's Pam?" he asked as they came in sight of the weir. "I thought you said—"

"I hope she's in the car with my wife."

"His rod's still where I last saw him," said Heathcote. "Whereabouts was he when you caught sight of him?"

"Look there, sir," shouted Hopping, pointing. They followed the line of his arm and saw that the body had been carried clear of the turmoil and was lying in shallow water on the other side of the river.

"Well, I'm damned," said Mr. Bobbin, "so we needn't have bothered with the punt after all."

It was difficult to get to the drowned man because on the far side of the river brambles came right to the water's edge. Heathcote and Blick, who had dashed over the bridge, had to hack their way through with sticks. It was a good many minutes before they had at last got Gringell up out of the water and over the bridge to where he could be laid out on the grass. He was a little ferret-faced man whose flannel shirt and grey trousers were so torn that they were only just clinging to him.

"You can sometimes bring people to life an amazing length of time afterwards by artificial respiration," Heathcote said, bending down.

"Not him you couldn't," said Blick, covering him with the ground sheet. "I seen too many of them in the Dardanelles."

"We'll have to take him up to the house," said Heathcote. "I think the best thing would be for us to carry him through the wood to the drive, and then for me to nip up to the garage for the shooting-brake."

"My car's at your disposal, if you want it," said Mr. Bobbin.

"That's awfully good of you; tell you what," said Heathcote, "if you could really spare the time perhaps you wouldn't mind taking Pam up to the house, that would save her having to go in the car with Gringell. Come with us to the drive, and then you can get to your car from there."

Heathcote and Blick went first, carrying the dripping body in the ground-sheet, and after them came Mr. Bobbin and Hopping with the effects, which included a very small dace which the rod had apparently caught itself during the interval. They took the path away from the mill which led them first in front of and then (sheering away from the river) into the heart of a wood whose closely knit trees held back the sunlight except for an occasional slender thread. After a while they came to a gate, also with its "Private" notice, and beyond that a grass border on which elms were growing, and then the drive, very unkempt.

"This is where we separate," said Heathcote to Mr. Bobbin. "You go down to the gates and turn left. Blick, you and Hopping wait here. Try to keep out of sight of Mrs. Gringell when she comes past."

A few minutes later the Bobbins and Mrs. Gringell were rattling up the drive in Candida. They crossed three bridges, one brick and two stone, over the three branches of the river and came to where another drive forked off to their left. In the angle between the two drives, with tracks leading to both, was a Dutch barn containing two stacks of hay, one behind the other, but with its roof so badly ripped open that it afforded hardly any protection. Just opposite the barn they overtook Heathcote and gave him a lift on the running-board as far as the turning off to the garage. Heathcote put his arm through the open window and patted the padding in the shoulder of Mrs. Bobbin's coat which was round Mrs. Gringell. Mrs. Gringell, who had been staring into space, gave a brief wan smile of gratitude.

They had hardly drawn up at the large portico of the house when another car—an old Daimler—which had been travelling very much faster, pulled up behind them with a great crunching of gravel. "That's Harry," said Mrs. Gringell faintly, "would you tell him, please?"

Mr. Bobbin got out and met the figure coming towards him, a tall, handsome, well-fed man in a dark grey, double-breasted suit. Mr. Bobbin gave him a brief account of what had happened, and Sir Henry thanked him profusely, adding, "I expect you could use a drink, I know I could. I'll get my housekeeper to see to Pam, and then perhaps you and your wife would join me in the library. Or are you in a fearful hurry to get on? I'm afraid all this will have rather eaten into your evening."

"We'd been to the sea," said Mr. Bobbin. "It all seems terribly long ago."

Sir Henry turned to Mrs. Gringell, a pale little figure who was walking slowly towards the house, leaning on Mrs. Bobbin's arm. "Pamela, I'm most dreadfully sorry . . . horrible, beastly affair. I expect you'd like to go straight to your room. I'll send Mrs. Crowl up with some whisky. These people seem to have been wonderfully kind and helpful."

The party went through the front door, Mr. Bobbin and Sir Henry wiping their shoes. Mr. Bobbin decided that Sir Henry's housekeeper must keep him under her thumb. Bachelors didn't usually bother with such refinements, or maybe, he thought, looking up at a glossy de Lazlo portrait in the front hall of a lovely but determined-looking woman, he was a widower.

In the library Sir Henry produced bottles and glasses from a cupboard. No butler, no decanter, Mrs. Bobbin noticed with regret, and the chairs wanted recovering badly. Stately homes weren't what they once were.

"Now tell me the whole thing again, slowly," said Sir Henry.

Mr. Bobbin left off admiring a collection of flint-lock pistols over the chimney-piece and told Sir Henry everything that seemed relevant. He was still answering questions when a noise from the hall told them that the others had arrived. The two men went to the door.

Heathcote had brought Blick with him to help carry. "In the gunroom, I should think, for the moment. Shocking business this," said Sir Henry, guiding Blick who was walking backwards. Blick was not used to highly polished floors and was embarrassed by not having a free hand to take off his cap. Just outside the library he trod on a button, and would have lost his balance if Sir Henry had not caught him.

When Blick had been sent on his way consoled by a ten-shilling note and the doctor had been summoned by telephone, Heathcote joined the others in the library.

"I still don't understand," said Sir Henry, handing Heathcote a drink, "what Cecil was doing on the bridge when you say his rod and stuff were farther down the bank."

Mrs. Bobbin, who had not spoken at all up till then, said, "Of course, people continually do things for reasons that are incomprehensible to others, like Mr. Heathcote here having the tail of a fish sticking out of his pocket. Mr. Gringell might have been chasing a rare butterfly or running about to cure himself of cramp."

Sir Henry, who had gone to sit at his knee-hole desk, looked at Mrs. Bobbin in mild astonishment and said, "I don't think Gringell went in for natural history much, but he was certainly unaccountable in his actions sometimes."

"Mr. Heathcote," said Mr. Bobbin, "has a suicide theory which I didn't want to mention when he wasn't with us." He turned to Heathcote, resting his glass on the corner of the desk. "I've already explained that Mrs. Gringell went with you to the gardens because Mr. Gringell was in such a vile temper."

Heathcote went very red. "I'm afraid I was talking a bit out of turn," he said. "I should have kept my big mouth shut. I think it's better to forget what I said."

"Unfortunately," said Mr. Bobbin, "you mentioned it in front of Blick and his father-in-law. The story is very likely gaining momentum in the Lamb and Flag at this very moment."

"Luckily neither Blick nor old Hopping go to the pub, and also"—Sir Henry looked hard at Heathcote—"Blick is a very loyal and devoted servant. I'm quite sure that he'd keep this matter to himself and see that his family did the same. However, to make quite sure"—he pressed a bell—"I'll send for him. For Pamela's sake we don't want any suggestion of suicide brought up. I think it's best to say simply that he was crossing the bridge and supported himself by the handrail, which gave way—which is no doubt what did in fact happen. With his gammy leg he often needed to hang on to something for support, and he may have gripped hold of the rail to steady himself, forgetting that it wasn't safe. We don't even have to mention that he left his rod on the bank. This suicide story is only a theory on Heathcote's part, and not I think a very good one.

After all, people don't usually kill themselves when they're in a towering rage. Don't you agree with me, Bobbin?"

Mr. Bobbin drew a little invisible spiral on the desk with his finger-nail. "You know," he said, "if you'll forgive my saying so, I think it would be very much better if at the inquest no attempt was made by anybody to suppress anything. It's all very well trying to spare people's feelings, but once you start concealing important facts about what happened before someone's death, the next thing you know you'll be suspected of having done the fellow in. Oh Lord!" Mr. Bobbin exclaimed, "I've committed a horrible crime myself by leaving a wet ring on the edge of your lovely walnut desk. I wonder if I might have a sheet of blotting-paper."

"Oh, it doesn't matter a damn! Mrs. Crowl will see to it," said Sir Henry, throwing over the top sheet out of his leather blotter all the same. Mr. Bobbin mopped up the wet and, being a tidy man, folded up the blotting-paper into an exact square, wet side inmost.

"Well," he said, "we must be on our way. Here's my card if you should want us." He looked round for a wastepaper-basket and not seeing one put the blotting-paper with his note-case in his breast pocket. As Sir Henry was showing them out, the maid, who gave the appearance of having come several miles at the run, arrived to answer the bell.

Neither Mr. nor Mrs. Bobbin spoke for a while as they chugged down the drive—Candida was getting very hot and tired—but as they reached the Dutch barn Mrs. Bobbin said, "I suppose the right fork takes you to Podbury," and added inconsequently, "You know I wouldn't be a bit surprised if it turned out that somebody pushed old Gringell in."

"How on earth do you make that out?" asked Mr. Bobbin, pulling up and looking intently at the roof of the Dutch barn.

"Well, of course," said Mrs. Bobbin, "I don't really suppose anybody did for a moment, but it wouldn't be at all hard to make out quite a good case."

"Wouldn't it?"

"No. For one thing," said Mrs. Bobbin, "why go all the way to the bridge and break the rail in order to kill yourself? If you must go to the bridge to die, then why not climb under the rail? But why bother to go that far? Why not jump in from the side where the rug was? And don't suicides always leave notes? If he wasn't committing suicide, then why on earth did he leave his line in the water and go and lean on a rail he knew very well to be rickety?"

"Well, you made some rather ill-timed suggestions on that point yourself in the library."

"Also," said Mrs. Bobbin, "if I may throw off a few maxims for a moment; women who are treated with disrespect look for consolation elsewhere. Attractive women are apt to find it. Superficially attractive women like Mrs. Gringell, who probably deserve all their husbands give them, usually make for undiscriminating youngsters like Heathcote, whose eager solicitude has been so much in evidence. Those two waltzing off together to the gardens and her coming back alone might easily have been done just to make it look as though Gringell had fallen in while they were away. Another thing—a filthy temper, as Sir Henry pointed out, isn't normally a prelude to suicide, but it's quite likely to exasperate a pair of guilty lovers to the point of murder. I should say by the look of his wife's rings that old Gringell was as rich as Croesus, which would make more of a motive."

"Jolly good," said Mr. Bobbin. "How was it done?"

"Well, not having actually been there I don't know, but I don't see why Heathcote and Mrs. Gringell might not have thought up some scheme for getting Gringell on to the bridge—like calling to him to look at a two-headed eel or something—and then have given him a good old-fashioned shove. Heathcote could have thought up the suicide story so that if anyone produced any powerful reasons why it couldn't have been an accident, then suicide rather than murder would be the next alternative. People with guilty consciences can never let well alone. Of course, if they'd had any sense they'd have brought the rod round on to the bridge to make it look as though he'd been fishing from there."

"Not if they knew anything about dry-fly fishing they wouldn't."

"Oh, wouldn't they? Of course they had to lay stress on the nasty temper, whether Gringell was really in one or not, in order to explain why Mrs. Gringell went off and left him; and they had to go past the mill so that the mill people could see them. I dare say you noticed that Mrs. Gringell appeared to have experimented with other objects to see how they reacted to being thrown into the weir. Very incriminating, that."

"Why didn't she get Heathcote to come back with her when she had this premonition, instead of coming back all alone to her husband's watery corpse? That would take a hell of a lot of nerve."

Mrs. Bobbin considered for a moment. "It would have looked suspicious the two of them walking off and then walking straight back again. The premonition story was much better. Anyway, she wouldn't have minded coming back alone, hard little bitch! I had more opportunity than you did of studying her. I wouldn't be surprised if it were she who did most of the shoving."

"How are you going to prove all this?"

"I don't suppose I am," said Mrs. Bobbin, laughing, "but perhaps if we went back to the weir to have a look round we could dig up a clue or two, unless the place is already black with sightseers. The cunning thing, you know, is that in a case like this the doctor will never be able to say within an hour when Gringell was drowned, and even supposing he could that wouldn't prove when he was pushed, would it? I don't know how I'm to prove that it all happened before they left for the kitchen garden. Incidentally, why have we stopped here?"

"I want to have a look round this barn."

"I never knew you were interested in barns."

"Didn't you? You know," said Mr. Bobbin reflectively, "you made rather a good point just now when you said that there was no need for Gringell to go as far as the bridge if he wanted to commit suicide, because that applies to his being pushed, too. If someone wanted to give him a push where he would be quite certain to drown, they'd only have to lure him as far as the rug and do it from there. Then they could go along afterwards and break the balustrade in order to make it look like an accident."

"Who's *they*? Have you got a murderer too? Is he the same as mine?"

"Well, he was abetted by Mrs. Gringell like yours, but according to my very latest theory Mrs. Gringell's alleged little affair with Heathcote may have just been part of a plot to remove suspicion from her real lover. My idea is that the murder was planned for Mrs. Gringell's first appearance at the river, but that it had to be postponed because of Heathcote turning up unexpectedly and accompanying her down. She didn't want to make him suspicious by trying to get rid of him so she let him come, very likely knowing he was on his way to the gardens, and in the meantime worked out a way of arriving at the river a second time—something of the sort, anyway."

"Doesn't sound much of a theory so far."

"Once she was back again at the weir," Mr. Bobbin went on, undaunted, "she could carry on with her original plan, which I believe was to sit on the rug and lure Gringell to his doom most likely by tantalizing him with an unstoppered pint of pale ale in danger of wasting. She presumably knew where he was going to fish, and also that she'd have to find a way of enticing him opposite the deeper water. Probably if Heathcote hadn't barged in, she and her accomplice would have pushed Gringell and then tidied up the rug and stuff to make it look as though she had only just arrived. I expect they would have taken the rod out of the water, too, to give the impression that Gringell hadn't yet begun to fish, but had parked his gear and was just hanging about on the bridge waiting for the evening rise or something. Once Heathcote had seen him fishing it wasn't so easy to explain his being on the bridge, especially as there was nowhere to fish from on the far bank."

"I still think it's a rotten theory and nothing like so convincing as mine and, anyway, who are you having as your murderer—the black-browed Blick? Did he have a secret crush on Mrs. Gringell?"

"I expect so. I've got a bit of a one myself. No, not Blick. Blick has a beautiful alibi supplied unintentionally by Mrs. Gringell, who said that he was scything immediately opposite the island. He couldn't have reached the point where I found him unless he'd been scything without stopping, and pretty expertly too."

"He could have told Mrs. Gringell to say he was opposite the island. You're no earthly good at this game."

"He couldn't have told her to say that, because he didn't know a thing about what was going on. You're mixing him up with Lady Chatterley's lover, and now I come to think of it the amount of scything he got through pretty well proves that Mrs. Gringell must have lingered by the river for quite a time before she came after us."

"Well, who was this man then and why didn't Heathcote see him?"

"Ah, that's the beauty of it. Nobody but Mrs. Gringell knew he was there, because all the time he was hidden in the bushes behind the rug."

"What makes you think that?"

"I know it. By the trampled look of the reeds and thistles and things, and two great muddy footmarks on the rug, you can see exactly which way he came."

"Are you trying to tell me there really *was* a man?"

"Certainly there was. I can even show you the crumbled bit of bank where he pushed Gringell over the edge. I expect he wrong-footed the wretched man just as he was reaching out for the beer. Mrs. Gringell presumably dropped it and went rapidly into reverse. Of course the noise of the water would have drowned the murderer's movements."

"How do you know it wasn't Heathcote hiding in the bushes?"

"Well, for one thing, whoever it was had much bigger feet, and for another he was with Mrs. Gringell just before she came for us. When he'd pushed poor Gringell in and made sure there was no chance of his getting out alive, he took Mrs. Gringell in his arms for a full three minutes, smoothing her highly doctored hair with his free hand, the left one, and no doubt making quite sure that she had got her last-minute instructions absolutely pat."

"Now you're being simply silly."

"No, I'm not. Do you see that track leading between the two stacks in the barn to the other drive? Do you notice those tyre marks in the mud curling round this way? Those are the tyre marks of the murderer's car, which he parked out of sight between the stacks. Come with me and I'll show you where he probably stopped. Last night's rain and that hole in the roof have made all this child's play.

"See," said Mr. Bobbin as they picked their way over the muddy ruts, "just as I thought; he got out of his car here and climbed up this ladder. Look at the fresh mud on the rungs. From up here"— he had scuttled up the ladder and was speaking from the top of the stack—"he could look up and down the drive and see that the coast was clear, although I notice that the gate where Blick and Hopping were waiting is quite hidden by those elms. He obviously came up here twice; once when he first arrived back from Podbury by the other drive, and again after the murder, when he must have hidden here to see how things developed. I dare say that when he saw Candida chugging up the drive in Heathcote's wake, he presumed that we had the body on board, and it would be a good moment to arrive back from his committee meeting and his odd jobs. Whether he was already in position by the weir when Mrs. Gringell and Heathcote arrived I wouldn't know, but I should think he probably meant to meet her somewhere and go with her most of the way himself. He must have been a bit nonplussed when he saw Heathcote was there too, unless of course Heathcote and Mrs. Gringell came to the weir the long way round by the mill and Sir Henry didn't see Heathcote until he was already in his hide-out. I ought to have checked up on that. In either case, Sir Henry must have been at rather a loss until Mrs. Gringell re-appeared on her own, unless of course they'd managed to exchange signals unknown to Heathcote and Gringell."

"And why pick on poor Sir Henry? A little smug but such a poppet."

"You and your poppets!" said Mr. Bobbin, climbing down the ladder. "Well, for one thing, those are his tyre marks there, though, of course, it wasn't those that put me on the scent because I've only just had a chance to examine them. What made me suspect him almost as soon as his name was mentioned was the fact that he'd been to a committee meeting. I was looking for a man in a

Sunday-go-to-meeting suit. Such a suit as would normally have
four cuff buttons, but in this case had the second one from the top
on the right sleeve apparently dangling by a thread. Someone in a
suit of this sort had clasped Mrs. Gringell to him for long enough to
leave strong impressions of three firm and one boss-eyed button
between her bare shoulder-blades. What's more, he'd done it recently enough for the marks to be still very much in evidence when
we arrived.

"Of course," Mr. Bobbin went on, "I had a pull over you
through having had more chance to examine the ground. When we
were taking the body through the trees to the drive I was able to see
how Sir Henry could have got from the drive to the weir without
once having to come into the open. All I had to know after that
was where the car was hidden. The moment I saw the barn, I
realized that it would be pretty well the only possible place."

"And what did you want the blotting-paper for?"

"Oh, the blotting-paper," said Mr. Bobbin, taking it from his
pocket and spreading it out on Candida's bonnet; "now kindly
observe how this button which I picked up from the floor of the
hall exactly fits into each of these circles which Sir Henry kindly
printed for me by leaning heavily on his blotter. Without exhibit
'A,' Mrs. Gringell's back as it was this afternoon, I'm afraid this
blotting-paper and this button will only amount to hearsay evidence, but luckily Sir Henry has left other damaging clues. There
are these tracks and, better still, the rug with his footprints, which
I put in Candida's boot and forgot to take out; and there should still
be enough mud on his shoes to keep the laboratory busy. It was all
I could do to stop myself saying it must have been a very muddy
meeting."

"Well, well. I hope you didn't put Sir Henry on the scent by
giving him your professional card. Just the kind of senseless thing
you would do."

"I wonder," said Mr. Bobbin, "if he'd be offended if I wrote and
asked him to sell me some of those pistols. He can't have much use
for them now unless he wants to shoot himself, and I should think
the estate could do with all the money it can get. I expect it was

partly the clamour of creditors which drove him to do poor Gringell in. I presume that in spite of their differences Gringell had left all to Mrs. G."

"Gosh!" exclaimed Mrs. Bobbin, only half listening as usual, "fancy putting on a two-piece sun-suit to assist at a murder."

The Homesick Buick

BY JOHN D. MACDONALD

To get to Leeman, Texas, you go southwest from Beaumont on Route 90 for approximately thirty miles and then turn right on a two-lane concrete farm road. Five minutes from the time you turn, you will reach Leeman. The main part of town is six lanes wide and five blocks long. If the hand of a careless giant should remove the six gas stations, the two theaters, Willows' Hardware Store, the Leeman National Bank, the two big air-conditioned five-and-dimes, the Sears store, four cafés, Rightsinger's dress shop, and The Leeman House, a twenty-room hotel, there would be very little left except the supermarket and four assorted drugstores.

On October 3rd, 1949, a Mr. Stanley Woods arrived by bus and carried his suitcase over to The Leeman House. In Leeman there is no social distinction of bus, train, or plane, since Leeman has neither airport facilities nor railroad station.

On all those who were questioned later, Mr. Stanley Woods seemed to have made very little impression. They all spoke of kind of a medium-size fella in his thirties, or it might be his forties. No, he wasn't fat, but he wasn't thin either. Blue eyes? Could be brown. Wore a gray suit, I think. Can't remember whether his glasses had rims or not. If they did have rims, they were probably gold.

But all were agreed that Mr. Stanley Woods radiated quiet confidence and the smell of money. According to the cards that were collected here and there, Mr. Woods represented the Groston Precision Tool Company of Atlanta, Georgia. He had deposited in the Leeman National a certified check for twelve hundred dollars and the bank had made the routine check of looking up the credit standing of Groston. It was Dun & Bradstreet double-A, but, of course, the company explained later that they had never heard of Mr. Stanley Woods. Nor could the fake calling cards be traced. They were of a type of paper and type face which could be duplicated sixty or a hundred times in every big city in the country.

Mr. Woods' story, which all agreed on, was that he was ". . . nosing around to find a good location for a small plant. Decentralization, you know. No, we don't want it right in town."

He rented Tod Bishner's car during the day. Tod works at the Shell station on the corner of Beaumont and Lone Star Streets and doesn't have any use for his Plymouth sedan during the day. Mr. Woods drove around all the roads leading out of town and, of course, real estate prices were jacked to a considerable degree during his stay.

Mr. Stanley Woods left Leeman rather suddenly on the morning of October 17th under unusual circumstances.

The first person to note a certain oddness was Miss Trilla Price on the switchboard at the phone company. Her local calls were all right but she couldn't place Charley Anderson's call to Houston, nor, when she tried, could she raise Beaumont. Charley was upset because he wanted to wangle an invitation to go visit his sister over the coming week end.

That was at five minutes of nine. It was probably at the same time that a car with two men in it parked on Beaumont Street, diagonally across from the bank, and one of the two men lifted the hood and began to fiddle with the electrical system.

Nobody agrees from what direction the Buick came into town.

There was a man and a girl in it and they parked near the drugstore. No one seems to know where the third car parked, or even what kind of car it was.

The girl and the man got out of the Buick slowly, just as Stanley Woods came down the street from the hotel.

In Leeman the bank is open on weekdays from nine until two. And so, at nine o'clock, C. F. Hethridge, who is, or was, the chief teller, raised the green shades on the inside of the bank doors and unlocked the doors. He greeted Mr. Woods, who went on over to the high counter at the east wall and began to ponder over his check book.

At this point, out on the street, a very peculiar thing happened. One of the two men in the first car strolled casually over and stood beside the Buick. The other man started the motor of the first car, drove down the street, and made a wide U-turn to swing in and park behind the Buick.

The girl and the man had gone over to Bob Kimball's window. Bob is second teller, and the only thing he can remember about the girl is that she was blonde and a little hard-looking around the mouth, and that she wore a great big alligator shoulder-bag. The man with her made no impression on Bob at all, except that Bob thinks the man was on the heavy side.

Old Rod Harrigan, the bank guard, was standing beside the front door, yawning, and picking his teeth with a broken match.

At this point C. F. Hethridge heard the buzzer on the big time-vault and went over and swung the door wide and went in to get the money for the cages. He was out almost immediately, carrying Bob's tray over to him. The girl was saying something about cashing a check and Bob had asked her for identification. She had opened the big shoulder-bag as her escort strolled over to the guard. At the same moment the girl pulled out a small vicious-looking revolver and aimed it between Bob's eyes, her escort sapped Old Rod Harrigan with such gusto that it was four that same afternoon before he came out of it enough to talk. And then, of course, he knew nothing.

C. F. Hethridge bolted for the vault and Bob, wondering whether he should step on the alarm, looked over the girl's shoulder just in time to see Stanley Woods aim carefully and bring Hethridge down with a slug through the head, catching him on the fly, so to speak.

Bob says that things were pretty confusing and that the sight of Hethridge dying so suddenly sort of took the heart out of him. Anyway, there was a third car and it contained three men, two of them equipped with empty black-leather suitcases. They went into the vault, acting as though they had been all through the bank fifty times. They stepped over Hethridge on the way in, and on the way out again.

About the only cash they overlooked was the cash right in front of Bob, in his teller's drawer.

As they all broke for the door, Bob dropped and pressed the alarm button. He said later that he held his hands over his eyes, though what good that would do him, he couldn't say.

Henry Willows is the real hero. He was fuddying around in his hardware store when he heard the alarm. With a reaction-time remarkable in a man close to seventy, he took a little twenty-two rifle, slapped a clip into it, trotted to his store door, and quickly analyzed the situation. He saw Mr. Woods, whom he recognized, plus three strangers and a blonde woman coming out of the bank pretty fast. Three cars were lined up, each one with a driver. Two of the men coming out of the bank carried heavy suitcases. Henry leveled on the driver of the lead car, the Buick, and shot him in the left temple, killing him outright. The man slumped over the wheel, his body resting against the horn ring, which, of course, added its blare to the clanging of the bank alarm.

At that point a slug, later identified as having come from a Smith & Wesson Police Positive, smashed a neat hole in Henry's plate-glass store window, radiating cracks in all directions. Henry ducked, and by the time he got ready to take a second shot, the two other cars were gone. The Buick was still there. He saw Bob run out of the bank, and later on he told his wife that he had his finger on the trigger and his sights lined up before it came to him that it was Bob Kimball.

It was agreed that the two cars headed out toward Route 90 and, within two minutes, Hod Abrams and Lefty Quinn had roared out of town in the same direction in the only police car. They were followed by belligerent amateurs to whom Henry Willows had doled out firearms. But on the edge of town all cars ran into an odd obstacle. The road was liberally sprinkled with metal objects shaped exactly like the jacks that little girls pick up when they bounce a ball, except they were four times normal size and all the points were sharpened. No matter how a tire hit one, it was certain to be punctured.

The police car swerved to a screaming stop, nearly tipping over. The Stein twins, boys of nineteen, managed to avoid the jacks in their souped-up heap until they were hitting eighty. When they finally hit one, the heap rolled over an estimated ten times, killing the twins outright.

So that made four dead. Hethridge, the Stein twins, and one unidentified bank robber.

Nobody wanted to touch the robber, and he stayed right where he was until the battery almost ran down and the horn squawked into silence. Hod Abrams commandeered a car, and he and Lefty rode back into town and took charge. They couldn't get word out by phone and within a very short time they found that some sharpshooter with a highpowered rifle had gone to work on the towers of local station WLEE and had put the station out of business.

Thus, by the time the Texas Rangers were alerted and ready to set up road blocks, indecision and confusion had permitted an entire hour to pass.

The Houston office of the FBI assigned a detail of men to the case and, from the Washington headquarters, two bank-robbery experts were dispatched by plane to Beaumont. Reporters came from Houston and Beaumont and the two national press services, and Leeman found itself on the front pages all over the country because the planning behind the job seemed to fascinate the average joe.

Mr. Woods left town on that particular Thursday morning. The FBI from Houston was there by noon, and the Washington contingent arrived late Friday. Everyone was very confident. There was a corpse and a car to work on. These would certainly provide the necessary clues to indicate which outfit had pulled the job, even though the method of the robbery did not point to any particular group whose habits were known.

Investigation headquarters were set up in the local police station and Hod and Lefty, very important in the beginning, had to stand around outside trying to look as though they knew what was going on.

Hethridge, who had been a cold, reserved, unpopular man, had, within twenty-four hours, fifty stories invented about his human kindness and generosity. The Stein twins, heretofore considered to be trash who would be better off in prison, suddenly became proper sons of old Texas.

Special Agent Randolph A. Sternweister who, fifteen years before, had found a law office to be a dull place, was in charge of the case, being the senior of the two experts who had flown down from Washington. He was forty-one years old, a chain smoker, a chubby man with incongruous hollow cheeks and hair of a shade of gray which his wife, Claire, tells him is distinguished.

The corpse was the first clue. Age between thirty and thirty-two. Brown hair, thinning on top. Good teeth, with only four small cavities, two of them filled. Height, five foot eight and a quarter, weight a hundred and forty-eight. No distinguishing scars or tattoos. X-ray plates showed that the right arm had been fractured years before. His clothes were neither new nor old. The suit had been purchased in Chicago. The shirt, underwear, socks, and shoes were all national brands, in the medium-price range. In his pockets they found an almost full pack of cigarettes, a battered Zippo lighter, three fives and a one in a cheap, trick billclip, eighty-five cents in change, a book of matches advertising a nationally known laxative, a white bone button, two wooden kitchen matches with blue and white heads, and a penciled map, on cheap notebook paper, of the main drag of Leeman—with no indication as to escape route. His fingerprint classification was teletyped to the Central Bureau files and the answer came back that there was no record of him. It was at this point that fellow workers noted that Mr. Sternweister became a shade irritable.

The next search of the corpse was more minute. No specific occupational calluses were found on his hands. The absence of laundry marks indicated that his linen, if it had been sent out, had been cleaned by a neighborhood laundress. Since Willows had used a .22 hollow-point, the hydraulic pressure on the brain fluids had caused the eyes of Mr. X to bulge in a disconcerting fashion. A local undertaker, experienced in the damage caused by the average Texas automobile accident, replaced the bulging eyeballs and smoothed out the expression for a series of pictures which were sent to many points. The Chicago office reported that the clothing store which had sold the suit was large and that the daily traffic was such that no clerk could identify the customer from the picture; nor was the youngish man known to the Chicago police.

Fingernail scrapings were put in a labeled glassine envelope, as well as the dust vacuumed from pants cuffs and other portions of the clothing likely to collect dust. The excellent lab in Houston reported back that the dust and scrapings were negative to the extent that the man could not be tied down to any particular locality.

In the meantime the Buick had been the object of equal scrutiny. The outside was a mass of prints from the citizens of Leeman who had peered morbidly in at the man leaning against the horn ring. The plates were Mississippi license plates and, in checking with the Bureau of Motor Vehicle Registration, it was found that the plates had been issued for a 1949 Mercury convertible which had been almost totally destroyed in a head-on collision in June, 1949. The motor number and serial number of the Buick were checked against central records and it was discovered that the Buick was one which had disappeared from Chapel Hill, North Carolina, on the 5th of July, 1949. The insurance company, having already replaced the vehicle, was anxious to take possession of the stolen car.

Pictures of Mr. X, relayed to Chapel Hill, North Carolina, and to myriad points in Mississippi, drew a large blank. In the meantime a careful dusting of the car had brought out six prints, all different. Two of them turned out to be on record. The first was on record through the cross-classification of Army prints. The man in question was found working in a gas station in Lake Charles, Louisiana. He had a very difficult two hours until a bright police officer had him demonstrate his procedure for brushing out the front of a car. Ex-Sergeant Golden braced his left hand against the dashboard in almost the precise place where the print had been found. He was given a picture of Mr. X to study. By that time he was so thoroughly annoyed at the forces of law and order that it was impossible to ascertain whether or not he had ever seen the man in question. But due to the apparent freshness of the print it was established—a reasonable assumption—that the gangsters had driven into Texas from the East.

The second print on record was an old print, visible when dust was carefully blown off the braces under the dismantled front seat. It belonged to a garage mechanic in Chapel Hill who once had a small misunderstanding with the forces of law and order and who was able to prove, through the garage work orders, that he had repaired the front seat mechanism when it had jammed in April, 1949.

The samples of road dirt and dust taken from the fender wells and the frame members proved nothing. The dust was proved, spectroscopically, to be from deep in the heart of Texas, and the valid assumption, after checking old weather reports, was that the car had come through some brisk thunderstorms en route.

Butts in the ashtray of the car showed that either two women, or one woman with two brands of lipstick, had ridden recently as a passenger. Both brands of lipstick were of shades which would go with a fair-complexioned blonde, and both brands were available in Woolworth's, Kress, Kresge, Walgreens—in fact, in every chain outfit of any importance.

One large crumb of stale whole-wheat bread was found on the floor mat, and even Sternweister could make little of that, despite the fact that the lab was able to report that the bread had been eaten in conjunction with liverwurst.

Attention was given to the oversized jacks which had so neatly punctured the tires. An ex-OSS officer reported that similar items had been scattered on enemy roads in Burma during the late war and, after examining the samples, he stated confidently that the OSS merchandise had been better made. A competent machinist looked them over and stated with assurance that they had been made by cutting eighth-inch rod into short lengths, grinding them on a wheel, putting them in a jig, and spot-welding them. He said that the maker did not do much of a job on either the grinding or the welding, and that the jig itself was a little out of line. An analysis of the steel showed that it was a Jones & Laughlin product that could be bought in quantity at any wholesaler and in a great many hardware stores.

The auditors, after a careful examination of the situation at the bank, reported that the sum of exactly $94,725 had disappeared. They recommended that the balance remaining in Stanley Woods' account of $982.80 be considered as forfeited, thus reducing the loss to $93,742.20. The good citizens of Leeman preferred to think that Stanley had withdrawn his account.

Every person who had a glimpse of the gang was cross-examined. Sternweister was appalled at the difficulty involved in even establishing how many there had been. Woods, the blonde, and the stocky citizen were definite. And then there were two with suitcases—generally agreed upon. Total, so far—five. The big question was whether each car had a driver waiting. Some said no—that the last car in line had been empty. Willows insisted angrily that there had been a driver behind each wheel. Sternweister at last settled for a total of eight, seven of whom escaped.

No one had taken down a single license number. But it was positively established that the other two cars had been either two- or four-door sedans in dark blue, black, green, or maroon, and that they had been either Buicks, Nashes, Oldsmobiles, Chryslers, Pontiacs, or Packards—or maybe Hudsons. And one lone woman held out for convertible Cadillacs. For each person that insisted that they had Mississippi registration, there was one equally insistent on Louisiana, Texas, Alabama, New Mexico, and Oklahoma. And one old lady said that she guessed she knew a California plate when she saw one.

On Saturday morning, nine days after the sudden blow to the FDIC, Randolph Sternweister paced back and forth in his suite at the hotel, which he shared with the number two man from the Washington end, one Buckley Weed. Weed was reading through the transcripts of the testimony of the witnesses, in vain hope of finding something to which insufficient importance had been given. Weed, though lean, a bit stooped, and only thirty-one, had, through osmosis, acquired most of the personal mannerisms of his superior. Sternweister had noticed this and for the past year had been on the verge of mentioning it. As Weed had acquired Sternweister's habit of lighting one cigarette off the last half-inch of the preceding one, any room in which the two of them remained for more than an hour took on the look and smell of any hotel room after a Legion convention.

"Nothing," Sternweister said. "Not one censored, unmentionable, unprintable, unspeakable thing! My God, if I ever want to kill anybody, I'll do it in the Pennsy Station at five-fifteen.

"The Bureau has cracked cases when the only thing it had to go on was a human hair or a milligram of dust. My God, we've got a whole automobile that weighs nearly two tons, and a whole corpse! They'll think we're down here learning to rope calves. You know what?"

"What, Ran?"

"I think this was done by a bunch of amateurs. There ought to be a law restricting the practice of crime to professionals. A bunch of wise amateurs. And you can bet your loudest argyles, my boy, that they established identity, hideout, the works, before they knocked off that vault. Right now, blast their souls, they're being seven average citizens in some average community, making no splash with that ninety-four grand. People didn't used to move around so much. Since the war they've been migrating all over the place. Strangers don't stick out like sore thumbs any more. See anything in those transcripts?"

"Nothing."

"Then stop rattling paper. I can't think. Since a week ago Thursday fifty-one stolen cars have been recovered in the South and

Southwest. And we don't know which two, if any, belonged to this mob. We don't even know which route they took away from here. Believe it or not—nobody saw 'em!"

As the two specialists stared bleakly at each other, a young man of fourteen named Pink Dee was sidling inconspicuously through the shadows in the rear of Louie's Garage. (Tow car service—open 24 hours.) Pink was considered to have been the least beautiful baby, the most unprepossessing child, in Leeman, and he gave frank promise of growing up to be a rather coarse joke on the entire human race. Born with a milk-blue skin, dead white hair, little reddish weak eyes, pipe-cleaner bones, narrow forehead, no chin, beaver teeth, a voice like an unoiled hinge, nature had made the usual compensation. His reaction-time was exceptional. Plenty of more rugged and more normal children had found out that Pink Dee could hit you by the time you had the word out of your mouth. The blow came from an outsize, knobbly fist at the end of a long thin arm, and he swung it with all the abandon of a bag of rocks on the end of a rope. The second important item about Pink Dee came to light when the Leeman School System started giving IQ's. Pink's was higher than they were willing to admit the first time, as it did not seem proper that the only genius in Leeman should be old Homer Dee's only son. Pink caught on, and the second time he was rated he got it down into the cretin class. The third rating was ninety-nine and everybody seemed happy with that.

At fourteen Pink was six foot tall and weighed a hundred and twenty pounds. He peered at the world through heavy lenses and maintained, in the back room of his home on Fountain Street, myriad items of apparatus, some made, some purchased. There he investigated certain electrical and magnetic phenomena, having tired of building radios, and carried on a fairly virulent correspondence on the quantum theory with a Cal Tech professor who was under the impression that he was arguing with someone of more mature years.

Dressed in his khakis, the uniform of Texas, Pink moved through the shadows, inserted the key he had filched into the Buick door, and then into the ignition lock. He turned it on in order to activate the electrical gimmicks, and then turned on the car radio. As soon as it warmed up he pushed the selective buttons, carefully noting the dial. When he had the readings he tuned it to WLEE to check the accuracy of the dial. When WLEE roared into a farm report, Louis appeared and dragged Pink out by the thin scruff of his neck.

"What the hell?" Louie said.

Being unable to think of any adequate explanation, Pink wriggled away and loped out.

Pink's next stop was WLEE, where he was well known. He found the manual he wanted and spent the next twenty minutes with it.

Having been subjected to a certain amount of sarcasm from both Sternweister and Weed, Hod Abrams and Lefty Quinn were in no mood for the approach Pink Dee used.

"I demand to see the FBI," Pink said firmly, the effect spoiled a bit by the fact that his voice change was so recent that the final syllable was a reversion to his childhood squeaky-hinge voice.

"He demands," Hod said to Lefty.

"Go away, Pink," Lefty growled, "before I stomp on your glasses."

"I am a citizen who wishes to speak to a member of a Federal agency," Pink said with dignity.

"A citizen, maybe. A taxpayer, no. You give me trouble kid, and I'm going to warm your pants right here in this lobby."

Maybe the potential indignity did it. Pink darted for the stairs leading up from the lobby. Hod went roaring up the stairs after him and Lefty grabbed the elevator. They both snared him outside Sternweister's suite and found that they had a job on their hands. Pink bucked and contorted like a picnic on which a hornet's nest has just fallen.

The door to the suite opened and both Sternweister and Weed glared out, their mouths open.

"Just ... just a fresh ... kid," Hod Adams panted.

"I know where the crooks are!" Pink screamed.

"He's nuts," Lefty yelled.

"Wait a minute," Randolph Sternweister ordered sharply. They stopped dragging Pink but still clung to him. "I admit he doesn't look as though he knew his way home, but you can't tell. You two wait outside. Come in here, young man."

Pink marched erectly into the suite, selected the most comfortable chair, and sank into it, looking smug.

"Where are they?"

"Well, I don't know exactly . . ."

"Outside!" Weed said with a thumb motion.

". . . but I know how to find out."

"Oh, you know how to find out, eh? Keep talking, I haven't laughed in nine days," Sternweister said.

"Oh, I had to do a little checking first," Pink said in a lofty manner. "I stole the key to the Buick and got into it to test something."

"Kid, experts have been over that car, half-inch by half-inch."

"Please don't interrupt me, sir. And don't take that attitude. Because, if it turns out I have something, and I know I have, you're going to look as silly as anything."

Sternweister flushed and then turned pale. He held hard to the edge of a table. "Go ahead," he said thickly.

"I am making an assumption that the people who robbed our bank started out from some hideout and then went back to the same one. I am further assuming that they were in their hideout some time, while they were planning the robbery."

Weed and Sternweister exchanged glances. "Go on."

"So my plan has certain possible flaws based on these assumptions, but at least it uncovers one possible pattern of investigation. I know that the car was stolen from Chapel Hill. That was in the paper. And I know the dead man was in Chicago. So I checked Chicago and Chapel Hill a little while ago."

"Checked them?"

"At the radio station, of course. Modern car radios are easy to set to new stations by altering the push buttons. The current settings of the push buttons do not conform either to the Chicago or the Chapel Hill areas. There are six stations that the radio in the Buick is set for and . . ."

Sternweister sat down on the couch as though somebody had clubbed him behind the knees. "Agh!" he said.

"So all you have to do," Pink said calmly, "is to check areas against the push-button settings until you find an area *where all six frequencies are represented by radio stations in the immediate geographical vicinity*. It will take a bit of statistical work, of course, and a map of the country, and a supply of push pins should simplify things, I would imagine. Then, after the area is located, I would take the Buick there and, due to variations in individual sets and receiving conditions, you might be able to narrow it down to within a mile or two. Then, by showing the photograph of the dead gangster around at bars and such places . . ."

And that was why, on the following Wednesday, a repainted Buick with new plates and containing two agents of the Bureau roamed through the small towns near Tampa on the West Florida Coast, and how they found that the car radio in the repainted Buick brought in Tampa, Clearwater, St. Pete, Orlando, Winter Haven, and Dunedin on the push buttons with remarkable clarity the closer they came to a little resort town called Tarpon Springs. On Thursday morning at four, the portable floodlights bathed three beach cottages in a white glare, and the metallic voice of the P.A. system said, "You are surrounded. Come out with your hands high. You are surrounded."

The shots, a few moments later, cracked with a thin bitterness against the heavier sighing of the Gulf of Mexico. Mr. Stanley Woods, or, as the blonde later stated, Mr. Grebbs Fainstock, was shot, with poetic justice, through the head, and that was the end of resistance.

On Pink Dee Day in Leeman, the president of the Leeman National Bank turned over the envelope containing the reward. It came to a bit less than six per cent of the recovered funds, and it is ample to guarantee, at some later date, a Cal Tech degree.

In December the Sternweisters bought a new car. When Claire demanded to know why Randolph insisted on delivery *sans* car radio, his only answer was a hollow laugh.

She feels that he has probably been working too hard.

Otherwhere

Seven o'clock

The gathering darkness was accentuated by a fog which had appeared dispiritingly at about tea-time. Looking across the river, you could no longer make out the half-demolished Festival buildings on the far side; and although October was still young, the sooty trees on the Embankment had already surrendered their stoic green to the first spears of the cold, and there were few homekeeping folk hardy enough to resist the temptation of a fire. Presently, to a servile nation-wide juggling with clocks, Summer Time would officially end. In the meanwhile, it seemed that Nature's edict had anticipated Parliament's by a matter of several days; so that more than one belated office-worker, scurrying to catch his bus in Whitehall or the Strand, shivered a little, and hunched his shoulders, as he met the cold vapour creeping into London from the Thames. . . .

In a room high up in a corner of New Scotland Yard, a room where the lights had had to be turned on more than two hours ago, Detective-Inspector Humbleby produced a sherry decanter and two glasses from a filing-cabinet implausibly marked 'Jewel Thefts,' and displayed them to his visitor, who said: "I didn't know you were allowed to keep drink on the premises."

"We're not." Humbleby poured the sherry without any special sign of perturbation. "And I," he added, "am the only officer in the entire building who does. There's discipline for you. . . . But look here, Gervase, are you sure you wouldn't like to go on to the club, or wherever we're dining, and let me join you as soon as this call has come through?"

"No, no." And Gervase Fen, Professor of English Language and Literature in the University of Oxford, shook his head emphatically. "It's perfectly comfortable here. What's more, your sherry"—he sipped experimentally, and his face brightened—"your sherry is too good to leave. But what is the call? Anything important?"

"A routine report. From a pleasant though rather ponderous colleague called Bolsover, of the Mid-Wessex C.I.D. They dragged me in to work with him on a case," said Humbleby without relish, "arising out of primitive rustic passions. Tuesday and Wednesday I was on the spot where the thing happened, but then yesterday I had to travel back here so as to give evidence this morning at the Elderton trial, and Bolsover promised to telephone me here this evening and let me know if there was anything new."

"What sort of a case?"

"Murder. It makes my twentieth this year. There are times when I wish I'd specialised in art forgeries, or something peaceful and infrequent like that. Lloyd Jones, who's our best man for that kind of thing, has done practically damn-all for the last six months. . . . However, it's no use moaning, I suppose."

"Will you have to go back to Wessex?"

"Yes, tomorrow—unless in the meantime Bolsover's solved the thing on his own. I'm rather hoping he has, and that that's why he's late with this call." Humbleby raised his sherry-glass to the light and contemplated its contents with solemn gloom. "It's been an exasperating business, and the sooner it's done with, the better I shall be pleased. I don't like Wessex, either. I don't like any sort of bucolic place."

"Well, but what is the problem?"

"An alibi. We know who *did* the killing—we're morally certain, that is—but the wretched fellow has an alibi and I can't for the life of me see the flaw in it."

A little superciliously, Fen sniffed. His long, lean form was sprawled gracelessly in the office's only tolerable chair, his ruddy, clean-shaven face wore an expression of incredulity, and his brown hair, ineffectually plastered down with water, stood up, as usual, in mutinous spikes at the crown of his head. "Perhaps there isn't a flaw in it," he suggested. "It wouldn't be the first time a moral certainty had turned out to be a total delusion. What sort of a moral certainty is it, anyway?"

"It's a question," said Humbleby, "of fingerprints. A certain man's fingerprints were found on the weapon with which the murder was committed. The prints were slightly blurred, I'll grant you; someone wearing gloves *could* have used the gun subsequently, and left them intact. But then, this man's explanation of how they came to be there is a demonstrable lie—and what's more, he has a strong motive for the crime. So you see how it is."

"I'm not sure that I do," said Fen. "Not so far. But since we've got to wait for our dinner, we may as well pass the time usefully: tell me about it."

Humbleby sighed, glancing first at his wrist-watch and then at the telephone which stood mute by his elbow. Then, abruptly reaching a decision, he got up, pulled the curtains to across the windows, dispensed more sherry, and finally settled himself back into the desk-chair with the air of one who is now prepared to stand a long siege. Groping for a cheroot, "Cassibury Bardwell," he began suddenly, "is the scene. I don't know if you've ever been there?" Fen shook his head. "Well, it's a hybrid sort of place, too big to be a village and too small to be a town. The houses are almost all built of a damp-looking grey stone, and the rain-water pours down the surrounding hill-slopes into the main street from all points of the compass, all year round. The nearest railway-station is miles away, and the people are in every sense inbred. They're chiefly occupied with—well, *farming*, I suppose," said Humbleby dubiously. "But it's not, in any event, a very prosperous locality. In the countryside round about there are, apart from the farms, a few remote, inaccessible, horrid little cottages, and in one of these, tended only by a sister of advancing years, lived the protagonist of my tale."

"More matter," said Fen somewhat restively, "with less art."

"Unconscious of his doom"—Humbleby had at last found a cheroot, and was applying fire to it from a desk lighter—"unconscious of his doom, the little victim, aged about thirty and by name Joshua Ledlow, which goes to show the potency of the tradition of Biblical nomenclature in these less accessible rural places—the little victim.... What was I saying?"

"Really, Humbleby ..."

"Here is this Joshua, then." All at once Humbleby abandoned frivolity and became business-like. "Thirty years old, unmarried, of a rather sombre and savage temperament, socially a cut above the farm labourer and living modestly on money left him by a farmer father. He is looked after by his sister Cicely, five to ten years older than he, who shows no particular fondness for him and who would in any case prefer to be looking after a husband, but who remains unwooed and, having no fortune of her own, housekeeps for Joshua as a respectable substitute for earning a living. Joshua, meanwhile, is courting, the object of his fancy being a heavily-built girl called Vashti Winterbourne, who appears to have cast herself for the role of Cassibury Bardwell's *femme fatale*. She didn't seem to me, when I met her, to be physically very well suited for this task, but the local standard of female beauty is extraordinarily low, so I suppose.... Well, anyway, you see what I mean.

"Now, as you'd expect, Johsua isn't alone in his admiration for this rustic charmer. He has a rival, by name Arthur Penge, by vocation the local ironmonger; and it is clear that Vashti will soon have to make up her mind which of these suitors she is going to marry. In the meantime, relations between the two men degenerate into something like open hostility, the situation being complicated latterly by the fact that Joshua's sister Cicely has fallen in love with Penge, thereby converting the original triangle into a sort of—um—a quadrangle. So there you have all the ingredients for a thoroughly explosive mixture—and in due course it does in fact explode.

"With that much preliminary," continued Humbleby rather grandly, "I can go on to describe what happened last Saturday and Sunday. What happened on *Saturday* was a public quarrel, of epic proportions, between Joshua, Cicely and Penge. This enormous row took place in the entrance-hall of *The Jolly Ploughboy*, which is by just a fraction the less repellent of Cassibury's two pubs, and consisted of (*a*) Penge telling Joshua to lay off Vashti, (*b*) Cicely telling Penge to lay off Vashti and take her, Cicely, to wife instead, (*c*) Penge telling Cicely that no man not demonstrably insane would ever dream of marrying *her*, and (*d*) Joshua telling Penge that if he didn't keep away from Vashti in future, he, Joshua, would have much pleasure in slitting his, Penge's, throat for him. Various other issues were raised, apparently, of a supplementary kind, but these were the chief items; and when the quarrellers at last separated and went home, they were all, not unnaturally, in a far from forgiving frame of mind.

"Note, please, that this quarrel was quite certainly genuine. I mention the point because Bolsover and I wasted a good deal of energy investigating the possibility that Penge and Cicely were somehow in cahoots together—that the quarrel so far as they were concerned was a fake. However, the witnesses we questioned weren't having any of that; they told us roundly that if Cicely was acting, they were Dutchmen, and we were forced to believe them, the more so as one of them was the local doctor, who had to be called in to deal with Cicely's subsequent fit of hysterics. No chance of collusion in that department, then. Mind you, I'm not saying that if Penge had visited Cicely afterwards, and abased himself and asked her to marry him, she mightn't have forgiven him: she's not, poor soul, of an age at which you can afford to take too much umbrage at the past behaviour of a repentant suitor. But the established fact is that between the quarrel and the murder next day he definitely didn't visit her or communicate with her in any way. With the exception of a single interlude of one hour (and of the half-hour during which he must have been committing the crime), his movements are completely accounted for from the moment of the quarrel up to midnight on the Sunday; and *during* that one hour, when he *might* (for all we know) have gone to make his apologies to the woman, she was occupied with entertaining two visitors who can swear that he never came near her."

"I take it," Fen interposed, "that this hypothesis of Cicely and Penge working together would have solved your alibi problem for you."

"It would have, certainly, if there'd been evidence for it. But in actual fact, the evidence completely excludes it—and you must just accept that, I'm afraid. . . . But now let me get on with the story." ("I haven't been stopping you," Fen muttered.) "The next event of any consequence was on Sunday morning, when Cicely broke her ankle by falling out of a tree."

"A *tree?*"

"An apple-tree. She'd been picking the fruit, it seems. Anyway, the effect of this accident was of course to immobilise her and hence, in the event, to free her from any possible suspicion of having herself murdered her brother Joshua, since his body was found some considerable distance away from their cottage."

"You think the killing was done at the place where the body was found, do you?"

"We're certain of it. The bullet went clean through the wretched man's head and buried itself in a tree-trunk behind him—and that's a set-up which you can't fake convincingly, however hard you try: it's no use just firing a second bullet into the tree, because it's got to have traces of human blood and brains on it. . . . Cicely, then, is in the clear, unless you feel inclined to postulate her hobbling a couple of miles on crutches with a view to doing her brother in.

"The crime was discovered at about ten o'clock that evening by several people in a party, one of whom fell over Joshua's corpse in the dark: none of these people features in any other way in the affair, so I needn't specify them at all. The *place* was a little-frequented footpath on the direct route between Joshua's cottage and the centre of Cassibury, approximately two miles from the former and a mile from the latter. And I may as well say at once, to avoid describing the scene in detail, that all the obvious lines of investigation—footprints, position of the body, threads of clothing on brambles and so forth—led absolutely nowhere. However, there was just one substantial clue: I mean the revolver—a great cannon of a thing, an old .45—which Bolsover found shoved into the hedge a little distance away, with a fine set of prints on it.

"Now, we haven't, I'm afraid, so far discovered anything about this gun—its ownership and history and all the rest of it. It may belong to the Prime Minister or the Archbishop of Canterbury, for all we know. But in view of the fingerprints we could afford to defer the problem of the gun's origin for a few days anyway; our immediate plan of action was of course to uncover possible motives for Joshua's death, get by guile the fingerprints of anyone suspicious, and compare them with the prints on the gun—and that led us straight away to Penge, because it was impossible to be in Cassibury five minutes without hearing about the Penge-Vashti-Joshua triangle in all its sumptuous detail. Penge, then, had this motive of jealousy—Vashti isn't the sort of girl I personally would do murder for, but then, I've known a *crime passionnel* be committed for possession of a penniless old lady of sixty-eight, and statistics show sex to be the motive for quite half the murders committed in this country, so that in that particular department I try not to be surprised at anything—Penge had this motive, then. And a comparison of his fingerprints with those on the revolver showed the two sets to be the same.

"When eventually he was asked to explain this circumstance he told, as I've mentioned, a demonstrable lie: saying that he'd handled the gun three days previously when Joshua (of all people!) had brought it into his ironmonger's shop to ask if a crack in the butt could be repaired. On its being pointed out to him that Joshua had quite certainly been in Dorchester during the whole of the day mentioned, and so couldn't possibly have visited the Cassibury ironmonger's, he wavered and started contradicting himself and eventually shut up altogether; in which oyster-like condition he's been ever since—and very wise of him, too.

"However, I'm anticipating: we didn't ask him about the gun until after we'd gone into the problem of the time of Joshua's death.

There was delay in getting a doctor to look at the body, so that the medical verdict was too vague to be helpful—between six and ten was the best reckoning we could get. But then two women came forward to tell us that they'd seen Joshua alive at seven. They said that on hearing of Cicely's accident they'd visited the cottage to condole with her, and had glimpsed Joshua on arrival; though he'd disappeared almost at once (having met the two ladies, I can see why) and they hadn't set eyes on him again. So clearly the next thing to do was to talk to Cicely herself. By early on Monday morning—the morning after the murder—Bolsover had taken over; and the local Sergeant, an intelligent lad, had the sense to warn him before he set off for Cicely's cottage that she was a hysterical type who'd have to be handled carefully if her evidence was to be of any use—a diagnosis which the event confirmed. However, it turned out that by a great stroke of luck she hadn't heard of the murder yet; the reasons for this being (*a*) the fact that Joshua had planned to be away from home that night in any case, so that his absence had not alarmed her, and (*b*) the fact that the local Sergeant, a temperamentally secretive person, had sworn everyone who knew of the murder to silence until a higher authority should release them from the vow. Consequently, Bolsover was able to put his most important questions to Cicely *before* telling her his reason for asking them— and a good thing too, because she had a fit of the horrors as soon as she heard her brother was dead, and the doctors have refused to allow her to talk to anyone since. Anyway, her testimony was that Joshua, having seen her settled for the night, had left the cottage at about eight-fifteen on the Sunday evening (a quarter of an hour or so after her own visitors had gone), with a view to walking into Cassibury and catching a bus to Dorchester, where he was to stay with friends. And that, of course, meant that he could hardly have reached the spot where he was killed much earlier than a quarter to nine.

"So the next thing, naturally enough, was to find out where Penge had been all the evening. And what it amounted to was that there were two periods of his time not vouched for by independent witnesses—the period from seven to eight (which didn't concern us) and the period from eight-thirty to nine. Well, the latter, of course, fitted beautifully; and when we heard that he'd actually been *seen*, at about a quarter to nine, close to the place where the murder was committed, we started getting the warrant out without any more ado.

"And that, my dear Gervase, was the point at which the entire case fell to pieces.

"Penge had lied about his whereabouts between eight-thirty and nine: we knew that. What we didn't know was that from twenty-past eight to ten past nine two couples were making love no more than a few feet from the place of the murder; and that not one of those four people, during the time they were there, heard a shot.

"It's no use talking about silencers, either; even a silenced report would have been heard, on a quiet night. And so that, as they say, was that. Penge certainly shot Joshua. But he didn't do it between eight-thirty and nine. And unless Cicely was lying in order to help him—which is inconceivable; and in any case, Bolsover's ready to swear on the Book that her brother's death was an unspeakable shock to her—unless that, then he didn't do it between seven and eight, either."

Humbleby stubbed out his cheroot and leaned forward earnestly. "But he worked it somehow, Gervase. His lies alone would make me certain that he's guilty. And the thought that he's invented some ingenious trick or other, which I can't for the life of me see, makes me writhe."

There was a long silence when he had finished speaking. In Whitehall, the traffic had diminished from a continuous to an intermittent roar, and they could hear Big Ben striking a quarter to eight. Presently Fen cleared his throat and said diffidently:

"There are lots of things one wants to ask, of course. But on the evidence you've given me so far the trick looks fairly simple."

Humbleby made an incoherent noise.

"If Penge's alibi is watertight," Fen went on, "then it's watertight. But just the same, it's easy to see how he killed Joshua."

"Indeed." Humbleby spoke with considerable restraint.

"Yes. You've been looking at it upside down, you see. The situation, as I understand it, *must* be that it isn't Penge who has the alibi. It's the corpse."

"The *corpse?*" Humbleby echoed, dumbfounded.

"Why not? If Cicely was lying about the time Joshua left the cottage—if in fact he left much earlier—then Penge could have killed him between seven and eight."

"But I've already explained—"

"That it's inconceivable she'd lie on Penge's behalf. I quite agree. But mightn't she lie on her brother's? Suppose that Joshua, with a revolver in his pocket, is setting out to commit a crime. And suppose he tells Cicely, if any questions are asked, to swear he left her much later than in fact he did. And suppose that a policeman questions Cicely on this point *before* she learns that it's her brother, and not the man he set out to kill, who is dead. Wouldn't that account for it all?"

"You mean—"

"I mean that Joshua intended to murder Penge, his rival in this young woman's affections; that he arranged for his sister (whom Penge had just humiliated publicly) to give him, if necessary, a simple alibi; and that then—"

"Ah yes. 'Then'..."

"Well, one doesn't *know*, of course. But it looks as if the plan misfired—as if Penge struggled with Joshua, got hold of the gun, and killed his assailant in self-defence. Behold him, then, with a watertight alibi created—charming irony—by his enemy. If the lovers hadn't been hanging about, he would have spoiled that alibi by going back afterwards—and one wonders why he *did* go back, though I imagine—"

"Morbid attraction," Humbleby interposed. "I've seen it happen time and time again. . . . But good God, Gervase, what a fool I've been. And it is the only explanation. The one trouble about it is that there's no *proof*."

"I should think there will be," said Fen, "as soon as Cicely ceases to be incommunicado and learns what's happened. If what you say about her dislike of Penge is true, she won't persist in the lie which exonerates him from killing her brother." All at once Fen was pensive. "Though come to think of it, if I were *Penge*—"

Shatteringly, the telephone rang, and Humbleby snatched it from its cradle. "Yes," he said. "Yes, put him on. . . . Bolsover?" A long pause. "Oh, you've seen that, have you? So have I—though only just. . . . Allowed to talk to people again, yes, so you— *What?*" And with this squeak of mingled rage and astonishment Humbleby fell abruptly silent, listening while the telephone crackled despairingly at his ear. When at last he rang off, his round face was a painter's allegory of gloom.

"Bolsover thought of it too," he said sombrely. "But not soon enough. By the time he got to Cicely's bedside, Penge had been there for hours. . . . They're going to get married: Cicely and Penge, I mean. She's forgiven him about the quarrel—I told you she doted on him, didn't I? Bolsover says he's never seen a more obsequious, considerate, dutiful, loving bridegroom-to-be. And of course, she's sticking to her story about the time Joshua left the house. Very definite about it, Bolsover says, and if she weren't, there are always Penge's *beaux yeux* to make her so."

And Fen got to his feet. "Well, well," he said, "you'll never put him in the dock now. And yet I suppose that if he'd had the courage to tell the truth, he'd probably have got away with it."

"All I can say is"—Humbleby, too, had risen—"that I hope it really was self-defence. In the interests of justice—"

"Justice?" Fen reached for his hat. "I shouldn't worry too much about that, if I were you. Here's a wife who knows her husband killed her brother. And here's a husband who knows his wife can by saying a word deprive him of his liberty and just possibly—if things didn't go well—of his life. And each knows that the other knows. And the wife is in love with the husband, but one day she won't be any longer, and then he'll begin to be afraid. And the wife thinks her husband is in love with her, but one day she'll find out that he isn't, and then she'll begin to hate him and to wonder what she can do to harm him, and he will know this, and she will know that he knows it and will be afraid of what he may do. . . .

"Justice? My dear Humbleby, come and have some dinner. Justice has already been done."

One Word at a Time

BY BAYARD WENDELL

"That same evening, in the presence of the whole family, a turnip fell from the ceiling."

We all burst out laughing except Lovell, who was holding the place in the book with his finger. His tone when he spoke held a reproof: "It's not a fairy tale. It happened, in Stratford, Connecticut—where they now play Shakespeare—"

"In colonial times, I suppose?" asked Trenner regretfully.

"Not at all. In 1850. At the house of a very intelligent clergyman, Dr. Phelps. His son was a Yale professor and tells about it. He says that the spirit, poltergeist, whatever it was, could read their minds and do the opposite of what they were thinking of."

"As good as a wife, eh?" put in Klotz, who was the club cynic.

The conversation had taken off from the afternoon papers, which reported an outbreak of "events" in the house of a Long Island plumber. Lovell, who made his living writing American history, cited a number of cases. Because he seemed to believe them, we argued. So he started to take books down from the shelves.

"What bothers me," said Theodore Morley, "is the turnip. It lacks style."

"That's because you're a drama critic of the old school," said Trenner with a certain intensity. He was the youngest of us.

"That's right," added Klotz. "Turnips strike me as very modern. You see them on the stage all the time."

"All right, we'll call it symbolic and then it will be in style." Ted's tired brown face broke into a disarming grin. "But what do you fellows think?" He was addressing the two men who had not yet spoken, George Scudder the lawyer and Sholto Williams, the research scientist who some years before had won a Nobel prize.

Scudder made a gesture toward his neighbor. "Sholto's the only man here qualified to pass judgment. I don't mean about what happened last century. I mean about yesterday on Long Island."

Williams stirred a bit and his yellow-white hair and thin pale face caught the firelight. "Well, you know, chemistry doesn't specialize in poltergeists. All I can say you know already. And it's simply that the chances are against any report of supernatural events being true. When plates and vegetables fly through the air, the assumption is that some ordinary motive power is at work."

"You start out expecting fraud?" Trenner again hung forward in his chair.

"Perhaps not entirely conscious—"

"Ah!" It was Lovell seizing his advantage. "You do grant the possibility of purely mental force, ESP and so on. And if thoughts can be read—"

Ted Morley gave an explosive "Ha!" which made everybody turn. "Sorry. I didn't mean to interrupt, but your words, Arthur, made me think of some people Sholto and I once knew, who got into a weird mess over this sort of thing—the science of telepathy. In fact we had quite an adventure, Sholto and I, during that weekend in the pines. Do you remember?"

"I do." Williams spoke gravely. "Hocus-pocus, scandal, suicide—it was complete."

"Then you must tell us." There was a chorus of assent to Trenner's suggestion, though Lovell looked a trifle put out. And at first both Sholto and Ted demurred, pleading their aging memories. But we insisted that they piece them together and we finally got the story.

The first indication that anything was wrong at Melbury came to Sholto Williams in the form of a wire from his old friend and classmate Tom Sherwood, whom the chemist had not seen for two years or more. The wire read:

NEED ADVICE CAN YOU COME WEEKEND BRING TED IF AVAILABLE TOUGH PROPOSITION

Sherwood could have telephoned and made the problem clear at once, but those were the days before the Second World War, when the habit of ringing up friends in distant cities was less common than now. It was Ted, newspaperman with few inhibitions, who called up the great house in the South Carolina pine country, and got the gist of the difficulty. That something serious was afoot both Ted and Sholto knew from their friend's use of the final phrase in his message. In college it had been for their little group Tom's nickname as well as a signal that he was not fooling: "Tough proposition." But what trouble could have descended on the household of the debonair, handsome, generous man who was wealthy enough to have retired in middle age, who was happily married, and whose one grievance against life could only be the loss, two years before, of his one son and only child? The boy had just turned seventeen and had died of septicemia from an infected blister on the foot, acquired in playing tennis. Tom and his wife had been unconsolable. After a time they had gone on a trip around the world and had been back at Melbury but a few months.

As Ted explained it to Sholto on the train south, Tom's present worry seemed incredibly out of character. "Just think, he has these two living in the house already and feeding him this bilge—"

"But does he believe it?"

Ted hesitated. "I'm not sure. My impression was—and I didn't catch it all because the connection was poor—that it's Mary who is going all out for it. She thinks she can eventually talk to Evan in the next world. She feels guilty, because she didn't take the boy's infection seriously enough in the first days. Thinks she killed him."

"Dear, dear! But you haven't really answered my question. How does Tom take all this? He cared about the boy as much as she did. Does he think these people can put *him* in touch?"

"That's the strange part. He's confident they're honest. He says their attitude is scientific. And yet he doesn't sound convinced— thank God! He says he's in a terrible dilemma, because of Mary and because of what he calls 'his own situation,' which he wouldn't discuss over the phone. To me the nub of the thing is that they want him to subsidize their research—all right, don't go rigid over a word—they're working on telepathy and they want a wad of Tom's money."

Williams was silent for a moment, then came out of his reverie with a gesture showing an impatience quite alien to his ways. "Tom is the last man this ought to happen to. You know how open-handed he can be—what does he mean by 'scientific' anyway? Well, there's no use speculating."

"Yes, we'll soon know the worst, though I tell you I don't like the idea of sharing a bathroom with a medium—probably goes right through a locked door."

"This is no joking matter."

"Don't tell me you believe these artists are genuine?"

"I keep an open mind, as you know, but what worries me is not what they are, or even what they want, but what they do—or are about to do—to Tom and Mary."

The visitors had rather steeled themselves, as one does, against the first contact with unpleasantness. But their host proved to be everything they had ever thought him—big in every way. Whatever he felt, he had put on a big smile to welcome them and from his grip and his words no stranger could have suspected that this autumn reunion had any other purpose than conviviality, golf, and the best duck-shooting in the country. Only to the eyes of his especially observant friends, the one a critic, the other a man of science, did Tom Sherwood seem overwrought.

When Mary appeared a few moments later, the cause was evident. Sherwood kept stealing apprehensive little glances at his unseeing wife. They were both pitiable. The last time they had seen Mary Sherwood she had been a strikingly elegant woman, beautiful in face and carriage, a fit model for Sargent. Now there was only one word for her—she was undone. Her eyes were dead and her lips out of control. Her handshake was unpleasantly moist, and she kept repeating meaningless little words. "The poor dears want to go to their rooms, Tom. The poor dears, the poor dears . . ."

It is true there was just time to change and dress, but having plumbed his friend's misery, Sholto Williams could not bear the thought of behaving as if nothing had happened. "Perhaps," he said to Mary, "Tom will take me up, though Ted and I know our way."

Upstairs and alone with his host, Williams came straight to the point. "Now, Tom, what *is* this situation you are in?"

Sherwood seemed relieved at being asked. "It's quite simple— and devilish. Mary, as you can see, hasn't recovered—the trip did no good. It did harm, because she kept brooding on a possibility that hadn't occurred to her before, of establishing communication with Evan."

"What put that into her mind?"

"Not long after we left, Jim Thorne—you know, our great friend in Philadelphia—wrote to say he'd heard of a medium who was unlike any other. Got advance notice of people's deaths and so on. He suggested the link might work in reverse. This took hold of Mary and—"

"Is this the medium we're going to meet here?"

"One of them. But that's not all. I had another blow from Thorne when I returned, or rather, he let me know in London that he had serious news for me. He's a good businessman, in spite of con- sorting with mediums—has wonderful tips and he's attended to my affairs for years. Well, it seems that during those months I was away, a number of stocks went bad. He tried to recoup and got in deeper.

The result is, I'm not in any permanent danger, but we must be careful and retrench."

"Well, why doesn't that solve your problem? You're temporarily strapped. Surely that's not the time to subsidize psychical research?"

"There's Mary. In the first place, I'd do anything—anything—to take that look from her face and give her back some peace of mind. She used to be so—" He broke off helplessly. "The final twist is this: when Mary and I got married we pooled our holdings under the law of community property; I invested hers with mine. Now she naturally feels she has a claim on her share, just when—"

"She's made this claim, outright?"

"Yes."

The monosyllable told Sholto all. "I see. There's only one thing, Tom, these mediums of yours must be proved fraudulent beyond a doubt."

"That's the way I see it too. It took me long enough to figure out. I haven't been exactly at my best. Meantime they've made themselves at home. Mary has taken a shine to the young one. Sometimes, from a distance, he looks a little like Evan—the way he walks."

"Oh Lord," muttered Williams, "you mean no matter what we do we're bound to—"

"Exactly. But I see no other way. Cruel to be kind—you agree with me? Mary and I can't go on living like this. These last six months! She talks of selling the house—the money is nothing: I want her to be—well—my wife again—in spite of—" he made a cosmic gesture—"everything."

Williams returned the other's somber look. "We'll try—everything." He gave the departing Sherwood a gentle tap on the shoulder and was alone. There would be a chance later to tell Morley what he had learned. He must hurry if he was not to hold up dinner.

Meanwhile Ted, nearly dressed, had found that his mind wandered willingly as his eyes took in the last glow of the sun setting behind a palisade of innumerable pines, the dark expanse of lawn below his windows, and other signs of spaciousness within and without. He let out a deep breath as he relaxed under these influences, surprised at the warmth of contentment that crept into him. He chided himself, gave a last pull to his tie, and went downstairs without waiting for the gong.

Ted had first come to the place when Tom was unmarried and his parents still living. Memories, he reflected, made one quickly feel at home again. He stepped into the small sitting room at the left of the stairs to find a cigarette. As he walked in, Mary Sherwood was standing with her back to him, and in the half gloom he had a swift impression of the figure of a man, blond and slight, disappearing into the room beyond, unquestionably the dining room. Mary turned, looking transfigured, and said, "Oh!" Then her eyes focused and she went past Ted to the hall door, saying, "Excuse me, dear, I must speak to Tom first."

Ted found and lit a cigarette and crossed the corridor to the living room. Nobody was down, but soon there were voices in the hall. A very tall, stooped southern gentleman with a huge head appeared, preceded by a thin woman, also with an outsize head, who strongly resembled him. Ted introduced himself and was told that he was speaking to Miss Rainsford and her brother Judge Leigh Rainsford, whom he had indeed met in this same house years before. The Judge was disposed to talk about the weather in a reedy voice that seemed out of keeping with his size and public dignity. The lady, whose hair, clothes, and voice alike conveyed an impression of gunmetal, did not beat around the bush: "Are you here to witness the experiment too?"

Morley was nonplussed. "The experiment?"

"Yes, the demonstration or whatever you choose to call it, which Tom and Mary want us to see before they take the plunge."

"Now, Letitia, you mustn't—"

What she mustn't remained unsaid, for just then a stout man of forty-eight or so, with quickly roving eyes and a misleading air of being unshaved, came into the room with Tom and Mary and was introduced.

"How nice it is," said Tom, "to have guests who are prompt!" He was shaking hands with Letitia as he said this and she took him up:

"You say that as if you were a martinet, but the real reason is that you love your friends so much you can't wait to see them."

"Hear, hear!" said the fat man in a penetrating voice. He turned to Sholto Williams, who had quietly come in, and held out a hand. "My name's Thorne. I'm Tom's trustee. You don't know the word, eh? In these parts and as far as Philadelphia, where I come from, it means broker, lawyer, man of business all in one. It's cheaper—"

"But not safer," said Letitia, again looking at Tom. Thorne took no notice. He was eying the cocktails which the butler was passing around.

The conversation went on by spurts, as it will when everybody is thinking of something else. The obvious subject was being avoided, and when Ted finally stood behind his chair in the dining room, his thought still was: "Where *are* those charlatans?" And it was clear from Sholto's expression across the table that at least one act of mind-reading had already been accomplished.

The performers made their entrance after dinner, but not before Tom had prepared the stage. He forbore, he said, to thank his good friends who were there to help him; they were like members of the family and would, he knew, give him and Mary their frankest advice. Right now they must concentrate on the one point which might mean so much for her happiness and his.

"I already owe to Jim Thorne," he went on, "the opportunity of knowing Melvin Addison, whom you will shortly meet. He is a Ph.D. in psychology from Tulane and has taught the subject at various colleges. In one of them he found that his young assistant, Alan Wright, was frequently able to read his mind. At first they thought it was coincidence, or subvocal talking, or some other familiar phenomenon. But they took measures to exclude all this and established the fact that young Wright is a medium. Not only is he remarkably in tune with Addison, but when Addison's father died, eight hundred miles away, young Wright got the news—so to speak—before the wire came."

Morley had been watching as well as listening, and he caught on Thorne's face a look which he could not interpret. All he knew was that the man's restless eyes now stood out and his forehead was glistening. Mary Sherwood was still in another world, as she had been throughout dinner. The Judge, his legs outstretched and his eyes shut, seemed bored or possibly dead. Letitia's expression spelled polite derision. Only Sholto kept his customary detachment. But Sherwood was going on.

"—true scientific test is to arrange things so that the effect can be repeated at will. That is what they have done. Addison doesn't profess to explain what goes on, but he has got his method to a point where under controlled conditions he can invariably transmit to Wright one word in the space of eight to ten hours. He can tell you more himself, and he will of course answer any questions— but here they are."

Though well turned out in evening clothes, Addison was in no way spectacular. He was of middle height, on the stocky side, and had the earnest homely look that often characterizes the man of science. Sholto's first impression—and even Ted's—was good: the man did not look slick. Perhaps his hair was a bit too black and flourishing, but that might only be a sign of health. By contrast Alan Wright was a cipher. Blond, willowy, good-looking in a common, vacuous way, he was evidently dependent on every thought and wish of his more masculine companion.

"If that's what's required for ESP," said Morley to himself, "I'd rather not have it." He was quite sure now that this youngster was the figure he had seen in private conversation with Mary Sherwood. Well, why not? No reason, certainly, but why vanish when someone else came in—and through the *dining room*?

Ted's mind switched back to more solid ground. Hadn't someone said at dinner that the assistant was about twenty-five? This chap barely looked nineteen and not very bright. No wonder the other could imprint any word he chose upon that blank tablet. Yes, they were a pair, and on the subject of pairs Ted could be as prejudiced as any woman.

But the black-haired Ph.D. had launched into his lecture. It would be a long one, too, judging from the conventional opening words, "I'll try to be brief...."

"It must bore my good friends the Sherwoods to hear again what I have so often gone over before. My excuse must be that this is my first opportunity here to be speaking of my work to another man of science."

He made a little bow to Sholto, who acknowledged it: "I am not a psychologist," he said pleasantly, "but I think I can follow you on the general principles."

Addison bowed again. "My claim is not a large one, and any success that has attended my studies is only a small part of what I must have before I can publish any results. That is why, with Mr. Sherwood's generous help, I hope to convince you that the little I have got hold of in mental telepathy is a fragment on which it would be well to build. It is only a fragment, but it is solid. I want you all to assure yourselves of this. Any suspicion of trickery naturally ruins any hope of support or of serious attention, either by patrons or by anyone who may be on the same track in the same spirit of science.

"I shan't detail the course of my experiments during the last six years. And I can't analyze for you very far the actual mechanism of the transference, for I have not yet been able to put it on a quantitative basis. I have simply found that certain methods produce certain results, not occasionally but invariably. Lately, when I have failed I have always been able to relate it to the absence of one of the numerous bodily factors, in myself or in my assistant, which are essential to success. Blood pressure, for example, is very important. This is my contribution so far: I know the physiological requirements of thought transference. I can check their presence in the performers, and so I can predict the certainty of the outcome even though I cannot explain it. And of course I cannot produce at will the delicate physiological balance that is required."

The speaker paused. The listeners were impressed in spite of themselves. Addison continued.

"As you have been told, I shall demonstrate the process in its simplest form, during the course of an ordinary night of eight hours. During that time Mr. Wright falls into a perfectly normal sleep—I have just checked all his responses as well as mine—and in the morning the word I have spent part of the night endeavoring to transfer will occur to him if he is asked for it as soon as he wakes.

"I repeat that his sleeping is entirely normal. He is not hypnotized. And you see the advantage, from our point of view, of this nighttime procedure. You have no cause to suspect signals, motions, or other visual tricks to deceive you and convey the word. I shall be out of the room when you choose it. You will give it to me, in my room, on a slip of paper, and will at once set up any guard you wish outside my door. Mr. Wright's room is several doors down on the other side of the hall. There can be no collusion.

"I might add that if the word is not asked for fairly promptly, its memory fades very rapidly, which suggests to me that the transfer is from my conscious mind to the receiver's unconscious. The word comes into his conscious mind only because it is asked for—and because Mr. Wright cannot help knowing that we are conducting experiments—yes, Dr. Williams?"

"Forgive me, I was just wondering what you inferred from these observations?"

"My tentative conclusion is that in the beginning of evolution we all read one another's minds as easily as we hear one another's voices. Animals are aware of their fellows' needs, certainly, and so are we to a certain extent. But with us social convention keeps a great deal of this—er—material repressed in the unconscious."

"Very ingenious," piped Judge Rainsford with eyes shut.

"How ghastly for everybody if this wholesome repression should stop," said his sister.

"But some people—some people can break through it," croaked Thorne the trustee.

"That is so." It was the first word that Alan Wright had spoken since shaking hands. His voice was unusually vibrant for his slight frame and everybody seemed surprised except Mary. She had come to life during the explanations, familiar as they must have been to her. "But Alan, dear," she said, "you haven't mentioned your greater powers—you know—breaking the barrier and speaking with—with those who—who have gone before."

It was Tom Sherwood's turn to look hunted. He gave a violent headshake, then said briskly, "It's ten o'clock. We ought to get under way if you young men and our other guests are going to get their beauty sleep. Addison, you go upstairs with Wright. We'll see you shortly with the word."

The pair left with appropriate murmurs, and rather self-consciously one little group fell to discussing desirable words. "Short but not too common," said Letitia decisively.

Ted cleared his throat. "I wonder, could we beforehand have a look at the rooms where the scientific gentlemen concentrate and—er—receive?"

"Certainly. But Ted, you know this house. There are no secret passages, no hidden wires or tubes. Mary and I have been all over it before. You'll only have your trouble for nothing—oh, all right," he laughed. "I know that mulish look on your face, go on up. You too, Sholto, it's only fair after dragging you down here. At the head of the stairs and then across, three doors down."

The would-be investigators went up silently. Addison showed them in with calm courtesy. His bedroom was small and simply furnished, but off it, in a larger space, he had set up his "laboratory"—a mass of apparatus on two large trestle tables, with more of it attached to a plain wooden armchair. Addison let them explore alone. Williams recognized a basal metabolism machine, a sphygmomanometer, an encephalograph or brain-wave recorder, coils, batteries, and other electric meters, including a galvanometer. Ted slapped his hand down on a black box with a number of jacks. "This," he announced confidently, "is an electrocardiograph."

"How do you know?"

"It says so on a little brass plate."

They took care to trace every wire to its attachment, moved the few boxes on the floor, scanned the walls and windows, lifted the plain carpet, and made sure that nothing illicit led out of either the laboratory or the bedroom. They repeated their search in Wright's quarters, while the young man looked at them in silence. Then they rejoined the others downstairs.

"Satisfied?" cried Tom.

"Yes," said Sholto.

"Then give us a word. We didn't want to choose without you."

"If you don't mind, I'd rather stay on the outside—the complete observer, you know. Perhaps Miss Rainsford will be good enough to help us."

Letitia drew her mouth in a line and held out a hand to Tom, who was already reaching for his pen and a slip from his notebook. She made a few angular marks on the paper and passed it around so that everyone could make out the word "Euchre."

The next morning at 8:30 the five men, led by Sherwood, knocked on Wright's door and went in. Four of them had slept on army cots placed opposite the doors of the two telepathists, Morley having won the toss-up for the privilege of a night's sleep in a proper bed. Alan Wright, when he greeted the group, also seemed to have had a good night. He smiled, stretched, and hoisted himself a little on his pillows. "I know what you gentlemen want," he said, "it's 'Euchre.' "

Williams and Morley exchanged glances, then turned to read their companions' expressions. Thorne, Ted decided, must come naturally by his look of perpetual alarm, and also by a greasy skin; the Judge was giving nothing away; Sherwood seemed torn between disappointment and a secret satisfaction. Alan Wright looked bland. In the silence he slid out of bed and shut the window. Meanwhile Sholto had wandered a little away from the rest and was refreshing his observations of the evening before. The room could hardly be called bare, but it afforded no means of concealment—no corners, no heavy hangings, no balcony. Casually, the scientist confirmed his impression that the assistant, whether a mind reader or not, was something of a reader of books. The bedside table held more volumes than he would have supposed a medium could want: four or five novels, a manual of woodcraft, two of Richard Halliburton's travel adventures, a Bible, and—wise precaution—a desk dictionary.

Half-listening, he heard Ted giving the telepathist congratulations on his receptivity. Ted also prophesied fame to Sherwood if he should prove to be the first patron of a new science. "By the way," added Morley, turning back to Wright, "which do you find it easier to summon up, images or sounds?"

The youth stopped with a vacuous grin, as if he felt flattered without knowing why. "Afraid I don't get you."

"I mean, does the consciousness you acquire of somebody else's thought come to you as a picture, to which you then put a name, or do you hear in your mind certain sounds forming a word which is the name of an idea or object?"

This seemed to nonplus—as well it might—the human tabula rasa. As Wright struggled for an answer, Addison's black mane and lantern jaws appeared at the door. Williams took a quick decision. "May I add a word to my friend Morley's expression of interest? It was a very striking demonstration—beautifully simple, like the de-cisive first steps of a new science."

As Addison bowed, Sherwood took charge. "Successful, as usual," he said to Addison, and with a gesture he urged everybody out. "Let's let Alan get dressed. He must be hungry. And I bet you're all wanting your breakfast too."

Morley edged over and, making a sign to Sholto to draw near, he spoke in an undertone to Sherwood. "Get their noses into their plates and join us in the downstairs sitting room."

A few minutes later the three friends were together. "Tom," said Theodore, "you can be absolutely sure that this dodge is a fake from beginning to end."

Sherwood looked from the one to the other.

"I agree," said the scientist slowly. "The trouble is, I can prove it to myself and perhaps to you, but until I can show how the thing is worked, I can't convince a real believer like Mary."

"Or Thorne," put in Ted. "By the way, what's the matter with your friend? His eyes start out of his head every time this subject comes up."

Sherwood gave a brief laugh. "You have to get used to Jim. He is —always has been—the most superstitious man alive. Black cats, Fridays, omens of all sorts. I don't know how he does it, but he runs his brokerage office on the advice of one woman clairvoyant after another. I thought his familiarity with the breed might help tell us whether Wright is the genuine article."

Morley made a sound in his throat. "That little rat is a phony."

"Why are you so sure?"

"Listen: if I sit up half the night trying to get 'Euchre' into your mind, I am thinking either of the game itself—the cards, the rules, the terminology—or else I am concentrating on the two sounds— 'you-cur'. Very well. Now, suppose I'm the receiver: either I see something or I hear something. And if the telepathic process has taken place a dozen or a score of times I can't help knowing which it is, sound or picture, that rises from my unconscious." He paused. "I have a hunch the picture would take a little longer to identify and give a name to, whereas the sound would come out automatically. Now, I don't believe for a moment this booby had ever heard of euchre in his life before last night. I was dying to ask him—"

"I was afraid you might," put in Sholto. "It's very important to make them think we are taken in."

"But Ted, if it all works through the unconscious—"

"That's hogwash. Of course our thoughts come out of some dark hole or other—unconscious or memory. When you try to recall a name you've temporarily forgotten, you grope and grope and suddenly it's there. And when it comes you know that it's what you've been looking for because it *fits*. The sound and the meaning are those you wanted. But this chap doesn't want any particular word—he has no idea what is going to be wafted to him—so when he gets ready to open his mouth with that sleepy look on his face, he must feel some surprise at hearing an unexpected word sounding in his ear—or else he must be seeing a picture. And I repeat: if he does either of these things he can tell me which it is when I ask him. You saw that he had no idea what I was talking about."

There was a pause. Then Sherwood looked up sharply. "I can see Sholto agrees with you. But aren't you proving too much? If Alan doesn't become aware of a sound or a picture, how does he get the right word every time? He does that, you know, without a fail or a stumble."

"There's only one possible answer," said Sholto, "he gets it in some written form."

"Yes," added Morley, "the civilized way. Men first made sounds, then drew pictures, and finally invented letters."

"But how—how? It isn't as if they had only a couple of amateurs like Mary and me to deal with. You've looked at the rooms. I know the house like the palm of my hand. They've had no chance to instal anything—how do they do it?"

"That's what we have to find out. At the moment," Sholto gave a dim smile, "if I may use Addison's own words, 'I can't analyze for you the actual mechanism of transference.' But can you possibly manage to get everybody out of the way—I don't mean Mary—so as to give me a free run of the second floor? Just for the afternoon. I may be able to tell you something when you come back."

"I bet you won't pry Addison loose from his laboratory without a pickax."

"You're wrong, Ted. Addison's a golfer. I'll get them all out to the country club for lunch. Then eighteen holes, which I'll drag out as much as I can. Alan doesn't play but I'll plant him on some nice girls for tennis."

"I'm for the girls, too," said Ted, "—rather more, I suspect, than your young friend. My point is, I want to keep an eye on him. I have an idea there's a story in that boy I'd give a good deal to know."

Tom looked up again and gave an embarrassed cough. "I may as well tell you the latest—development."

"You haven't already forked up?" Ted was aghast.

"No, not the way you think. But Mary—well, Mary's feelings are easily worked on and Wright's been getting money from her."

Ted had a flash of understanding. "Last night—?"

"Yes, last night again, and she let drop something that might turn really serious. You see, there is—there was something—irregular about Evan's birth. The Rainsfords know, but it's been a well-guarded secret, and now—now Mary has confided in this young cub—God knows why!" The exclamation burst from Tom as if for the first time he were angry with his wife.

"That *is* bad," agreed Sholto. "I wondered whether Dr. Addison was just a plain fraud. It looks now as if he had a sideline—"

But Sherwood had quickly recovered himself. "I see what you mean, but I don't think so. I'm on edge and I probably jumped too soon. They'd need proof, you see. We adopted Evan in due form, and they wouldn't get far on hearsay." Tom's voice held a menace.

"I don't like the looks of it, just the same." Theodore was equally grim. "I want that little crook turned inside out. Wait till this afternoon!"

After a solitary lunch—Mrs. Sherwood not having come down since the night before—Sholto Williams began his wanderings from room to room. In his quiet methodical way, he picked up objects, tested a few pieces among the litter of apparatus in Melvin Addison's laboratory, followed with his eye the moldings of the elegantly appointed bedrooms of the old house, opened windows and leaned out over balconies, lifted rugs by one corner, and read the titles of a good many scattered books. On his first survey he did not pry into the papers on Addison's desk. They were exposed to anyone's eye and the drawers were unlocked: it was obvious the psychologist would not be caught with compromising documents at the very time he was inviting a search.

But as Sholto came the second time around, it occurred to him that even though everybody has read Poe's "Purloined Letter" some may think themselves alone in valuing its lesson. So he glanced briefly at the tidy packet of letter-size sheets. They were notes, most of them too abbreviated to be read, mixed with differential equations. The rest were four or five reprints from psychological journals, none by Addison himself. It was all pure science and no occult lore. This was a shrewd move—and revealing. The lab, Williams was convinced, must hold the clue, since Addison operated either from it or from the adjoining bedroom, and the bedroom held nothing suspicious. Yet in the lab, two objects and only two could be considered not quite what they seemed.

It was after five when Sherwood's car came up the gravel drive and the slim figure of the scientist made his way back to his own room. Morley joined him there. "You're the one that looks tired," he panted, "but I'm the one who's done the hard work."

"On the tennis court?"

"In a telephone booth. I can't understand why the long-lines people spend millions of dollars rigging up the best equipment along the highways and then allow some local company to put in three miles of condemned wire across country—it must be clothesline they've used to connect the country-club—you can't hear yourself for the hum."

"You heard something, anyway, or you wouldn't be looking so pleased with yourself."

"I have. I am. For a Saturday I did pretty well. I had some luck at Tulane, because it's still late registration time and the offices were open. They told me that Addison *was* one of their Ph.D.'s and had taught there for a couple of years. I got on to the head of the department and he couldn't tell me anything, being a senior man, but he found a mere colonel, or maybe a sergeant of science, who remembered young Addison about ten years ago. And what do you think he told me?"

"I have no idea, but if it's bad I wonder that he should tell it to a stranger over the phone."

"He told me *because* it was bad—and because a representative of the press is never a stranger. To be brief, they thought Addison a very bright lad indeed but he couldn't keep his hands off other people's results, so they sacked him. This chap said it wasn't even safe to talk over your ideas with our Melvin, he would snap them up, work them out faster than lightning, and be in print before you'd get your own wires properly soldered."

"That's a help." Sholto spoke a little abstractedly. "I mean it should help to make him vacate the premises when—"

"When we blow the gaff? You mean you've got something too?"

"I think I have a glimmer. But go on, if there's more to come."

"There is. You know how I worry an idea like a dog with a bone? Well, ever since I laid eyes on Thorne I've been ridden by the notion that something or somebody was eating him alive. And I didn't like what Tom told us of the homecoming this 'great friend' had prepared for him. I don't know much about stocks, but they have no business going down when their owner is taking a long trip."

"Do come to the point."

"The point is this: I rang up a couple of my colleagues in New York and Philly and found that James Lavengro Thorne is, to use a technical term, in the soup. What's more, the Philadelphia man says gossip attributes this to Thorne's ex-wife, who is said to have some hold on him. But in New York they think it's the fortune tellers who have finally let him down."

"Well, gossip is often diverting, but how does this help Tom—or get us any farther with our two impostors?"

"Why, don't you see? Tom's got to be warned. He's the victim of a conspiracy. I don't believe for a minute that Thorne's lost any of Tom's money—yet. But these three are in cahoots to clean him out. The boy works on Mary and the quack gets the rest, part hocus-pocus, part blackmail. Tom must file a complaint at once. The Judge—"

"Not so fast, Ted. If we aren't careful and concentrate our fire, we'll play into their hands. Our confusion will be their smokescreen. I don't minimize your results, but so far they're mostly suspicion. Did you carry out your threats about Wright, by the way?"

"Not a chance. He's a damned good tennis player and the girls found him ducky—that was the word. I couldn't get near him for the skirts."

"Well, better luck next time, though I think that even if you knew all about him you'd only pile up more suspicion."

"What have you got that's better?"

"I have a plan. I want to force a showdown on this telepathy business, right here, tomorrow morning."

"Well, I'm all for blowing up the sleeping beauty and finishing the fairy tale, but how are you going to do it overnight? You said you only had a glimmer."

"It's a trifle more than that. In the first place, that laboratory is a meaningless collection of junk. It can't possibly be used for any intelligent purpose, and it lacks certain essentials. Secondly, in the midst of what's there I came across a very curious object."

"A transmitter of some sort?"

"No, nothing like that. Last night when we were looking around I found an oblong wooden box containing an ordinary armband, gauge, and stethoscope such as doctors use to measure blood pressure."

"What about it?"

"Just this: it looks all right when you open it. But as you know I have a chemist's nose and I noticed the characteristic smell of perished rubber. Today I took it out. The thing is really old, probably bought second-hand, and it certainly cannot be used to take anybody's blood pressure. The tube and bulb are rotted through."

"That fits in with what I heard. Addison hasn't a cent. But I don't see what you make of a negative fact like that—"

"Just cast your mind back to last night and you'll see. No, I shan't tell you. I'm going to drop a word to Tom—no, not about what you or I have found, about something else I hope will develop of its own accord."

Man proposes but God disposes. Ted at cocktails was brooding about Sholto's secretiveness and also about the quick exchange between Addison and Thorne, of which he had caught a glimpse when he had looked up instinctively from the landing. They came down behind him, without Wright. How did these comings and goings fit together? And how was Sholto going to—? At this point the lights went out. Instead of a hubbub there was uncommon quiet, followed by desultory talk until Sherwood returned to apologize. It was not a fuse but a more awkward breakdown at the plant. Help had been sent for, though Helder, the chauffeur, might be able to make temporary repairs.

As the dinner-table candles were brought in, Sherwood expressed the hope that they would all be willing to carry on with the experiment as planned. He glanced briefly at Addison in the gloom.

"As planned?" echoed the psychologist. "I wonder just what was planned." He paused. "As you know, I am not able to control the delicate—"

"—physiological balance," finished Ted. "Yes, we know, but

until the lights went out you were going to try. I heard you say so to Thorne at the head of the stairs." The lie might catch a lie.

"You're mistaken. What I said about a long shot referred to golf."

"That's right," said Thorne, too quickly.

Sherwood did not miss the implication and his face grew stony. "That's fine," he said a little harshly. "Golf tomorrow. Tonight, business as usual. I may as well tell you, Addison, that I attach special importance to this one experiment. In fact, I make it a condition of my continued interest in your project."

"Oh, Tom, you can't!" Mary had half risen, but no one paid attention, because of the rasp in Addison's voice as he broke in. "I accept the challenge, Mr. Sherwood. But let me add that whether I fail or succeed, I have reason to think your interest in my work will continue." He rose and the darkness seemed to lend him stature. "I think all of you will continue to be *greatly* interested in my work. Now I have tests to run and must ask to be excused."

Thorne let out a hissing sigh. Letitia went to Tom and murmured some words Ted did not catch. Her brother was talking to himself and Ted did hear something about "his game." Sholto had gone to Mary Sherwood and seemed to be entreating her, but she interrupted to remind them of dinner. As Sherwood sat down, his face a pattern of dark lines, he said: "I apologize again. I never meant to involve you in such a messy business. But tomorrow morning should see the end of it."

Dinner and coffee were despatched with little cheer. A word was chosen by Sholto, with clucking appreciation from Letitia Rainsford, and the guard of four—now including Morley in place of Sherwood—settled one by one on their narrow couches.

The next day being Sunday, the hour for the recovery of the winged word had been moved to 9.30. Twenty minutes before that time Morley was pacing in and out of his room, lighting cigarettes he did not finish. Williams was awake too, but Thorne still snored covertly and the Judge, flat on his back, looked like an effigy on a cathedral tomb. Ten minutes before the time, Theodore roused the two older men and shook and bundled them into their gowns and slippers. Williams looked on with grim amusement, occasionally glancing at his wrist watch.

It was perhaps five minutes after the half hour when the party trooped into the assistant's bedroom. Alan Wright was sleeping evenly. Ted rattled the foot of the bed without mercy and the boy awoke with a start. His eyes opened wide but he saw nothing. He made an inarticulate noise and turned over on his side. But Morley was adamant. "Wake up!" he cried. "The word, the word!" and he shook him again, by the shoulder this time.

The boy reopened his eyes and yawned painfully. With a jerk he sat up and a cloud of apprehension passed over his face. He swallowed and gave a sidelong glance at the pile of books on the bedside table. Then he uttered a sound so indistinct that no one understood it. "Say it again," urged Morley.

"*Sis-toll,*" said the boy looking desperately into the unkempt, accusing faces.

"What's that?" thundered Morley.

"I think there is no need to shout." It was Addison, calm and somehow light on his feet, like a boxer. "My assistant is due the same consideration that you have been good enough to accord to me. Do I understand Alan has not got the right word?"

"You are to understand that your confidence game is over." Ted's dark face was suffused with anger. "Your stooge was not only out of touch with his unconscious when we woke him just now, but his conscious mind has muffed the cue for lack of sufficient coaching. We gave you the three-syllable word *systole;* he gave it to us in two syllables riming with—with 'bean-pole.' When you spelled it out to him in the night he was too lazy or too sleepy to look it up in his dictionary, and when he overslept this morning he gave the show away." Ted broke off and rounded on the boy: "What *does* 'systole' mean?"

No answer came but only a sinking glance at Addison. The assistant could see that his mentor had eliminated him from his own strategy. Addison seemed curiously jaunty. "May I be told, Mr. Morley, how—if the process is a fraud—I have managed to convey the words—the unusual and difficult words—that have so far been communicated?"

Before Ted had to admit that he didn't know, Williams coolly interposed. "You could do it quite easily by using the regular communication systems of the house."

"But Sholto, the only two phones are downstairs." As Tom spoke, he moved to the door; his wife was coming down the hall toward the commotion.

"I never said it was the phone. Communication is a subtle thing, as you can tell when you see two deaf mutes conversing, or two ships at sea. Words take many shapes. For example, on Friday night and, I imagine, every time before that, Dr. Addison used the electric light to carry his message in Morse."

"How could you do that?" Judge Rainsford thrust his big head forward.

Sholto bowed to Melvin Addison, whose poise was unruffled save for a slight working of the dark jaws. "Perhaps you would care to explain? Well then, I must. In going through the apparatus in the other room I came across a small hand vibrator of a common type. I plugged it in. It did not work. Though I applied a good practical knowledge of electrical equipment I could find no visible defect. It looked clean and used, but what could it be used for in its present condition? The more I thought of the make-believe laboratory, the surer I was that this blocked motor held a clue. The thing in my hand was still plugged in and I felt it grow warm. That told me what I should have guessed: it was being used as a resistance coil. Plug it in while the assistant's lamp is turned on by his bedside and the lamp will dim. Pull it out and it brightens again. Long and short will flash any word you can spell, even if the recipient cannot pronounce it."

Addison's expression now showed contempt. "You may recall there was no electricity last night."

"True," replied Sholto evenly. "I asked our host to throw the switch and announce a breakdown. I do not know, strictly speaking, how the code was worked last night in spite of the—"

"—then what right have you—"

"—I was about to say—" a faint smile played on Sholto's thin lips, "science gives the practitioner confidence in general propositions. When you have eliminated the impossible, as Poe said before Sherlock Holmes, what remains is the truth. You see, there *are* 'hidden wires and tubes' in this house—in any modern house. If the electrical system was useless, you must have used the second large system of conveyors, the water pipes. They too will indicate varying pressures. It would not surprise me to hear that last night Dr. Addison and his assistant took excessively thorough baths."

The scientist turned from his friends to the man he was accusing, but it was Letitia, just arrived, who spoke.

"You are right, Dr. Williams. The noise woke me about three. The shower was running and it did not stop till a quarter to four."

"Who is next door to you?" asked Morley.

"That young man." She pointed at Alan Wright. "By far the worse of the two."

"No, no, Letitia. He's done nothing wrong. He's only a boy. He's been so kind to me. He's explained very patiently. Sometimes there is fraud, but it grows out of the real thing. He's told me things about Evan only you and I know. No, Tom, don't try to stop me, he's told the truth. He admits the science is faked, but the messages come just the same, on earth and from beyond." Mary's sobs wrenched her body from her husband's arm and she rocked on the doorjamb, her head on her crossed hands.

Letitia took hold of her and shook her head at Sherwood. "No, you call the doctor." Then, from the threshold, she turned on the mind readers. "Now that you've seen your handiwork, you two— go, go, go, go!"

Alan Wright fled through the bath, but Addison held his ground. "Mr. Sherwood, I warned you last night. I have stood enough from hysterical women and," his glance flicked Sholto and Ted, "interfering busybodies. If I had only myself to consider, I would withdraw. But I have to think of my work. It must go on—in spite of the envy of petty minds. To a searcher after truth the end justifies the means. If I cannot get the support I need fairly on the merits, I shall get it by—pressure." He paused. "Today is Sunday and the banks are closed. By tomorrow at twelve o'clock, Mr. Sherwood, you will let me have a cashier's check for $75,000." He turned to go.

"This is pure bluff. You will regret it." Sherwood was livid.

"I never bluff. The proofs of your turpitude are all in order. You know my terms."

"Just a moment." The Judge's high-pitched voice was as controlled as Addison's. "You have uttered threats in front of witnesses. You are in effect blackmailing Sherwood. I shall advise him to prosecute."

Addison gave a wintry smile. "Get some better advice—from *him*." He pointed at Thorne and left the room.

Sherwood gave his friend a stony look, as he had done the night before. "What does he mean, Jim?"

Thorne darted his eyes at all in turn. The veins in his temples were throbbing. "I'd better make a clean breast, Tom. It had to come out some time. While you were gone, I had to—to realize on your reserves—in your other box. Otherwise your quarterly income would have been down. I couldn't explain while you were abroad—"

"*I—want—to know—about—Addison!*"

"I'm coming to that. I met him through—never mind—he gave a demonstration at her house. I believed him. He—he got hold—through her—of some things—facts—about my business. He had me. He knew more than he could prove, but a word from him would have brought everything toppling down. So he forced me to send him to you—he knew I had your power of attorney and he—he demanded that I open up your deposit boxes. He had me—I couldn't refuse—he took your—your private papers." The Judge groaned and swung aside on his stool. Thorne went on. "I'm a worm, Tom. I can't live with myself for thinking what I've done to you. My money's gone—my clients'—it's—there's no way back."

The silence grew unbearable. Tom knocked his dead pipe on the fender and rose. "I must call the doctor. This other thing is pretty bad too, but I can stand it if we don't all go to jail first. Leigh, you tell them."

The Judge hesitated only an instant. "There is a secret between the four of us—the Sherwoods, my sister, and me. It goes back a long time and has to do with Letitia's—with Mary's son. That's one reason she's so miserable. The truth isn't much worse than you'll find in the history of many good families, but there's one damaging fact: the adoption certificate was fraudulent. If the story comes out, other people than ourselves will suffer—"

"What proofs were in your box, Tom?" It was Sholto who asked the returning Sherwood.

"I don't exactly know. There was a birth certificate, genuine, made out in Switzerland. Then, one or two papers, copies of affidavits, which could establish the perjury. There may be a photograph too, of Evan's father, but I'm not sure. I don't suppose Addison has them here."

"I disagree." Morley seemed relieved to be able to speak. "They'd be safer in a vault, of course, but Addison's got no home base. Besides, he can't collect from you unless he can deliver for money received."

"That's a good point." Sherwood showed animation. "It means there's something we can do."

"I looked through his desk yesterday," put in Sholto. "Nothing there, I am sure."

Morley was annoyed. "We're not going to let that ugly mug get away with it."

"Not if we can help it, but I confess I have no ideas—and the time is short. Are you sure the statute of limitations won't cover your—er—misdemeanors?"

"It isn't that," replied Rainsford tonelessly. "Just lodging the complaint—or even if Addison simply made inquiries—the whole story would come out. You couldn't stop tongues wagging. Adultery, bastardy, forged documents—there's no closed season on scandal."

"In that case, the goose is cooked, no matter what we do." Ted was beginning to see it like Sholto.

"Nothing's hopeless till you're dead." Sherwood had evidently overcome whatever weakness his wife's condition had induced in him. "Without documentary proof Addison can't get to first base. No court, no newspaper around here will listen to a damn Yankee venting his spite. So—we must get those bits of paper back. As I think about it, the birth certificate is the only one that can't be explained away. Queer that I kept it. I couldn't tell you why."

"Never mind, Tom, you've given me an idea." Morley's confidence was only partly put on. "We *can* get it back. Thank God it's Sunday—and—let me think—that's it: Thorne will take Wright for a walk. Meanwhile Sholto has to get back to town. Now listen. . . ."

Williams left at midday, as conspicuously as possible, and, smuggled back in the car, was now cooling his heels in the garage. The only question left was the proper time to spring the trap. The decision was: in the morning. Addison would be in a hurry to make his getaway with the loot. Right now, Sherwood would notify the man that he expected him in the second-floor sitting room at nine the next morning, "to negotiate."

By ten-fifteen on Monday the discussion seemed to have reached a deadlock. Only one thing was clear. Addison wanted the money so badly he was not going to lose his temper. He would gain his point by tireless repetition. As he kept saying, he had no wish for revenge—else he would have also required a signed testimonial from Sholto Williams declaring his belief in the experimental "results." Nor did he want to destroy people's reputations. But if his hand was forced—who could tell where it would land them all? Mrs. Sherwood, he thought, was already unwell. Miss Rainsford's one reason for existence he knew to be her good works in the community. The Judge—surely there was no need to go on with this, when a miserable sum would settle it all and remove him from their sight. No, it could not be less than $75,000—they could make it up together any way they liked in exchange for the documents. No, he would not produce them; he did not have them on him. He was one against three, a mild scientist among a trio of athletes whom he could not trust.

Morley, who had spoken only when Rainsford and Sherwood seemed to need a breathing spell, leaned back in the window seat, his hand hanging carelessly outside the open dormer. Suddenly he stood up. "I've had about enough. Addison! You'd better start packing, you and your boy. You have no documents. I mean," he amended, seeing the other's mocking look, "you had them until three and a half or four minutes ago. At this minute your threats are of no effect—except against yourself. We will testify to extortion, conspiracy, fraud—whenever Mr. Sherwood decides to prefer charges. What do you say, Tom?"

"Oh, let him go, let him go. I don't want to hear another word. He's a poor devil, only a little worse than the rest of us—"

"—nonsense!" said the Judge in a scream of relief.

But Addison had recovered from Ted's announcement. "You're a clever actor, Mr. Morley, and for a second you had me fooled. But you're bluffing. How would you know if I no longer had my proofs? Tell me where they are if you know so much."

"I can't. All I know is that Dr. Williams informed me just now that he had found your cache and had secured the property you stole from Mr. Sherwood's deposit box."

"Dr. Williams? But he's in New York. And you haven't left the room!"

"Oh, didn't you know? We're mind-readers. Here is Williams himself. He'll tell you."

Sholto, stepping in quietly behind the psychologist, was now at his elbow and saying something in his ear. Addison's only response was to clamp his jaws as he raked the four men with a remembering look. Then he was gone.

The Judge slumped sideways in a chair. It was Sherwood who broke the silence. "By God, we pulled it off. I don't know what I'd have done without you. But I still can't imagine how you found those bloody papers in the time, Sholto—or where."

"It was really not so hard as it looks. What made it possible at all was those earlier searches in connection with the so-called experiments. Addison simply couldn't afford to keep any secrets in the desk or under a loose board or in any of the traditional places. He couldn't slit your mattresses or tamper with any part of your

house or furnishings, because you or your friends were in and out
of his quarters, bent on examining all the things that one ordinarily
takes for granted."

"I can see that. It cut down your job, but it didn't tell you where
to look. When I think of all that electrical apparatus—"

"My dear Tom, you mustn't exaggerate or I shall grow con-
ceited. As regards the apparatus, I also started with an advantage.
On Saturday I examined with great care that miscellaneous lot of
discarded equipment which Addison called a laboratory. Knowing
what the pieces were, I knew ahead of time what *could not* be
used for concealment. Some have bakelite cases that cannot be
opened; other cases, which do open, contain parts so tightly fitted
together that you could not insert sheets of any size without
crumpling or tearing them."

"I suppose," Ted broke in, "you thought all this out in the
garage yesterday. Then today you went straight to the one piece of
junk that did have a crack and made it in one."

"Not quite—in fact I nearly missed it. Addison was no scientist
but he had his wits about him and was good with his hands. I
had made up my mind from what I knew that the papers—a few
sheets at most—must be on or near the *surface* of some largish
object. For instance, he had an old-fashioned balance there. Suppose the inside back panel, which would be almost always in the
dark, was covered with a thin sheet of decalcomania of the right
color; the papers could be between the wood and the sheet. You
could poke inside and outside the case, you might look right at it
and never notice anything, especially in a hurried search."

"Is that where you found it?" the Judge wanted to know.

"No, it wasn't. I told you—or rather Ted—that Addison's ob-
solete equipment first put me on to him. You remember he spoke
of taking blood pressures on Friday night, yet his gauge had certainly not been used for many years; it was completely unusable."

Ted snapped his fingers—he had never put together Sholto's
observation and the psychologist's remark.

"Now this morning my eye fell again on one of those wooden

drums mounted on a pivot and fitted with a writing arm—the kind of thing you see on a recording barometer but about twice as high. What physiological test of the nineties it was originally meant for, I can't tell you. The armature was absurdly connected to a pair of dead dry cells. It couldn't work. Yet the drum was properly covered with a sheet of graph paper showing a jagged "curve" on it. I had noticed on Saturday that this sheet was fresh and the curve inked in by hand. And the sheet, too, was homemade. The margins showed it had been cut from a larger sheet to fit the drum."

"These technicians!" exclaimed Ted, raising his eyes to heaven.

"Don't interrupt," said Sherwood.

"Well, after I had dismissed a couple of other likely places, I pitched on this drum. I thought there was a good chance that the documents might be between its surface and the graph paper. I removed the writing arm, took off the paper, and found—the drum. Nothing between. The paper, however, kept its curl and rolled off the table to the floor. It fell upright, a cylinder open down one side. I found myself looking at it because of some oddity that baffled me. Then I knew. The whole thing was too stiff to be natural. Addison had taken the trouble to seal together a sort of sandwich of documents and graph paper. He used as a seal one of those transparent cellulose sheets that adhere on being warmed. He had carefully filled in all the edges with slips of blank paper, and smoothed and flattened the filler of the sandwich, so that when you looked at any edge all you saw was a thickish piece of paper. When fitted on the drum the top and bottom edges were not even visible. A perfect hiding place."

"Nice work," said Ted, "but how did you get this laminated job unstuck?"

"That's what took a little time. Anyhow, the papers are now in a manila envelope in your hall mailbox. I made sure it was locked and I know your butler doesn't clear it till two o'clock."

"Speaking of clearing," said Morley, "we ought to make sure those scientists are on their way."

"Helder is seeing to it. He has the car out in front. But Sholto, what I still don't understand is how you gave Ted the signal that all was safe."

"Ah, that," cried Ted, "is *my* little secret. Would you like to see a demonstration of telepathy, guaranteed all wool—to pull over your eyes?"

"Pipe down. I want to hear Sholto."

"Ted is always trying to save my life, you know. As we'd originally planned it, I was to come in and confront Addison with the papers in my hand. Well, Ted thought the brute might turn nasty or at least try to snatch the documents from my feeble grasp, so he devised this scheme. Tell them."

"No, no. I'm entitled to my theatricals too. You two think of a word. Go with Sholto to his room and tell him what it is. Leave him alone for a minute of powerful concentration. Then come back here and I'll give you the word."

Within a few moments Ted was on the landing, announcing gravely, "The word is 'Fake.' And that, dear old Tom, should be a lesson to you. City slickers always have another trick up their sleeve. Yes, I'll tell you, but promise you won't brain me." Ted held up a ping-pong ball. "I abstracted this from the billiard room and gave it to Sholto. When he finally had the papers he let it roll along the gutter outside his window and down to the sitting room, where I stopped it with my hand. Just now, of course, when he did it again, he penciled your word on it—*le mot juste* if ever there was one."

The club fire had nearly gone out for lack of attention. We noticed it only when Ted and Sholto had finished, and by that time the belief in mental telepathy seemed no longer to have any advocates. The actualities of life held us instead. Once again it was Hugh Trenner who spoke the question in all our minds.

"What finally happened to these unfortunate friends of yours? Did Mrs. Sherwood recover? And all his money—that is, if you feel free to tell us."

"I can't tell you everything," Morley replied. "But there was one more agony for Tom to endure—the full blast of scandal where no scandal existed. You see, when I got back the next night to the city room—my paper was then *The Globe*—almost the first thing I read on the teletype was: PHILADELPHIA BUSINESSMAN SHOOTS SELF IN SO. CAROLINA MANSION AS HOSTESS TAKES OVERDOSE OF DRUGS IN NEXT ROOM."

The Oyster Catcher

BY MICHAEL GILBERT

The table was the first thing that caught your eye as you came into the room. Its legs were of green-painted angle-iron, bolted to the floor; its top, a block of polished teak. Overhead shone five white fluorescent lights.

On the wide, shadowless, aseptic surface the raincoat looked out of place, like some jolly, seedy old tramp who has strayed into an operating-theatre. A coat is such a personal thing, almost a second skin. As it loses its own shape and takes on the outlines of its wearer, as its pockets become a repository of tobacco flakes and sand and fragments of leaves, and its exterior spotted with more unexpected things than rain, so does it take on an intimate life all of its own.

There was an element of indecency, Petrella thought, in tearing this life from it. The earnest man in rimless glasses and a white laboratory overall had just finished going over the lining with a pocket-sized vacuum cleaner with a thimble-shaped container. Now he was at work on the exterior. He cut a broad strip of adhesive tape and laid it on the outside of the coat, pressing it firmly down. Then he marked the area with a special pencil, and pulled the tape off. There was nothing visible to the naked eye on the under surface of the tape, but he seemed satisfied.

"We'll make a few micro-slides," he said. "They'll tell us anything we want to know. There's no need for you to hang about if you don't want to."

Sergeant Petrella disliked being told, even indirectly, that he was wasting his time. Let the truth be told, he did not care for Scientific Assistant Worsley at all. Worsley had the very slightly patronizing manner of one who has himself been admitted to the inner circles of knowledge and is speaking to unfortunates who are still outside the pale—a habit, Petrella had noticed, that was very marked at the outset of a scientific career, but diminished as a man gained more experience and realized how little certainty there was, even under the eye of the microscope.

"All right," he said. "I'll push off and come back in a couple of hours."

"To do the job completely," said Worsley, "will take about six days." He looked complacently at the neat range of Petri dishes round the table, and the samples he had so far extracted. "Perhaps another three to tabulate the results."

"All the same," said Petrella, "I'll look in this evening and see what you have got for me."

"As long as you appreciate," said Worsley, "that the results I give you will be unchecked."

"I'll take a chance on that."

"That, of course, is for you to decide." His voice contained a reproof. Impetuous people, police officers. Unschooled in the discipline of the laboratory. Jumpers to conclusions. People on whom careful, controlled research was usually wasted. Worsley sighed audibly.

Sergeant Petrella said nothing at all. He had long ago found out that it was a waste of time antagonizing people who were in a position to help you.

He consulted his watch, his notebook, and his stomach. He had a call to make in Wandsworth, another in Acton, and a third in

South Harrow. Then he would come back to the Forensic Science Laboratory to see what Worsley had got for them. Then he would go back to Highside and report to Superintendent Haxtell. He might have time for lunch between Acton and South Harrow. If not, the prospect of food was remote, for once he reached Highside, there was no saying that Haxtell would not have a lot more visits lined up for him.

All this activity—and, indirectly, the coat lying on Worsley's table—stemmed from a discovery made by a milkman at No. 39 Carhow Mansions. Carhow Mansions is a tall block of flats overlooking the southern edge of Helenwood Common.

Miss Martin, who lived alone at No. 39, was a woman of about thirty. Neither beautiful, nor clever; nor ugly, nor stupid. She was secretary to Dr. Hunter, who had a house and consulting-room in Wimpole Street. She did her work well, and was well paid for it.

The flat, which was tucked away on the top storey and was smaller than the others in the block, was known as a "single," which means that it had about as little accommodation as one person could actually exist in. A living-room that was also a dining-room; an annexe that served as a bedroom; one cupboard, called a kitchen, and another called a bathroom. Not that Miss Martin had ever been heard to complain. She had no time to waste on housework and ate most of her meals out. Her interests were Shakespeare and tennis.

Which brings us to the milkman, who, finding Friday's milk bottle still unused outside the door of Flat 39 on Saturday, mentioned the matter to the caretaker.

The caretaker was not immediately worried. Tenants often went away without telling him, although Miss Martin was usually punctilious about such matters. Later in the morning his rounds took him up to No. 39, and he looked at the two milk bottles and found the sight faintly disturbing. Fortunately, he had his passkey with him.

Which brought Superintendent Haxtell onto the scene in a fast car. And Chief Superintendent Barstow, from District Headquarters. And photographic and fingerprint detachments, and a well-known pathologist, and a crowd on the pavement, and a uniformed policeman to control them. And eventually, since Carhow Mansions was in his manor, Sergeant Petrella.

Junior detective sergeants do not conduct investigations into murders, but they are allowed to help, in much the same way as a junior officer helps to run a war. They are allowed to do the work, while their superiors do the thinking. In this case, there was a lot of work to do.

"I don't like it," said Barstow, in the explosive rumble that was his normal conversational voice. "Here's this girl, as ordinary as apples-and-custard. No one's got a word to say against her. Life's an open book. Then someone comes in and hits her on the head, not once, but five or six times."

"Any one of the blows might have caused death," agreed the pathologist. "She's been dead more than twenty-four hours. Probably killed on Friday morning. And I think there's no doubt that that was the weapon." He indicated a heavy long-handled screwdriver.

"It could have belonged to her," said Haxtell. "Funny thing to find in a flat, though. More like a piece of workshop equipment."

"All right," said Barstow. "Suppose the murderer brought it with him. Ideal for the job. You could force a front door with a thing like that. Then, if the owner comes out, it's just as handy as a weapon. But it's still—" he boggled over the word and its implications—"it's still mad."

And the further they looked, and the wider they spread their net, the madder it did seem.

Certain facts came to light at once. Haxtell was talking to Doctor Hunter, of Wimpole Street, within the hour. The doctor explained that Miss Martin had not come to work on Friday because he himself had ordered her to stay in bed.

"I think she'd been over-using her eyes," said the doctor. "That gave her a headache, and the headache in turn affected her stomach. It was a form of migraine. What she needed was forty-eight hours on her back, with the blinds down. I told her to take Friday off, and come back on Monday if she felt well enough. She's been with me for nearly ten years now. An excellent secretary, and such a nice girl."

He spoke with so much warmth that Haxtell, who was a cynic, made a mental note of a possible line of inquiry. Nothing came of it. The doctor, it transpired, was very happily married.

"That part of it fits all right," said Haxtell to Chief Superintendent Barstow. "She was in bed when the intruder arrived. He hit her as she was coming out of her bedroom."

"Then you think he was a housebreaker?"

"I'd imagined so, yes," said Haxtell. "The screwdriver looks like the sort of thing a housebreaker would carry. You could force an ordinary mortise lock right off with it. He didn't have to use it in this instance, because she'd got a simple catch-lock that a child of five could open. I don't doubt he slipped it with a piece of talc."

"Why did he choose her flat?"

"Because it was an isolated one, on the top floor. Or because he knew her habits. Just bad luck that she should have been there at all."

"Bad luck for her," agreed Barstow sourly. "Well, we've got the machine working. We may turn something up."

Haxtell was an experienced police officer. He knew that investigating a murder was like dropping a stone into a pool of water. He started two inquiries at once. Everybody within a hundred yards of the flat was asked what they had been doing and whether they had noticed anything. And everyone remotely connected with Miss Martin, by ties of blood, friendship, or business, was sought out and questioned.

It is a system that involves an enormous amount of work for a large number of people, and has got only one thing in its favour. It is nearly always successful in the end.

To Sergeant Petrella fell the task of questioning all the other tenants in the block. This involved seven visits. In each case at least one person, it appeared, had been at home all Friday morning. And no one had heard anything, which was disappointing. Had anything unusual happened on Friday morning? The first six people to whom this inquiry was addressed scratched their heads and said that they didn't think anything had. The seventh mentioned the gentleman who had left census papers.

Now Petrella was by then both hot and tired. He was, according to which way you looked at it, either very late for his lunch or rather early for his tea. He was on the point of dismissing the man with the census papers when the instinct that guides all good policemen drove him to persevere with one further inquiry. Had he not, the Martin case would probably have remained unsolved.

As he probed, a curious little story emerged. The man had not actually left any papers behind him. He had been making preliminary inquiries as to the number of people on the premises so that arrangements for the census could be put in hand. The papers would be issued later.

Petrella trudged down three flights of stairs—it is only in grave emergency that a policeman is allowed to use a private telephone—and rang up the Municipal Returning Officer from a call box.

After that he revisited the first six flats. The occupants unanimously agreed that a "man from the Council" had called on them that Friday morning. They had not mentioned it because Petrella had asked if anything "unusual" had happened. There was nothing in the least unusual in men from the Council snooping round.

Petrella asked for a description and collated, from his six informants, the following items. The man in question was young, youngish, sort of middle-aged—this was from the teen-aged daughter in No. 37. He was bareheaded and had tousled hair. He was wearing a hat. He had a shifty look—No. 34; a nice smile—teen-aged daughter; couldn't say, didn't really look at him—the remainder. He was about six foot—five foot nine—five foot six—didn't notice. He had an ordinary sort of voice. He was wearing an Old Harrovian tie—gentleman in ground-floor flat No. 34. He seemed to walk with rather a stiff sort of leg, almost a limp—four out of six informants.

Petrella hurried back to Highside Police Station, where he found Haxtell and Barstow in conference.

"There doesn't seem to be much doubt," he reported, "that it was a sneak thief. Posing as a Council employee. I've checked with them and they are certain that he couldn't have been genuine. His plan would be to knock once or twice. If he got no answer he'd either slip the lock or force it. He drew a blank at the other seven. Someone answered the door in each of them. When he got to No. 39, I expect Miss Martin didn't hear him. The migraine must have made her pretty blind and deaf."

"That's right," said Barstow. "And then she came out and caught him at it, and he hit her."

"The descriptions aren't a lot of good," said Haxtell, "but we'll get all the pictures from the C.R.O. of people known to go in for this sort of lark. They may sort someone out for us."

"Don't forget the most important item," said Barstow. "The limp."

Petrella said, "It did occur to me to wonder whether we ought to place much reliance on the limp, sir."

He received a glare that would have daunted a less self-confident man.

"He would have to have somewhere to hide that big screwdriver. It was almost two foot long. The natural place would be a pocket inside his trouser leg. That might account for the appearance of a stiff leg."

Haxtell avoided Barstow's eye. "It's an idea," he said. "Now just get along and start checking on this list of Miss Martin's known relations."

"There was one other thing—"

"Do you know," observed Chief Superintendent Barstow unkindly, "why God gave young policemen two feet but only one head?"

Petrella accepted the hint and departed.

Nevertheless, the idea persisted; and later that day, when he was alone with Superintendent Haxtell, he voiced it to him.

"Do you remember," he said, "about six months ago, I think it was, we had an outbreak of this sort of thing in the Cholderton

Road, Park Branch area? A man cleared out three or four blocks of flats, and we never caught him. He was posing as a pools salesman then."

"The man who left his coat behind."

"That's right," said Petrella. "With Colonel Wing."

Colonel Wing was nearly ninety and rather deaf, but still spry. He had fought in the Afghan campaign, and one Zulu war, and the walls of his top-floor living-room in Cholderton Mansions were adorned with a fine selection of assegais, yataghans, and knopkieries. Six months before this story opens he had had an experience that might have unnerved a less seasoned warrior.

Pottering out of his bedroom one fine morning at about eleven o'clock—he was not an early riser—he had observed a man kneeling in front of his sideboard and quitely sorting out the silver. It was difficult to say who had been more taken aback. The man had jumped up, and run from the room. Colonel Wing had regretfully dismissed the idea of trying to spear him with an assegai from the balcony as he left the front door of the flats, and had rung up the police. They had made one curious discovery.

Hanging in the hall was a strange raincoat.

"Never seen it before in my life," said Colonel Wing. "D'you mean to say the damn feller had the cheek to hang his coat up before starting work? Wonder he didn't help himself to a whisky-and-soda while he was about it."

Haxtell said that he had known housebreakers to do just that. He talked to the Colonel at length about the habits of criminals; and removed the coat for examination. Since the crime was only an attempted robbery, it was not thought worth while wasting too much time on it. A superficial examination produced no results in the way of name tabs or tailors' marks, the coat was carefully placed in a cellophane bag and stored.

"I'd better have a word with him," said Petrella.

He found the Colonel engaged in writing a letter to the *United Services' Journal* on the comparative fighting qualities of Zulus and Russians. He listened to the descriptions of the intruder, and said that, as far as one could tell, they sounded like the same man.

His intruder had been on the younger side of middle age, of medium height, and strongly built.

"There's one thing," said the Colonel. "I saw him in a good light and I may be deaf, but I've got excellent eyesight. There's a tiny spot on his left eye. A little red spot, like a fire opal. You couldn't mistake it. If you catch him, I'll identify him for you fast enough."

"The trouble is," said Petrella, "that it looks as if he's never been through our hands. Almost the only real lead we've got is that coat he left behind him at your place. We're going over it again now, much more thoroughly."

Thus had the coat grown in importance. It had improved its status. It had become a possible exhibit in a murder case.

"Give it everything," said Haxtell to the scientists. And the scientists prepared to oblige.

That evening, after a weary afternoon spent interrogating Miss Martin's father's relatives in Acton and South Harrow, Petrella found himself back on the Embankment. The Forensic Science Laboratory observes civilized hours and Mr. Worsley was on the point of removing his long white overall and replacing it with a rather deplorable green tweed coat with matching leather patches on the elbows.

"I've finished my preliminary work on the right-hand pocket," he said. "We have isolated arrowroot starch, pipe tobacco, and a quantity of common silver sand."

"Splendid," said Petrella. "Splendid. All I have got to do now is to find a housewife who smokes a pipe and has recently been to the seaside and we shall be home and dry."

"What use you make of the data we provide must be entirely a matter for you," said Mr. Worsley coldly. He was already late for a meeting of the South Wimbledon Medico-Legal Society, to whom he had promised a paper entitled, *The Part of the Laboratory in Modern Crime Detection*.

Petrella went back to Highside.

There he found a note from Superintendent Haxtell that ran: "A friend of Miss Martin has suggested that some or other of these were, or might have been, boy-friends of the deceased. I am seeing ones marked with cross. Would you tackle the others?" There followed a list of names and addresses ranging from Welwyn Garden City to Morden.

He looked at his watch. It was half past seven. With any luck he could knock off a few of them before midnight.

In the ensuing days the ripples spread wider and wider, diminishing in size and importance as they became more distant from the centre of the disturbance.

Petrella worked his way from near relatives and close friends, who said, "How terrible! Who ever would have thought of anything like that happening to Marjorie!" through more distant connections who said, "Miss Martin? Yes, I know her. I haven't seen her for a long time," right out to the circumference where there were people who simply looked bewildered and said, "Miss Martin—I'm sorry, I don't think I remember anyone of that name," and on being reminded that they had danced with her at a tennis-club dance two years before said, "If you say so, I expect it's right, but I'm dashed if I can remember what she looked like."

It was in the course of the third day that Petrella called at a nice little house in Herne Hill. The name was Taylor. Mr. Taylor was not at home, but the door was opened by his wife, a cheerful redhead, who banished her two children to the kitchen when she understood what Petrella was after.

Her reactions were the standard ones. Apprehension, followed, as soon as she understood that what Petrella wanted was nothing to do with her, by a cheerful communicativeness. Miss Martin was, she believed, her husband's cousin. That is to say not his cousin, but his second cousin, or something like that. Her husband's father's married sister's husband's niece. So far as she knew they had only met her once, and that was quite by chance, six months before, at the funeral of Miss Martin's mother who was, of course, sister to her husband's uncle by marriage.

Petrella disentangled this complicated relationship without difficulty. He was already a considerable expert on the Martin family tree. Unfortunately, Mrs. Taylor could tell him nothing. Her acquaintance with Miss Martin was confined to this single occasion and she had not set eyes on her since. Her husband, who was a commercial traveller for Joblox, the London paint firm, was unlikely to be back until very late. He was on a tour in the Midlands, and it depended on the traffic, when he got home. Petrella said he quite understood. The interview remained in his memory chiefly because it was on his way back from it that he picked up his copy of the laboratory report on the coat.

The scientists had done themselves proud. No inch of its surface, interior or exterior, had escaped their microscopic gaze. Petrella cast his eye desperately over the eight closely-typed foolscap pages. Stains on the exterior had been isolated and chemically tested and proved beyond reasonable doubt to be in two cases ink, in one case rabbit blood, and in one case varnish. A quantity of sisal-hemp fluff had been recovered from the seam of the left-hand cuff and some marmalade from the right-hand one.

A sliver of soft wood, originally identified on the Chaterton Key Card as ordinary *pinus sylvestris*, was now believed to be *chamaecyparis lawsoniana*. In the right-hand pocket had been discovered a number of fragments of oyster shell, and a stain of oil shown by quantitative analysis to be a thick oil of a sort much used in marine engineering.

Petrella read the report in the underground between Charing Cross and Highside. When he reached the Police Station he found Haxtell in the C.I.D. room. He had in front of him the reports of all visits so far made. There were two hundred and thirty of them. Petrella added the five he had completed that afternoon, and was about to retire when he remembered the laboratory report, and cautiously added that too to the pile. He was conscious of thunder in the air.

"Don't bother," said Haxtell. "I've had a copy." His eyes were red-rimmed from lack of proper sleep. "So has the Chief Superintendent. He's just been here. He wants us to take some action on it."

"Action, sir?"

"He suggests," said Haxtell, in ominously quiet tones, "that we re-examine all persons interviewed so far—" his hand flickered for a moment over the pile of paper on the table—"to ascertain whether they have ever been interested in the oyster-fishing industry. He feels that the coincidence of oyster shell and marine oil must have some significance."

"I see, sir," said Petrella. "When do we start?"

Haxtell stopped himself within an ace of saying something that would have been both indiscreet and insubordinate. Then, to his eternal credit, he laughed instead. "We are both," he said, "going to get one good night's rest first. We'll start tomorrow morning."

"I wonder if I could borrow the reports until then," said Petrella, wondering at himself as he did so.

"Do what you like with them," said Haxtell, "I've got three days' routine work to catch up with."

Petrella took them back with him to Mrs. Catt's, where that worthy widow had prepared a high tea for him, his first leisured meal for three days. Sustained by a mountainous dish of sausages and eggs and refreshed by his third cup of strong tea, he started on the task of proving to himself the theory that had come to him.

Each paper was skimmed, and put on one side. Every now and then he would stop, extract one, and add it to a much smaller pile beside his plate. At the end of an hour, Petrella looked at the results of his work with satisfaction. In the small pile were six papers, six summaries of interviews with friends or relations of the murdered girl. If his idea was right, he had thus, at a stroke, reduced the possibles from two hundred and thirty-five to six. And of those six possibles, only one, he knew in his heart of hearts, was a probable.

There came back into his mind the visit that he had made that afternoon. There it was, in that place and no other, that the answer lay. There he had glimpsed, without realizing it, the end of the scarlet thread that led to the heart of this untidy, rambling labyrinth. He thought of a nice redheaded girl and two redheaded children, and unexpectedly he found himself shivering.

It was dusk before he got back to Herne Hill. The lights were on in the nice little house, upstairs and downstairs, and a muddy car stood in the gravel run-in in front of the garage. Sounds suggested that the redheaded children were being put to bed by both their parents and were enjoying it.

One hour went by, and then a second. Petrella had found an empty house opposite, and he was squatting in the garden, his back propped against a tree. The night was warm and he was quite comfortable, and his head was nodding on his chest when the front door of the house opposite opened, and Mr. Taylor appeared.

He stood for a moment, outlined against the light from the hall, saying something to his wife. He was too far off for Petrella to make out the words. Then he came down the path. He ignored the car, and made for the front gate, for which Petrella was thankful. He had made certain arrangements to cope with the contingency that Mr. Taylor might use his car, but it was much easier if he remained on foot.

A short walk took them both, pursuer and pursued, to the door of the King of France public house. Mr. Taylor went into the saloon. Petrella himself chose the private bar. Like most private bars, it had nothing to recommend it save its privacy, being narrow, bare, and quite empty. But it had the advantage of looking straight across the serving-counter into the saloon.

Petrella let his man order first. He was evidently a well-known character in the King of France. He called the landlord Sam, and the landlord called him Mr. Taylor.

Petrella drank his own beer slowly. Ten minutes later the moment for which he had been waiting arrived. Mr. Taylor picked up a couple of glasses and strolled across with them to the counter. Petrella also rose casually to his feet. For a moment they faced each other, a bare two paces apart, under the bright bar lights.

Petrella saw in front of him a man of early middle age, with a nondescript face and neutral-coloured tousled hair, perhaps five foot nine in height, and wearing some sort of old-school tie.

As if aware that he was being looked at, Mr. Taylor raised his head; and Petrella observed, in the left eye, a tiny red spot. It was, as the Colonel had said, exactly the colour of a fire opal.

"We showed his photograph to everyone in the block," said Haxtell with satisfaction, "and they all of them picked it out straight away, out of a set of six. Also the Colonel."

"Good enough," said Chief Superintendent Barstow. "Any background?"

"We made a very cautious inquiry at Joblox. Taylor certainly works for them. But he's what they call an outside commission man. He sells in his spare time, and gets a percentage on sales. Last year he made just under a hundred pounds."

"Which wouldn't keep him in his present style."

"Definitely not. And of course a job like that would be very useful cover for a criminal sideline. He would be out when and where he liked, and no questions asked by his family."

Barstow considered the matter slowly. The decision was his.

"Pull him in," he said. "Charge him with the job at Colonel Wing's. The rest will sort itself out quick enough when we search his house. Take a search-warrant with you. By the way, I never asked how you got onto him. Has he some connection with the oyster trade?"

Petrella said, cautiously, "Well . . . no, sir. As a matter of fact, he hadn't. But the report was very useful corroborative evidence."

"Clever chaps, these scientists," said Barstow.

"Come clean," said Haxtell, when the Chief Superintendent had departed. "It was nothing to do with that coat, was it?"

"Nothing at all," said Petrella. "What occurred to me was that it was a very curious murder. Presuming it was the same man both times. Take Colonel Wing—he's full of beans, but when all's said and done, he's a frail old man, over ninety. He saw the intruder in a clear light, and the man simply turned tail and bolted. Then he bumps into Miss Martin, who's a girl, but a muscular young tennis player, but he *kills* her, coldly and deliberately."

"From which you deduced that Miss Martin knew him, and he

was prepared to kill to preserve the secret of his identity. Particularly as he had never been in the hands of the police."

"There was a bit more to it than that," said Petrella. "It had to be someone who knew Miss Martin, but so casually that he would have no idea where she lived. Mightn't even remember her name. If he'd had any idea that it was the flat of someone who knew him he wouldn't have touched it with a barge pole. What I was looking for was someone who was distantly connected with Miss Martin, but happened to have renewed his acquaintance with her recently. He had to be a very distant connection, you see. But they had to know each other by sight. There were half a dozen who could have filled the bill. I had this one in my mind because I'd interviewed Mrs. Taylor only that afternoon. Of course, I'd have tried all the others afterwards. Only it wasn't necessary."

There was neither pleasure nor satisfaction in his voice. He was seeing nothing but a nice redheaded girl and two redheaded children.

It was perhaps six months later that Petrella ran across Colonel Wing again. The Taylor case was now only an uncomfortable memory, for Mr. Taylor had taken his own life in his cell, and the redheaded girl was now a widow. Petrella was on his way home, and he might not have noticed him, but the Colonel came right across the road to greet him, narrowly missing death at the hands of a motorcyclist of whose approach he had been blissfully unaware. "Good evening, Sergeant," the old man said. "How are you keeping?"

"Very well, thank you, Colonel," said Petrella. "And how are you?"

"I'm not getting any younger," said the Colonel. Petrella suddenly perceived to his surprise that the old man was covered with embarrassment. He waited patiently for him to speak.

"I wonder—" said the old man at last, "it's an awkward thing to have to ask, but could you get that coat back—you remember?"

"Get it *back*?" said Petrella. "I don't know. I suppose so."

"If it was mine, I wouldn't bother. But it isn't. I find it's my cousin Tom's. I'd forgotten all about it, until he reminded me."

Petrella stared at him.

"Do you mean to say—"

"Tom stayed the night with me—he does that sometimes, between trips. Just drops in. Of course, when he reminded me, I remembered—"

"Between trips . . ." said Petrella weakly. "He isn't by any chance an oyster fisherman?"

It was the Colonel's turn to stare. "Certainly not," he said. "He's one of the best-known breeders of budgerigars in the country."

"Budgerigars?"

"Very well-known for them. I believe I'm right in saying he introduced the foreign system of burnishing their feathers with oil. It's funny you should mention oysters, though. That's a thing he's very keen on. Powdered oyster shell in the feed. It improves their high notes."

Petrella removed his hat in a figurative but belated salute to the Forensic Science Laboratory.

"Certainly you shall have your coat back," he said. "It'll need a thorough clean and a little stitching, but I am delighted to think that it is going to be of use to someone at last."

Murder Is No Joke

I was a little disappointed in Flora Gallant when she arrived that
Tuesday morning for her eleven-o'clock appointment with Nero
Wolfe. Her getup was a letdown. One of my functions as Wolfe's
factotum is checking on people who phone for an appointment with
him, and when I had learned that Flora Gallant was one of the staff
of her brother Alec's establishment on East Fifty-fourth Street,
and remembered remarks a friend of mine named Lily Rowan had
made about Alec Gallant, I had phoned Lily for particulars.

And got them. Gallant was crowding two others for top rank-
ing in the world of high fashion. He thumbed his nose at Paris
and sneered at Rome, and was getting away with it. He had refused
to finish three dresses for the Duchess of Harwynd because she
postponed flying over from London for fittings. He declined to
make anything whatever for a certain famous movie actress because he didn't like the way she handled her hips when she walked.
He had been known to charge as little as eight hundred dollars for
an afternoon frock, but it had been for a favorite customer so he
practically gave it away.

301

And so forth. Therefore when I opened the door to admit his sister Flora that Tuesday morning it was a letdown to see a dumpy middle-aged female in a dark gray suit that was anything but spectacular. It needed pressing, and the shoulders were too tight, and her waist wasn't where it thought it was. As I ushered her down the hall to the office and introduced her to Wolfe, I was thinking that if the shoemaker's son went barefoot I supposed his sister could too, but all the same I felt cheated.

Her conversation was no more impressive than her costume, at least at the beginning. Seated on the edge of the red leather chair beyond the end of Wolfe's desk, the fingers of both hands gripping the rim of the gray leather bag on her lap, she apologized, in a low meek mumble with just a trace of a foreign accent, for asking such an important man as Nero Wolfe to give any of his valuable time to her and her troubles. That didn't sound promising, indicating as it did that she was looking for a bargain. As she went on with it Wolfe started a frown going, and soon he cut her off by saying that it would take less of his time if she would tell him what her troubles were.

She nodded. "I know. I just wanted you to understand that I don't expect anything for myself. I'm not anybody myself, but you know who my brother is? My brother Alec?"

"Yes. Mr. Goodwin has informed me. An illustrious dressmaker."

"He is not merely a dressmaker. He is an artist, a great artist." She wasn't arguing, just stating a fact. "This trouble is about him, and that's why I must be careful with it. That's why I come to you, and also"—she sent me a glance and then back to Wolfe—"also Mr. Archie Goodwin, because I know that although you are private detectives, you are gentlemen. I know you are worthy of confidence."

She stopped, apparently for acknowledgment. Wolfe obliged her. "Umph."

"Then it is understood I am trusting you?"

"Yes. You may."

She looked at me. "Mr. Goodwin?"

"Right. Whatever Mr. Wolfe says. I only work here."

She hesitated, seeming to consider if that was satisfactory, decided it was, and returned to Wolfe. "So I'll tell you. I must explain that in France, where my brother and I were born and brought up, our name was not 'Gallant.' What it was doesn't matter. I came to this country in nineteen-thirty-seven, when I was twenty-five years old, and Alec only came in nineteen-forty-five, after the war was over. He had changed his name to Gallant and entered legally under that name. Within seven years he had made a reputation as a designer, and then— Perhaps you remember his fall collection in nineteen-fifty-three?"

Wolfe grunted no.

Her right hand abandoned its grip on the bag to gesture. "But of course you are not married, and you have no mistress, feeling as you do about women. That collection showed what my brother was—an artist, a true creator. He got financial backing, more than he needed, and opened his place on Fifty-fourth Street. I had quit my job four years earlier—my job as a governess—in order to work with him and help him, and had changed my name to have it the same as his. From nineteen-fifty-three on it has been all a triumph, many triumphs. I will not say I had a hand in them, but I have been trying to help in my little way. The glory of great success has been my brother's, but I have been with him, and so have others. But now trouble has come."

Both hands were gripping the bag again. "The trouble," she said, "is a woman. A woman named Bianca Voss."

Wolfe made a face. She saw it and responded to it. "No, not an *affaire d'amour*, I'm sure it's not that. Though my brother has never married, he is by no means insensible to women, he is very healthy about women, but since you are worthy of confidence I may tell you that he has an *amie intime*, a young woman who is of importance in his establishment. It is impossible that Bianca Voss has attracted him that way. She first came there a little more than a year ago. My brother had told us to expect her, so he had met her somewhere. He designed a dress and a suit for her, and they were made there in the shop, but no bill was ever sent her. Then he gave her one of the rooms, the offices, on the third floor, and she started to come every day, and then the trouble began. My brother never told us she had any authority, but she took it and he allowed her to. Sometimes she interferes directly, and sometimes through him. She pokes her nose into everything. She got my brother to discharge a fitter, a very capable woman, who had been with him for years. She has a private telephone line in her office upstairs, but no one else has. About two months ago some of the others persuaded me to try to find out about her, what her standing is, and I asked my brother, but he wouldn't tell me. I begged him to, but he wouldn't."

"It sounds," Wolfe said, "as if she owns the business. Perhaps she bought it."

Flora Gallant shook her head. "No, she hasn't. I'm sure she hasn't. She wasn't one of the financial backers in nineteen-fifty-three, and since then there have been good profits, and anyway my brother has control. But now she's going to ruin it and he's going to let her, we don't know why. She wants him to design a factory line to be promoted by a chain of department stores using his name. She wants him to sponsor a line of Alec Gallant cosmetics on a royalty basis. And other things. We're against all of them, and my brother is too, really, but we think he's going to give in to her, and that will ruin it."

Her fingers tightened on the bag. "Mr. Wolfe, I want you to ruin *her*."

Wolfe grunted. "By wiggling a finger?"

"No, but you can. I'm sure you can. I'm sure she has some hold on him, but I don't know what. I don't know who she is or where she came from. I don't know what her real name is. She speaks with an accent, but not French; I'm not sure what it is. I don't know when she came to America; she may be here illegally. She may have known my brother in France, during the war. You can find out. If she has a hold on my brother you can find out what it is. If she is blackmailing him, isn't that against the law? Wouldn't that ruin her?"

"It might. It might ruin him too."

"Not unless you betrayed him." She swallowed that and added

hastily, "I don't mean that, I only mean I am trusting you, you said I could, and you could make her stop and that's all you would have to do. Couldn't you just do that?"

"Conceivably." Wolfe wasn't enthusiastic. "I fear, madam, that you're biting off more than you can chew. The procedure you suggest would be prolonged, laborious, and extremely expensive. It would probably require elaborate investigation abroad. Aside from my fee, which would not be modest, the outlay would be considerable and the outcome highly uncertain. Are you in a position to undertake it?"

"I am not rich myself, Mr. Wolfe. I have some savings. But my brother—if you get her away, if you release him from her—he is truly *généreux*—excuse me—he is a generous man. He is not stingy."

"But he isn't hiring me, and your assumption that she is galling him may be groundless." Wolfe shook his head. "No. Not a reasonable venture. Unless, of course, your brother himself consults me. If you care to bring him? Or send him?"

"Oh, I couldn't!" She gestured again. "You must see that isn't possible! When I asked him about her, I told you, he wouldn't tell me anything. He was annoyed. He is never abrupt with me, but he was then. I assure you, Mr. Wolfe, she is a villain. You are *sagace*— excuse me—you are an acute man. You would know it if you saw her, spoke with her."

"Perhaps." Wolfe was getting impatient. "Even so, my perception of her villainy wouldn't avail. No, madam."

"But you would know I am right." She opened her bag, fingered in it with both hands, came out with something, left her chair to step to Wolfe's desk, and put the something on his desk pad in front of him. "There," she said, "that is one hundred dollars. For you that is nothing, but it shows how I am in earnest. I can't ask her to come so you can speak with her, she would merely laugh at me, but you can. You can tell her you have been asked in confidence to discuss a matter with her and ask her to come to see you. You will not tell her what it is. She will come, she will be afraid not to, and that alone will show you she has a secret, perhaps many secrets. Then when she comes you will ask her whatever occurs to you. For that you do not need my suggestions. You are an acute man."

Wolfe grunted. "Everybody has secrets."

"Yes," she agreed, "but not secrets that would make them afraid not to come to see Nero Wolfe. When she comes and you have spoken with her, we shall see. That may be all or it may not. We shall see."

I do not say that the hundred bucks there on his desk in used twenties was no factor in Wolfe's decision. Even though income tax would reduce it to sixteen dollars, that would buy four days' supply of beer. Another factor was plain curiosity: would she come or wouldn't she? Still another was the chance that it might develop into a decent fee. But what really settled it was her saying, "We shall see," instead of "We'll see" or "We will see." He will always stretch a point, within reason, for people who use words as he thinks they should be used. So he muttered to her, "Where is she?"

"At my brother's place. She always is."

"Give Mr. Goodwin the phone number."

"I'll get it. She may be downstairs." She started a hand for the phone on Wolfe's desk, but I told her to use mine and left my chair, and she came and sat, lifted the receiver, and dialed.

In a moment she spoke. "Doris? Flora. Is Miss Voss around? . . . Oh. I thought she might have come down. . . . No, don't bother, I'll ring her there."

She pushed the button down, told us, "She's up in her office," waited a moment, released the button, and dialed again. When she spoke it was another voice, as she barely moved her lips and brought it out through her nose: "Miss Bianca Voss? Hold the line, please. Mr. Nero Wolfe wishes to speak with you. . . . Mr. Nero Wolfe, the private detective."

She looked at Wolfe and he got at his phone. Having my own share of curiosity, I extended a hand for my receiver, and she let me take it and left my chair. As I sat and got it to my ear Wolfe was speaking.

"This is Nero Wolfe. Is this Miss Bianca Voss?"

"Yes." It was more like "yiss." "What do you want?" The "wh" and the "w" were off.

"If my name is unknown to you, I should explain—"

"I know your name. What do you want?"

"I want to invite you to call on me at my office. I have been asked to discuss certain matters with you, and—"

"Who asked you?"

"I am not at liberty to say. I shall—"

"What matters?" The "wh" was more off.

"If you will let me finish. The matters are personal and confidential, and concern you closely. That's all I can say on the telephone. I am sure you—"

A snort stopped him, a snort that might be spelled "Tzchaahh!" followed by: "I know your name, yes! You are scum, I know, in your stinking sewer! Your slimy little ego in your big gob of fat! And you dare to—*owulggh!*"

That's the best I can do at spelling it. It was part scream, part groan, and part just noise. It was followed immediately by another noise, a mixture of crash and clatter, then others, faint rustlings, and then nothing. I looked at Wolfe and he looked at me. I spoke to my transmitter. "Hello hello hello. *Hello!* Hello?"

I cradled it and so did Wolfe. Flora Gallant was asking, "What is it? She hung up?"

We ignored her. Wolfe said, "Archie? You heard."

"Yes, sir. If you want a guess, something hit her and she dragged the phone along as she went down and it struck the floor. The other noises, not even a guess, except that at the end either she put the receiver back on and cut the connection or someone else did. I don't —Okay, Miss Gallant. Take it easy." She had grabbed my arm with both hands and was jabbering, "What is it? What happened?" I put a hand on her shoulder and made it emphatic. "Take a breath and let go. You heard what I told Mr. Wolfe. Apparently something fell on her and then hung up the phone."

"But it couldn't! It is not possible!"

"That's what it sounded like. What's the number? The one down-stairs?"

She just gawked at me. I looked at Wolfe and he gave me a nod, and I jerked my arm loose, sat at my desk, got the Manhattan book, flipped to the Gs and got the number, PL2-0330, and dialed it.

A cultured female voice came. "Alec Gallant Incorporated."

"This is a friend of Miss Voss," I told her. "I was just speaking to her on the phone, in her office, and from the sounds I got I think something may have happened to her. Will you send someone up to see? Right away, I'll hold the wire."

"Who is this speaking, please?"

"Never mind that. Step on it. She may be hurt."

I heard her calling to someone, then apparently she covered the transmitter. I sat and waited. Wolfe sat and scowled at me. Flora Gallant stood for a good five minutes at my elbow, staring down at me, then turned and went to the red leather chair and lowered her-self onto its edge. I looked at my wrist watch: 11:40. It had said 11:31 when the connection with Bianca Voss had been cut. More waiting, and then a male voice came.

"Hello?"

"Hello."

"This is Carl Drew. What is your name, please?"

"My name is Watson, John H. Watson. Is Miss Voss all right?"

"May I have your address, Mr. Watson, please?"

"What for? Miss Voss knows my address. Is she all right?"

"I must have your address, Mr. Watson. I must insist. You will understand the necessity when I tell you that Miss Voss is dead. She was assaulted in her office and is dead. Apparently, from what you said, the assault came while she was on the phone with you, and I want your address. I must insist."

I hung up, gently not to be rude, swiveled, and asked Flora Gallant, "Who is Carl Drew?"

"He's the business manager. What happened?"

I went to Wolfe. "My guess was close. Miss Voss is dead. In her office. He said she was assaulted, but he didn't say with what or by whom."

He glowered at me, then turned to let her have it. She was coming up from the chair, slow and stiff. When she was erect she said, "No. No. It isn't possible."

"I'm only quoting Carl Drew," I told her.

"It isn't possible. He said that?"

"Distinctly."

"But how—" She let it hang. She said, "But how—" stopped again, turned, and was going. When Wolfe called to her, "Here, Miss Gallant, your money," she paid no attention but kept on, and he poked it at me, and I took it and headed for the hall. I caught up with her halfway to the front door, but when I offered it she just kept going, so I blocked her off, took her bag and opened it and dropped the bills in and closed it, handed it back, and went and pulled the door open. She hadn't said a word. I stood on the sill and watched, thinking she might stumble going down the seven steps of the stoop, but she made it to the sidewalk and turned east, toward Ninth Avenue. When I got back to the office Wolfe was sitting with his eyes closed, breathing down to his big round middle. I went to my desk and put the phone book away.

"She is so stunned with joy," I remarked, "that she'll probably get run over. I should have gone and put her in a taxi."

He grunted.

"One thing," I remarked, "Miss Voss's last words weren't exactly *généreux*. I would call them catty."

He grunted.

"Another thing," I remarked, "in spite of the fact that I was John H. Watson on the phone, we'll certainly be called on by either Sergeant Stebbins or Inspector Cramer or both. When they go into whereabouts Flora will have to cough it up for her own protection. And we actually heard it. Also we'll have the honor of being summoned to the stand. Star witness."

He opened his eyes. "I'm quite aware of it," he growled. "Confound it. Bring me the records on *Laelia gouldiana*."

No orchid ever called a genius a slimy little ego in a big gob of fat. I remarked that too, but to myself.

II

"Sure I appreciate it," Cramer declared. "Why shouldn't I? Very thoughtful of you. Saves me time and trouble. So it was eleven-thirty-one when you heard the blow?"

Inspector Cramer, big and brawny with a round red face and all his hair, half of it gray, had nothing to be sarcastic about as he sat in the red leather chair at six-thirty that Tuesday afternoon, and he knew it, but he couldn't help it. It was his reaction, not to the present circumstances, but to his memory of other occasions, other experiences he had undergone in that room. He had to admit that we had saved him time and trouble when I had anticipated his visit by typing out a complete report of the session with Flora Gallant that morning, including the dialogue verbatim, and having it ready for him in duplicate, signed by both Wolfe and me. He had skimmed through it first, and then read it slowly and carefully.

"We heard no blow, identifiably," Wolfe objected. His bulk was comfortably arranged in his oversize chair back of his desk. "Mr. Goodwin wrote that statement, but I read it, and it does not say that we heard a blow."

Cramer found the place on page four and consulted it. "Okay. You heard a groan and a crash and rustles. But there *was* a blow. She was hit in the back of the head with a chunk of marble, a paperweight, and then a scarf was tied around her throat to stop her breathing. You say here at eleven-thirty-one."

"Not when we heard the groan," I corrected. "After that there were the other noises, then the connection went, and I said hello a few times, which was human but dumb. It was when I hung up that I looked at my watch and saw eleven-thirty-one. The groan had been maybe a minute earlier. Say eleven-thirty. If a minute is important."

"It isn't. But you didn't hear the blow?"

"Not to recognize it, no."

He went back to the statement, frowning at it, reading the whole first page and glancing at the others. He looked up, at Wolfe. "I know how good you are at arranging words. This implies that Flora

Gallant was a complete stranger to you, that you had never had anything to do with her or her brother or any of the people at that place, but it doesn't say so in so many words. I'd like to know."

"The implication is valid," Wolfe told him. "Except as related in that statement, I have never had any association with Miss Gallant or her brother, or, to my knowledge, with any of their colleagues. Nor has Mr. Goodwin. Archie?"

"Right," I agreed.

"Okay." Cramer folded the statement and put it in his pocket. "Then you had never heard Bianca Voss's voice before and you couldn't recognize it on the phone."

"Of course not."

"And you can't hear it now, since she's dead. So you can't swear it was her talking to you."

"Obviously."

"And that raises a point. If it was her talking to you, she was killed at exactly half past eleven. Now there are four important people in that organization who had it in for Bianca Voss. They have admitted it. Besides Flora Gallant, there is Anita Prince, fitter and designer, been with Gallant eight years; Emmy Thorne, in charge of contacts and promotion, been with him four years; and Carl Drew, business manager, been with him five years. None of them killed Bianca Voss at half past eleven. From eleven-fifteen on, until the call came from a man who said he was John H. Watson, Carl Drew was down on the main floor, constantly in view of four people, two of them customers. From eleven o'clock on Anita Prince was on the top floor, the workshop, with Alec Gallant and two models and a dozen employees. At eleven-twenty Emmy Thorne called on a man by appointment at his office on Forty-sixth Street, and was with him and two other men until a quarter to twelve. And Flora Gallant was here with you. All airtight."

"Very neat," Wolfe agreed.

"Yeah. Too damn neat. Of course there may be others who wanted Bianca Voss out of the way, but as it stands now those four are out in front. And they're all—"

"Why not five? Alec Gallant himself?"

"All right, five. They're all in the clear, including him, if she was killed at eleven-thirty. So suppose she wasn't. Suppose she was killed earlier, half an hour or so earlier. Suppose when Flora Gallant phoned her from here and put you on to talk with her, it wasn't her at all, it was someone else imitating her voice, and she pulled that stunt, the groan and the other noises, to make you think you had heard the murder at that time."

Wolfe's brows were up. "With the corpse there on the floor."

"Certainly."

"Then you're not much better off. Who did the impersonation? Their alibis still hold for eleven-thirty."

"I realize that. But there were nineteen women around there altogether, and a woman who wouldn't commit a murder might be willing to help cover up after it had been committed. You know that."

Wolfe wasn't impressed. "It's very tricky, Mr. Cramer. If you are supposing Flora Gallant killed her, it was elaborately planned. Miss Gallant phoned here yesterday morning to make an appointment for eleven this morning. Did she kill Miss Voss, station someone there beside the corpse to answer the phone, rush down here, and maneuver me into ringing Miss Voss's number? It seems a little farfetched."

"I didn't say it was Flora Gallant." Cramer hung on. "It could have been any of them. He or she didn't have to know you were going to ring that number. He might have intended to call it himself, before witnesses, to establish the time of the murder, and when your call came, whoever it was there by the phone got rattled and went ahead with the act. There are a dozen different ways it could have happened. Hell, I know it's tricky. I'm not asking you to work your brain on it. You must know why I brought it up."

Wolfe nodded. "Yes, I think I do. You want me to consider what I heard—and Mr. Goodwin. You want to know if we are satisfied that those sounds were authentic. You want to know if we will concede that they might have been bogus."

"That's it. Exactly."

Wolfe rubbed his nose with a knuckle, closing his eyes. In a moment he opened them. "I'm afraid I can't help you, Mr. Cramer. If they were bogus they were well executed. At the time, hearing them, I had no suspicion that it was flummery. Naturally, as soon as I learned that they served to fix the precise moment of a murder, I knew they were open to question, but I can't challenge them intrinsically. Archie?"

I shook my head. "I pass." To Cramer: "You've read the statement, so you know that right after I heard it my guess was that something hit her and she dragged the phone along as she went down and it struck the floor. I'm not going to go back on my guess now. As for our not hearing the blow, read the statement. It says that it started out as if it was going to be a scream but then it was a groan. She might have seen the blow coming and was going to scream, but it landed and turned it into a groan, and in that case we wouldn't hear the blow. A chunk of marble hitting a skull wouldn't make much noise. As for supposing she was killed half an hour or so earlier, I phoned within three minutes, or John H. Watson did, and in another six or seven minutes Carl Drew was talking to me, so he must have seen the body, or someone did, not more than five minutes after we heard the groan. Was she twitching?"

"No. You don't twitch long with a scarf as tight as that around your throat."

"What about the ME?"

"He got there a little after twelve. With blood he might have timed it pretty close, but there wasn't any. That's out."

"What about the setup? Someone left that room quick after we heard the sounds. If it was the murderer, he or she had to cradle the phone and tie the scarf, but that wouldn't take long. If it was a fill-in, as you want to suppose, all she had to do was cradle the phone. Whichever it was, wasn't there anyone else around?"

"No. If there was, they're saving it. As you know, Bianca Voss wasn't popular around there. Anyway, that place is a mess, with three different elevators, one in the store, one at the back for service and deliveries, and one in an outside hall with a separate entrance so they can go up to the offices without going through the store."

"That makes it nice. Then it's wide open."

"As wide as a barn door." Cramer stood up. To Wolfe: "So that's the best you can do. You thought the sounds were open to question."

"Not intrinsically. Circumstantially, of course."

"Yeah. Much obliged." He was going. After two steps he turned. "I don't like gags about homicide, murder is no joke, but I can mention that Bianca Voss had you wrong. Scum. Stinking sewer. Orchids don't smell." He went.

Apparently he hadn't really swallowed it that she was already dead when we heard the sounds.

III

The next morning, Wednesday, eating breakfast in the kitchen with the *Times* propped up in front of me, which is routine, of course I read the account of the Bianca Voss murder. There were various details that were news to me, but nothing startling or even helpful. It included the phone call from John H. Watson, but didn't add that he had been identified as Archie Goodwin, and there was no mention of Nero Wolfe. I admit that the cops and the DA have a right to save something for themselves, but it never hurts to have your name in the paper, and I had a notion to phone Lon Cohen at the *Gazette* and give him an exclusive. However, I would have to mention it to Wolfe first, so it would have to wait until eleven o'clock.

As a matter of fact, another item in the *Times* came closer to me. Sarah Yare had committed suicide. Her body had been found Tuesday evening in her little walk-up apartment on East Thirteenth Street. I had never written a fan letter to an actress, but I had been tempted to a couple of years back when I had seen Sarah Yare in *Thumb a Ride*. The first time I saw it I had a companion, but the next three times I was alone. The reason for repeating was that I had the impression I was infatuated and I wanted to wear it down, but when the impression still stuck after three tries I quit. Actresses should be seen and heard, but not touched. At that, I might have given the impression another test in a year or two if there had been an opportunity, but there wasn't. She quit *Thumb a Ride* abruptly some months later, and the talk was that she was an alco and done for.

So I read that item twice. It didn't say that it had been pronounced suicide officially and finally, since she had left no note, but a nearly empty Bourbon bottle had been there on a table, and on the floor by the couch she had died on there had been a glass with enough left in it to identify the cyanide. The picture of her was as she had been when I had got my impression. I asked Fritz if he had ever seen Sarah Yare, and he asked what movies she had been in, and I said none, she was much too good for a movie.

I didn't get to suggest phoning Lon Cohen to Wolfe because when he came down from the plant rooms at eleven o'clock I wasn't there. As I was finishing my second cup of coffee a phone call came from the District Attorney's office inviting me to drop in, and I went and spent a couple of hours at Leonard Street with an assistant DA named Brill. When we got through I knew slightly more than I had when we started, but he didn't. He had a copy of our statement on his desk, and what could I add to that? He had a lot of fun, though. He would pop a question at me and then spend nine minutes studying the statement to see if I had tripped.

Getting home a little before noon, I was prepared to find Wolfe grumpy. He likes me to be there when he comes down from the plant rooms to the office, and while he can't very well complain when the DA calls me on business that concerns us, this wasn't our affair. We had no client and no case and no fee in prospect. But I got a surprise. He wasn't grumpy; he was busy. He had the phone book open before him on his desk. He had actually gone to my desk, stooped to get the book, lifted it, and carried it around to his chair. Unheard of.

"Good morning," I said. "What's the emergency?"

"No emergency. I needed to know a number."

"Can I help?"

"Yes. I have instructions."

I sat. He wants you at his level because it's too much trouble to tilt his head back. "Nothing new," I said, "at the DA's office. Do you want a report?"

"No. You will go to Alec Gallant's place on Fifty-fourth Street and speak with Mr. Gallant, his sister, Miss Prince, Miss Thorne, and Mr. Drew. Separately if possible. You will tell each of them— You read the *Times* this morning as usual?"

"Certainly."

"You will tell each of them that I have engaged to make certain inquiries about Miss Sarah Yare, and that I shall be grateful for any information they may be able and willing to furnish. I would like to see any communications they may have received from her, say in the past month. Don't raise one brow like that. You know it disconcerts me."

"I've never seen you disconcerted yet." I let the brow down a little. "If they ask me who engaged you what do I say?"

"That you don't know. You are merely following instructions."

"If I ask you who engaged you what do you say?"

"I tell you the truth. No one. Or more accurately, I have engaged myself. I think I may have been hoodwinked and I intend to find out. You may be fishing where there are no fish. They may all say they have never had any association with Sarah Yare, and they may be telling the truth or they may not. You will have that in mind and form your conclusions. If any of them acknowledge association with her, pursue it enough to learn the degree of intimacy, but don't labor it. That can wait until we bait a hook. You are only to discover if there are any fish."

"Now?"

"Yes. The sooner the better."

I stood up. "It may take a while if the cops and the DA are working on them, and they probably are. How urgent is it? Do you want progress reports by phone?"

"Not unless you think it necessary. You must get all five of them."

"Right. Don't wait dinner for me." I went.

On the way uptown in the taxi I was using my brain. I will not explain at this point why Wolfe wanted to know if any of the subjects had known Sarah Yare, and if so how well, for two reasons:

first, you have certainly spotted it yourself; and second, since I am
not as smart as you are, I had not yet come up with the answer. It
was underneath. On top, what I was using my brain for, was the
phone book. Unquestionably it was connected with his being hoodwinked, since that was what was biting him, and therefore it probably had some bearing on the call that had been made from his
office to Bianca Voss, but what could he accomplish by consulting
the phone book? For that I had no decent guess, let alone an answer,
by the time I paid the hackie at Fifty-fourth and Fifth Avenue.

Alec Gallant Incorporated, on the north side of the street near
Madison Avenue, was no palace, either outside or in. The front was
maybe thirty feet, and five feet of that was taken by the separate
entrance to the side hall. The show window, all dark green, had just
one exhibit: a couple of yards of plain black fabric, silk or rayon or
nylon or Orlon or Dacron or cottonon or linenon, draped on a little
rack. Inside, nothing whatever was in sight—that is, nothing to buy.
The wall-to-wall carpet was the same dark green as the show window. There were mirrors and screens and tables and ash trays, and a
dozen or more chairs, not fancy, more to sit in than to look at. I
had taken three steps on the carpet when a woman standing with a
man by a table left him to come to meet me. I told her my name and
said I would like to see Mr. Gallant. The man, approaching, spoke.

"Mr. Gallant is not available. What do you want?"

That didn't strike me as a very tactful greeting to a man who, for
all he knew, might be set to pay eight hundred dollars for an afternoon frock, but of course he had had a tough twenty-four hours, so
I kept it pleasant. "I'm not a reporter," I assured him, "or a cop, or
a lawyer drumming up trade. I'm a private detective named Archie
Goodwin, sent by a private detective named Nero Wolfe to ask
Mr. Gallant a couple of harmless questions—not connected with the
death of Bianca Voss."

"Mr. Gallant is not available."

I hadn't heard his voice in person before, only on the phone, but
I recognized it. Also he looked like a business manager, with his neat
well-arranged face, his neat well-made dark suit, and his neat
shadow-stripe four-in-hand. He was a little puffy around the eyes,

but the city and county employees had probably kept him from getting much sleep.

"May I ask," I asked, "if you are Mr. Carl Drew?"

"Yes. I am."

"Then I'm in luck. I was instructed to see five different people here—Mr. Gallant, Miss Gallant, Miss Prince, Miss Thorne, and Mr. Carl Drew. Perhaps we could sit down?"

He ignored that. "See us about what?"

The woman had left us. She was in earshot if her hearing was good, but this was certainly no secret mission, with five of them on the list. "To get information," I told him, "if you have any, about a woman who died yesterday. Not Bianca Voss. Miss Sarah Yare."

"Oh." He blinked. "Yes. That was tragic. Information? What kind of information?"

"I don't exactly know." I was apologetic. "All I know is that someone has engaged Mr. Wolfe to make inquiries about her, and he sent me to ask you people if you had any messages or letters from her in the past month or so, and if so will you let him see them."

"Messages or letters?"

"Right."

"That seems a little— Who engaged him?"

"I don't know." I was not permitting my face or voice to show that I had caught sight of a fish. "If you have had messages or letters, and would like to know who wants to see them before you produce them, I suppose Mr. Wolfe would tell you. He would have to."

"I have no messages or letters."

I was disappointed. "None at all? I said the past month or so, but before that would help. Any time."

He shook his head. "I never have had any. I doubt if she ever wrote a letter—that is, to anyone here—or any messages, except phone messages. She always did everything by telephone. And for the past month, longer than that, more than a year, she hasn't been— uh—she hasn't been around."

"I know." I was sympathetic, and I meant it, though not for him. "Anyway, I don't think Mr. Wolfe would be interested in

letters about clothes. I think it's personal letters he wants, and he
thought you might have known her well enough personally to
have some."

"Well, I haven't. I can't say I didn't know her personally—she
was a very fine customer here for two years, and she was a very
personal person. But I never had a personal letter from her."

I had to resist temptation. I had him talking, and there was no
telling if or when I would get at the others. But Wolfe had said
not to labor it, and I disobey instructions only when I have reason
to think I know more about it than he does, and at that moment I
didn't even know why he had been consulting the phone book. So
I didn't press. I thanked him and said I would appreciate it if he
would tell me when Mr. Gallant would be available. He said he
would find out, and left me, going to the rear and disappearing
around the end of a screen, and soon I heard his voice, but too
faint to get any words. There was no other voice, so, being a detective, I figured it out that he was on a phone. That accomplished, I
decided to detect whether the woman, who was seated at a table
going through a portfolio, was either Anita Prince or Emmy
Thorne. I voted no, arriving at it by a process so subtle and complicated that I won't go into it.

Drew reappeared, and I met him in the middle of the room. He
said that Mr. Gallant was in his office with Miss Prince and could
let me have five minutes. Another fish. Certainly Drew had told
Gallant what my line was, and why did I rate even five seconds?
As Drew led me to an elevator and entered with me, and pushed the
button marked "2," I had to remember to look hopeful instead of
smug.

The second-floor hall was narrow, with bare walls, and not carpeted. As I said, not a palace. After following Drew down six
paces and through a door, I found myself in a pin-up paradise.
All available space on all four walls was covered with women,
drawings and prints and photographs, both black-and-white and
color, all sizes, and in one respect they were all alike: none of them
had a stitch on. It hadn't occurred to me that a designer of women's
clothes should understand female anatomy, but I admit it might

help. The effect was so striking that it took me four or five seconds to focus on the man and woman seated at a table. By that time Drew had pronounced my name and gone.

Though the man and woman were fully clothed, they were striking too. He reminded me of someone, but I didn't remember who until later: Lord Byron—a picture of Lord Byron in a book in my father's library that had impressed me at an early age. It was chiefly Gallant's dark curly hair backing up a wide sweeping forehead, but the nose and chin were in it too. The necktie was all wrong; instead of Byron's choker he was sporting a narrow ribbon tied in a bow with long ends hanging.

The woman didn't go with him. She was small and trim, in a tailored suit that had been fitted by an expert, and her face was all eyes. Not that they popped, but they ran the show. In spite of Alec Gallant's lordly presence, as I approached the table I found myself aiming at Anita Prince's eyes.

Gallant was speaking. "What's this? About Sarah Yare?"

"Just a couple of questions." He had eyes too, when you looked at them. "It shouldn't take even five minutes. I suppose Mr. Drew told you?"

"He said Nero Wolfe is making an inquiry and sent you. What about? About how she died?"

"I don't think so, but I'm not sure. The fact is, Mr. Gallant, on this I'm just an errand boy. My instructions were to ask if you got any messages or letters from her in the past month or so, and if so will you let Mr. Wolfe see them."

"My God." He closed his eyes, tilted his head back, and shook it—a lion pestered by a fly. He looked at the woman. "This is too much. Too much!" He looked at me. "You must know a woman was assassinated here yesterday. Of course you do!" He pointed at the door. "There!" His hand dropped to the desk like a dead bird. "And after that calamity, now this, the death of my old and valued friend. Miss Yare was not only my friend; in mold and frame she was perfection, in movement she was music, as a mannequin she would have been divine. My delight in her was completely

pure. I never had a letter from her." His head jerked to Anita
Prince. "Send him away," he muttered.

She put fingers on his arm. "You gave him five minutes, Alec,
and he has only had two." Her voice was smooth and sure. The
eyes came to me. "So you don't know the purpose of Mr. Wolfe's
inquiry?"

"No, Miss Prince, I don't. He only tells me what he thinks I
need to know."

"Nor who hired him to make it?"

So Drew had covered the ground. "No. Not that either. He'll
probably tell you, if you have what he wants, letters from her, and
you want to know why he wants to see them."

"I have no letters from her. I never had any. I had no personal
relations with Miss Yare." Her lips smiled, but the eyes didn't.
"Though I saw her many times, my contact with her was never
close. Mr. Gallant preferred to fit her himself. I just looked on. It
seems—" She stopped for a word, and found it. "It seems odd that
Nero Wolfe should be starting an inquiry immediately after her
death. Or did he start it before?"

"I couldn't say. The first I knew, he gave me this errand this
morning. This noon."

"You don't know much, do you?"

"No, I just take orders."

"Of course you do know that Miss Yare committed suicide?"

I didn't get an answer in. Gallant, hitting the table with a palm,
suddenly shouted at her, "Name of God! Must you? Send him
away!"

"I'm sorry, Mr. Gallant," I told him. "I guess my time's up. If
you'll tell me where to find your sister and Miss Thorne, that
will—"

I stopped because his hand had darted to an ash tray, a big metal
one that looked heavy, and since he wasn't smoking he was presumably going to let fly with it. Anita Prince beat him to it. With her
left hand she got his wrist, and with her right she got the ash tray
and moved it out of reach. It was very quick and deft. Then she

spoke, to me. "Miss Gallant is not here. Miss Thorne is busy, but
you can ask Mr. Drew downstairs. You had better go."

I went. In more favorable circumstances I might have spared
another five minutes for a survey of the pin-ups, but not then,
not if I had to dodge ash trays.

In the hall, having pulled the door shut, the indicated procedure,
indicated both by the situation and by Miss Prince's suggestion, was
to take the elevator down and see Drew again, but a detective is
supposed to have initiative. So when I heard a voice, female, float-
ing out through an open door, I went on past the elevator, to the
door, for a look. Not only did I see, I was seen, and a voice, anything but female, came at me.

"You. Huh?"

I could have kicked myself. While, as I said, my mission couldn't
be called secret with five people on the list, certainly Wolfe had
intended it to be private, and there was Sergeant Purley Stebbins
of Homicide West, glaring at me.

"Sightseeing?" he asked. Purley's idea of humor is a little primitive. "The scene of the crime?"

I descended to his level. "Just morbid," I told him, crossing the
sill. "Compulsion neurosis. Is this it?"

Evidently it was. The room was about the same size as Alec
Gallant's, but while his had been dominated by women without
clothes, this one ran to clothes without women. There were coats,
suits, dresses, everything. They were on dummies, scattered around;
on hangers, strung on a pole along a wall; and piled on a table. At
my right one dummy, wearing a skirt, was bare from the waist up;
she might have blushed if she had had a face to blush with. There
was one exception: a well-made tan wool dress standing by a
corner of a desk contained a woman—a very attractive specimen
in mold and frame, and in movement she could have been music.
Standing beside her was Carl Drew. Seated at the desk was Sergeant
Purley Stebbins, with a paper in his hand and other papers on the
desk. Also on the desk, at his left, was a telephone—the one, presumably, that Wolfe and I had heard hit the floor.

What I had stumbled into was obvious. Purley was examining the

effects, including papers, probably the second time over, of Bianca
Voss, deceased, under surveillance on behalf of Alec Gallant Incorporated.

"Actually," I said, advancing past the immodest dummy, "this
is one homicide I have no finger in. I'm on a fishing trip." I moved
my eyes. "Would you tell me, Mr. Drew, where I can find Miss
Thorne?"

"Right here," the tan wool dress said. "I am Miss Thorne."

"I'm Archie Goodwin of Nero Wolfe's office. May I have a
word with you?"

She exchanged glances with Carl Drew. Her glance told me that
Drew had told her about me; and his, if I am half as bright as I
ought to be, told me that if he was not on a more personal basis
with her than he had been with Sarah Yare it wasn't his fault. If
he wasn't he would like to be.

"Go ahead," Drew told her. "I'll stick around." She moved toward the door, and I was following when Purley pronounced my
name, my last name. He has on occasion called me Archie, but not
when I suddenly appeared, uninvited, when he was working on a
homicide. I turned.

"Who are you fishing for?" he demanded.

"If I knew," I said, "I might tell you, but don't hold your breath."
There was no point in trying to sugar him. The damage, if any, had
been done the second he saw me. "See you in court."

Emmy Thorne led me down the hall to a door, the next one, and
opened it. Walking, she could have been music at that, if her heels
had had any purchase. She held the door for me to enter, shut it,
went to a chair behind a desk, and sat. The room was less than half
the size of the others and displayed neither women nor clothes.

"Sit down," she said. "What is this nonsense about letters from
Sarah Yare?"

I took the chair at the end of her desk. "You know," I said, "my
tie must be crooked or I've got a grease spot. Mr. Drew resented me,
and Mr. Gallant was going to throw an ash tray at me. Now you.
Why is it nonsense to ask a simple question politely and respectfully?"

"Maybe 'nonsense' isn't the word. Maybe I should have said 'gall.' What right have you to march in here and ask questions at all? Polite or not."

"None. It's not a right, it's a liberty. I have no right to ask you to have dinner with me this evening, which might not be a bad idea, but I'm at liberty to, and you're at liberty to tell me you'd rather dine at the automat with a baboon, only that wouldn't be very polite. Also when I ask if you have any letters from Sarah Yare you're at liberty to tell me to go climb a tree if you find the question ticklish. I might add that I would be at liberty to climb a pole instead of a tree. Have you any letters from Sarah Yare?"

She laughed. She had fine teeth. She stopped laughing abruptly. "Good Lord," she said, "I didn't think I would laugh for a year. This mess, what happened here yesterday, and then Sarah. No, I have no letters from her. You don't have to climb a tree." The laughter was all gone, and her gray eyes, straight at me, were cool and keen. "What else?"

Again I had to resist temptation. With Drew the temptation had been purely professional; with her it was only partly professional and only partly pure. Cramer had said she was in charge of contacts, and one more might be good for her.

Having resisted, I shook my head. "Nothing else, unless you know of something. For instance, if you know of anyone who might have letters."

"I don't." She regarded me. "Of course I'm curious, if you want to call it that. I was very fond of Sarah, and this coming after all her trouble, naturally I'm wondering why you came here. You say Nero Wolfe is making an inquiry?"

"Yes, he sent me. I don't know who his client is, but my guess would be that it's some friend of Miss Yare's." I stood up. "Someone else may be curious. Thank you, Miss Thorne. I'm glad I don't have to climb a tree."

She got up and offered a hand. "You might tell me who it is."

"I might if I knew." Her hand was cool and firm and I kept it for a second. "I'm sorry I interrupted you in there." That was absolutely true. "By the way, one more liberty: is Miss Gallant around?"

She said no and came with me to the hall and left me, heading for the scene of the crime. I went the other way, to the elevator. Down on the main floor the woman was there alone, at a table with a portfolio. Not at all like Macy's main floor. Emerging, I turned left, found a phone booth on Madison Avenue, dialed the number I knew best, got Fritz, and asked for Wolfe.

His voice came. "Yes, Archie?"

"It's full of fish. Swarming. Sarah Yare bought her clothes there for two years and they all loved her. I'm phoning to ask about Flora Gallant. I've seen all the others, but Flora isn't around. My guess is that she's at the DA's office. Do I stick until she comes?"

"No. Satisfactory."

"Any further instructions?"

"No. Come home."

IV

In the office, after a late lunch of corned-beef hash with mushrooms, chicken livers, white wine, and grated cheese, which Fritz apologized for because he had had to keep it warm too long, I gave Wolfe a full report of the fishing trip, including all dialogue. When I had finished he nodded, took in air through his nose all the way down, and let it out through his mouth.

"Very well," he said, "that settles it. You will now go—"

"Just a minute," I cut in. "It doesn't settle it for me. It was bad enough up there, not knowing the score, and before I do any more going I want a little light. Why did you pick on Sarah Yare, and where did the phone book come in?"

"I have an errand for you."

"Yeah. Will it keep for ten minutes?"

"I suppose so."

"Then why?"

He leaned back. "As I told you this morning, I thought I might have been hoodwinked and I intended to find out. It was quite possible that that performance here yesterday—getting us on the phone just in time to hear a murder committed—was flummery. Indeed, it was more than possible. Must I expound that?"

"No. Even Cramer suspected it."

"So he did. But his theory that Bianca Voss had been killed earlier and that another woman, not the murderer, was there beside the corpse waiting for a phone call, was patently ridiculous. Must I expound that?"

"No, unless it was a lunatic. Anyone who would do that, even the murderer, with the chance that someone might come in any second, would be batty."

"Of course. But if she wasn't killed at the time we heard those sounds she must have been killed earlier, since you phoned almost immediately and sent someone to that room. Therefore the sounds didn't come from there. Miss Gallant did not dial that number. She dialed the number of some other person whom she had persuaded to perform that hocus-pocus."

He turned a hand over. "I had come to that conclusion, or call it surmise, before I went to bed last night, and I had found it intolerable. I will not be mistaken for a jackass. Reading the *Times* at breakfast this morning, the item about the death of Sarah Yare, my attention was caught by the fact that she had been an actress. An actress can act a part. Also she had been in distress. Also she had died. If she had been persuaded to act *that* part, it would be extremely convenient—for the one who persuaded her—for her to die before she learned that a murder had been committed and she had been an accessory after the fact. Certainly that was mere speculation, but it was not idle, and when I came down to the office I looked in the phone book to see if Sarah Yare was listed, found that she was, and dialed her number. Algonquin nine, one-eight-four-seven."

"What for? She was dead."

"I didn't lift the receiver. I merely dialed it, to hear it. Before doing so I strained my memory. I had to recall an experience that was filed somewhere in my brain, having reached it through my ears. As you know, I am trained to attend, to observe, and to register. So are you. That same experience is filed in your brain. Close your eyes and find it. Take your ears back to yesterday, when you were standing there, having surrendered your chair to Miss Gallant, and she was at the phone, dialing. Not the first number she dialed; you dialed that one yourself later. The second one, when, according to her, she was dialing the number of the direct line to Bianca Voss's office. Close your eyes and let your ears and brain take you back. Insist on it."

I did so. I got up and stood while she was dialing, shut my eyes, and brought it back. In ten seconds I said, "Okay."

"Keep your eyes closed. I'm going to dial it. Compare."

The sound came of his dialing. I held my breath till the end, then opened my eyes and said positively, "No. Wrong. The first and third and fourth were wrong. The second might—"

"Close your eyes and try it again. This will be another number. Say when."

I shut my eyes and took five seconds. "Go."

The dialing sound came, the seven units. I opened my eyes. "That's more like it. That was it, anyway the first four. Beyond that I'm a little lost. But in that case—"

"Satisfactory. The first four were enough. The first number, which you rejected, as I did this morning, was Plaza two, nine-oh-two-two, the number of Bianca Voss's direct line according to the phone book—the number which Miss Gallant pretended to be dialing. The second was Sarah Yare's number, Algonquin nine, one-eight-four-seven."

"Well." I sat down. "I'll be damned."

"So it was still a plausible surmise, somewhat strengthened, but no more than that. If those people, especially Miss Gallant, could not be shown to have had some association with Sarah Yare, it was untenable. So I sent you to explore, and what you found promoted the surmise to an assumption, and a weighty one. What time is it?"

He would have had to twist his neck a whole quarter-turn to look at the wall clock, whereas I had only to lower my eyes to see my wrist. I obliged. "Five to four."

"Then instructions for your errand must be brief, and they can be. You will go to Sarah Yare's address on Thirteenth Street and look at her apartment. Her phone might have been discontinued since that book was issued. I need to know that the instrument is still there and operable before I proceed. If I intend to see that whoever tried to make a fool of me regrets it, I must take care not to make a fool of myself. Have I furnished the light you wanted?"

I told him it was at least a glimmer and departed on the errand. If you think I might have shown fuller appreciation of his dialing display, I beg to differ. There is no point in assuring a man that he is a genius when he already knows it. Besides, I was too busy being sore at me. I should have thought of it myself. I certainly should have caught on when I saw him with the phone book.

It was not my day. At the address of the late Sarah Yare on East Thirteenth Street I stubbed my toe again. One thing I think I'm good at is sizing up people, and I was dead wrong about the janitor of that old walk-up. He looked as if anything would go, so I merely told him to let me into Sarah Yare's apartment to check the telephone, and the bum insisted on seeing my credentials. So I misjudged him again. I offered him a sawbuck and told him I only wanted two minutes for a look at the phone with him at my elbow, and when he turned me down I showed him a twenty. He just sneered at it. By that time we were bitter enemies, and if I had showed him a C he would probably have spit on it. The upshot was that I went back home for an assortment of keys, returned, posted myself across the street, waited nearly an hour to be sure the enemy was not peeking, and broke and entered, technically.

I won't describe it; it was too painful. It was a hell of a dump for a Sarah Yare, even for a down-and-outer who had once been Sarah Yare. But the telephone was there, and it was working. I dialed to make sure, and got Fritz, and told him I just wanted to say hello and would be home in fifteeen minutes, and he said that would please Mr. Wolfe because Inspector Cramer was there.

"No," I said.

"Yes," he said.

"When did he come?"

"Ten minutes ago. At six o'clock. Mr. Wolfe said to admit him and is with him in the office. Hurry home, Archie."

I did so.

I got a hackie who liked to take advantages, and it took a little less than the fifteen minutes. I ascended the stoop and let myself in, not banging the door, and tiptoed down the hall and stopped short of the office door, thinking to get a sniff of the atmosphere before entering. I got it. Wolfe's voice came.

". . . and I didn't say I have never known you to be wrong, Mr. Cramer. I said I have never known you to be more wrong. That is putting it charitably, under provocation. You have accused me of duplicity. Pfui!"

"Nuts." Cramer had worked up to his grittiest rasp. "I have accused you of nothing. I have merely stated facts. The time of the murder was supposed to be established by you and Goodwin hearing it on the phone. Is that a fact? Those five people all have alibis for that time. One of them was here with you. Is that a fact? When I put it to you yesterday that that phone business might have been faked, that she might have been killed earlier, all I got was a runaround. You could challenge it circumstantially but not intrinsically, whatever the hell that means. Is that a fact? So that if you and Goodwin got to the witness stand you might both swear that you were absolutely satisfied that you had heard her get it at exactly half past eleven. Is that a fact? Giving me to understand that you weren't interested, you weren't concerned, you had no—"

"No," Wolfe objected. "That was not broached."

"Nuts. You know damn well it was implied. You said you had never had any association with any of those people besides what was in your statement, so how could you be concerned, with Bianca Voss dead? Tell me this, did any of them approach you, directly or indirectly, between seven o'clock yesterday and noon today?"

"No."

"But—" He bore down on the 'but.' "*But* you sent Goodwin there today. He told Stebbins he was on a fishing trip. He talked with Drew, and Gallant, and Miss Prince, and he actually took Miss Thorne from under Stebbins' nose, took her out to talk with her. Is that a fact? And they all refuse to tell what Goodwin said to them or what they said to him. That *is* a fact. They say it was a private matter and had nothing to do with the murder of Bianca Voss. And when I come and ask you what you sent Goodwin there for, ask you plainly and politely, you say that you will— What are you laughing at?"

It wasn't a laugh, I just barely caught it, it was hardly even a chuckle, but all the same it could get under your skin, I knew.

"It escaped me, Mr. Cramer. Your choice of adverbs. Your conception of politeness. Pray continue."

"All right, I asked you. And you said you will probably be ready to tell me within twenty-four hours. And what I said was absolutely justified. I did not accuse you of duplicity. You know what I said."

"I do indeed, Mr. Cramer." I couldn't see Wolfe, but I knew he had upturned a palm. "This is childish and futile. If a connection is established between your murder investigation and the topic of Mr. Goodwin's talks with those people today, it will be only because I formed a conjecture and acted on it. I hope to establish it within twenty-four hours, and meanwhile it will do no harm to give you a hint. Have you any information on the death of a woman named Sarah Yare?"

"Some, yes. Presumed a suicide, but it's being checked. I have two men on it. What about it?"

"I suggest that you assign more men to it, good ones, and explore it thoroughly. I think we will both find it helpful. I may soon have a more concrete suggestion, but for the present that should serve. You know quite well—"

The doorbell rang. I about-faced and looked through the one-way glass panel of the front door. It wasn't a visitor on the stoop, it was a mob. All five of them were there: Gallant, his sister, Anita Prince, Emmy Thorne, and Carl Drew. Fritz appeared from the kitchen, saw me, and stopped. I got my notebook and pen from pockets and wrote:

That phone works. The five subjects are outside wanting
in.

AG

I told Fritz to stand by, tore out the sheet, entered the office and
crossed to Wolfe's desk, and handed it to him.

Wolfe read it, frowned at it for three seconds, turned his head
and called, "Fritz!"

Fritz appeared at the door. "Yes, sir?"

"Put the chain-bolt on and tell those people they will be admitted shortly. Stay there."

"Yes, sir." Fritz went.

Wolfe looked at Cramer. "Mr. Gallant, his sister, Miss Prince,
Miss Thorne, and Mr. Drew have arrived, uninvited and unexpected. You'll have to leave without being seen. In the front room
until they have entered. I'll communicate with you later."

"Like hell I'll leave." Cramer was on his feet. "Like hell they're
unexpected." He was moving, toward the hall, his intention plain—
taking over as receptionist.

"Mr. Cramer!" It snapped at his back, turning him. "Would I
lie so clumsily? If they had been expected would I have let you
in? Would I have sat here bickering with you? Either you leave or
I do. If you admit them you'll have them to yourself, and I wish
you luck."

Cramer was glaring. "You think I'm going to sneak out and sit
on your goddam stoop until you whistle?"

"That *would* be unseemly," Wolfe conceded. "Very well." He
pointed at a picture on the wall to his left behind him—a pretty
waterfall. "You know about that. You may take that station, but
only if you engage not to disclose yourself unless you are invited.
Unequivocally."

The waterfall covered a hole in the wall. On the other side, in a
wing of the hall across from the kitchen, the hole was covered by
nothing, and you could not only see through but also hear through.
Cramer had used it once before, a couple of years ago.

Cramer stood, considering. Wolfe demanded. "Well? They're
waiting. For you or for me?"

Cramer said, "Okay, we'll try it your way," turned and marched to the hall, and turned left.

Wolfe told me, "All right, Archie. Bring them in."

v

Lord Byron, alias Alec Gallant, and the red leather chair went together fine. He sat well back, unlike most people I have seen there. Usually they are either too mad or too upset. Any of the other four probably would have been; they looked it. They were on yellow chairs that I had moved up to make a row facing Wolfe, with Emmy Thorne nearest me, then Anita Prince, then Carl Drew, then Flora Gallant. That put Flora nearest her brother, which seemed appropriate.

Wolfe was turned to Gallant. "You ask me, sir, why I sent Mr. Goodwin to ask you people about Sarah Yare. Of course I'm under no compulsion to reply, and I'm not sure that I am prepared to. Instead, I may ask why his questions, certainly not provocative, so disturbed you. Apparently they have even impelled you to call on me in a body. Why?"

"Talk," Gallant said. "*Vent*. Wind." There was an ash tray on the little table at his elbow, but not a heavy one.

Anita Prince put in, "The police have insisted on knowing why he was there, what he wanted."

Wolfe nodded. "And you refused to say. Why?"

"Because," Emmy Thorne declared, "it was none of their business. And we have a right to know why you sent him, whether his questions were provocative or not." That girl was strong on rights.

Wolfe's eyes went from right to left and back again. "There's no point," he said, "in dragging this out. I'll grant your question priority and we'll go on from there. I sent Mr. Goodwin to see you because I suspected I had been gulled and wanted to find out; and further, because I had guessed that there was a connection between Sarah Yare, and her death, and the murder of Bianca Voss.

By coming here en masse you have made that guess a conviction, if any doubt had remained."

"I knew it," Flora Gallant mumbled.

"*Tais-toi,*" her brother commanded her. To Wolfe: "I'll tell you why we came here. We came for an explanation. We came—"

"For an understanding," Carl Drew cut in. "We're in trouble, all of us, you know that, and we need your help, and we're ready to pay for it. First we have to know what the connection is between Sarah Yare and what happened to Bianca Voss."

Wolfe shook his head. "You don't mean that. You mean you have to know whether I have established the connection, and if so, how. I'm willing to tell you, but before I do so I must clarify matters. There must be no misunderstanding. For instance, I understand that all of you thought yourselves gravely endangered by Miss Voss's presence. You, Miss Prince, you, Miss Thorne, and you, Mr. Drew—your dearest ambitions were threatened. Your future was committed to the success and glory of that enterprise, and you were convinced that Miss Voss was going to cheapen it, and perhaps destroy it. Do you challenge that?"

"Of course not." Emmy Thorne was scornful. "Everybody knew it."

"Then that's understood. That applies equally to you, Miss Gallant, but with special emphasis. You also had a more intimate concern, for your brother. You told me so. As for you, Mr. Gallant, you are not a man to truckle, yet you let the woman prevail. Presumably you were under severe constraint. Were you?"

Gallant opened his mouth and closed it. He looked at his sister, returned to Wolfe, and again opened his mouth and closed it. He was under constraint now, no doubt about that.

He forced it out. "I was under her heel." He clamped his jaw. He unclamped it. "The police know. They found out enough, and I have told them the rest. She was a bad woman. I met her in France, during the war. We were in the Resistance together when I married her. Only afterward I learned that she was *perfide.* She had been a traitor to France—I couldn't prove it, but I knew it. I left her and changed my name and came to America—and then last year she found me and made demands. I was under her heel."

Wolfe grunted. "That won't do, Mr. Gallant. I doubt if it has satisfied the police, and it certainly doesn't satisfy me. In that situation you might have killed her, but surely you wouldn't have let her take charge of your business and your life. What else was there?"

"Nothing. Nothing!"

"Pfui. Of course there was. And if the investigation is prolonged the police will discover it. I advise you to disclose it and let me get on and settle this affair. Didn't her death remove her heel?"

"Yes. Thank God, it did." Gallant hit the arms of the chair with his palms. "With her gone there is no evidence to fear. She had two brothers, and they, like her, were traitors, and I killed them. I would have killed her too, but she escaped me. During the war it would have been merely an episode, but it was later, much later, when I found out about them, and by then it was a crime. With her evidence I was an *assassin*, and I was doomed. Now she is gone, thank God, but I did not kill her. You know I did not. At half past eleven yesterday morning I was in my workshop with Miss Prince and many others, and you can swear that she was killed at that moment. That is why we came to see you, to arrange to pay—"

"Hold it, Alec." Anita Prince headed him off. "Mr. Wolfe wants to clarify matters. Let him."

"That cat's head is out," Wolfe told her, "but I had already heard it scratch. Let's get on. I cannot swear that Bianca Voss was killed 'at that moment.' On the contrary, I'm sure she wasn't, for a variety of reasons. There are such minor ones as the extraordinary billingsgate she spat at me on the phone, quite gratuitous; and her calling me a gob of fat. A woman who still spoke the language with so marked an accent would not have the word 'gob' so ready, and probably wouldn't have it at all."

He waved "gob" away. "But the major reasons are more cogent. In the first place, it was too pat. Since the complexities of nature permit a myriad of coincidences we cannot reject one offhand, but we can discriminate. That one—that the attack had come just at the moment when Miss Gallant had got Mr. Goodwin and me on the phone with her—was highly suspect. Besides, it was indiscreet to strike just then. Why not wait until she had hung up? Whoever was talking with her would certainly hear the sounds and take alarm. As I told Mr. Cramer, it was open to challenge circumstantially, though not intrinsically. However, there was another challenge, on surer ground. Miss Gallant did not dial Plaza two, nine-oh-two-two, Miss Voss's number, as she pretended. She dialed Algonquin nine, one-eight-four-seven, Sarah Yare's number."

A noise, a sort of low growl, came from the waterfall. I was farthest away, and I heard it distinctly, so it must have reached their ears too, but Wolfe's last words had so riveted their attention that it didn't register.

It did with Wolfe, and he added hastily, "I didn't know that yesterday. I became certain of it only after you rang my doorbell, when Mr. Goodwin handed me this note." He tapped it, there on his desk. "Its first words are 'That phone works.' I had sent him to learn if Sarah Yare's phone was in operation. Obviously, Miss Gallant had arranged with Miss Yare to impersonate Bianca Voss, and it is a reasonable—"

"Wait a minute." Gallant had come forward in the red leather chair. "You can't prove that."

"Directly, no. Inferentially, yes."

"And how do you know she dialed Sarah Yare's number? You weren't where you could see the dial, and neither was Goodwin."

Wolfe nodded. "Evidently you have discussed it with her. You're quite right, Mr. Gallant; we couldn't see the dial. Nevertheless, we can supply evidence, and we think it will be persuasive. I am not—"

"What kind of evidence?"

"That's no good, Alec." It was Emmy Thorne, the contact girl. "You can't push Nero Wolfe. He has his teeth in it, you can see that. You know what we decided."

"I'm not sure," Anita Prince objected, "that we decided right."

"I am. Carl?"

"Yes." Drew was chewing his lip. "I think so. Yes."

"Flora? It's up to you."

"I guess so." Flora's voice was cracked, and she tried again. "I guess so." A little better.

Emmy nodded. "Go ahead, Alec. You can't push him."

"My God." Gallant looked at his sister, and back at Wolfe. "All right. We will pay you to help us. *I* will pay you. My sister is innocent and she must not suffer. It would be an offense against nature, against God Himself. She has told me all about it, and she was stupid, but she is innocent. She did arrange with Sarah Yare, as you said, but only to move you. She had read much about you and had a great opinion of your abilities. She was desperate about Bianca Voss. She knew you demanded high fees, much beyond her resources, so she conceived a plan. She would persuade you to talk with Bianca Voss on the phone, and she would get Sarah instead, and Sarah would abuse you with such violence that you would be offended and resent it, and you would be moved to act against Bianca Voss. It was stupid, yes, very stupid, but it was not criminal."

Wolfe's eyes, at him, were half closed. "And you want to pay me to help her."

"Yes. When I told her you had sent your man to inquire about Sarah Yare I saw she was frightened and asked her why, and she told me. I consulted the others, and it was apparent that you knew something, and that was dangerous. We decided to come and ask you to help. My sister must not suffer."

Wolfe's eyes moved. "Miss Gallant. You heard your brother. Did he quote you correctly?"

"Yes!" That time it was too loud.

"You did those things? As he related them?"

"Yes!"

Wolfe returned to Gallant. "I agree with you, sir, that your sister was stupid, but you are not the one to proclaim it. You say that she arranged with Sarah Yare to abuse me on the phone, but Miss Yare didn't stop at that. She ended by making noises indicating that she had been violently attacked, and jerked the phone off onto the floor, and made other noises, and then hung up the phone and cut the connection. Was that on her own initiative? Her own idea?

Your sister's stupidity can bow to yours if you expected me to overlook that point—or worse, if you missed it yourself."

"I am not stupid, Mr. Wolfe."

"Then you are devious beyond my experience."

"Devious?"

"*Rusé. Subtil.*"

"No. I am not." Gallant clamped his jaw. He released it. "*Bien.* Suppose, only to suppose, she arranged that too, that comedy. Suppose even that she killed Bianca Voss. Was that a crime? No; it was justice; it was the hand of God. Bianca Voss was an evil woman. She was *vilaine.* Are you so virtuous that you must crucify my sister? Are you a paragon? For she is in your hands, at your mercy. You know about Sarah Yare, but the police do not. You know she dialed that number, but the police do not, and they will not unless you tell them. By your word it can be that my sister was here with you at the time that Bianca Voss was killed. As I have said, I will pay you. It will be a great service from you, and it deserves payment. I will trust you. I will pay you now."

Wolfe grunted. "That was quite a speech."

"It was not a speech. I do not make speeches. It was an appeal to your charity. From my heart."

"And to my cupidity." Wolfe shook his head. "No. I am not a paragon. I am not even a steward of the law. But you have ignored two important factors: one, my self-esteem. Even if Bianca Voss deserved to die, I will not permit a murderer to take me for a simpleton. Two, another woman died too. Was Sarah Yare also evil? Was she *vilaine?*"

"But she—Sarah killed herself!"

"No. I don't believe it. That's another coincidence I reject. Granted that she may have been wretched enough for that extreme, why did she choose that particular moment? Again too pat. According to the published account, she died between ten o'clock yesterday morning and two in the afternoon, but I can narrow it a little. Since she spoke with me on the phone at eleven-thirty, she died between that hour and two o'clock. I believe that the person who killed Bianca Voss at some time prior to eleven-thirty, and arranged with Sarah Yare to enact that comedy, as you call it, went to Sarah Yare's apartment later and killed her. Indeed, prudence demanded it. So you ask too much of my charity. If only Bianca Voss had died—"

"No!" Gallant exploded. "Impossible! Totally impossible! My sister loved Sarah! She killed her? Insane!"

"But you believe she killed Bianca Voss. You came here believing that. That was stupid too. She didn't."

Gallant gawked at him. Lord Byron shouldn't gawk, but he did. So did the others. Also they made noises. Carl Drew demanded, "Didn't? You say she *didn't?*" Emmy Thorne asked coolly, "What's this, Mr. Wolfe? A game?"

"No, madam, not a game. Nor a comedy—Mr. Gallant's word. As a man I know said yesterday, murder is no joke." Wolfe's eyes went to Flora. "There was much against you, Miss Gallant, especially the fact that you dialed that other number before you dialed Sarah Yare's, and asked someone you called Doris if Miss Voss was around. Are you too rattled to remember that?"

"No." She was clutching the rim of her bag with both hands. "I remember."

"Of course the reason for it was obvious, if you had killed Bianca Voss before you came here; you had to know that the body had not been found before you proceeded with your stratagem. Since you had *not* killed Bianca Voss, why did you make that call?"

"I wanted to make sure that she hadn't gone out. That she was there in her office. You might call her again after I left and find out she hadn't been there. I didn't care if you called her and she denied she had talked to you like that. I thought you would think she was lying. I suppose that was stupid." Her mouth worked. "How did you know I didn't kill her?"

"You told me. You showed me. If you had devised that elaborate humbug, certainly you would have decided how to act at the moment of crisis. You would have decided to be alarmed, and shocked, and even perhaps a little dazed. But it wasn't like that. You were utterly stunned with bewilderment. When Mr. Goodwin told us what Mr. Drew had said, what did you say? You said,

'But how—' And repeated it, 'But how—' If you had killed Bianca Voss you would have had to be a master dramatist to write such a line, and an actress of genius to deliver it as you did; and you are neither."

Wolfe waved it away. "But that was for me. For others, for a judge and jury, I must do better, and I think I can. If you are innocent, someone else is guilty. Someone else learned of the arrangement you had made with Sarah Yare, either from you or from her, and persuaded her to add a dramatic climax. Someone else killed Bianca Voss and then established an invulnerable alibi for the crucial period. Someone else had secured the required amount of cyanide—it doesn't take much. Someone else, having established the alibi, went to Sarah Yare's apartment and poisoned her glass of whisky. That was done before two o'clock, and that should make it simple. Indeed, it *has* made it simple. Shortly before you came I learned from Mr. Cramer of the police that you arrived at your brother's place yesterday a few minutes after noon. Since you left here at a quarter of twelve, you hadn't had time to go first to Thirteenth Street and dispose of Sarah Yare; and you were continuously under the eyes of policemen the rest of the afternoon. That is correct?"

"Yes." Flora's eyes were wet but she hadn't used a handkerchief. "I wanted to go and see what had happened to Sarah, but I was afraid—I didn't know—"

"It's a good thing you didn't, madam. I also learned from Mr. Cramer that you, Mr. Gallant, you, Mr. Drew, and you, Miss Prince, were also constantly under surveillance, for hours, from the time the police arrived. That leaves you, Miss Thorne." His eyes were narrowed at her. "You were with three men in an office on Forty-sixth Street from eleven-twenty until a quarter to twelve. You arrived at Mr. Gallant's place, and found the police there, shortly before three o'clock. You may be able to account for the interim satisfactorily. Do you want to try?"

"I don't have to try." Emmy Thorne's gray eyes were not as cool and keen as they had been when she had told me I didn't have to climb a tree. She had to blink to keep them at Wolfe. "So it *is* a game."

"Not one you'll enjoy, I fear. Nor will I; I'm out of it now. To disclose your acquisition of the cyanide you would need for Sarah Yare; to show that you entered Bianca Voss's room yesterday morning, or could have, before you left for your business appointment; to find evidence of your visit to Thirteenth Street after your business appointment; to decide which homicide you will be put on trial for—all that is for others. You must see now that it was a mistake— *Archie!*"

I was up and moving, but halted. Gallant, out of his chair and advancing, wasn't going to touch her. His fists were doubled, but not to swing; they were pressed against his chest. He stopped square in front of her and commanded, "Look at me, Emmy."

To do so she would have had to move her head, tilt it back, and she moved nothing.

"I have loved you," he said. "Did you kill Sarah?"

Her lips moved but no sound came.

His fists opened for his fingers to spread on his chest. "So you heard us that day, and you knew I couldn't marry you because I was married to her, and you killed her. That I can understand, for I loved you. But that you killed Sarah, no. No! And even that is not the worst! Today, when I told you and the others what Flora had told me, you accepted it, you allowed us to accept it, that she had killed Bianca. You would have let her suffer for it. Look at me! You would have let my sister—"

Flora was there, tugging at his sleeve, sputtering at him, "You love her, Alex, don't hurt her now, don't—"

Gallant jerked loose, backed up, folded his arms, and breathed; and Emmy Thorne moved. She came up out of her chair, stood rigid long enough to give Gallant a straight, hard look, shook her head, spun away from him, and headed for the door, brushing against Flora. Her route took her past Anita Prince, who tilted her head back to look up at her, and past Carl Drew, who had to pull his feet back not to trip her.

I didn't budge, thinking I wasn't needed, and I was right. In movement she might have been music, but if so, the music got stopped. As she made the hall and turned toward the front a hand gripped her arm—a hand that had had plenty of practice gripping arms.

"Take it easy, Miss Thorne," Cramer said. "We'll have to have a talk."

"*Grand Dieu,*" Gallant groaned, and covered his face with his hands.

HISTORIC TALES

Cloak Without Dagger (1776)*

BY PIERRE-AUGUSTIN CARON
DE BEAUMARCHAIS

London, May 6, 1776

To the Editor of the *Morning Chronicle*

Sir:

I am a foreigner, French, and a man of honor. If this does not tell you in full who I am, at least it tells you in more ways than one who I am not. In these days and in London it is not pointless to do so.

The day before yesterday, after the concert at the Pantheon, when people had started dancing, I found under my feet a woman's cloak. It was of black taffeta, lined with the same material and edged with lace. I do not know to whom the cloak belongs. I never saw, at the Pantheon or elsewhere, the person who wore it, and since that day all my efforts to learn something about her have been in vain.

I therefore beg you, sir, to advertise in your paper that the cloak

---

* *Gaîté faite à Londres* in Beaumarchais, *Oeuvres Complètes,* Paris, 1809, VII, 157–164. Translated by the Editor.

has been found, so that the rightful owner may come forward to claim it.

But in order that there may be no mistake about who this is, I must inform you that the person who wore the cloak was also wearing that day a headdress of pink feathers and, I believe, long diamond earrings. Of this last detail I am not so certain as of the rest, but I may add that she is tall and has a good figure; that her hair is a silvery blond and her complexion dazzlingly light; that her neck is slim and fine, and likewise her waist. As for her foot, it is the prettiest in the world. I observe also that she is quite young, rather lively, and a trifle heedless; that she has a light step and a great fondness for dancing.

If you ask me, sir, why if I took such close notice I did not return her cloak to her on the spot, I must repeat what I said above, namely, that I never saw the lady; I know neither her face, nor her look, clothes, or bearing. I do not know who she is, nor what her mien may be. If you insist on knowing how without seeing her I can describe her so thoroughly, it will be my turn to express surprise that such an observer as yourself does not know how readily a woman's cloak affords the means of recognizing her.

Without boasting of a talent which is one no longer since the late Zadig of happy memory disclosed its method, I would ask you, Sir, to believe that while examining the cloak in question I found clinging to the material of the hood a few hairs of a beautiful blond color, as well as a few wisps of pink feather obviously parted from a headdress. You will surely grant that it took no great effort of genius to conclude that the hair and coiffure of this blonde must be like the samples thereof that had become detached. You follow my reasoning, I have no doubt.

And since such hair never grew upon a dark brow or a dark skin, analogy would suggest to you as it did to me that this beauty with the silver-blond hair must have a dazzling complexion. No observer can question this without making his own judgment questionable.

Similarly, a very slight pulling of the threads in the taffeta, on each inner side of the hood (such as cannot have been produced except by the constant friction of two small, hard objects in motion) told me, not that she wore long earrings on that day (I did not say she did), but that she usually wears them. And between you and me it is not likely that she would forgo these ornaments on a day of show, conquest, and large assembly. If my reasoning is false, do not, Sir, spare me. Strictness is no injustice.

The rest goes without saying. Anyone can see that I had only to examine the ribbon which fastens the cloak about the neck, and to tie the knot at the place shown by the wrinkling, to observe that the space thus bounded was slight. Hence the neck daily enclosed therein must be slim and fine—no difficulty here.

Measuring then most carefully the distance between the top of the cloak (at the back) and the horizontal fold or wrinkling produced (below) by the tying of it, French fashion, to set off the waist and mould the upper part above the hips, while the lower falls softly in lace flounces over a rounded and well-defined posterior, I decided as would any connoisseur that with such a tapered waist and rich bust the owner must be tall and well made. The thing speaks for itself: the artist detects the nude beneath the drapery.

Suppose further, Sir, that while examining the middle of the cloak, you had found on the black taffeta the print of a very pretty shoe outlined in grey dust. Would you not have reasoned that if some other woman had stepped on the cloak after it had slipped to the floor she would have deprived me of the pleasure of picking it up? After this conclusion you could no longer doubt that the charming print was that of the owner of the cloak herself. Whereupon you would reflect that if her shoe is so small, her pretty foot must be still smaller. I take no credit for inferring this fact: any observer, a child itself, could make this sort of discovery.

But this print, which was made in stride and without being even noticed, implies (besides a great liveliness of gait) a strong preoccupation of mind, to which persons that are grave, old, or cold-blooded are seldom liable. From this I deduced that my charming blonde is in the flower of youth, most animated, and proportionately heedless. Would you not, Sir, have thought the same? I ask for fear of being over-persuaded by my own theory.

Finally, remembering that the place where I found her cloak led to the spot where the dancing was growing liveliest, I argued that the lady must be very fond indeed of that pastime, for only its powerful spell could have made her forget her cloak and step upon it. No other conclusion was, I think, possible. Though French, I appeal on this point to the conscience of all fair-minded Englishmen.

And when, the next day, I recalled that in a place where so many people came and went I had been the one who chanced to pick up this cloak (proof enough that it had just been dropped), without being able to find its owner (sufficient indication that she had already gone a considerable distance), I said to myself: Assuredly this young lady is the most vivacious beauty in England, Scotland, and Ireland. And if I do not add America it is only because the people of that country have recently shown signs of devilish vivacity.

By pushing my inquiries further, I might perhaps have found out from the cloak what the owner's rank and station are. But when a man has ascertained about a woman that she is young and beautiful, is that not all he needs to know? At least such was the custom in my day in certain well-known towns of France, and even in a few villages, such as Marly, Versailles, etc.

Do not therefore be surprised, Sir, that a Frenchman who has made a lifelong philosophic (as well as intimate) study of the fair sex should have been able to discover, without sight of her and solely from the appearance of her cloak, that the beautiful blonde who lost it unites in herself the glamour of Venus, the slender neck of a nymph, the bearing of the Graces, and the youth of Hebe. She is quick and thoughtless, she loves to dance to the point of distraction, and she runs towards this pleasure with a foot small as Cinderella's, light as Atalanta's.

As I stand ready to return that most particular cloak, allow me, Sir, to wrap myself up in my own; and to subscribe myself as merely

A French Amateur

The Rifle (1828)*

BY WILLIAM LEGGETT

The traveller who passes, during the summer or autumn months
of the year, through the States of our union that lie west of the
Ohio river, Indiana and Illinois in particular, will often pause in
his journey, with feelings of irrepressible admiration, to gaze
upon the ten thousand beauties which nature has spread through
these regions with an uncommonly liberal hand. The majestic
mountain, upholding the heavens on its cloudy top, does not, to be
sure, arrest his astonished eye; and the roaring cataract, dashing
from a dizzy height, and thundering down into whirling depths
below, then rising again in upward showers, forms no part of the
character of their quiet scenes. But the wide-spread prairie, level
as some waveless lake, from whose fertile soil the grass springs up
with a luxuriance unparalleled in any other part of our country, and
whose beautiful green is besprinkled with myriads and myriads of
flowers, ravishing the sight with their loveliness, and filling the air

* Originally published in *Tales and Sketches of a Country Schoolmaster*,
Harper, 1829; reprinted in Mary Mitford's *Stories of American Life*, 3 vols.,
1830, III, 279 ff. The story has been slightly abridged by the Editor. Omissions
are shown by dots.

with their sweets; and, again, on either side of these immense savannas, standing arrayed, "like host to host opposed," the leafy forests, whose silence has not often been broken by the voice of man, and through whose verdant recesses the deer stalk in herds, with the boldness of primeval nature,—these are some of the scenes that call forth a passing tribute of praise from every beholder. Such is their summer aspect; but when winter "has taken angrily his waste inheritance," not even the painter's pencil can convey a just conception of the bleakness and desolation of the change. Then those extensive plains, lately covered with the infinitely diversified charms of nature, become one white unvaried waste; through the vistas of the naked trees, nothing meets the glance but snow; and if from the chilly monotony of earth, the wearied eye looks up to heaven, thick and heavy clouds, driven along upon the wind, seem overcharged to bursting, with the same frigid element. It was during the latter season that the incidents of our story took place.

About the middle of December, some ten or twelve years ago, before Illinois was admitted a sister State into the union, on the afternoon of a day that had been uncommonly severe, and during the morning of which there had occurred a light fall of snow, two persons were seen riding along one of the immense prairies, in a northern direction. The elder seemed advanced in years, and was dressed in the usual habiliments of the country. He wore a cap made of the skin of the otter, and a hunting-shirt of blue linsey-wolsey covered his body, descending nearly to the knees, and trimmed with red woollen fringe. It was fastened round the waist by a girdle of buckskin, to which was also appended a bullet pouch, made of the same material with the cap. His feet were covered with buckskin moccasins, and leggings of stout cloth were wrapped several times round his legs, fastened above the knee and at the ancle with strings of green worsted. The horse he bestrode was so small, that his rider's feet almost draggled on the ground, and he had that artificial gait, which is denominated rocking. The old man's hair fell in long and uncombed locks beneath his cap, and was white with the frosts of many winters; while the sallowness of his complexion gave **proof** of a long residence in those uncultivated parts of the country where the excessive vegetable decay, and the stagnation of large bodies of water, produce perennial agues. His companion was a young man, dressed according to the prevailing fashion of the cities of the eastern States, and his rosy cheeks, and bright blue eyes, evinced that he had not suffered from the effects of climate. He was mounted on a spirited horse, and carried in his hand, the butt resting on his toe, a heavy looking rifle.

"Well, Doctor Rivington," said the elder person, "I should no more ha' looked to see one of you Yankees taking about wi' you a rail Kentuck rifle, than I should ha' thought I'd be riding myself without one. If I didn't see it in your hands, I could almost swear that it's Jim Buckhorn's."

"You have guessed correctly, Mr. Silversight," replied the young physician; "I believe you know almost every rifle in this part of the territory."

"Why, I have handled a power of 'em in my time, Doctor," said the old man, "and there a'n't many good ones atwixt Sangano and the Mississip', that I don't know the vally on. I reckon, now, that same rifle seems to you but a clumsy sort of shooting-iron, but it's brought down a smart chance of deer, first and last. That lock's a rail screamer, and there a'n't a truer bore, except mine, that I left down in the settlement, to get a new sight to—no, not atwixt this and Major Marsham's. It carries just ninety-eight, and mine a little over ninety-four to the pound. Jim has used my bullets often, when we've been out hunting together."

"I was unacquainted with the worth of the gun," resumed Charles Rivington; "but stepping into the gunsmith's this morning, I heard him lament that he had missed a chance of sending it out to Jimmy Buckhorn's; so, intending to come this way, I offered to take charge of it myself. In this wilderness country, we must stand ready to do such little offices of friendship, Mr. Silversight."

" 'Twas no doubt kindly meant, Doctor, and Jim will be monstrous glad to git his piece again," said the hunter. "But my wonderment is, and I don't mean no harm by it, how that tinker would trust such a screamer as that 'ere with a Yankee doctor. Do give it to me; I can't 'bide seeing a good rifle in a man's hand that don't know the vally on it."

Doctor Rivington resigned the weapon with a good-humoured smile; for he had been some time in the country, and partly understood the love which a hunter always feels for a piece, of the character of that he had been carrying; he knew, too, though the old man's manners were rough, there was nothing like roughness in his heart. Indeed, the very person who was loath to trust his young companion with a gun, intrinsically worth but a trifle, would nevertheless, as we shall presently see, have unhesitatingly placed in his charge, without witness or receipt, an uncounted or unlimited amount of money. The term Yankee, which we have heard him applying, in rather a contemptuous manner, was then, and for years after, used indiscriminately in reference to all such as emigrated from the States east of the Alleghany mountains. Handing his rifle across his horse to the old hunter, Charles Rivington observed, "I am glad you have offered to take it, Mr. Silversight, for there appears to be a storm coming up, and as I wish to reach Mr. Wentworth's to-night, I can make the distance shorter, by crossing through the timber into the other prairie, before I get to Buckhorn's."

"Will you be going to town, to-morrow, Doctor?" asked Silversight.

"I shall."

"Well, then, you can do me a good turn. Here," said the old man, handing a little leathern bag, "is fifteen dollars in specie; and the rest, four hundred and eighty-five in Shawnee-town paper, is wrapped in this bit of rug. Want you to pay it into the land-office, to clear out old Richly's land: I was going to take it in; but you'll do just as well, and save me a long ride."

The physician promised to attend to the business, and they kept on together, conversing about such subjects as the nature of the scene suggested, until they reached the place where the path, dividing, pursued opposite directions.

"This is my nearest way, I believe?" said Charles.

"It is," answered the old man. "This first track, that we noticed awhile ago, lies on my route; so I'll push my nag a little, soon as I load this rifle, and it may so be, that I'll overtake company. Doctor, look here, and you'll know how an old hunter loads his piece—it may stand you in stead some day; I put on a double patch, because my bullets are a leetle smaller than Jim's, you mind I told you. There," said he, as he shoved the ball into its place, and carefully poured some priming into the pan, "it's done in quick time by them what have slept, year in and year out, with red Indians on every side of 'em. Good night to ye, Doctor; you needn't lift the certificates—the register may as well keep 'em till old Richly goes in himself."

So saying, the two travellers parted, each urging his horse to greater speed, as the night threatened to set in dark and stormy. The old hunter, acknowledging to himself in mental soliloquy, that the doctor was "a right nice and cute young fellow, considering he was raised among Yankees," rode briskly along the path. He had proceeded about four or five miles further on his way, when he perceived that the track he before observed turned aside: "So, so," said he, "Slaymush has been out among the deer, to-day; I was in hopes 'twas some one going up to the head-waters;" and he kept rocking along the road, when, directly, the report of a musket was heard reverberating through the night, and the old man, writhing and mortally wounded, fell from his horse, which, scared by the occurrence, ran wildly over the prairie. A form was seen a few minutes after, cautiously approaching the place, fearful lest his victim should not yet be dead; but apparently satisfied in this particular, by his motionless silence, he advanced, and proceeded immediately to examine the pockets of the deceased.

"Damnation!" muttered he at length, when a fruitless search was finished, "the old curmudgeon hasn't got the money after all; and I've put a bullet through his head for nothing. I'm sure, I heard him say, in Brown's tavern, down in the settlement, that old Richly give it to him to carry; well, it's his own fault, for telling a bragging lie about it; and the grey-headed scoundrel won't never jeer me again, for using a smooth-bore, before a whole company of Kentuck-squatters—it carried true enough to do his business. I'm sorry I dropped that flask, any how; but this powder-horn will make some amends," grumbled the wretch, as he tore the article he spoke of from the breast, where it had hung for forty years. "What the devil have we here!" said he again, as he struck his foot against the rifle that the murdered man had dropped; "ho, ho," discharging it into the air, "if the worst comes to worst, they'll think his piece went off by accident, and shot him. But there's no danger—it will snow by day light, and cover the trail; and the prairie-wolves will finish the job."

Thus muttering, the ruffian remounted the animal he held by the bridle, and trotted across the prairie, nearly at right angles with the path, along which the unfortunate hunter had been travelling.

It was in a log-house, larger, and of rather more comfortable construction, than was usually seen in that wilderness country, beside a fire that sent a broad and crackling flame half way up the spacious chimney, that there was seated, on the evening of this atrocious murder, in addition to its ordinary inmates, the young physician from whom we have lately parted. His great-coat, hat, and overalls were laid aside, and he was conversing with that agreeable fluency, and pleased expression of countenance, which denoted that he was happy in the society around him. Opposite, and busily employed in knitting, sat a beautiful girl of eighteen. From her work, which seemed to engross an unusual portion of her attention, she every now and then would send a furtive glance to their guest, thus telling, in the silent language of love, the tale she never could have found words to utter. We say she was beautiful; and if a complexion so clear, that

> The eloquent blood spoke through her cheek, and so
>   distinctly wrought,
> That we might say of her, her body thought;

if laughing blue eyes, lighted up by intelligence and affection; if smooth and glossy auburn ringlets; teeth white as the snow around her father's dwelling, and a person which, though not tall, was well formed and graceful;—if all these traits combined, constitute a claim to the epithet, it certainly belonged to her. She was modestly attired in a dress of no costly material; and the little feet that peeped from underneath it, were clothed in white stockings of her own fabrication, and in shoes of too coarse a texture ever to have been purchased from the shelves of a fashionable city mechanic. Yet that same form had been arrayed in richer apparel, and had been followed by glances of warmer admiration, than perhaps ever fell to the share of those, who are ready to condemn her on account of her simple garb.

Catharine Wentworth was the daughter (at the time of our story, the only one), of a gentleman who had formerly been a wealthy merchant in the city of New York; but to whom misfortune in business had suddenly befallen, and had stripped him of all his fortune. While surrounded by affluence, he had been considered remarkably meek and affable; but became proud and miserable in adversity: and not caring to remain among scenes that continually brought to mind the sad change in his condition, he emigrated, with his whole family, to the wilds of Illinois. He was actuated in part, no doubt, by a higher and better motive. At that time he was the father of another daughter. Louisa, older than Catharine, was fast falling a victim to that disease, which comes over the human form, like autumn over the earth, imparting to it additional graces, but too truly whispering that the winter of death is nigh. The medical attendant of the family, perhaps to favour the design which he knew Mr. Wentworth entertained, intimated that a change of climate was their only hope. The change was tried and failed, and the fair Louisa reposed beneath the turf of the prairie.

How strangely does the human mind accommodate itself to almost any situation! The man who had spent his life hitherto in a sumptuous mansion, surrounded by all those elegances and means of enjoyment, which, in a large city, are always to be procured by fortune, now experienced, in a log cabin, divided into but four apartments, and those of the roughest kind, a degree of happiness that he had never known before. And well he might be happy; for he was rich, not in money, but in a better, a more enduring kind of wealth. His wife, two hardy and active sons, and his remaining daughter, Catharine, were all around him, smiling in contentment, and ruddy with health. We can only estimate our condition in this life by comparison with others; and his plantation was as large, and as well cultivated, his crops as abundant, his stock as good as any of the settlers on that prairie. He had still a better source of consolation: Louisa's death, the quiet of the country, and the natural wish of every active mind to create to itself modes of employment, had led him more frequently to read and search the sacred scriptures, than he had found leisure to do before; and this was attended, as it always is, with the happiest result, a knowledge and love of Him, "whom to know is life eternal." But we are digressing.

The family of Mr. Wentworth, with the addition of Charles Rivington (whom, indeed, we might almost speak of as one of its members, for, on the coming New Year's Day, he was to receive the hand of their "saucy Kate," as the happy parents fondly called her), were gathered round the fireside, conversing cheerfully on every topic that presented itself, when a light tap was heard at the door, and Mr. Rumley, the deputy-sheriff of the county, entered the apartment. He apologized for his intrusion, by saying, that having had business to attend to at a cabin farther up the prairie, which detained him longer than he expected, he should not be able, on account of the darkness of the night, to return to town until the following morning; he therefore hoped that he might be accommodated with a bed. His request was, of course, readily complied with.

He was a tall, dark person, dressed much in the manner of the unfortunate hunter, except that his leggings were of buckskin. He had lost an eye when a young man, in a scuffle with an Indian, two of whom sprung upon him from an ambush; this, with a deep scar upon his forehead, received in a tavern-brawl at New Orleans, two or three years before, and the wrinkles that age, or more likely, his manner of life, had ploughed, gave to his countenance a sinister and disagreeable expression. At this time, the haggard appearance of his face was increased, either from having been a long while exposed to the cold, or from some latent sickness working on him, for his lip quivered, and was of a bloodless hue, and he was remarkably pale.

Charles Rivington, who often met him in his rides, was the first to notice the change from his usual appearance.

"You look pale and fatigued, Mr. Rumley; I hope you are not unwell?"

"No, sir—that is—yes, I do feel a little sickish; and should be glad to go to bed, if it's convenient," answered Mr. Rumley.

"Perhaps there is something we can do for you, sir?" said the maternal Mrs. Wentworth.

"No, ma'am, I thank ye. I reckon a good night's sleep will be best for me; it's what cures all my ailings."

And in compliance with his wish the guest was shown to his apartment.

One by one the different members of this peaceful family sought their pillows, till soon Charles Rivington and the blushing Catharine were left sole occupants of the room.

But though alone, they were not lonely; he had many an interesting tale to whisper into the maiden's ear (for it was almost a week since they met), and she, though something of a chatterbox, when none but her mother and brothers were present, on this occasion betrayed a wonderful aptitude for listening. The hours glided happily away; and the gray morning was already advancing, when the happy young man, imprinting a good-night kiss upon her cheek, left her to those sweet dreams which slumber bestows only on the young and innocent.

It was late in the afternoon of the following day, that Charles Rivington, being returned to the town where he resided, was seated in his office, employed in counting a roll of notes, a pile of dollars lying, at the same time, on the table before him, when three men abruptly entered the apartment.

"You are our prisoner," cried the foremost of the party. "By heavens, Jim! Look there; there's the very money itself. I can swear to that pouch."

And here he rudely seized our hero by the collar.

"Stand back, sir, and lay hold of me at your peril," returned Charles Rivington, sternly, as, shaking the man from him, he gave him a blow that sent him to the other side of the office; "What is it that you have to say? If I am to be made prisoner, produce your warrant."

"You may as well submit quietly, Doctor Rivington," said another of the party, who was a constable. "You perhaps can explain every thing; but you must come with us before Squire Lawton. This is my authority (showing a paper), and it is only necessary to say that suspicion rests on you, as the murderer of old Silversight, who was found shot through the head, on the road this morning."

"Is it possible?—poor old man! has he really been killed! When I parted from him last night he was not only well, but seemed in excellent spirits," said the doctor.

"He parted from him last night! mark that, Buckhorn," said the one who had just received so severe a repulse from our hero, and whose name was Carlock. "He left him in excellent spirits! mark what the villain says!"

"There needs no jeering about it," replied Buckhorn. "Doctor Rivington, you tended me in my bad fever last spring, and again when I had the chills in the fall, and you stuck by me truer than any friend I've had since my old mother died, except this ere rifle; and I am monstrous sorry I found it where I did. It may so be that you've got a clear conscience yet; but whether or no, though old Silversight and me has hunted together many and many's the day, you shall have fair play any how, damn me if you sha'n't. That 'ere money looks bad; if it had been a fair fight, we mought a hushed it up somehow or 'nother."

Our hero, while Buckhorn was speaking, had time to reflect that if Silversight were indeed dead, circumstances would really authorize his arrest. The rifle, which he was known to have carried with him from town, had been found, it seems, beside the murdered body. The money that the unfortunate man had entrusted to him, was discovered in his possession; and how could it be proved for what purpose it had been given to him? As these thoughts rushed rapidly through his mind, he turned to the officer, and observed,

"Mr. Pyke, I yield myself your prisoner. I perceive there are some circumstances that cause suspicion to rest on me. I must rely, for awhile upon the character which, I trust, I have acquired since my residence among you, for honour and fair dealing, until I shall be enabled to prove my innocence, or till heaven places in the hands of justice the real perpetrator of the deed."

So saying, he gathered up the money from the table, and departed with the officer and his companions, to the house of Mr. Lawton, who, being a justice of the peace, had issued a warrant for his apprehension.

"I have always been glad to see you heretofore, Doctor Rivington," said the magistrate, politely, on the appearance of that person before him, "and should be so now, were it not that you are charged with a crime, which, if proved, will call down the severest vengeance of the law. I hope and believe, however, that you can establish your innocence. Where were you, sir, on the afternoon of yesterday?"

"I went out to visit some patients, meaning to continue my ride as far as Mr. Buckhorn's; and took his rifle with me, from the gunsmith's, with the intention of stopping and leaving it; but I met with old Mr. Silversight at the cross-roads, who was going up from the New Settlements, and he offered to take charge of it. I gave it to him. We parted at the Fork, and I crossed over to Mr. Wentworth's."

"Did Mr. Silversight continue on his journey, having Jim Buckhorn's rifle with him?" asked the justice.

"Yes, sir; but before we separated he gave me this money," (handing the notes and specie to the magistrate), "requesting me to pay it into the land-office to-day, to clear out Mr. Richly's land. He said there were five hundred dollars in all, and I was counting it when arrested."

"There is a most unfortunate coincidence of circumstance against you, Doctor. The man is found murdered, the rifle which you were known to have carried laying near him, and you arrived in town on the next day, with the money of the deceased in your possession. The poor old man's horse going home without his rider, excited alarm; Buckhorn and Carlock, with other neighbours, set out upon the track; they found the murdered victim, stark and bloody, lying on the snow, which was scarcely whiter than his aged head; they divided—some bearing the body back, while the others followed on the trail; it led them to Mr. Wentworth's, where you acknowledge you passed the night; they there inquired what person made the track which they had followed, and were answered it was you; they continued on your trail until they arrived in town; they make affidavit of these facts, and procure a warrant for your arrest; when, to complete the chain of evidence, you are found counting the spoils of the murdered man. Now, sir, what answer can you make to these appalling circumstances?"

"They are appalling, indeed, sir," said our hero; "and I can only reply to them—I am innocent. If the poor man was murdered, the one who did it must certainly have left tracks; and I fear they have fallen upon his trail and taken it for mine. But it is in my power to prove that I had no weapons with me, except that unlucky rifle, and the gunsmith will testify that he gave me no balls with it."

"The gunsmith has already been before me," said Mr. Lawton, "for I was loath to have you apprehended, except on an application backed by such proof as could not be rejected. He states that when he gave you the gun, the lock had been repaired and polished, and that since that time it has certainly been discharged. I am sorry to do it, but my duty compels me to commit you."

．　．　．　．

He came into court, arm in arm with the attorney, who was employed to plead his cause; and slightly bowing to those whose friendly salute indicated that they believed him innocent, he passed through the crowd, and took a seat behind the lawyers within the bar. From the high and exemplary character which he had sustained invariably, from his first settling in the place until the present black suspicion rested on him, a degree of intuitive respect was accorded by all, that must have been highly gratifying to his feelings. A plea of not guilty was entered, and the examination of witnesses commenced.

George Carlock was the nephew of the deceased. On the night of the sixteenth of December, he was surprised to see the horse of his uncle arrive, with saddle and bridle on, but without a rider. He

thought that the deceased had stopped, perhaps, for awhile at Buckhorn's, who lived a mile or so further down the timber; but, as the
night passed away without his returning home, he started early in
the morning with the intention of tracking the horse. He called for
Buckhorn, and they got upon the trail, and followed it till they
found the dead body. It led them to Mr. Wentworth's. They inquired if any person had been there, that crossed over from the other
side of the stream. They were answered that Doctor Rivington had
crossed the stream, and remained the night with them. That Mr.
Rumley, the deputy-sheriff, had also remained the night, but that
he had come from farther up on the same side. They followed on
the trail till they arrived in town. Being informed, by Mr. Drill, the
gunsmith, that Doctor Rivington had taken Buckhorn's rifle out
with him, they immediately procured a warrant for his apprehension. They found him employed in counting the identical
money, which had been taken from the unfortunate Silversight.

James Buckhorn's testimony was in full corroboration of the
preceding. He mentioned, in addition, that he examined the lock
and barrel of his rifle, on finding it lying near the murdered man,
and discovered that it certainly had been discharged but a short
time before.

The gunsmith deposed to his having given the rifle to the prisoner,
on his offering to carry it out to Buckhorn, and that it had been
discharged since.

"Mr. Drill," said Lawyer Blandly, who was counsel for our hero,
"you mention having given the gun to Doctor Rivington; did you
also give him a bullet that would fit the bore?"

"I did not."

"Did he exhibit any anxiety to obtain the weapon?" again asked
the lawyer.

"By no means," replied the gunsmith; "I considered, at the time,
that the doctor's offer was one of mere kindness; and he had previously mentioned he was going out that way to visit his patients."

"The bore of this rifle, Mr. Drill," continued the sagacious lawyer, "is very small. I presume that you are familiar with the size and
qualities of all that are owned on the road out to Mr. Buckhorn's. Is

there any house at which Doctor Rivington could have stopped, and procured a ball of sufficient smallness?"

"John Guntry's rifle," answered Mr. Drill, "carries eighty-seven or eight to the pound, and one of his bullets, with a thick patch, would suit Buckhorn's pretty well. That is the only one any where near the size."

The attorney for the people here asked another question.

"For what purpose did the prisoner go into your shop, on the morning of the sixteenth of December?"

"I was employed in repairing a pair of pocket pistols for him, and fitting a bullet mould to them. He came in, I believe, to inquire if they were finished."

"Please to note that answer, gentlemen of the jury," said the prosecuting attorney. "Mr. Drill, you may stand aside."

Samuel Cochrane was next called. He was one of the young men, who had returned with the body of Silversight. On his way back, and about two hundred yards from the place where the murder had been committed, he found a copper powder flask, (which was shown to him, and he identified it), the letters C. R. M. D. being cut upon one of its sides, apparently with a knife. There was but one more witness on the part of the people, Mr. Lawton, the magistrate before whom the unfortunate prisoner had been examined. He testified as to the facts which were deposed before him, together with the acknowledgment of Doctor Rivington, that he had been in company with Mr. Silversight, &c. But we may pass over these circumstances, as the reader is already acquainted with them. The prisoner was now put on his defence, and all that talent or ingenuity could devise, was done by his skilful counsel. The witnesses were cross-examined, and re-cross-examined; but their answers were uniformly the same. A large number of respectable persons came forward to testify to the excellence of our hero's general character; but their evidence was rendered unnecessary by the attorney for the people admitting, in unequivocal terms, that previous to this horrid occurrence, it had been exemplary in a high degree. At length, wearied by his exertions and distressed at the result, Mr. Blandly discontinued his examination: he had one more weapon to try in behalf of his client—the powerful one of eloquence; and it was used by a master of the art; but, alas! was used in vain. He dwelt much on the fact that his unfortunate client had wished his route to be trailed from the village, and that Buckhorn had started for the purpose, when the disastrous snowstorm occurred, and took away the only hope he had of proving his innocence. He cited many cases to the jury, in which circumstances, even stronger than these, had been falsified, when their victim, murdered by the laws, was slumbering in his grave. He appealed to them as parents, to know if they would believe, that a son, who had been so filial, whose character had previously been without stain or blemish, could suddenly turn aside from the path of rectitude and honour, to commit such an atrocious crime? But it were useless to recapitulate the arguments that were made use of on this interesting occasion—they were ineffectual. The attorney for the prosecution summed up very briefly. He assured the jury that the evidence was so clear in its nature, so concatenated, so incontrovertible, as to amount to moral certainty. Near the body of the murdered man, a powder flask, such as the eastern people principally use, had been found, with the initials of the prisoner's name and medical degree, engraved upon it— C. R. M. D.—Charles Rivington, Doctor of Medicine. The trail is pursued, and it leads them to the house of Mr. Wentworth, where the prisoner arrived on the evening of the bloody deed, and remained all night. They continue on the trail, till at last they find him, with greedy eyes, bending over the plunder he had torn from his grey-haired victim. "Such," concluded he, "is a rapid outline of the facts; and deeply as I deplore the wretched young man's guilt, yet, believing him guilty, it is my sacred duty to display his enormity; but further than the imperious call of justice requires, I will not go, I cannot go."

The charge of the judge, who was evidently very much affected, occupied but a few minutes; and the jury retired to make up their verdict. We have already told the reader that the prisoner was pale, in consequence of sickness, produced by his exposed situation in prison; but the appalling events of the trial had caused no alteration in his appearance. He sat firm and collected; and there was a melan-

choly sweetness in the expression of his countenance, which told
that all was calm within.

.   .   .   .

The assembled crowd was still anxiously awaiting the return of
the verdict, when the mother of Charles Rivington, leaning on the
arm of Catharine Wentworth, entered the courthouse of Edgarton.
A passage was instantly opened for them, with that intuitive respect
which almost all men are ready to yield to misfortune, even when
accompanied by guilt. They had not been long seated in the part
of the room, where they could be most screened from observation,
when the jury returned, and, handing a sealed verdict to the clerk,
resumed their places. The clerk arose, and read in a faltering voice,
"We find the prisoner, Charles Rivington, guilty." The words had
scarcely left his lips, when a piercing shriek ran through the
apartment, and Catharine Wentworth fell lifeless on the floor. Not
so with that Christian mother; with an unwonted strength she
darted through the assembly, till she reached her child.

"My boy!" she cried, "my boy! be of good cheer; your heavenly
Father knows your inmost soul, and sees that you are guiltless. We
shall lie down together, for think not I can survive you. We shall lie
down together, to wake with the Lord! My boy! my boy! little did
I think to see this bitter day!"

Exhausted nature could endure no more, and the mother fainted
in the arms of her son.

We shall not attempt to describe the situation of our unhappy
hero, for words are inadequate to the task. The insensible forms of
his mother and his beloved Catharine, were conveyed from the
scene; and when some degree of silence was restored among the
sympathizing multitude, the judge proceeded to pronounce sentence upon him. He had nothing to say to avert it, except a reiterated
declaration of his innocence; and he besought the court that the
time previous to his execution might be as brief as possible, in mercy
to his bereaved parent, who would be but dying a continual death
while he survived. It was accordingly fixed to take place on that day
three weeks.

It was near midnight of that important day—the busy throng which the trial had collected together were dispersed, and the moon, high in heaven, was wading on her silent course, through the clouds of a wintry sky, when Charles Rivington, startled from unquiet slumber, by a noise at the door of his prison, and sitting up in bed, that he might more intently listen, heard his own name whispered from the outer side.

"Will you wake, Mr. Charles?" was softly uttered in the sweet accents of our little Irish acquaintance, Judy. "Was there iver the like," continued she, "and he asleeping at that rate, when his friends are opening the door for him?"

"Be quiet, Judy," responded a masculine voice, but modulated to its softest tone, "and stand more in the shadow, the doctor'll awake fast enough, as soon as I get this bolt sawed out; but if ye git that tavern-keeper's dog a-barking, there's no telling but it may wake the jailer instead of the doctor."

"And you're right, Jimmy dear," responded Judy; "there now, leave go with your fingers, man, you can't pull it off that ere way. Here, take this bit of a stake for a pry—and now, that's your sort," continued she, adding her strength to his, and a large end of the log, to which the fastenings of the door were appended, fell to the ground: "Now, one more pull, Jimmy, and the day's our own."

They accordingly made another exertion of united strength, when the prison door flying open, Buckhorn and Judy stood before the prisoner.

"There, Mister Charles, say nothing at all, at all about it; but jist take Jimmy's nag, that's down in the hollow, and git clare as well as ye can. There's a steam-boat, Jimmy says, at St. Louis going right down the river; and here's all the money we could git, but it's enough to pay your passage any how," said the affectionate girl, tears standing in her eyes as she reached to her respected, and, as she firmly believed, guiltless master, all her own hoardings, together with the sum which Buckhorn had been accumulating, ever since he became a suitor for her hand.

"You are a kind and excellent girl," answered Rivington, sensibly affected by the heroism and attachment of his domestic, "and you are a noble fellow, Buckhorn; but you forget that by flying I should only confirm those in the belief of my guilt who are wavering now; besides, I could hardly expect to escape; for my life being forfeit to the laws, a proclamation would be immediately issued, and apprehension and death then, as now, would be my doom. No, no, my good friends, you mean me well, but I cannot consent to live, unless I can live with an unsullied fame."

"Ah, dear doctor," sobbed out poor Judy, whose heart seemed almost broken; "what's the use of spaking about it? If you stay, you've but a few days to live; and if you take your chance now, who knows but the rail murderer may be found out, and then you might come back, Mr. Charles, and all would go well again."

"That is a powerful argument, Judy; but my trust is in him who beholds all my actions," returned our hero; "and I must confess that I cannot divest myself of the hope that the truth will yet be brought to light before I die the death of a felon."

"Doctor Rivington," said Buckhorn, going up to him, and taking him warmly by the hand, "I've been wavering all along about you; but I'm sartin now. The man that murdered Silversight in cold blood, wouldn't be agoing to stand shilly-shally, and the jail door wide open. I always was dub'ous about it, though the proof seemed so sure. My nag is down in the hollow, with saddle bags on him, and Judy has filled 'em full of your clothes; you may take him, Doctor, if ye will; you may take the money and welcome—but I that come here to set you clear, advise you to stay; and if I don't find out somethin' to turn the tables before hanging day, it shan't be because I don't try."

Our hero exchanged with the honest hunter one of those warm pressures of the hand, which may be termed the language of the soul, and conveyed to him, by the eloquent action, more than he could readily have found words to express. They were now alarmed by the report of two rifles near them, fired in quick succession, and two persons issuing from the shadow of a neighbouring horse shed, at the same moment made directly towards the door of the jail, crying out in a loud voice, "The prisoner has broke out! the prisoner has broke out!" Our friends, Judy and Buckhorn, were enabled to make good their retreat, as the object of the alarm seemed more to secure the prisoner than to arrest his intended deliverers. It was not many minutes before a considerable number of the idle and curious were collected by this clamour around the insufficient place of confinement, and effectual means were devised to prevent any danger of a further attempt at rescue.

The glimmer of hope which had been lighted up in our hero's heart by the last words of Buckhorn, and the confident manner in which they were uttered, gradually declined as day after day rolled by, and no trace could be discovered of the real perpetrator of the crime. To add to the anguish of his situation, he learned that his beloved Catharine was confined by a wasting fever to her bed, and that his mother, though she still bore up and uttered not a murmur against the Almighty's will, was fast sinking with a broken heart into the grave. The evening previous to the fatal day which was to terminate his earthly career at length arrived, but brought no cheering promise with it, and the unhappy young man, therefore, humbling himself before the throne of heaven, and beseeching that mercy there which he could no longer hope for on earth, devoted the greater part of the night to prayer.

It was on the same evening, in a little mean looking cabin, called "Brown's Tavern," in the place which we have before had occasion to speak of as the New Settlements, that two men were sitting at a table, with a bottle of whiskey between them, conversing on the general topic, the execution that was to take place on the morrow, when a third person entered, and, calling for a dram, took a seat at some distance from them. He was a tall, dark man, dressed in a hunting frock and buckskin leggings, and held in his hand one of those mongrel weapons, which partaking of the characters both of rifle and musket, are called smooth bores by the hunters of our western frontier, who, generally speaking, hold them in great contempt. The apartment of the little grocery, or tavern, where these three persons were assembled, was lighted, in addition to the blaze of a large wood fire, by a single long-dipped tallow candle, held in an iron candlestick; and its only furniture consisted of the aforementioned table, with the rude benches on which the guests were seated. The conversation had been interrupted by the entry of the third person, but was now resumed.

"For my part, as I was saying," observed one of the persons, in continuation of some remark he had previously made, "I think the thing's been too hasty altogether. The doctor's character, which every body respected, should have made 'em more cautious how they acted; especially as he wanted 'em to go right out on his trail, and said they'd find he'd kept straight on to Mr. Wentworth's. Now he wouldn't a told 'em that if it wasn't so; and I am half a mind to believe that he's not guilty after all."

"That's damned unlikely," said the stranger, in a gruff voice.

"Why bless me, Mr. Rumley," continued the first speaker, "I didn't know it was you, you set so in the dark. How have you been this long time? Let me see, why, yes, bless me, so it was—it was you and I that was talking with poor old Silversight the day he started from here with the money. I havn't seen you since. Why, a'n't you a going to be over in Edgarton to see the doctor hung tomorrow?"

"I don't know whether I shall go or not," replied Rumley.

"Well, I've a great notion to ride over there, though I'm monstrous sorry for the poor man."

"Sorry—the devil! hang all the cursed Yankees, say I," responded the amiable deputy-sheriff.

"Come, that's too bad—though I like to see you angry on account of the old man's murder, because ye wasn't very good friends with him when he was alive—but bless me, Mr. Rumley, that powder-horn looks mighty like old Silversight's," taking hold of it to examine it, as he said so.

"Stand off!" cried Rumley; "what do you s'pose I'd be doing with the old scoundrel's powder-horn? It's not his—it never was his—he never seen it."

"It's a lie!" cried a person, who had glided in during the foregoing conversation, and had obtained a view of the horn in question, as the deputy-sheriff jerked it away from the other. "It's a lie!—I know it well—I've hunted with the old man often; I know it as well as I do my own. Bill Brown, and you, John Gillam," addressing himself to the one who first recognized the horn, "I accuse Cale Rumley of old Silversight's murder—help me to secure him."

The deputy-sheriff stood motionless for a moment; and turned as pale as death (from surprise, perhaps), then suddenly recovering his powers, he darted across the room, and seizing his gun, before any one was aware of his intention, levelled and fired at his accuser. The apartment became instantly filled with smoke, which, as it slowly rolled away, discovered to the astonished beholders the stiff and bleeding form of Caleb Rumley, stretched at full length upon the floor. As soon as he discharged his piece, the infuriated man had sprung towards the door, designing to make an immediate escape; but the motion was anticipated by our friend Jimmy Buckhorn (for it was he who charged his fallen antagonist with murder, and who luckily was not touched by the ball that was meant to destroy him), and with one blow of his powerful arm he felled the scoundrel to the earth. He now rapidly explained to the wondering trio the nature of the proof he had obtained of Rumley's guilt; and succeeded in satisfying them that he ought to be made prisoner, and immediately conveyed to Edgarton.

The morning which our hero believed was to be the last of his earthly existence, rose with unwonted brightness; and throngs of males and females came pouring into the little village, impelled by the mysterious principle of our nature, which incites us to look on that we nevertheless must shudder to behold. But no sounds of obstreperous merriment, no untimely jokes, were uttered, as they passed along the road, to grate upon the ear of the unfortunate Charles, and break him off from his communion with heaven: on the contrary, many a tear was shed that morning by the bright eyes of rustic maidens, who were "all unused to the melting mood:" and many a manly breast heaved a sigh of sympathy for the culprit, who was that day to make expiation to the offended laws. Indeed, since the sentence of the court was passed, a wonderful change had been wrought among the ever-changing multitude, by various rumours that were whispered from one part of these wide prairies to another, and spread with almost incredible velocity. A thousand acts of un-asked benevolence were now remembered, in favour of him, who was soon to suffer. Here was an aged and afflicted woman, whom he had not only visited without hope of reward, but upon whom he had conferred pecuniary, as well as medical comforts. There was an industrious cripple, who had received a receipt in full from the young physician, when creditors to a less amount were levying upon his farm. And many similar acts of bounty were proclaimed abroad, by the grateful hearts on which they had been conferred; all helping to produce the change of sentiment which was manifestly wrought. Still the general impression seemed to be unshaken, (so strong had been the proofs), that, in an evil hour, he had yielded to temptation, and embrued his hands in a fellow-creature's blood.

The hour at last arrived when Charles Rivington was to suffer the sentence of the law. A rude gallows was erected at about a quarter of a mile from the public square; and thither the sad procession moved. He was decently dressed in a black suit, and walked to the fatal place with a firm step. He was very pale; but from no other outward sign might the spectators guess that he shrunk from the horrors of such a death; for his eye had a calm expression, and the muscles of his face were as motionless as an infant's in slumber. They reached the spot: a prayer, a solemn prayer was offered up to heaven for the murderer's soul; in which every hearer joined with unaccustomed fervour. The sheriff's attendant stood in waiting with the fatal cord, while the agonised mother, vainly endeavouring to emulate the firmness of her heroic son, approached with trembling steps, to bid a last farewell—when hark! a shout was heard; all eyes were turned to catch its meaning; another shout, and the words "Stop, stop the execution!" were distinctly audible. In less than an instant after, the death-pale form of Jimmy Buckhorn tumbled from his horse with just sufficient strength remaining to reach towards the sheriff, with an order from the judge to stay the execution.

Reader, our tale is nearly at an end. Jimmy Buckhorn had been faithful to his word: he had sought for some clue to the real murderer, with an earnestness, which nothing but a firm conviction of our hero's innocence, superadded to his love for Judy, could possibly have enkindled. For some time he was unsuccessful. At length the thought struck him, that the track on the side of the stream

where Mr. Wentworth resided, might have been caused by a traveller passing along, on the morning after the fatal deed, and the
deputy-sheriff, in that case, might be the real culprit. He immediately set out to visit every cabin above Mr. Wentworth's, to see if
his story that he had been further up the stream was correct. This
took a considerable time; but the result satisfied him that that tale
was false. He then procured the assistance of a surgeon, imposing
upon him secrecy, until the proper time for disclosure; and proceeded to disinter the body of Silversight. This was more successful
that he had even dared to hope: the ball had lodged in a cavity of the
head; and being produced, Buckhorn pronounced at once, from its
great size, that it could have been discharged only from Rumley's
smooth-bore. He set out directly for Edgarton, choosing to go by
the way of the New Settlements, for a two-fold reason. He had
heard that Rumley was in that neighbourhood; and to get possession
of him or of his gun, at any rate, he deemed very essential. Besides,
that route would take him by the house of the judge, and from him
it would be necessary to procure an order to delay the proceedings.
We have seen the result. But the chain of evidence was not yet
complete.

A wild and dissipated young man, by the name of Michael Davis,
who had just returned up the river from New Orleans, entered the
office of the clerk of the county, on his way back to the tavern,
from the place where the execution was to have taken place, in order
to while away an hour, until the time for dinner should arrive. The
powder-flask, which had been brought in evidence against our hero,
was lying on the table, the graven side downwards. There is a restless kind of persons in the world, who can never be easy, let them
be sitting where they will, without fingering and examining whatever is in their reach—and such an one was Michael Davis: he
accordingly took up the flask in a careless manner, and turning it
over in his hand, his eye fell upon the letters.

"Why, halloo! what the devil are you doing with my powder-
flask?" asked he.

"I wish the unlucky article had been your's, or any body's, except
the unfortunate Dr. Rivington's," returned the clerk, who was a

friend of our hero, and deeply deplored the circumstances that had lately transpired.

"Unfortunate devil's," reiterated Michael; "I tell you it's my flask, or article, as you prefer calling it; or rather it was mine and Cale Rumley's together. We bought it when him and me went down to New Orleans—let's see, that's three years, come spring. I ought to know the cursed thing, for I broke a bran new knife in scratching them letters on it."

The clerk started from his seat—he snatched the flask out of the hand of Davis—he gazed at it a moment intently—then, the truth suddenly flashing on his mind, he rushed out into the road, forgetting his hat, forgetting every thing but the letters on the flask. The magistrate, who grieved as much as any one, at the supposed dereliction of their young friend, the physician, was amazed to see the clerk enter his apartment in such a plight.

"There!" cried he, as he threw down the flask on the table, "C. R. M. D. spells something beside Rivington. Send your servant out of the room."

As soon as he was gone, and the door carefully closed, the clerk continued in a low, confidential tone, "That flask is Caleb Rumley's, and Caleb Rumley is the murderer (no wonder he has kept himself away all this while). It belonged to him, and that imp of Satan, Mich. Davis, together, and Mich. Davis told me so, with his own mouth, not three minutes ago—and Charles Rivington's an honest man—huzza! huzza! huzza!" concluded he, as he danced and skipped about the apartment, with the delirious joy true friendship inspired. The magistrate was a man of middle age, and very large and corpulent, but a mountain of flesh could not have kept him down, when such thrilling news tingled in his ears, and he, too, began to dance a jig, that shook the tenement to its foundation.

It became the duty of the worthy magistrate, to commit, in the course of that very day, our respected friend, Caleb Rumley, Esq., deputy-sheriff of the county of —— to the same capacious tenement which Dr. Rivington had lately inhabited; he, with the consent of the judge, being more safely disposed of in the prison of his own house. A bill was immediately found by the Grand Jury, and the trial of the real murderer came on shortly after. For a long time he obstinately denied any knowledge of the death of Silversight; but as proofs after proofs were disclosed against him, he first became doggedly silent, then greatly intimidated, and at last made a full disclosure of his crime. He was found guilty, and executed on the same gallows that had been erected for our calumniated hero.

The sickness of Catharine Wentworth was long and severe; but our friend Charles was her physician, and the reader will not wonder that it yielded at last to his skill. The Christian parent of our hero had been condemned, at different periods of her life, to drink deeply of the cup of affliction, and she had bowed with a noble humility to the decree of heaven; it was thence she now derived support in this more trying hour of joy. Spring had gone forth, warbling with her thousand voices of delight, over these wide-extended prairies, and the flowers had sprung into a beautiful existence at her call, when the hand of the blushing Catharine, herself a lovelier flower, was bestowed in marriage on the transported Charles Rivington. Never did there stand before the holy man, a happier, a more affectionate pair. Their hearts had been tried—severely tried; they had been weighed in the balance, and not found wanting. The house of Mr. Wentworth was the scene of their union; and, on the same evening, and by the same hand that had bound her dear "Mister Charles" to his blooming bride, our little Irish friend Judy was united to the worthy Buckhorn, who had been prevailed upon, reluctantly, to lay aside his hunting shirt and leather leggings on the joyful occasion. The evening glided rapidly away, urged along by tales of mirth, and song, and jest; and it was observed, that though Charles and Catharine took but little share in the rattling conversation of the hour, they appeared to enjoy the scene with happiness that admitted of no increase. Indeed, often did the tender blue eyes of the beautiful bride become suffused with crystal drops of joy, as she raised them in thankfulness to her heavenly Father, who had conducted them safely through all the perils of the past, and at last brought them together under the shelter of his love.

"The whole trouble come out of your being so kind, Dr. Rivington," said the manly, though, in his new suit, rather awkward-looking Buckhorn; "it was all of your kindness to offer to bring out my plaguy rifle. If it hadn't been for that, suspicion wouldn't a lighted on you at all."

"Now hould your tongue, Jimmy dear," answered his loquacious little wife; "I thought so myself, till Mister Charles explained it to me, and then I found out how 'twas the wisdom of the Almighty put it into his head to carry your gun; for how would you iver got on the true scent, if the big bullet hadn't a tould ye for sartain that it was niver the small-bored rifle that kilt him. No, blessed be his name, that made then, as he always will, goodness its own reward, and put it into the heart of my dear, kind master, to carry out a great clumsy gun, to an old ranger like you, Buckhorn. And, under heaven, the cause of all our present happiness, take my word for it, is THE RIFLE."

The King's Private Eye (1848)*

BY ALEXANDRE DUMAS

While the King was making final preparations to discover the truth, d'Artagnan, without wasting a second, ran to the stables, took down the lantern, saddled his horse himself, and was making his way toward the spot indicated by His Majesty.

As promised, he had seen and talked to nobody, and as we just saw, he carried precaution to the point of doing what he had to do without the help of grooms and stable boys. For he was of those who in moments of stress like to surpass themselves.

After five minutes' gallop he had reached the wood, fastened his horse to the nearest tree and walked to the clearing. He began by going, lantern in hand, over the entire ground, on foot. He went back and forth, took measurements, scrutinized, and after half an hour's minute inspection, he quietly remounted. At a walking pace and in deep thought he made his way back to Fontainebleau.

The King was waiting in his private room, alone and scribbling

*From *Le Vicomte de Bragelonne ou Dix Ans Plus Tard*. Paris, 1848; new ed. Michel-Lévy, 1869, IV, 23, 172–9. Translated by the Editor.

sentences which to D'Artagnan's glance looked uneven and much scratched over. The musketeer inferred that they were verses. The King raised his head and saw D'Artagnan.

"Well, Captain, what news? Did you see anything?"

"Yes."

"What."

"I can only report probabilities."

"But I asked you for certainties."

"I shall get as close to certainty as I can. The weather was favorable to the kind of inquiry I was making: it had been raining and the ground was moist."

"My dear sir, come to the point."

"Your Majesty told me that there was a dead horse at the cross-roads where one enters Rochin Wood. So I began studying the roads—I say "roads" because the spot can be reached from four directions. The one I came by was the only one to show fresh tracks. Two horses had gone along it side by side; the eight hoof-marks were clearly marked in the clay. One of the riders was impatient; his tracks were always half a length ahead of the other."

"You are sure they were traveling together?" asked the King.

"Yes, sire. Both horses were large animals, of equal pace, and trained for maneuvers, for they wheeled in perfect formation around the fence at the clearing."

"And then?"

"At that point the horsemen stopped a moment, doubtless to settle the terms of the duel. The horses grew restless. One gentleman was speaking, the other listened and put in a word from time to time. His horse pawed the ground, which shows that his master's attention was so taken up with listening that he let the bridle fall on the horse's neck."

"Then a duel took place?"

"That is certain."

"Go on. You are a good observer."

"One of the pair stayed where he was—it was the listener. The other crossed the clearing, turned and faced his adversary. Where-upon the other galloped two-thirds of the way across the place, thinking to charge his enemy, but the latter had gone along the outer circle."

"You don't know who they were, I suppose."

"No, I do not. Only, the one who went around rode a black horse."

"How do you know?"

"A few hairs from his tail caught on the brambles that border the ditch."

"Go on."

"As for the other horse, it's easy to identify him since he was left dead on the field of battle."

"How was he killed?"

"By a ball through the head."

"From a pistol or a musket?"

"From a pistol. What is more, the wound showed the tactics used by the man who fired the shot. He went around the outer circle so as to flank his enemy. Besides I could also see his tracks on the grass."

"The tracks of the black horse, you mean?"

"Yes, sire."

"What then?"

"Now that your Majesty perceives the positions of the two men, I must turn from the stationary one to the one who started off at a gallop."

"Do so."

"The horse of the man who was charging his enemy was killed on the spot."

"How can you tell?"

"The horseman had no time to leap off and so fell with the beast. I saw the impression of his leg, which he had trouble pulling out from under the horse. The spur plowed up the ground."

"Excellent! What did he do when he got up?"

"He walked straight up to his opponent."

"Who was still on the verge of the wood?"

"Yes, sire. When well within range, the walking man stopped, his heels solidly planted on the ground. He fired and missed."

"How do you know he missed?"

"I found a hat with a hole in it."

"Ah, that would be proof, wouldn't it?"

"Not proof enough, sire," replied D'Artagnan coldly. "The hat is unmarked, no insignia, just a red feather, like all other hats; the braid itself is ordinary."

"And did the man with the perforated hat fire his second shot?"

"Oh, sire, he had already shot twice."

"How can you be sure?"

"I found the wadding of each shot."

"What happened to the ball that did not hit the horse?"

"It cut the other man's feather in half, and shattered a young birch on the far side of the clearing."

"So the man with the black horse was helpless, while his enemy still had one shot?"

"Sire, while the dismounted man was getting to his feet the other reloaded. But he was upset and his hand was shaking."

"Tell me how you ascertained that?"

"Half the powder fell on the ground and he threw away the rod, he was in such a state."

"Monsieur D'Artagnan, your account is wonderful!"

"It is mere observation, sire; any experienced scout could do the same."

"I can see the scene from just hearing you talk."

"It is at any rate the way I reconstruct it in my mind, by approximation."

"Go back to the man who was unhorsed. You said he walked straight up to his opponent while the latter reloaded."

"That is true, but just as he was taking aim, the other fired."

"Oh!" exclaimed the King. "And the shot?"

"The shot was deadly, sire. The unhorsed man fell on his face after staggering three paces."

"Where was he hit?"

"In two places, first in the right hand, then through it in the chest."

"But how could you find all this out?" asked the King, full of admiration.

"It is quite simple: the butt of the pistol was all bloodied. In it was a groove made by the ball and a piece from a broken ring. Hence the probability is that the wounded man had his ring finger and little finger shattered."

"That tells us about the hand. What of the chest?"

"Sire, there were two pools of blood about two and a half feet apart. Near one the grass was pulled out as by a clenching of the fingers; near the other, the grass was merely pressed down by the weight of the body."

"Poor De Guiche!" cried the King.

"Ah, it was Monsieur de Guiche, then," said the musketeer calmly. "I suspected it but did not venture to mention it to your Majesty."

"But what made you suspect?"

"I recognized the armorial bearings of the Grammont family on the holsters of the dead horse."

"Do you think the wound was serious?"

"Very serious, since he fell at once and lay a good while in one place. Nevertheless he was able to walk away when supported by two friends."

"You met them on the way back?"

"No, but I saw the footprints of three men; those on the left and on the right walked normally; the one in the middle dragged his feet and blood was spattered along his track."

"Well, now, since you saw the engagement so distinctly that no detail escapes you, tell me something of De Guiche's opponent."

"Sire, I have no idea who he was."

"Yet you see everything else quite clearly."

"Yes, sire, I see. But I do not tell all I see. And since the poor devil got away, I beg Your Majesty to permit me to state that I will not inform upon him."

"But, Captain, whoever fights a duel is a criminal!"

"Not to me, sire," replied D'Artagnan coldly.

"Sir, do you know what you are saying?"

"Perfectly, sire, but in my eyes a man who fights a duel is a brave man. That is what I think. You may think otherwise. It is but natural—you are the King."

"But sir, did I not order you to—"

D'Artagnan broke in with a gesture full of respect. "You ordered me to gather what I could of a reported fight. I have reported in my turn. If you now order me to arrest the opponent of Monsieur de Guiche, I shall obey. But please do not order me to inform upon him, for I will not obey."

"Very well. Go and arrest him!"

"First give me his name, sire."

Louis stamped his foot. Then, after a moment's thought, "You are right," he said, "altogether right."

"That is my opinion, sire. I am happy that it is also Your Majesty's."

"One word more: who went to help De Guiche?"

"I do not know."

"But you mentioned two men. There was a witness, then, acting as second."

"There was no second. Moreover, after Monsieur de Guiche fell, his opponent fled without giving help."

"The scoundrel!"

"That is but the result of your decrees, sire. A man fights a fair fight; having survived a first chance of death, he naturally wants to avoid a second. Egad, people can't forget what happened to Monsieur de Boutteville!"

"And that's how men turn cowards."

"No, they only turn prudent."

"And so he took to his heels."

"Yes, that is, he and his horse, as fast as they could go."

"In what direction?"

"Toward the castle."

"And when they'd gone?"

"When they had gone, as I had the honor of saying to Your Majesty, two men came on foot and assisted Monsieur de Guiche off the field."

"What evidence have you that they came after the fight?"

"Clear evidence, sire: at the time of the fight the rain had just stopped. The ground had not soaked it all up and was quite muddy, so footprints were deep. But after the fight, while Monsieur de Guiche lay fainting on the ground, the soil hardened a little and footprints were shallower."

Louis clapped his hands in admiration. "Captain D'Artagnan, you are positively the cleverest man in our kingdom."

"That is what Cardinal Richelieu used to think, sire, and what Cardinal Mazarin used to say."